I0575563

Edward Healy Thompson, Marie Lataste, Pascal Darbins

**The Life of Marie Lataste**

Edward Healy Thompson, Marie Lataste, Pascal Darbins

**The Life of Marie Lataste**

ISBN/EAN: 9783744659895

Printed in Europe, USA, Canada, Australia, Japan

Cover: Foto ©Raphael Reischuk / pixelio.de

More available books at **www.hansebooks.com**

# LIBRARY

OF

# RELIGIOUS BIOGRAPHY.

EDITED BY

## EDWARD HEALY THOMPSON.

———

VOLUME VI.

## MARIE LATASTE.

𝕭𝖆𝖑𝖑𝖆𝖓𝖙𝖞𝖓𝖊 𝕻𝖗𝖊𝖘𝖘
BALLANTYNE, HANSON AND CO.
EDINBURGH AND LONDON

# THE LIFE

OF

# MARIE LATASTE,

*LAY-SISTER OF THE CONGREGATION OF THE
SACRED HEART.*

WITH

𝔄 𝔅𝔯𝔦𝔢𝔣 𝔑𝔬𝔱𝔦𝔠𝔢 𝔬𝔣 𝔥𝔢𝔯 𝔖𝔦𝔰𝔱𝔢𝔯 ℭ𝔲𝔦𝔱𝔱𝔢𝔯𝔦𝔢.

"Declaratio sermonum tuorum illuminat, et intellectum dat parvulis. '
—*Psalm* cxviii. 130.

LONDON : BURNS & OATES,
PORTMAN STREET AND PATERNOSTER ROW.
DUBLIN: W. B. KELLY, 8 GRAFTON STREET.
1877.

# ADVERTISEMENT.

MARIE LATASTE, the subject of this biography, appears to be comparatively little known in England, although her Life and Writings, published fifteen years ago in France, have excited a lively interest among Catholics in the land of her birth, and have, we are assured on all hands, produced abundant fruits of edification in that country. They have already gone through four editions, a practical proof of the estimation in which they are held. Nor can this be matter of surprise; for that an uneducated peasant girl, engaged in field occupations from her very infancy in an obscure hamlet, situated in a most isolated district, should, while so employed, pen a work on theological subjects which would have reflected credit on the most devout and learned ecclesiastic, is in itself a marvel; and the explanation of that marvel which will be found in her Life and Letters only introduces a prodigy of another and a higher order. For there we learn that in all she wrote she was simply retailing knowledge which she had supernaturally received.

It would be almost impossible to possess stronger guarantees of authenticity than can be alleged in the case of Marie Lataste's Works and Letters. The latter, addressed to her director, were carefully preserved by him, and her papers were handed over to

him at the time they were written, sheet by sheet, as
she was able to find some private opportunity to
compose them. At a very early stage they were
shown to an eminent priest of the neighbourhood,
and afterwards to the Bishop of the Diocese, by whose
desire they were also privately submitted to the
scrutiny of several learned ecclesiastics. All this will
be found detailed at length in the biography.

For our materials we have referred to the last
edition of her Life and Works, that of 1872, and also
to the earliest, which was published in 1862. The
editor of the several editions was the Abbé Pascal
Darbins,* nephew of Marie's director, the Abbé Pierre
Darbins; for the latter, having been removed to a
populous parish, had not the necessary leisure personally to undertake the task. It was executed, however,
under his close superintendence, and it was not until
a short time before his death, in 1867, that he formally
handed over the custody of the manuscripts to his
nephew. To the first edition a Life of Marie was pre-
fixed, written by M. Pascal Darbins, his uncle acting
as his guide throughout. It was illustrated by copious references to the Works and Letters. All this
was in accordance with our Lord's own directions, as
reported by Marie ; but, as the number of quotations
involved much repetition, it was considered advisable
subsequently to have the Life re-written in a shorter
form, giving chiefly what may be considered as Marie's

* "La Vie et les Œuvres de Marie Lataste, Religieuse Coadjutrice
du Sacré Cœur, publiées par M. l'Abbé Pascal Darbins, avec
l'approbation de Mgr. l'Evêque d'Aire. Quatrième edition : revue
avec le plus grand soin et collationée sur les manuscrits; augmentée
d'une Introduction sur les Révélations Privées et de Notes Théo-
logiques composées par deux Pères de la Compagnie de Jésus."
Paris : Bray et Retaux, 1872.
   The Abbé Pascal Darbins is now occupying the important position of Vicar-General to the Archbishop of Santiago, in Chili.

external relations; the letters of a historical kind, as they may be called, being appended thereto, and serving to supply what was omitted of interior details in the Life. This work was undertaken by a Religious of the Sacred Heart. For ourselves, we have endeavoured to steer a middle course. As the Life here given to the English public is detached from the Works and Letters, it became necessary to return, in a measure, to the original plan, without, however, quoting more largely than was necessary for the purpose.

By the desire of the Bishop of Aire, and with the consent of Marie's director, M. Pascal Darbins had, previously to bringing out the later editions, subjected her papers to the examination of several Fathers of the Company of Jesus, who were thus able scrupulously to compare what had been printed with the originals, and consequently to furnish a fresh guarantee of the authenticity of the writings which passed under her name. They are, therefore, without a shadow of doubt, the genuine productions of the illiterate peasant girl of the Landes.

The appellation of Lay-Sister has been given to Marie Lataste on the Title-page because the second class of Religious in the Congregation of the Sacred Heart are so styled in England. In France they continue to be called Sœurs Coadjutrices, or Assistant-Sisters, a name accorded to them, apparently, because their position differs in certain respects from that of the ordinary Sœur Converse, or Lay-Sister.

The brief memoir of her sister Quitterie has been taken from that which is appended to Marie's Life in the French edition of 1872. Of the third sister, Marguerite, nothing more is known than appears in the few scattered notices of her which will be found

in the present volume. Quitterie became a Sister of
Charity; Marguerite abode with her parents at home.
But what is so remarkable is that these three sisters
should have been chosen by our Blessed Lord, as He
revealed to Marie, to represent what He himself
called His three Lives: viz., His hidden Life at Nazareth; His active Life during His public ministry;
His interior Life with His Heavenly Father; Marie
being privileged to represent the last, the highest of
the three. This, indeed, it is which, irrespective of
the other supernatural elements, gives such a peculiar
and quite exceptional interest to the history of a life
apparently so devoid of incident as that which is related in the following pages.

We may here add that, with the generous permission of the Parisian publishers, Messrs. Bray and
Retaux, in whom the copyright is vested, an English
translation of Marie Lataste's Letters and Works has
been undertaken by the editor of this series. A
translation has already appeared both in Spain and
Germany.

---

In obedience to the decrees of Urban VIII. and
other Sovereign Pontiffs, we declare that, in all we
have written of the holy life and exalted virtues
of Marie Lataste, as also of her sister Quitterie, we
submit ourselves without reserve to the infallible
judgment of the Apostolic See, which alone has
authority to pronounce to whom rightly belong the
character and title of saint.

# CONTENTS.

## CHAPTER VIII.

### MARIE'S VISIONS OF THE MOTHER OF GOD.

## CHAPTER IX.

### JESUS INSTRUCTS MARIE IN PARABLES, AND SPEAKS TO HER OF FRANCE.

## CHAPTER X.

### FOREWARNINGS OF TRIALS AND SUFFERINGS, AND WITHDRAWAL OF SENSIBLE VISIONS.

## CHAPTER XI.

### FRESH LIGHTS AND THE BEGINNING OF TRIALS.

## CHAPTER XII.

### MARIE IS ADVANCED TO A HIGHER STATE.

## CHAPTER XIII.

### PRAYER AND COMMUNION.

## CHAPTER XIV.

## CHAPTER XV.

## CHAPTER XVI.

## CHAPTER XVII.

## CHAPTER XVIII.

### RECOLLECTIONS OF MARIE AS A POSTULANT DURING HER STAY AT PARIS.

## CHAPTER XIX.

### MARIE AT CONFLANS.

## CHAPTER XX.

### MARIE A NOVICE.

## CHAPTER XXI.

### MARIE IS SENT TO RENNES.

## CHAPTER XXII.

### MARIE'S LAST ILLNESS AND DEATH.

## CHAPTER XXIII.

### HER WRITINGS.

## Quitterie Lataste.

# CHAPTER I.

## CHILDHOOD OF MARIE LATASTE.

THE life of Marie Lataste, the subject of this biography, was a short life, and, apart from the supernatural element which enters so largely into it, was an uneventful life. Regarded, however, from this superior point of view, it must be considered as most remarkable; for, surely, of no life could anything more surprising be recorded than is exhibited in every stage of her short earthly career. That our Lord should Himself, personally, not only undertake the guidance of a soul, as by His Spirit He does of every faithful son and daughter of His Church—not only communicate Himself by occasional revelations or manifestations, as He has done from time to time to certain chosen individuals—but assume the entire instruction and training of that soul, from childhood upwards, by means of the most familiar and sensible communications, and this too, so to say, in the most painstaking, systematic, and persevering manner, is surely an event to which no incident in human life can compare for interest. Such a relation manifested between the God-Man and an individual soul places the person thus favoured in a position which must awaken in us a holy curiosity to know all that

A

can be known with reference to one so singularly privileged.

When we speak of our Lord having made these personal communications to the soul of Marie Lataste, we
wish once for all, in order to avoid all ambiguity and to
preclude the necessity of repetition, to say that we do
not pretend in any way to prejudge a question upon
which the highest authority has not as yet pronounced ;
we must, therefore, always be understood as expressing
ourselves with a corresponding reserve.   Those who examined and tested the spirit of this girl, and to whom she
gave her whole confidence, certainly believed her to be
entirely free from any mental illusion and quite incapable of deceit.   They had frequent opportunity of veri-
fying the truth of many things which she communicated
to them, and the knowledge of which she could not have
obtained by natural means ; and she gave, on a thousand
occasions, the best of proofs that the spirit which guided
her was good, by an unalterable and childlike humility
as well as by the practice in an eminent degree of the
other Christian virtues.   It is many years now since she
has gone to her rest ; and the published record of her
life, her works, and her letters, have been in the hands
of thousands during this interval, and have proved the
source of spiritual profit to numbers, by their own acknowledgment, and of edification to all by general consent.   Had Marie Lataste been either a dupe or an
impostor, the evil one would strangely have overshot
his mark, and would have laboured for his own discom-
fiture.   Add to this, her writings have been published
with the sanction and approbation of the bishop of the
diocese to which she belonged ; not, of course, as pronouncing upon the truth or the character of the revelations to which they refer, but simply recommending

them as edifying works, containing doctrine conformable to Scripture, and calculated to nourish piety in the souls of those who read them. This is sufficient for our purpose, and we need not again advert to the subject.

Marie Lataste's life, then, possesses a singular interest, from the peculiar dealings of God with her soul. It has often pleased our Lord, as we know from the records of hagiology, to select persons of low estate and homely occupations, ignorant of all that knowledge which secular education imparts, but simple and docile in proportion to this ignorance, in order to reveal to them the treasures of His heavenly wisdom. That very simplicity and docility, we may believe, helped to attract to them, so far as we are allowed to catch a glimpse of the mysterious and inscrutable secrets of God's electing grace, the privileged communications of which they were the recipients. At any rate simplicity is very dear to God, and seems to be almost a condition of any familiar approach or intimate manifestation on the part of Him whose adorable essence is simplicity itself. Moreover, the absence of this simplicity, it would seem, cannot be compensated by any other quality, however exalted, whether intellectual or moral ; and where we see our Lord favouring persons of a high order of mind, and such as have enjoyed the benefits of education, with similar sweet and familiar visits, we shall find that they have never been wanting in this disposition, which, when alien to their nature, has been taught and acquired by grace. We may the more confidently make this assertion, because we have our Lord's own warrant for the fact that God hides Himself from the wise and prudent in their own eyes and makes Himself known to those who are babes in spirit. It was the subject of one of those great acts of

thanksgiving which He uttered aloud to His Eternal
Father. "In that same hour He rejoiced in the Holy
Ghost, and said : I confess to Thee, O Father, Lord of
heaven and earth, because Thou hast hidden these
things from the wise and prudent, and hast revealed
them to little ones. Yea, Father, for so it hath seemed
good in Thy sight."* We have also the concordant
testimony of all the eminent masters and directors in
the ways of perfection, that nothing is a greater hindrance to advance in the school of Christ, that nothing
keeps us farther off from Him, nothing conduces more
certainly to deprive us of His choicest favours and
communications, than the being full of our own ideas.
It is not question here of self manifesting its predo-
minance in its grosser forms, but of a much subtler
exhibition of its influence, in which there appears to
be nothing sinful, and which assumes not seldom the
plausible appearance of a busy intellectual activity
directed to good ends. Those who were well acquainted
with the lamented Father Faber will remember how
strongly he used to express himself on this subject.
To be "viewy" was in his estimation an insuperable
obstacle, so long as that habit of mind remained, to
spiritual progress. The poor are seldom "viewy," and
this may be reckoned amongst their other inappreciable,
and, not seldom, unappreciated advantages.

By her position in life and her education, or rather
deficiency of education, Marie Lataste belonged to the
class in which our Lord has been thus pleased to seek
out some of the most favoured recipients of exceptional
graces. Nevertheless, to our superficial observation she
would have seemed unlikely, from her natural disposition, to be called to partake of such special privi-

* Luke x. 21.

leges. The soil did not appear favourable, and her faults were of that very character which we should have judged beforehand to stand peculiarly in the way, not only of so high a vocation, but even of ordinary piety. God, however, who reads the depths of the heart, sees not as we see. He may discern there, how much soever overlaid with what is evil, a real good will and a sterling sincerity which is beyond our ken, even in our own case ; how much more in that of others ! And where there is this good will the grace of God can do all, and is never more glorified than in the transformation of souls in which the rebellion of the old nature has made itself most palpable.

Marie Lataste was born on February 21st, 1822, at Mimbaste, a little village in the department of the Landes, distant a few kilometres from Dax, a small town near the base of the Pyrenees, the name of which few perhaps would remember were it not that it gives its title, conjoined with Aire, to the diocese in which it is situated, but which ought any way to possess an interest in the eyes of Catholics, because not far from it are the birthplace of St. Vincent de Paul and the celebrated sanctuary of Our Lady of Buglosse. Amidst its desolated ruins, for it had been burned by the Huguenots, and while the miraculous image which pious hands had saved from destruction was still lying concealed in the depths of a morass, the future saint, when a child, would worship for hours. Here he made a little oratory of a hollow in an old oak-tree, which still survives, the object of a veneration which no centuries of existence could have conferred upon it. The peculiar character of the district known as the Landes, the description of which is probably familiar to most of

our readers, has tended to isolate it from the busy
world, and thus to keep its poor and scattered population in a very primitive condition. Mimbaste is an in-
considerable village,—if it might not rather be called a
hamlet. Its houses are not gathered in a street, but
dispersed here and there in a picturesque manner. This
circumstance, combined with its unfrequented and solitary situation, restricts the inhabitants generally, so far
as regards society, to their own immediate families.
They are poor and have to work for their living, and
seldom meet save at church. .Whatever the friends of
so-called progress may think of a social state like this,
it is undoubtedly favourable to the maintenance of purity
and piety amongst a Catholic people, who, if ignorant
of much which the men of our day deem it so essential
to know, are not untaught as regards the knowledge
alone necessary. Accordingly the rural population of
the Landes, generally speaking, and this little village in
particular, have continued almost entirely strangers to
the movement going on in the great centres of industry,
and, remaining so, have also remained simple, religious,
and laborious like their forefathers. Modern ideas have
made little way among them ; they lend a docile ear to
their pastors, and, for the most part, live at peace with
God and with each other.

The father and mother of Marie, François Lataste
and Elisabeth Pourlet, were good specimens of this type.
They had a small scrap of ground of their own, desig-
nated as the Gran Cassou, or Grand Chêne, which they
cultivated diligently, and upon the produce of which
they managed to support themselves and their family.
They were not, however, absorbed by these cares to the
prejudice of higher objects, but neglected nothing in
their power to bring up their children in the fear of

God and the practice of their duty. Elisabeth Pourlet had herself enjoyed very slender advantages in the way of education, even of such as her humble birthplace afforded. Having lost her father when she was but ten years of age, she had to leave school that she might help her mother and take her share of labour in providing for the subsistence of the family. She had, therefore, but a very small stock of knowledge to impart to her own children; it might be summed up in reading, writing, sewing, and spinning : this was all she knew, and this was all she could teach. She was, however, a good and devout Christian, and solicitous to bring up her three daughters in the way in which they should go; striving to nourish their faith and to form their hearts to piety, in which undertaking, doubtless, her example was more eloquent than her words. The two elder ones, Quitterie and Marguerite, gave her no trouble, and repaid her care abundantly, but it was not so with the youngest, Marie. With her she had a very hard task. The child's temper was very quick; she was disobedient and wilful; and, notwithstanding the exemplary patience which her mother displayed in teaching her, it was impossible to get her to learn her catechism, or listen to its explanation. Marguerite, of whom Marie always spoke as her good angel, was a little more successful as an instructress. Perhaps from the very circumstance of being her sister, and so possessing no authority, her influence was somewhat more acceptable to this young rebellious spirit; at any rate, she was more willing to listen to her advice, but it was almost immediately forgotten.

To Elisabeth the intractable spirit of her youngest child was a source of much anxiety and the subject of frequent prayer. When Marie, however, arrived at the age of developed reason, and had reached her eighth

year, there was an improvement as respected her
behaviour. She was less passionate and more tract-
able, but the amelioration was not really of a satisfactory kind. The child had remarkably good sense;
it is not surprising, therefore, that those infantine faults
which result from the imperfect development of the
reasonable faculties should in a great measure disappear.
The desires of the heart also shift their objects with
every stage of advancing life, and there is a corresponding change of outward bearing. A baby will cry for
the moon, and beat with its tiny hand the " naughty "
chair which it has fallen against. The older child will
commit neither of these follies, but it does not follow
that it has ceased to long for the unattainable, or has
its angry passions under any better control. Marie
had certainly not ceased to long for the unattainable:
this was the secret of the grave and almost gloomy
temper manifested by her when its infantine violence
and wilfulness abated. But she kept her thoughts to
herself; they were, probably, indeed, at first of a rather
vague and indistinct character; she was discontented,
yet might have found it difficult to state the precise
cause of her discontent. But, as she grew older, and
became competent to observe, to compare, and to
reflect, her dissatisfaction assumed a more definite
shape. The human soul has an insatiable longing for
happiness, and is filled with aspirations after self-eleva-
tion. Whatever form these desires may take, and they
take very different forms according to the nature of the
individual, noble spirits aiming high, while the ignobler
seek baser objects, they proceed alike from a secret
instinct of our great destiny. We were made for God,
the All-Great and the All-Perfect; and the fallen soul
of man retains the impress of this destiny in these two

propensities. The devil takes occasion thereby to tempt it to seek their gratification amidst finite objects ; in lofty spirits he excites ambition, and, where this passion has no scope for operation, he endeavours to fix the sting of repining discontent.

So it was with this poor peasant girl. She had become alive to the temporal disadvantages of her position in life. Restricted as was her sphere, her powers of observation were very keen ; gifted with an ardent imagination and a precocious intellect, she realised what duller children would have failed to perceive, or to which they would at that early age have been quite indifferent. She instinctively longed to know and to learn, and she had neither knowledge nor the means of acquiring it. She felt this deeply, and the result was that kind of dissatisfaction with self which is apt to lead to a certain awkwardness and embarrassment in the behaviour. The same pride which urges some to push themselves forward, drives other natures into a peculiar species of reserve, a reserve more or less unamiable according to the individual temper. With Marie this reserve assumed an unpleasing character. The poor child, quite ignorant of her own mental powers and gifts, mistook the awkwardness and shyness under which she laboured for stupidity, and this conviction added to her mortification. The pleasing qualities which she observed in others, and which won for them love and admiration, equally saddened her, because she was conscious of being devoid of them herself. Again, the poverty of her family weighed heavily upon her, there seemed no prospect of ever emerging from a routine of grinding toil, and, little as Marie knew of the world, she caught sufficient glimpses of it to perceive that easy circumstances extended the sphere of

earthly enjoyments, while to her the pleasures attached
to riches were for ever barred. And so she began to
dislike everything around her, and the very sight of her
humble village was disagreeable and repulsive to her.

She thus adverts in after years, when writing to her
director, to these secret longings of her heart even in
her earliest childhood :—"From my early infancy, I
always felt myself attracted towards what was high,
and far above anything to which I could aspire. I did
not believe that I was made to lead an obscure life in a
little village like Mimbaste. How often did I wish that
I belonged to a rich and noble family, which could have
given me a brilliant education, and thus facilitated for
me the means of distinguishing myself! But I hid all
this in the depths of my heart, and communicated my
thoughts to no one. I nourished these secret ideas in
my soul, and suffered because they could not be realised."
The consequence was that she became silent and moody ;
but what was passing in this little girl's mind none
guessed. To neither mother nor sisters did she manifest the source of her discontent, and all the efforts of
Marguerite, who redoubled her affectionate care and
solicitude, could not succeed in winning her confidence.
There are certain thoughts which do not seek or desire
a confidant, and to this class proud and discontented
aspirations belong. The foolish, it is true, will betray
them, but Marie was not foolish ; she kept her own
counsel, and retained her inexplicable gloom, the source
of which, but for her subsequent avowals, would never
have been known.

While poor Marguerite was toiling to dispel the
cloud, the mother was praying for her child with that
persevering earnestness and strong faith which is a
pledge of success. Marie was now approaching her

twelfth year, the usual time for children to make their first communion, and at this period a change came over her. She felt the necessity of a fitting preparation for so solemn an act. Now, preparation to be worth anything must be real; Marie had a truthful nature, and knew this; if, therefore, she addressed herself to the work of preparation, she must do so with sincerity and diligence. Accordingly she now studied her catechism assiduously, and listened attentively to the explanation. What was commenced from a sense of duty, love, however, soon rendered easy and delightful. The beauty of the truths of the Faith, when once she had given her mind seriously to consider them, found access to her heart, which till then had been closed against their influence by worldly desires and the evil passions which had been roused by those desires into activity. The germs of virtue which existed in her, although hitherto overlaid and choked, were now able, under the vivifying action of grace, to develop themselves. She began to endeavour to correct her faults, and before long she found in the practices of piety a sweetness which she had never tasted either in them or in aught else beside. A corresponding change was soon visible on her young face. The expression of her countenance became more serene; the clouds gradually cleared away, and the sun shone forth. The outward transformation, in short, corresponded with that which had been worked internally.

At last the happy day of communion arrived, and we learn from her own lips that, in thus uniting herself to her Lord for the first time, Marie had a very lively impression of His presence, and that He vouchsafed to communicate to her some of that sweetness of which He designed hereafter to give her such abundant

participation. She did not conceal her joy. Heretofore so reserved, when tempted by the dumb demon of
sadness, she now spoke to her mother artlessly and
confidingly of what was passing within her. "Mother,"
she said, "how sweet it is (qu'il fait bon) to receive
Jesus, and bear Him within us!" "True, my child,"
replied Elisabeth; and now you must try for the
future to be very good, and to live in such a way as to
deserve to communicate often." And Marie was faithful to this maternal counsel. She had longed for
happiness, as the human heart always longs, more or
less consciously, and she had found it. Blessed child;
doubly blessed in her poor condition, which had saved
her from having the cup of false worldly pleasure presented to her acceptance before she came to know the
true and only good!

She prepared herself with the same diligence and
fervour for the sacrament of Confirmation, which she
received shortly after in the church of Pouillon, an
adjoining parish to Mimbaste, from the hands of
Monseigneur Savy, the Bishop of Aire. Marie opened
her heart to receive in abundance the effusion of the
gifts of the Holy Ghost, and the effects were manifestly
visible in her whole conduct and demeanour. Every
day seemed marked by progress in virtue, and all
noted and admired her modesty, her gentleness, her
graceful attention to the wishes of others, her prompt
obedience, her industry. All this was the more striking
as her previous deficiency in the sweetest graces of the
Christian character had been so observable. But, above
all, her fervour in the performance of her acts of
devotion, and, in particular, her singular recollection in
presence of the Blessed Sacrament, edified all who saw
her. A strong faith, causing her to realise intensely

this adorable Presence, was the inward source of her remarkable composure when present at Mass, or when she had the consolation of visiting our Lord in the Sacrament of His Love.   Thither she felt herself drawn more and more every day, and every day she there imbibed fresh draughts of love.   Such was Marie between the ages of twelve and thirteen years.

———◆———

## CHAPTER II.

### FIRST FAVOURS AND TEMPTATIONS.

ABOUT a year after her first communion, Marie one day, at the moment of the elevation, perceived a brilliant light over the altar, and, while her eyes were contemplating it, she felt her heart penetrated with love for the God of the Eucharist.   This love, as has been said, had been day by day increasing in her, and now, along with its increase, increased also the splendour of the light which she continued to behold.   She has herself described her interior colloquies with her Divine Lord at that period.

"For a long time," she says, "I only talked *to* Him. I said very little.   I did not know anything to say to Him, except these words : ' O my Jesus, I love Thee ; ' or ' Jesus, I give Thee my heart ; ' or ' Saviour Jesus, increase my love for Thee.'   Then, on leaving Him, I used to bid Him farewell, saying, ' My Saviour, bless Thy most humble servant.' "

We have an instance here of the simplicity which Jesus loves so much.   These short ejaculations are like arrows sent to His Divine Heart, which, we may believe, reach It more surely than many elaborate prayers, however beautiful they may be, and however fervent the sentiments they may embody. For a long time Marie received no sensibly audible reply from the lips of her Saviour, nor, as we may readily imagine, had she any such presumptious expectation ; nevertheless, she felt that He spoke to her heart. "I heard," she says, "as it were, an interior voice which pronounced no words ; and this voice, full of gentleness and sweetness, said to me, ' My daughter, I love thee. My daughter, I accept the offering of thy heart. My daughter, I bless thee ; ' and then I retired happy."

We see here the dawn of those signal favours which were reserved for this dear child by her Lord. But it seems in accordance with His dealings in like cases, after giving a soul a first taste, more or less sweet, of His love, to send trials or temptations to purify and prepare it for higher graces and closer and clearer manifestations of Himself. And so it was with Marie Lataste : she was to pass through a painful interior ordeal. First, she had to contend with the uprisings of her own rebellious nature; for, notwithstanding the change which had been worked in her,—a change the results of which were so palpable that to those around her she seemed like another being,—the old Adam was not yet subdued. He is not put to death in a day, or at so small a cost ; nay, he is never thoroughly put to death even in the most perfect until they quit this body of sin, in which the roots of evil tarry, ready to bud and sprout again, if the knife be not constantly applied to them. True, while enjoying the sweetness of divine grace, and while supported sensibly by God's almighty arm, the soul, in the first fervours of her conversion, might imagine that her enemy was prostrated under her feet for ever, never more to arise and molest her. This is an error which she has to unlearn by experience, that she may recognise most intimately her own weakness, and thus become grounded in humility and self-contempt, and at the same time be strengthened in faith and confidence in Him who will never allow those to be " put to confusion " who have hoped in Him. Emerging from these trials, the soul is fitted to receive the gifts of God without secretly appropriating anything to herself ; then can she take up safely the song of triumph, and exclaim, with David, " How great troubles hast Thou shown me, many and grievous : and turning Thou hast brought me to life, and hast brought me back again from the depths of the earth : Thou hast multiplied Thy magnificence, and turning to me Thou hast comforted me. For I will also confess to Thee, Thy truth with the instruments of psaltery : O God, I will sing to Thee with the harp, Thou Holy One of Israel. My lips shall greatly rejoice, when I shall sing to Thee ; and my soul which Thou hast redeemed."*

Marie's predominant passion seems to have been pride, and she had now to contend with its continual assaults. To these temptations, scruples presently came to add their peculiar torture. Scruples, as we know, are of two kinds : the one sort are defects, and not the less hard to cure that they partake at the same time of the nature of infirmities ; the other sort are temptations, with which God has permitted some of His greatest saints to be assailed for their more entire purification and the increase of their merits. Of the latter character, we may believe, were the scruples with which Marie was harassed at this time. The profound impression which the truths of the Faith made upon her mind, her

* Psalm lxx.

conviction of the purity of God's law, and of its high requirements, coupled with the increased perception of her own shortcomings, became to her so many occasions of alarm and self-reproach; the enemy of souls availing himself of this disposition to bewilder her mind with a thousand fears and to set her actions before her as all soiled by sin.

Marie, however, was no longer shut up within the limits of a shy and cold reserve; she made no secret, therefore, of her apprehensions to her sister Marguerite, and, when preparing to approach the tribunal of penance, used to submit to her the different subjects of self-accusation which she was about to carry thither. Marguerite often had difficulty in discerning any matter of confession in these avowals of her sister, and still more difficulty in reassuring her, which she strove to do to the best of her knowledge and ability; all her endeavours failing to calm the mental anguish of Marie. The poor child was unable even to place any reliance on the sincerity of her confessions, for she experienced no sensible sorrow for her faults, and feared, therefore, that she should not obtain the pardon which she sought. As yet her piety needed guidance and enlightenment, and her ignorance accordingly made her regard the absence of affective emotions as a sign that she was rejected by God. The bitter grief which this fear occasioned to her was, however, sufficient proof of the ardour with which she in truth aspired to Him. Her confessor was happily a man skilled in the science of direction; he was watching attentively the progress of grace in this child's soul; and in her simple abandonment to his teachings and counsels she was to find the effectual antidote to her scruples.

A still more painful trial, however, had now assailed

her.   It has pleased God by a special favour to exempt
some of His saints from temptations against the most
delicate and precious of virtues, but many others have
been allowed to pass through this torturing crucible.
Marie Lataste, young as she was,—for by her own
account her scruples attacked her when she was between
thirteen and fourteen years of age, and these temptations against purity appear to have come upon her
almost, if not quite, simultaneously—was not spared this
ordeal.   She says that they were well-nigh continual;
and, if we could have any doubt of the quarter whence
they proceeded, it would suffice to note that, while her
soul was thus filled with images and suggestions of evil,
she was every day growing in the strongest love of the
very virtue which they assailed, and in estrangement
from worldly things.   " God," she said, " was seeking to
fashion my heart by these terrible trials, sent to me at
so tender an age.   He inspired me with sentiments of
disinclination for the world ; He taught me the danger
of yielding to my passions, and daily increased in me
the love of virginity.   It offered to my mind an indis-
cribable secret charm, which attached me to it and
made me fear to lose it."   While these temptations lasted,
however, she suffered intensely.   " My soul," she says,
in the letter to her director, written some years later,
from which we have just quoted, " was oppressed with
trouble, weariness, and dryness.   I found consolation
nowhere : neither in God, nor in my mother, who
suffered from my suffering, which she could not understand, but which she perceived.   My sister Marguerite
alone was like a consoling angel, whom Heaven had
placed near me ; but, ignorant as she was of what was
passing within me, how could she, notwithstanding all
her love for me, give me the support I needed ? "

B

In regard to this temptation, Marie, who was open and frank with her sister about the state of her soul on other points, was silent, and spoke of it only to her confessor. She was very anxious to bind herself by a vow of perpetual chastity; but this, from prudence, he did not allow her to do, in spite of her earnest desire and frequent solicitations. Much discretion, of course, is always requisite in such cases with respect to persons living in the world, and Marie's extreme youth rendered caution doubly necessary. At last her confessor so far acceded to her wishes as to permit her to make this vow from year to year. From the moment she was allowed to contract this solemn engagement, temporary as it was, the trouble and uneasiness which she had experienced began gradually to diminish. Nevertheless, though she enjoyed this relief from the most afflicting of her interior trials, her dryness in prayer still continued, and, so far from finding any consolation in communion, which she received monthly, it used to be the occasion of a renewal of inward suffering, accompanied with an increase of sadness.

Soon she was to be called to endure fiercer assaults. When she had completed her seventeenth year she was quite freed from the distressing temptations against purity, but she had now to encounter an almost general revolt of all the other passions. The pride which had been so dominant throughout her childhood seemed to revive, and to rise within her with redoubled strength; and her heart felt embittered with anger to such an excess that she compares the pains she endured from her inward struggle to dying, as it were, every moment. "My sensibility and susceptibility," she adds, "became extreme : a word, a look, a gesture, a mere nothing, would displease me in others and put me out of patience.

What I suffered, and what a life I led at this time, not knowing what to do, or which way to turn myself!" Perhaps there is no harder temptation to bear than this unreasoning and unreasonable bitterness of spirit; and it is one, moreover, for which little allowance is sure to be made, not only by others, if they perceive it, but by the soul which suffers from it. We are speaking, of course, of those who are innocently the subjects of this temptation, whether it proceed from mere natural and physical causes, or be an interior cross and a temptation permitted for their purification. It is very humiliating for the soul to feel itself thus the victim of a general sense of irritation, for which it can assign no causes but such as when stated, if capable of being so, sound puerile or despicable; and for this very reason, doubt-less,—that is, because such temptations are so peculiarly calculated to lower us in our own esteem,—has it often pleased God to subject His most favoured servants, at certain periods of their spiritual progress, to these re-volts of their most ignoble passions, apparently long subdued, withdrawing at the same time all sensible sweetness from their souls.

In the midst of these fierce assaults with which Satan was permitted to afflict Marie and try her fidelity, Jesus was casting a look of compassion on His servant, and preparing for her the sweetest of cordials and the most powerful of supports. This cordial and support was the extraordinary love which He infused into her for Himself in the Adorable Sacrament. "He hath brought me up," says the royal Psalmist, "on the water of refreshment. Though I should walk in the midst of the shadow of death, I will fear no evils, for Thou art with me. Thy rod and Thy staff, they have comforted me. Thou hast prepared a table before me, against

them that afflict me. Thou hast anointed my head
with oil; and my chalice which inebriateth me, how
goodly is it!"* Marie had ever since her conversion
felt a strong devotion springing up in her heart towards
Jesus in His Sacrament, but the tabernacle where He
abides was henceforth to become a magnet continually
attracting to itself all her thoughts and affections.

We cannot do better than give her own account of
this grace which was vouchsafed to her. She has been
speaking of the bitterness of spirit and universal irritation which, as has been said, was one of her most
excruciating trials, when she exclaims, "Oh, the providence and mercy of God! This amiable Father cast a
look of compassion on me, He had pity on my wretch-
edness, He attracted my heart to the Divine Sacrament
of the Altar. He took it to bind it so firmly to Himself that it was no longer easy for me to wander from
Him; I mean in thought. Sleeping or waking, whether
working or not, alone or in company, conversing with
God or with men, my mind and my heart remained near
Jesus. How many pains, torments, tribulations, sufferings of all kinds, did I experience even then! But I
was with Jesus, and it was a happiness for my soul to
suffer in His presence, and to offer myself to Him as a
victim, beholding Him a victim of love for me in His
Eucharist." This was, indeed, a very great grace,
especially if we are to understand the assertion literally—and we know not how otherwise to understand
it—that even when sleeping this realisation of her
nearness to Jesus on the altar was not interrupted.
Such a privilege certainly has been accorded to few.†

* Psalm xxii. 2, 4, 5.

† Père Nouet, in his "Homme d'Oraison," tells us that that
holy man, Brother Alphonsus Rodriguez, who was raised to the

Again, we find her thus describing, or, at least, endeavouring to describe, what the Tabernacle of Jesus had become to her soul: "The Tabernacle of Jesus is the place to which I love to retire, there to hide myself and take my repose. There I find a life which I cannot define, a joy which I cannot comprehend, a peace the like of which is not to be met with under the hospitable roofs of the dearest friends. The Tabernacle of Jesus is a shelter to me against my enemies, against the devil, against the world, against my passions, against my ill-regulated inclinations; it is a support to me in my weakness, a consolation in sorrow, a weapon in conflict, a refreshment in heat, a nourishment in hunger, a recreation in fatigue, a heaven upon earth. The Tabernacle of Jesus is my riches in poverty, my treasure in want, my clothing in nakedness, my crown in affliction. The Tabernacle of Jesus is my God and my All, my Jesus and my Saviour." No wonder that Marie should ever have considered this grace as amongst the greatest and highest which her Lord bestowed upon her. Yet we shall soon see with what extraordinary liberality He was to communicate Himself to this chosen soul.

sublimest degrees of contemplation, enjoyed this singular favour. For this we have his own testimony. He said that he truly prayed to God even while sleeping, making sweet colloquies with Him without being at first able to persuade himself that his sleep was accompanied by prayer; but he subsequently recognised that all his joy in life being to walk in the presence of God, God also communicated Himself to him everywhere, and that the time of slumber was peculiarly favourable to infused prayer, because the soul being then, as it were, disengaged from the body is more capable of seeing God present with it, and of uniting itself to Him in secrecy and in silence. See "The Life of Blessed Alphonsus Rodriguez, Lay-Brother of the Society of Jesus," by a Lay-Brother of the same Society, pp. 75, 76.

# CHAPTER III.

## Jesus Appears to Marie.

At the close of the year 1839, Marie one day, under the influence of the attraction which had taken possession of her whole being, took her way towards the church. In the act itself there seems nothing extraordinary ; nevertheless, it was not a common act, nor one performed deliberately from ordinary motives. These are her own words, when giving an account to her director three years later, of what then occurred :— "What was my happiness on that day, when I felt my soul illuminated by a light altogether interior, and my whole being attracted towards the Holy Sacrament of the Altar ! I could not resist this attraction. My feet carried me thither, so to say, naturally, and without effort." So absorbed was she by the inward vision which occupied her, that she seemed to herself to be already before the Blessed Sacrament, and was unconscious of seeing anything on her way.

"I saw," she says, "neither gardens, nor fields, nor meadows, neither men, nor women—nothing but the Tabernacle in all places, everywhere.. I walked, but believed myself to be before the Tabernacle." She adds, in explanation, that she beheld it, not with the eyes of the body, but with those of the soul. As yet there was no vision of which the senses took cognisance ; only their action seems to have been suspended by reason of her fixed internal contemplation.

But when she entered the church it was to be otherwise. Here a magnificent vision awaited her. She beheld our Lord Himself upon the altar, surrounded by His Angels. She did not, however, see Him at first with perfect distinctness. A thin cloud, like an almost imperceptible veil, appeared partially to conceal Him from her sight. The joy which filled Marie's heart was indescribable, yet she did not dare to draw near, nor even to continue facing this marvellous spectacle, but retired bashfully into a corner of the sacred building, where she remained with her eyes riveted on her Lord. Meanwhile her heart seemed each instant to be drawn more closely to Him; and, as the ardour of her love waxed stronger, so did the vision become more and more luminous to her bodily eyes. At last Jesus descended from the altar and approached, calling her benignantly by her name, and raising His hand to bless her. Then she beheld Him with perfect clearness in the brilliant light with which He was invested. His whole aspect was full of majesty and sweetness, and His countenance breathed nothing but love, benignity, and tenderness.

"From that moment," she said, " the society of men has never ceased to be displeasing to me ; I should wish to fly from them for ever and shut myself up in the Tabernacle with Him." She had seen Him whom her soul loved ; and how loveless did the world now seem to her! Had Jesus but once thus drawn aside the veil, and vouchsafed her only this one short vision of His Sacred Humanity, it would have sufficed for the memory of a whole life. That one glimpse of Him who is Beauty, Glory, Sweetness, Love, would have dimmed for ever in her eyes all the charms of earth and of the creature; but this extraordinary favour was to be now of almost daily renewal, and was but an instalment of still greater favours to come.

Nevertheless, although she almost always beheld
Him when assisting at Mass, she was not allowed to
depend upon this grace as a certainty.  Jesus sometimes tried her by His absence.  We learn from herself
the effect which this subtraction of His sensible presence produced upon her ; but first she describes to her
director the precious fruits which had been its results.
" Until the day," she writes, " when it was given to me
to adore Jesus Christ sensibly present to my sight, I
had only lived my child's life.  When the Saviour
Jesus appeared before my eyes the first time, I suddenly
experienced within myself greater firmness, vigour, and
courage ; I felt myself more drawn towards God, more
detached from the world, more at enmity with myself,
more amenable to others, more severe to myself, and
this with scarcely any effort on my part.  These dispositions of my soul increased every day, in proportion
as my eyes more and more contemplated the Saviour,
and my ears hearkened to His voice, and the darkness
of my understanding was dissipated.  I looked upon
myself as a tree which the morning dew and the sunshine of the day render fruitful without any merit on
its part; and willingly would I have lived this life for
a thousand years."  This account which Marie so
simply gives of what passed within her, suggests the
idea of an infusion of grace in which her soul, although
passive, was conscious of what was taking place while
simply yielding its consent.  It reminds one of what
the Apostle says to the Corinthians : " We all, beholding the glory of the Lord with open face, are transformed into the same image, from glory to glory, as by
the Spirit of the Lord." *  The soul, beholding Jesus, is
transfigured into His likeness.  It is true that in this

* 2 Cor. iii. 18.

case there was an actual vision, with an extraordinary favour accompanying it; nevertheless, the vision in itself would have had no transforming effect had there not been a preparation of heart; and the same transformation might have taken place, had it so pleased God, through an interior analogous manifestation to the soul. This may perhaps suggest to us a thought that we may sometimes mar God's work by our over-activity in prayer. We give Him no scope to form His image in us, by becoming like the ruffled lake, which ceases to be a mirror. All, doubtless, are not called to or capable of, contemplation, still a recipient and expectant attitude of mind, prevailing at times over the perpetual bustle of petition, might be within ordinary reach, and perhaps would prove to be a great secret for growing spiritually rich. It would be the " Ecce ancilla Domini" of the soul.

After describing, then (as we have seen), how her soul drank in grace in the sunshine of her Lord's countenance, Marie goes on to relate what were her painful experiences when He for a time withdrew His visible and sensible presence. " God's thoughts," she continues, " are not like those of us poor creatures, who know not what is for our good, or what is most profitable for us. He deprived me of His sensible presence, and I sank into a state of weakness, languor, and cowardice. I was oppressed with fatigue, and could rest nowhere; my heart was in a state of suffering, sadness, and continual impatience. I should easily have fallen into discouragement. I felt my passions and perverse inclinations raising their voices within me; I dreaded losing my soul, and becoming the miserable victim of sin." Marie was thus made experimentally to realise her own weakness and nothingness;

nevertheless, she was secretly sustained by grace, which never fails those who retain a good will, however fiercely they may be tried, or however great may be their sense of abandonment. " One day," she proceeds, "making an effort, I said to myself, 'How cowardly and fearful I am! Ah! certainly God will not abandon me.' I fell on my knees, and cried aloud to Heaven, 'Lord, Thy will be done, and do Thou have pity on me.' The Saviour Jesus was probably only waiting for this proof of my perfect resignation, for He did not delay to present Himself again to my eyes. What a beautiful soft light encompassed His throne and His person! How happy I was again at that moment! This light was reflected upon me, penetrated, illuminated, fortified me, and inflamed me with the love of God. Nevertheless, I had the resolution every day to say to Jesus, ' Lord, I sacrifice, if such be Thy pleasure, the sweetness of Thy presence.'" It was in the year 1842 that she wrote thus, when giving an account of what had occurred in the first year that she was favoured with these visions. She adds, " He continues to manifest Himself to me, but soon I shall see Him no more ; this He has Himself announced to me. His will be done !"

It was on the feast of the Epiphany, in the year 1840, that our Lord restored to her the vision which He had withdrawn ; and from this time, until the close of the year 1842, she was to behold Him daily at the moment of the elevation. She thus describes, in another letter, what took place on that occasion. "At the beginning of the year 1840, on the feast of the Epiphany, I had the happiness of receiving communion. I felt within me a happiness such as I had never before experienced. I turned my eyes to the altar : there, on a chair of gold, Jesus was seated, resplendent with glory and majesty. I saw Him smile upon me with kindness, and I said to Him interiorly, 'Lord Jesus, bless me, and take pity on a poor sinner like me.'" Although this absence appears to have been the longest in duration, Jesus had several times put the obedience and love of His servant to the test in similar ways. Some of these trials we will here relate in her own words. "One day Jesus appeared to me as He was wont; He called me to His tabernacle; then, all of a sudden, the splendour of His light vanished from my sight, and I heard His voice saying to me, 'Withdraw, my daughter.' I retired with pain and sorrow in my heart. For several days I returned without seeing Him. How grievously did I suffer from this privation of the sight of Jesus! I said to myself, 'It is your sins which have made you lose this favour;' and I humbled myself before the Lord, presenting Him, as an expiation of my sins and iniquities, my perfect submission to all His desires. Sometime afterwards I perceived Jesus on the altar. The priest was celebrating Holy Mass. 'Daughter,' said the Saviour to me after the Communion, 'remain at the rails. You must never approach nearer unless I direct you to do so.' 'Lord,' I replied, 'I will ever do Thy will.' Immediately, in order to try me, He drove me from the church; I remained without on my knees, waiting until He would admit me once more. After a good space of time He called me; He permitted me to prostrate myself at His feet, and to embrace them."

It will be seen from the foregoing extract that her visions were not all external to her; she had others of the imaginary class; the two kinds seeming often to pass the one into the other. When she speaks of

remaining at the rails of the sanctuary, it is evident
that we are not to understand her as being commanded
by our Lord to kneel always there; this would have
been an act of singularity; still less, can we interpret
in a literal sense the direction to advance within the
sanctuary.  She moved in spirit to these different
places, and often beheld Jesus within her own heart, to
which, as if it were something apart from herself, she
seemed to be admitted.  But all this will be best
described in her own words.  " For about a year," she
writes, " my place was at the railing.  I had not the
right to advance further.  Only sometimes Jesus manifested Himself to me in my heart, which then became
to me like a magnificent temple, the entrance to which
was never forbidden me.  I saw Him as really as I
do in the church, and I offered to Him my acts of
reverence and adoration.  There was in my heart an
altar, a tabernacle, a throne, a railing.  The altar was
of gold, the tabernacle of gold, the throne of gold, the
railing of gold.  There was also a magnificent lamp, the
light of which was more brilliant than that of the sun.
My angel guardian used to light it before Jesus entered
into my heart."  We shall quote by and by another
similar description of these interior visions.

Again, when giving an account, in obedience to her
director, of the manner in which Jesus had manifested
Himself to her, she thus describes His daily appearance
at the elevation, as already mentioned : " At the moment of the elevation, when the priest made his genu-
flexion, after having pronounced the words of consecration, I used to see an exceeding brightness filling the
sanctuary, and beheld Jesus appear upon the altar, where
He remained until the Communion.  His countenance
was usually full of benignity and sweetness, but some-

times He looked grave, and seemed to be displeased. His splendour surpassed that of the sun ; His majesty was such that on earth there is nothing comparable to it ; His throne was of the most refulgent gold, His robe was not formed of any stuff, not even of the finest, or, if it was of stuff, I have never seen the like ; it looked as though it were transparent, and sparkled with light like a diamond or precious stone. He was seated on His throne ; His left Hand rested on His Heart, and the right Hand reposed gently on His knees. His eyes were generally fixed on the people, and at certain moments—for example, during the Pater and the Agnus Dei—always on the priest. During this time I was allowed to approach close to the altar, and Jesus spoke to me in the manner I have related. Sometimes He permitted me to draw near to Him : then there was for me no longer railing, or steps, or priest, or altar ; I saw Jesus only, and I advanced towards Him as on solid ground. I placed myself on my knees, and He addressed me with kindness."

She then goes on to relate how Jesus sometimes manifested Himself to her in her heart, when He had disappeared from the altar. " After the Communion, Jesus was no longer on the altar. One day I sought Him elsewhere, and found Him in my heart. Now, strange to say, my heart appeared to me like the sanctuary and altar of the Tabernacle. It resembled a small vaulted chamber, in the midst of which I saw a chair of gold, like that of the altar, and Jesus was seated thereon. A balustrade surrounded His throne like that of the sanctuary, only it was neither of wood nor of stone, but of the finest gold. The brilliancy which I had seen on the altar of the church, I now saw in my heart. I desired to enter my heart ; I felt a powerful attraction

drawing me to penetrate into it, which I followed. I
began to walk towards my heart, as if it had been a
thing apart from myself, and I penetrated into it as
before I had penetrated into the sanctuary. Sometimes
Jesus kept me from Him on my knees before the balustrade which surrounded His throne. Thence He spoke
to me, as upon the altar and during Holy Mass. I will
not here describe the manner in which I beheld my
heart, nor the precipices which I encountered and which
I often perceived; the different accounts I have given
faithfully describe them." To some of these we shall
subsequently allude, when we come to speak more particularly of her visions. She proceeds to mention
another occasion on which she was in the habit of seeing Jesus in a sensible manner. "When I meditated,"
she continues, "I always transported myself to the foot
of the Tabernacle, there to pay my homage. When I
was engaged in mental prayer, my attraction drew me to
penetrate into the Tabernacle, and I used to find Jesus
as on the altar, and as in my heart after communion.
I beheld Jesus, I was within the Tabernacle with Him,
I spoke to Him, I was on my knees at His feet, or
standing before Him, and He discoursed with me as
He was wont."

In the early beginnings of these manifestations, the
simple girl imagined, as she herself afterwards said, that
she was not the object of any special privilege; she
thought that others enjoyed similar favours.* The
same modest reserve which made her practise silence,

---

* The writer has been told of a case, well authenticated, in which
a child was in the constant habit of seeing angels kneeling in adoration around the altar during Mass. She never thought of mentioning the circumstance because she supposed that others saw
them as well as herself. But upon her happening to allude to these
celestial adorers she never beheld them again.

she would naturally impute to every one, so that the secrecy observed on the subject did not surprise her; to her confessor alone did she allude to these things, and to him merely in a general way. It was afterwards, in obedience to the commands of her second director, that she furnished the details on which we have drawn. The priest of Mimbaste, who had known her from her infancy, and was well acquainted with her innocence and truthfulness of soul, thought it better to leave her to receive without disquietude the favours which it pleased God to bestow upon her, always avoiding the appearance of attaching much importance to them. But, although she never even to the most intimate of her companions gave a hint of what passed within her, or of the marvellous things which she was privileged to behold, nevertheless her demeanour attracted their observation. Ever since she had been favoured with these heavenly visits, she might be seen, while in the church, always upon her knees, immovable, with her hands joined, and her eyes usually fixed on the tabernacle or the altar. When on her way thither to pray, the joy she felt was so great that it revealed itself in her countenance, and when she left the church after her communings face to face with the Saviour, the radiant expression she wore could not but strike all who looked at her. This was the more remarkable in her, because Marie was of a grave temperament and by no means given to joyousness.

One of her friends spoke to her once on the subject. "Marie," she said, "you always look so extremely happy when you are entering or leaving the church." "I do not know whether I seem so outwardly," she replied, "but I frankly own that I am so inwardly. The reason is very simple. The church is the house of God; when

I enter it, I seem to be drawing nearer to God, to our Lord, to the Blessed Virgin, to the angels, and to the saints. When I leave it, I feel very happy at having been so near to God, to our Lord, to the Blessed Virgin, to the angels, and to the saints; and especially at having been able to converse for a few moments with them. I do not know many things to say to them; but I say what I know. What would you? I am going through my apprenticeship here below for Heaven; there we shall speak better than on earth. At present I only know how to stammer, but I do it with great pleasure." Thus did Marie ingeniously succeed in concealing the favours she received, while strictly adhering to the truth. But what if, when thus directly questioned, she had simply revealed the whole truth? would she have sinned? He who searches hearts and scans their secret motives and intentions could alone have judged; but probably she might never again have seen the glory and the vision. The Spirit of God is sensitive and jealous beyond conception with those to whom He vouchsafes His special communications; and, even as in close and intimate friendship there are indiscretions, whether of word or act, such as that of manifesting to others its tender familiarities and outpourings, which would hurt and wound it more than would faults of a seemingly graver character, so it is with the Friend who is nearer to us than a brother. The chosen servants of God have ever instinctively felt this, and have hid their treasure, like the man in the parable who found the pearl of great price. *"Secretum meum mihi."*

Having mentioned the appearance which Marie's devotion presented when kneeling in God's house, and the simple explanation of her happiness which she gave to her inquisitive friend, we will here subjoin the full and sincere avowal which, under obedience, she afterwards made to those who were entitled to her confidence. Her director (we mean her second director) had recommended her to put herself in communication with another priest, as will be hereafter noticed; and, fearing that she had perhaps not replied with sufficient clearness to two questions which he had addressed to her, Marie repeats her explanation in a letter to him. One of these inquiries related to what she experienced, physically speaking, when Jesus addressed her, or when she saw Him face to face; to which she thus replies :— "I experience no distressing bodily sensation either when Jesus speaks to me or previously. My body seems neither active nor passive. I cannot tell you precisely what is its state. It appears to me that it is without movement; that it has not the use of its senses; that all activity remains within my soul. When Jesus wishes to speak to me, or desires to manifest Himself to me, I feel myself attracted towards Him, towards His tabernacle, and I move towards Him either bodily or in spirit.* When able to go to the church, I kneel either on the floor or on a chair; I think of Jesus, I adore Him, I give Him my heart, I turn my eyes towards the tabernacle : then all disappears—church, altar, tabernacle; I see only Jesus and the priest, if it is during Mass. It is a wholly new world. I walk, I kneel down, I go to Jesus, I place myself near His throne, I listen to His words; and when Jesus has ceased to speak to me, and I am no longer speaking to

---

* By this she evidently means that when this attraction takes place, if she happens to be elsewhere, she turns her steps, if possible, to the church. A case of this kind is described by her the first time she was favoured with the vision of our Lord.

C

Him, I feel myself drawn to return Him thanks, and then I find myself still on my knees, on the floor or on a chair, in the same position as at the moment when I knelt down in His presence. All this occurs without any disturbance or bodily suffering; only I feel a certain sweetness following on these relations of my soul with the Saviour."

It could hardly be that she should thus inwardly behold and hear such glorious things, and that there should be no outward reflex to excite the observation of those around her. In her own room at home, when she was engaged in prayer and Jesus spoke to her, she had, she said, never been interrupted, but she had occasionally been surprised by the entrance of some one just at the moment when He had ceased speaking. She owned that on such occasions she had felt a little put out. "But now," she adds (she is writing in the beginning of 1843), "I have, thanks to the Divine Saviour, been enabled to overcome this kind of sensitiveness." However, although these visions seemed to cause neither strain nor suffering to her bodily frame, yet she remarked that, when they had passed, they left a kind of temporary indisposition to work. This seems to have been partly mental and partly bodily. "I think of Jesus," she says, "for a long time after I have heard Him; I should wish to be still with Jesus; I should wish to occupy myself with nothing but Jesus; I feel this attraction sensibly, and it throws my body into a sort of languor, which renders work harder and more irksome to me."

# CHAPTER IV.

## Jesus becomes Marie's Instructor.

WE have seen how the very sight of Jesus filled
Marie's soul with light, fervour, and fortitude to battle
with and overcome self. But, great as was this favour,
it was far from all which the liberality of our Lord
deigned to bestow upon her. He condescended to become her instructor in a manner perfectly marvellous.
The writings which, under obedience, Marie penned, record the lessons she thus supernaturally received. They
have been published under the title of "The Works of
Marie Lataste." Whoever, on hearing that these writings contain the account of what she heard from the
lips of Jesus during her visions, should open them
under the impression that their pious curiosity will be
gratified by wonderful and mysterious revelations, will
perhaps for a moment experience a certain sense of disappointment, when they find far the greater portion of
these communications to be simply an elaborate detail
of Christian doctrine; yet further consideration will
assuredly cause a feeling of wonder to arise in the
mind. When it is remembered that this poor girl had
only been taught her Catechism, like any other child of
poverty and ignorance, with such common explanation
as she was capable of receiving; that in her early
childhood it was difficult even to teach her the simplest
elements of the faith; that her mother was wholly
illiterate, and could not afford to put her to school;
that the greater part of her time was spent in looking
after animals in the fields or helping in some household

toil, no one can help feeling most strongly how utterly inadequate her unassisted powers and unenlightened intellect would have been to write one page of these two volumes.

In them we have not only a full explanation of all the mysteries of the faith,—simply and familiarly given, it is true, yet all in a strictly theological form,—but a thorough instruction concerning the spiritual life and the duties of the Christian state; prayer, the doctrines of grace, the theological and moral virtues, the gifts of the Holy Ghost, the chief types of the Old Testament, the exalted prerogatives of the Blessed Mother of God, the admirable relations which exist between God, the holy angels, and men ; and many other cognate subjects. Sometimes we find our Lord condescending to question His disciple just as a careful teacher interrogates his scholar to ascertain the amount of his knowledge on some point, or his retention and understanding of the instruction that had been conveyed to him. Sometimes He enlightens her by means of a symbolic vision, of which we shall hereafter give a few specimens. Our admiration increases as we read, and then we are led to make the following reflection. Here, it is true, was a favoured soul, whom it pleased Jesus to lift out of the dust of poverty and ignorance, and Himself directly to instruct without any intermediary. This is a miracle of grace and love as exceptional as it is marvellous ; still, in the main, we may recognise herein a touching example of what our Lord does, or is willing to do, for the soul of each and all of us in our several degrees. For we are, every one of us, singularly dear to Him, being purchased by His Precious Blood and called to learn of Him. The instruction which our external ears receive must be accompanied by the inward teaching and enforcement of His Spirit, or it fails of its effect. Jesus must speak to us by His Spirit, and we must hearken, or we shall hear and learn in vain, and this inward teaching He never withholds, nay, is most desirous to give, and will give in proportion to the simplicity and sincerity with which we throw open to Him, so to say, the avenues of our soul; not, indeed, as sensibly or perceptibly as to the poor peasant-girl of Mimbaste, yet as truly and effectually, if only we will permit Him. If this be so, as indeed, there can be no doubt, we may certainly derive not a little consolation and encouragement from this record of His divine condescensions.

Let us hear how Marie speaks of herself before entering on the task which had been laid upon her. "I am a poor humble country-girl, knowing nothing but what my mother has taught me; my whole knowledge in the natural order consists in knowing how to read and write, and use my needle and spindle. I am also a great sinner, upon whom Jesus has taken pity; for, first of all, He redeemed me at the price of His Blood, and He has since loaded me with the most signal favours. My knowledge in the supernatural order long consisted only in a simple acquaintance with the principal truths of salvation. I had learned them in my childhood with much pleasure. I often thought of them; my mind found rest in them; my soul took delight in them. By degrees the light has spread like that of a capacious hearth upon which wood is being continually piled, the wind at the same time blowing impetuously on it from all sides. It is the Saviour Jesus, the Light of the world, who has been the light of my soul; He has educated me, as a mother educates her daughter, with patience and perseverance; and, if I know something more now, I owe it all to Him."

It was during the first year of these visions, at the time when Jesus tried her by occasional absences, that Marie learned how to meditate. It was Jesus Himself who taught her. "He taught me," she writes, "three ways at three different times and places." The first was at the beginning, when her station near the altar railing was assigned to her. "My daughter," Jesus said to her, "I have given the first example to men, in order that they might act as I acted. I will be an example to you as to all men. Look at Me, and desire to follow on My steps. Think of My humble and private life at Nazareth; of My public life in Judæa and Galilee; of My Passion; of My Death. Regard My Life as a picture, and reproduce this picture in yourself, by the desire of your heart and of your soul." Marie followed the Saviour's instruction. She reflected on the Life of Jesus, praying for grace to copy it as perfectly as she was able, according to her age and state in life. But some time afterwards she seemed entirely to lose sight of how to meditate in this way, and remained before her Lord, as she describes it, "like a being devoid of reason and intellect." The time was come for a change. Jesus hearkened to her prayer for assistance and instruction, light broke in on her mind along with His words, as He taught her a higher mode of mental prayer. She now prepared herself for her meditation by going in spirit to the foot of the altar. She here banished every irrelevant thought from her mind, that she might become penetrated with the presence of God and the subject of her meditation. Generally, she selected some circumstance of the Passion, and, when she had viewed and considered it as though present at it,— whether it were in the Garden of Olives, in the Pre- torium, on Calvary, or near the Sepulchre hewn in the rock,—she returned in spirit to the altar, near to Jesus, there to elicit her affections and offer them to Him. This done, she implored the effusion of His graces in her soul, and finished her meditation. "I followed this method," she writes, "for about a year. The Saviour Jesus taught it me one day when He permitted me to pass beyond the railing, and to go up to the altar, where He was seated on His throne."

"One day," she continues, "I found the Saviour Jesus in my heart. He looked all smiling. I threw myself on my knees, saying to Him, 'I love Thee, Lord; take pity on Thy humble servant.' At that moment He taught me a new way of meditating." This new way seemed to differ from the former chiefly in containing closer sentiments of union with Jesus. It no longer consisted in a pictorial consideration of her subject, with a view to imitation or to the eliciting of devout affections, but in a more attentive hearkening to the words which it might please her Lord to address to her, and in a laying open of her heart to the receiving of His inspirations. It must not, however, be understood that this was unaccompanied by affections, acts of self-oblation, and petitions. This third manner of meditating, she thought, was the most perfect of the three, and, writing in the early spring of 1842, she says that it is the one which she had practised ever since. Later, however, she was raised to one of a more simple and higher character. Writing in November of the year 1843, and speaking of her meditation, she says, "It is, properly speaking, nothing but a simple elevation of my mind towards God, without considerations, without reflections, without affections, without resolutions. I raise my soul towards God, I unite myself to Him as my principle and my end. My whole occupation is to keep myself united to Him purely and simply, to repose peacefully in His Infinite Being, and to receive the different operations of His grace. However, I never close my meditation without making to Him an oblation of all my actions, or without recommending to Him my neighbours, both generally and in particular, soliciting for them, as for myself, the graces and benedictions of God."

We shall return to this subject in the course of the narrative. In the meantime, two observations may be made as to this mode of mental prayer. The one is that the absence of reflections, and even of affections, which were prominent and sensible in her previous practice, must not be regarded as a deficiency. All that was included in the former methods was supereminently comprised in the more advanced form of prayer. Discursive reflections, which are but means to the eliciting of affections, were indeed no longer needed; while the affections themselves, though less sensible, were really more intimately present, but of a simpler and more subtle character. The other observation which suggests itself is this: that it is clear that none can by their own choice raise themselves to this kind of prayer. They would run the risk of falling into idleness and dangerous illusion. For this reason it is— we mean the risk of illusion, or, on the other hand, the risk, not uncommon we believe, of refusing through ignorance an offer made, and resisting the attraction of grace which would lead on to a higher mode of prayer— that a qualified director, skilful and experienced in the spiritual ways, is much needed by persons who would make progress in the inner life. Where such may not be had, one safe resource remains : to yield ourselves humbly and obediently to the inward attraction, begging for light, as Marie Lataste did, and, next, to watch ourselves. The prayer which leads to no improvement, no increase in self-knowledge, no growing hatred of sin, no increase in humility and the love of God, ought to be mistrusted. An Italian proverb says, " Se son rose, fioriranno—If they are roses, they will bloom." Had Marie's conduct not borne this test, her visions themselves would have lacked that evidence which alone could satisfactorily stamp their divine origin. We have seen, however, how entire was the change produced in her by their means, and what a complete transformation of her whole being they effected.

We have already quoted what she said to her director of her natural desires of exaltation, and of the pride of her heart even in her tender childhood. We will here add what she stated concerning the results, in this respect, of the divine teaching which she received. " I do not know if the Saviour Jesus has completely modified by His grace what was defective in me. I know not if I may hope to continue always advancing towards perfection ; but it seems to me that the work of Jesus in me has not been in vain. I still love greatness, exaltation, glory, honour; but it is the greatness of God, the exaltation of God, the glory of God, the honour of God. Formerly, I loved only myself, my own person, all that appertained to me ; now, I desire to love, and I do love, so it seems to me, God alone. I do not wish for riches ; God suffices me. I do not wish for fame ; my glory is to live unknown and hidden in the most amiable Heart of Jesus. A throne, a crown, would not tempt me, and I should prefer the poverty of Jesus, the cross of Jesus, the thorny crown of Jesus, the service of Jesus, to everything of the kind here below." Such is the work of the Spirit in souls: it does not change their natures or characteristics in any way which

would imply the destruction of what is essential to
them, but it gives a new and right bent to all, building
on nature, not crushing it, transforming and transfigur-
ing, not extirpating it. " Never," she continues, " were
my heart, my mind, my soul more attached to God and
more devoted to Him than at this present ; never have
I more loved the virtues which my Saviour has taught
me to know ; never have I more loved my vocation ;
never have I more hated the world."

She then proceeds to describe the stages through
which her hatred of the world had proceeded ; for she
declares that she had hated the world with all her
heart, she might almost say during her whole life, but
at first it was from a widely different cause. " I hated
the world at first, because it was to me impossible to
love it ; but if I had possessed those things which are
necessary to make it an object of love—I say this to my
shame—I should have loved it, miserable creature that
I was, because I did not know it. I hated the world,
then, because it mortified my self-love. The world
requires an easy deportment, and, because I was timid,
I hated the world ; the world loves wit and intelligence,
and, because I was ignorant and stupid, I hated the
world ; the world esteems riches, and, because I was
poor, I hated the world. I had nothing which was
requisite to fit me for the world, and so I said within
my heart, Hatred to the world which despises you and
tramples you under foot ! This hatred was not good ;
it had no other foundation than my self-love. Later, I
still hated the world ; I had become disgusted with it
on account of the numerous obstacles which I found
in it to the working out my salvation, and the many
dangers which are to be met with at every step ; so I
desired to separate myself from it in order to live

more united to God, and to save my soul with more facility."

Hatred of the world on this account, that is to say, on account of its enmity against God and opposition to our own true interests, whether or no it lead to the desire of actually retiring from it, is essential to the Christian. Without this hatred we cannot be the friends of God. But those who go on to perfection, as did this holy soul, arrive at a further stage. At the time she wrote this account of her previous state of mind, she added that her wish to leave the world was no longer owing to her fear of losing her soul, for she believed that the grace of God would always be with her to protect her, but only in order to divest herself of everything, that she might give all to God, and love Him without interruption and for ever. It is not that persons, however far advanced in perfection, are insensible to the danger of losing their souls from presumption of having attained security; on the contrary, the more they know themselves and the better they know God, the more convinced they are of their own nothingness and frailty ; but, on the other hand, their confidence in God is far more entire, and love tends to swallow up and absorb into itself every other feeling and motive ; that love which the beloved disciple tells us " casteth our fear."

Our Lord's dealing with Marie varied according to the needs of her soul, and the dispositions in which He found her. It was, generally speaking, full of gentleness and kindness, but occasionally, when not satisfied with her, He evinced a marked displeasure. When He had traced out a line of conduct for her, she was very fearful of swerving from it, yet sometimes she failed in this respect ; then He immediately reproaches her, and exhorts her to be more faithful for the future. He was especially severe in any case of inattention. One day, in particular, she relates that her mind was in a very dissipated state, and her heart in consequence full of indifference; this caused her to listen to the words which Jesus addressed to her without the reverence due to them. "I then," she says, "saw His countenance become grave, and He looked fixedly at me. He paused, and said to me in a tone of anger, 'Who are you, to receive with so much negligence the words which I speak to you? Daughter, full of pride, do you well know yourself? You are only nothingness, sin, and corruption, and it is thus that you hearken to My words! Do you imagine that it is on account of any merits of your own that I come to converse with you? It is from My pure mercy alone that I come to teach you. This instruction is in no way your due. Beware of despising it, beware of valuing yourself upon it, beware of elevating yourself on that account above others. My word alone will not save you; your co-operation is needed. My word will not impart merit to you; your merit will be in corresponding with what it tells you. My word must not return to Me void. What I say to you would suffice to convert millions of ido-laters. Woe to you if you derive no profit from it! Know that you ought always to humble yourself before Me; for you are but dust and ashes, sin and corruption; and Jesus is God all-powerful, God infinitely perfect, God thrice holy, the Saint of saints, Sanctity Itself. I make kings. I cause monarchs and rulers to tremble on their thrones. I prove the heart and the reins; nothing which men do escapes My sight; I know their most secret thoughts. Be faithful to Me, then, and give Me your attention.'"

At other times, when through timidity she hesitated to draw near, her heart being oppressed with discouragement and sadness, Jesus would speak to her with the kindness and sweetness of the tenderest father. "Come, My child," He would say, "come to Me trustfully; raise up your heart. Speak to Me with confidence, fear nothing, disclose your sorrows to Me, and I will remove them. Come to Me, I will change your troubles into joy, your sighs and groans into songs of gladness. Your sufferings and tribulations will pass away; they are but for a time, and in heaven you will find only happiness and bliss." At the sound of these words joy would revisit her soul, and it seemed to her (to use her own words) as if she drew with abundance from the Heart of Jesus as from a well, or as if from His lips a refreshing dew descended upon her which quenched her thirst and penetrated her whole being.

On one occasion Jesus called on Marie to make a definitive choice of His service. It was on a Sunday before Mass had begun. She first of all heard the Saviour address the faithful present, pointing out to them the vanity of earthly things and the emptiness of worldly pleasures. "I had not," she said, "lost one of His words. All of a sudden He turned towards me, and said to me in a grave and earnest tone, 'To which side do you wish to belong? that of the world and the devil, or that of your Saviour and your God? If you take part with the world and the devil, eternal misery awaits you, but this you will escape if you take My side. Under my banner, you will have to endure all kinds of suffering, tribulations, and conflicts, but the cross will conduct you to heaven: choose!'" She describes herself as at that moment entirely abandoned to herself, and as if God had left her alone, perfectly mistress of her own will. In this state she remained suspended for an instant, like one who is reflecting and deliberating; then she experienced a sweet attraction drawing her towards God. It was an attraction which her will, free as it was, felt to be irresistible, and so, she adds, "My will made the happy choice of declaring itself on the side of Jesus." The Saviour further told her that it was not sufficient to range herself on His side; she must also never leave Him, and be faithful to Him for ever.

He then engaged her to promise never to commit a voluntary and deliberate sin, and to avoid all such circumstances as might lead her into sin. "I was at that moment," she says, "near the altar, for the Saviour called me to Him. I did not feel the courage to make this promise. Then Jesus made it in my name: 'I promise to avoid sin, however small it may be; and henceforward nothing shall be capable of inducing me to commit it deliberately. I promise to be faithful to God. I call as witness of my promise the stone of this altar, on which Jesus Christ immolates Himself every day to expiate the sins of the world. Let this altar be the sensible monument of my promise, and let it recall it to my mind whenever my eyes shall rest upon it.' Then I myself pronounced the promise, after thus hearing it from the lips of Jesus." He now told her that she must also never be ashamed of belonging to Him. "Lord," she promptly replied, "with Thy grace I promise this with all my heart." "If this be so," He added, "always wear My cross in sight, as a proof of the sincerity of your promise." From that moment, she declared, she had experienced a sensation of fresh strength, of new vigour; from that moment she felt that she had sincerely given herself to God.   She had made this offering through Jesus, and through Him she knew it was perpetuated.   She had, indeed, become more and more convinced that of herself she could do nothing, but that in Jesus she could do all ; it was in His strength and His grace that she had promised fidelity, and to Him she abandoned herself with the fullest confidence.

"For some time past," she says, writing in the early portion of the year 1842, "He has ceased to reproach me with anything, and treats me with increased gentleness, affection, and familiarity.   He continues to instruct and enlighten me ; moreover, He tranquillises my mind, calms my agitation, dispels what might disturb my peace, warns me when it is the devil who is seeking to trouble me, and forbids me to listen to his voice.   He invites me to abandon myself to His Providence, to cast myself into His arms with the confidence of a child, to deposit all my troubles and afflictions in His Heart.   Then He speaks to me of the most beautiful virtues ; He makes known to me their nature and effects ; He exhorts me to cherish them in my heart when God has planted them there, and to merit them, if I have not yet acquired them, by an increase of fervour."

In the dealings of Jesus with Marie, all exceptional as they were from the marvels attending upon them and giving them an outward and sensible manifestation, we seem to behold, as has been already observed, a picture of His inward work in the souls of all the members of His mystical body ; for, different as that work may indefinitely be, according to the vocation of each, still in kind it is the same, and we may, therefore, venture to conjecture that when Jesus, as we learn, expressly

declared that He desired that what He had done for the
soul of His servant Marie should be made known to the
world, and that it would conduce to the spiritual profit
of many, He desired, in His love for us, to bring this
most encouraging truth before us, and to draw our
hearts thereby to a more confiding and grateful
sense of this favour, as well as to a fuller realisation of
the responsibility which it involves in the way of
co-operation on our part. For though it be true that
all the favours shown to His saints in all ages have
been admirable evidences of His love for His Church,
nevertheless, there seems to be something very peculiar in the picture of His condescending and patient
instruction of a humble and simple soul thus mirrored
before us in what we may call His education of Marie
Lataste. We may conceive that it is intended to
have, in its measure, a general application. In these
latter days, Jesus seems to be making, as it were, His
last and most touching appeals for our love, as He has
done in the manifestation of His Sacred Heart to the
nun of Paray le Monial; and, while awaiting the
judgment of the Church concerning the poor peasant-
girl of Mimbaste, we may perhaps be allowed piously
to believe that we have here another pathetic proof
of this longing of His Adorable Heart to be known
and loved in return by those for whom every drop of
Its Precious Blood was poured forth. What can be
more simply touching than the following words of
our Lord, extracted from a most loving intimation
which He made to her one day after communion,
when He besought her in the tenderest terms to perform all, even the least of her actions, out of love to
Him ? " My daughter, let us draw closer and closer
the sweet ties which bind us to each other ; let nothing

be able to separate us, neither life nor death, neither men nor devils. Love Me each day more and more; as for Me, I shall not love you to-morrow more than I do to-day, but I will give you more sensible marks of My love. Open your soul to all the ardours of divine love; let its flames circulate with your blood in your veins. Offer yourself as a victim, and let your sacrifice be consumed by the fire of divine love. Love Me as I loved you when I was on earth. What pains, what fatigues, what sufferings, you have cost Me! I gave My Life and My Blood to save you; and, not satisfied with having died once for you, I am ever with you in the Sacrament of My Love. I abide here constantly, with My Body, My Soul, and My Divinity, out of love for you; abide here in thought out of love for Me. When I instituted this sacrament I already knew all the outrages, the irreverences, the sacrileges, and insults which I was to receive in it, but I knew how to content Myself with the small number of faithful souls who would honour Me therein and testify to Me their love. Be of this number, my daughter. Compensate Me by your love for the indifference and the insensibility of so many bad Christians. I have the right, and a very special right, to expect this from you. O sacred love, extend thyself over the earth and inflame all hearts! Let it, above all, inflame your heart, My daughter. Let it be to you the most precious of all treasures. Let it be the supreme beauty of your soul. Let it be the relief, the consolation, and the repose of your heart in all your sufferings and afflictions. O power of divine love over men! O power of divine love over God! It forms men to God; it makes God die for men. I died for the love of you, My daughter. Give yourself, then, to your Saviour, to your God, for the

D

love of Him. Respond to My love by your love ; live
for the love of Me ; die for the love of Me. I have
lived, I have suffered, I have died, for the love of you."
After that He asked for her heart, and this request
was followed by a beautiful representative vision, at
the conclusion of which Jesus told her that He had
chosen her for His spouse.

The following extract from one of Marie's letters
describes the happiness she enjoyed from the divine
communications made to her ; sentiments the less liable
to illusion inasmuch as her peace of mind, as we may
note, did not proceed from the absence of temptation,
or from that repose in which the soul is disposed to
indulge when unsolicited by evil and consoled by
spiritual sweetness. After speaking of the frequent
occasions on which Jesus came to her aid, fortifying
and calming her when she seemed utterly abandoned
and left to herself in face of her enemies, or a prey
to self-reproach and to scruples, she thus concludes :—
"Jesus is the happiness of my life in my affliction and
distress ; I say it, and it is the truth. How should He
not, in effect, make me happy, since He manifests
Himself to me as the only true good, the possession of
which is promised to fidelity, as the sole being who can
fill up the immensity of my insatiable thirst for
happiness and bliss? Joy and blessedness are only in
Jesus. To possess Jesus for ever and immediately,
willingly would I give my life, willingly would I
behold it fade away and come to an end in its spring-
time, in order to hasten my perpetual union to this
Friend so devoted, to this Father so full of affection,
to this Spouse so tender, to this Saviour so compassionate, to this God so holy and so perfect. To die and
possess Jesus ; to die and leave the stormy sea of life in

order to enter the harbour; to die and go far from this sad place of exile to our true country, which is heaven; to die and see God; to die and know God; to die and love God for all eternity—such is my ambition at this hour, such is the most intimate desire of my heart. Oh, who will give me to see the happy, the blessed day when my soul shall be separated from my body and be united with Jesus! Then shall I be plunged in the immense charity of God; here, on earth, I feel myself immersed in the immensity of my pride and my self-love. Pride is in my soul; it seeks to rule it, to bring it into bondage, to become master of it. Proud creature! Who then am I? Who am I, to believe myself anything, and not to remember every instant that I hold all from Jesus, from His mercy, from His goodness, and from His love. What a labour it is to repress pride, that mortal enemy of my soul, of my repose, of my peace!"

Marie's humility and self-distrust is in itself a strong proof that she was not under the influence of delusion or in any way carried away by her imagination; and of this she furnishes also another proof in the very fear which she acknowledges to have felt of any self-deception or diabolical illusion. It is true that while Jesus was speaking to her such an idea could not find entrance, but at times, when left to herself, she was not free from apprehension. "I often ask myself," she says, "if all this may not be the effect of the imagination or a snare of the devil, and whether or no I ought to yield my belief to it." Whenever such misgivings suggested themselves, Jesus immediately removed them, assuring her that there was no illusion, and bidding her tell all to her director and abide by his judgment. "I have often done so," she adds, "but without entering into many details. He urges me now more strongly than ever, since you have been amongst us, to make everything known to you, and do whatever you shall enjoin me." It is in one of her letters, written to M. Darbins, her second director, in the beginning of 1842, that she makes these observations. In order to recount what had taken place in her inner life—for her external life had not varied in its uneventful course—between the close of 1839 and the commencement of 1842, we have had to draw upon these letters, but much remains still to be told in order to give a just idea of the way in which Jesus was pleased in so marvellous a manner to instruct this simple soul during these two years. We must, however, interrupt our account awhile for the purpose of explaining how these details were placed on record.

## CHAPTER V.

### The New Director.

Towards the close of the year 1841, M. Forbas, the worthy priest who had prepared Marie for her first communion, and who had hitherto been the sole recipient of the extraordinary confidences which she was called to make, was removed to another parish. Marie naturally felt this deeply. All persons are disposed to regret the loss of their habitual confessor, but in the case of the poor and uneducated it is often difficult to conceive how great a trial such an occurrence is to them, particularly when, like Marie, they have from their childhood known no other. She had an additional trouble in being under the necessity of communicating to fresh ears the exceptional favours she was receiving. She esteemed herself utterly unworthy of them, and this conviction rendered it painful to her beyond expression to have to speak of them. We have seen how her first pastor dealt with her. Cautious of interfering with the work of God, and fully persuaded of her simplicity and sincerity, he had done little more than listen to what she told him ; moreover, her account had been, as we have seen, merely general. But how would this priest, to whom she was quite unknown, regard the subject? We can hardly wonder at her repugnance to open her heart to him ; and, had not our Lord impressed upon her the highest idea of the sacerdotal office, teaching her to behold in the priest His own representative and her appointed guide in the ways of grace, a guide the more needed in her case in order to guard her from all illusion, she might very likely have shrunk from the obligation.

Certainly there was little in this poor girl to prepare her pastor for what he was about to hear. Indeed he had remarked nothing in her except that she was a good, modest, and well-conducted young woman, very regular and devout in the observance of her religious duties. We can imagine, therefore, that he was a good deal surprised when Marie, whom our Lord had urged to be full and explicit in her manifestation of His dealings with her, laid before him in detail her spiritual experiences of the last two years. Daily visions, oral instruction from the lips of Jesus Himself, whom her eyes were favoured to behold,—these were strange things indeed ; strange, not merely because visions and revelations are rare and unusual occurrences, but also on account of their exceptional frequency. M. Darbins,

however, was not one of those good, but more or less
narrow-minded, men who set limits, as it were, to the
power and liberality of God, and prejudge to be in-
credible what as yet has not come under their notice.
Neither did he belong to an opposite and more dangerous class, who are liable to be deceived by plausible
appearances, and, too easily welcoming the marvellous
in their penitents, are ready to credit anything apparently supernatural without due examination. Besides,
by nature he was thoughtful and reserved; accordingly,
without pronouncing upon the character of the manifestations of which Marie declared herself the recipient,
he resolved at once to subject her to close scrutiny and
put her obedience and humility to the test. The first
thing he did was to forbid her to continue the austerities which she had imposed upon herself, for he had
required an account of her mode of life, and to retrench
the number of her communions. Marie obeyed without permitting herself to make the slightest observation.

We may here transcribe the rule she followed daily,
as recorded in one of her letters. " In the morning, on
rising, I transport myself in spirit before the Blessed
Sacrament; I offer to Jesus my heart and all my
actions during the day. I have no fixed time for either
getting up or going to bed. I rise in the morning
when my parents do, or as soon as I awake. I lie
down to rest in the evening when all has been well set
to rights in the house, when no more work remains to
be done, and I feel the need of taking the rest necessary
for restoring my strength. Every morning, on rising,
if I have the time at my disposal, I make half an
hour's meditation, for which I prepare myself by vocal
prayer. In the course of the day I read some devout

book; I say the Rosary; thrice I repeat seven times the Gloria Patri, as being a member of the Confraternity of the Most Holy Trinity, besides offering some prayers to the Blessed Virgin, as member of the Confraternity of the Scapular. All these different pious exercises I perform at the first leisure time I have during the day. In the evening I make my prayer, my examination of conscience, and a spiritual communion to unite myself to Jesus. I also make a spiritual communion in the morning after rising, and sometimes during the day. At mid-day I cast an eye back on the morning, in order that I may unite myself more closely to God until the evening, that I may avoid offending Him, and love Him from my inmost heart. I fast twice in the week; once in honour of Mary, and again in honour of the suffering Heart of Jesus. I do this, however, only with the permission of my director." She was also in the frequent habit of sleeping on the hard floor. This was one of the austerities which M. Darbins forbade. She attended Mass whenever she was able, but her laborious life, which took her out into the fields, did not always permit her to do so.

She had been in the habit, from the times she was eighteen, of communicating once a fortnight. It seems to us at first sight almost a matter of surprise that, with her edifying and mortified life, and her devotion to the Adorable Sacrament—not to speak of the peculiar graces with which she had been favoured by our Lord in connection with that great mystery of His love—she should not have been encouraged or permitted to communicate more frequently. Once a week is not reckoned by spiritual writers as frequent communion. The probable explanation is that this was the usual number of times that the good Catholic youth of her native village approached the altar. It is a very common interval amongst a large class of our own people, and perhaps her confessor did not desire to make any difference in her respect, lest it might be misinterpreted. We have seen that, while listening kindly to the brief allusion she made in confession to the favours which she received, he affected to attach slight importance to them.

But why did not Marie herself ask to be allowed to communicate more frequently? Here we are not left to conjecture, as we have her own account of the matter in one of her letters written in the beginning of 1842. She here tells her director that she had often desired to receive the Adorable Eucharist more frequently, but that she had constantly stifled the wish, thinking that possibly it proceeded from her self-love. It is clear that she never acted on her own impulse, and as yet she had received no command on the subject from our Lord. The desire, however, became so strong about four or five months previous to that date, that she prayed the Saviour to acquaint her with His will. "My daughter," He said, "I not only desire but I command you to communicate every week. I call you to live a more perfect life, and it is by My sacraments that you will attain this perfection." From the moment Marie received this command, strange to say, the pressing desire vanished. Jesus, however, spoke again to her, bidding her inform her confessor of His will and abide by what he should say. He added many promises to her if she should open her heart to him who directed her, and severe threatenings should she abuse His favours or treat them with negligence. Upon this she spoke to her confessor, M. Darbins's predecessor, at that time still resident at Mimbaste, who replied that he considered she had the necessary, or sufficient, dispositions for weekly communion, but that she was to continue to confess only once a fortnight.

Such was her practice when M. Darbins arrived, who restricted her for a time, in order to try her, to a monthly communion. This must have been a severe trial to her, although her humility and submission did not permit her to offer the slightest remonstrance, or so much as to make a simple observation on the subject. Our Lord, doubtless, supported and comforted her under this deprivation, and seems to have fed her, as it were, mysteriously with the light of His countenance, for she often speaks of these visions of His Sacred Humanity as if her soul was nourished and fortified, as well as enlightened, by them. We ought here to add, when speaking of the account of her state, which she laid in all its fulness before her confessor, that she told him that the Saviour had made known to her that He had chosen her for His spouse, and had hidden designs concerning her; that He purposed to withdraw her from the world, and to give her a place in the religious family dedicated to His Sacred Heart. " I will hide you," He had said to her, " as My dove in the hole of the rock; I will bear you away from the world, and will give you a place in the Holy Family consecrated to My Divine Heart: there you will be all Mine and I shall be all yours."

Marie would have wished to endeavour to comply at once with the gracious call of her Lord, but M. Darbins would not even entertain the question of her vocation until he had tried and satisfied himself regarding the spirit which was working in his penitent. For two years she had to undergo this ordeal. From the first, M. Darbins had set himself to watch her very

closely, but he could never discover in her behaviour anything which was not edifying. In her exterior nothing
singular or extraordinary betrayed itself : there was but
one sign indicating anything remarkable, and that was
her deep recollection while in church. M. Darbins
had early sought advice on the subject, and, with the
permission of his penitent, had conferred with a learned
priest of much discernment and experience, the Abbé
Dupérier, director and professor of theology at the
great seminary of Dax. Acting in conformity with his
opinion, he subjected Marie to numerous examinations.
Both of them separately interrogated her, trying to
embarrass her by subtle questions. They would also,
by agreement, ask her the same questions, couched in
different forms and at considerable intervals of time,
and they would then compare the answers they had re-
spectively received ; but never could they surprise her
in the least contradiction. Her replies were always
simple, precise, and unvarying in their substance.

Often, from the fear of not having been sufficiently
explicit, or in compliance with the expressed desire of
her confessor, she would write to him, for he had given
her strict orders to make him acquainted with everything ; to which our Lord had added His own formal
injunction, bidding her repeat faithfully all His words
and report all her own sentiments. She was not to
consider whether what He said to her was in praise or
blame, whether it might seem extraordinary and extravagant or wise and prudent ; nothing was to be kept
back. And she obeyed with that straightforward simplicity and sincerity which distinguished her. Nor can
any one read what she has written without feeling convinced that her one predominant object was to record
accurately all that had passed in her visions, and dis-

close the inmost recesses of her soul to him whom she
regarded as her father and guide. Plainly there was
no after-thought, no fear of what he might think; she
repeats her own commendations, as uttered by the lips
of Jesus, with as much fulness and ease as she records
any censure He may have pronounced; there is no
apology, no disclaimer. Such passages as the following
abound :—"This is, in all sincerity, what the Saviour
Jesus said to me ; you will think what you judge proper of it." Or again, "I submit to you what I experienced ; you will think what you please of it."

The tone of her letters is always humble and respectful ; they always go right to the point, without preface,
circumlocution, or comment ; no extraneous matter is
ever introduced ; you do not even meet with a super-
fluous word. Again, so entirely free does she show
herself to be from all attachment to her own opinion,
that in her later letters, written at the time when those
to whom her case was submitted judged it advisable to
affect great doubts and uncertainty, she thought herself
obliged to enter into their views by adopting a different
form of expression, and, instead of any longer saying,
" the Saviour Jesus spoke thus to me," she would say
" the voice which speaks to me said ;" or, " it appears
to me that the Saviour Jesus has said this to me ;" or
" he who speaks to me, if it be not Jesus, I know
not who it is :" these and similar expressions are of
frequent occurrence.

A large number of letters exist which form a kind of
supplement, as she herself said they would, to what was
omitted in her works. Of these works we must now
give some account. The works, be it observed, of an
illiterate peasant girl, who had never left her own
obscure village ; whose native tongue was not even good

French but a Gascon *patois !* The reader may well feel some astonishment at the idea of any literary production emanating from such a quarter. We proceed to account for their existence.

The two priests, after consulting together, agreed to require this young girl to give them a written narration of all that she had seen and heard in the supernatural order, as also to record in the same way all that she should hear, see, and experience of the same kind in the future. A moment's consideration will show what an arduous task they were imposing upon her. Marie could write, it is true, but facility in writing is acquired only by practice; while to the uneducated, to write the most ordinary letter is an arduous undertaking. They are not accustomed to put their ideas together in a formal shape; even narration itself is very difficult to them; they seldom know how to condense or abridge, or how to relate the slightest incident without the incumbrance of much repetition and irrelevant matter. But more than this—the subjects which Marie was desired to commit to paper related to what was highest and most sublime. How was her uncultivated memory accurately to recall the words addressed to her during these visions which had been continually occurring during the last two years, and of which she had preserved no note whatever? Another difficulty was her want of leisure. Hers was a life of toil, what we are used to call drudgery. During the greater part of the day she was out in the fields, watching the cattle. Morning and evening she had house-work to do. And again, how was she to escape notice? Hours of privacy are not easily secured in the cottages of the poor. Excuses, therefore, were not wanting to Marie for avoiding compliance with the order she had received.

Many would judge that she might have urged the un-
answerable plea of utter inability to comply with it;
nevertheless, regarding the command as coming to her
from God, speaking by the mouth of His minister, she
submitted, and acquiesced without a murmur, reckoning
on that help which is pledged to the obedient, for God
never commands impossibilities. She was not deceived
in her hope. As regarded her remembrance of the past,
our Lord came to her aid to revive her recollection in a
manner which we shall presently describe in her own
words. As regarded the time and opportunity, she rose,
by His directions, very early, and she also gave a great
portion of the night to this occupation, while the rest
of the family were sleeping. Even when looking after
the cattle, she was able during the day to profit by
many a calm and solitary hour.

Thus it was that in the course of two years she succeeded in placing on record, with a rapidity which under
her peculiarly disadvantageous circumstances was truly
surprising, the instructions which our Lord had deigned
to give her. But it must not be supposed that all
this cost her nothing, or that, because she was assisted
from above, she was spared all labour and difficulty.
Far from it; and so great was the repugnance she
experienced, that she afterwards declared that many
a time she would have preferred to take a spade
and dig, or pull up weeds. Submissive and obedient
as she was, she allowed herself to complain to Jesus.
Sometimes He would severely chide her for her
pusillanimity; at other times He would kindly encourage her, and then her task would become sweet
and easy. We may add that Marie carefully concealed
from her family what she had written until she was
able to hand it over to her director. On one sole occa-

sion some leaves were found and read by Marguerite.
Marie exacted of her sister a solemn promise that she
would never mention the circumstance, nor ever read
any similar papers she might hereafter chance to find;
and Marguerite faithfully kept her word.

We will here insert a letter, written at the close of
the year 1842, in which she explains to M. Darbins
the manner in which our Lord assisted her memory.

"Monsieur le Curé, I have never thought of telling
you the way in which I furnish you the writings which
you have required of me, and of explaining to you
how, after the lapse of so much time, I am able to
recall the discourses and words of the Saviour Jesus as
if He had almost just addressed them to me. It is
thus. One day, about two years ago, Jesus appeared
to me and said, ' My daughter, come to Me.' I drew
nigh to Him. He held in His hand a book and a
casket. He presented them to me, saying, 'I desire
you, My daughter, to preserve preciously the memory
of My words, and the good effect of the virtuous movements with which I shall inspire your heart. This
book contains all the words that I shall address to you.
I forbid you ever to open it without My permission.
Open it now.' I opened it; it was written on throughout, from the first page to the last; I closed it again
immediately. ' This casket,' He continued, ' contains
the perfume which shall exhale from the words which
I may address to you. You will never open it without My permission. Open it, My daughter.' I opened
it, and perceived the most beautiful flowers which I
had ever beheld. And, in fact, a sweet and delicious
fragrance proceeded from them. ' My daughter,' then
said the Saviour Jesus to me, ' take this book of knowledge and of wisdom and this casket; conceal them in

your heart. Later you will have need to open them, and they will be of great use to you.'"

It is scarcely necessary to observe, as our Lord's own words sufficiently demonstrate the fact, that He gave her no actual book or casket which she could open with her hands. They were mentally stored up, and the opening or shutting of them was a mental act, followed, however, by the results which have been indicated. Marie continues: "This is quite true,"—that is, it is true that she has found in these possessions what her Lord had promised,—"and it is to this book and this casket that I have recourse when I wish to write what I remit to you in my papers, or when I address a letter to you. I open the book at hazard, I read, and I write. Sometimes Jesus will not allow me to open it; I then take the casket, smell the flowers, and write whatever comes into my mind. Now, I have noticed that the book contains the different instructions which the Saviour has given me, whether for myself or for those who may come to be acquainted with them, while the casket contains and inspires me with only that which concerns myself. It was but a few days ago that the Lord said to me, 'The book and the casket which I have given you are granaries of plenty, which will avail you in time of dearth; that is to say, in case of forgetfulness or the insufficiency of your memory. Your writings and your virtues will also be two granaries of plenty, whence the Egyptians, that is, sinners and burdened souls, will come and take ample provisions.'" Here we have one of those instances in which she reports our Lord's words of commendation as calmly and simply as if they related to any one else. "'Neglect, therefore, nothing,' He continued; 'receive My word, and preserve it in your mind. The book and the casket which I have given you will profit you only so far as you shall have deserved it by your attention to what I have said.'"

"When I cannot remember," proceeds Marie, "what I ought to say, I have recourse to my granaries of plenty. Alas! Monsieur le Curé, sometimes I find the door of these granaries closed. I know well that it has been my own fault. I have not always hearkened attentively to the word of the Saviour. May He deign to have mercy on me and forgive me. Nevertheless, I always tell you what I can remember, and all that presents itself to my mind, in the sincere desire of my soul to hide nothing from you and to tell you the whole truth. You will think what you please of this. I relate to you all that passes in me. Pray for me, most revered Father of my soul, to the Saviour Jesus, that I may sanctify myself, and ever correspond to all the good cautions and all the holy counsels which you may give me." Her letters and papers constantly end with similar passages, expressive of her total disengagement from any private view or opinion of her own, and her entire submission to the judgment of God's appointed minister, who was Christ's representative to her. Nothing can be considered as a more reliable test of the goodness of the spirit actuating those who have received special lights than this absence of all pertinacity and attachment to their own convictions, and to the revelations of which they believe themselves the recipients, upon encountering any mistrust on the part of their confessors or being subjected to trial by them. We shall see by and by how completely satisfactory was Marie's behaviour on an occasion of this kind.

In the meantime we will subjoin one other short passage from a letter written to the Curé of Mimbaste a little later, as having reference to the subject of which we have been speaking, namely, the assistance which her memory received. It contains answers to two questions addressed to her by M. Dupérier in an interview which he had desired to have with her. To one of these questions and her reply we have already adverted. It concerns what took place in her sensibly during the visions in which Jesus appeared and spoke to her. The other regards her study of Holy Scripture. To this question, which was the first in order, she also replies first, giving her reasons for fearing that she may not have been sufficiently explicit. "Monsieur le Curé, I have had a conversation at Dax with the venerable priest to whom you referred me. I answered the questions he put to me as well as I could. Now, you know that I always feel difficulty in speaking, and, indeed, am unable to speak, of what I experience to any one but yourself. You have considered it well, for my good, to engage me to consult M. Dupérier. I have done so with the deference which I always have had, and which I always shall have, for your advice, and I acknowledge that I have had no reason to repent of this. Nevertheless, perhaps I may not have explained myself in a sufficiently precise and clear manner with regard to two questions which he addressed to me." One of these questions she now proceeds to answer. She had been asked whether she had learnt from our Lord Himself the passages of Scripture which were to be found in her writings. "I must observe, in the first place," she says, "that I have read the whole of the Bible, with the exception of certain portions which my previous director, as well as yourself, recommended me not to read. Having stated this, I add that there are passages of which I was ignorant, or which I had

E

entirely forgotten; others, again, which I remembered. In cases where I was ignorant, Jesus would tell me to open my Bible or my Paroissien, and would then comment on the passage upon which my eye had fallen. Where I had forgotten, He would recall the passage to my mind, and give me the explanation of it; but in cases where I had remembered, He would only comment on the passage, so as to impress it on my mind without further dwelling upon it. I have but one remark to make as to those texts of Scripture with which I was not acquainted, and which the Saviour was pleased to make the subject of His instruction. Frequently my eye rested on the verse itself; at other times I had to read several verses. I always recognised the one which was to form the subject of the Saviour's discourse by a special attraction which imprinted it on my mind, while the others made no such impression. I have nothing else to observe in reply to 'this first question."

----◆----

# CHAPTER VI.

## OUR LORD'S INSTRUCTIONS.

BEFORE proceeding further, we feel that some idea ought to be presented to the reader of the instructions which our Lord deigned to impart to this humble village girl; but here we are met by a difficulty. Marie Lataste's writings, including those letters which may be regarded as their supplement, fill two 12mo volumes, of about 400 pages each. To give samples of our Lord's method in teaching this simple soul, which is all that is possible in this biography, is scarcely to do justice to the subject; nor does it seem easy thereby to furnish an adequate conception of the value of the teaching as a whole. For this teaching is not distinguished by what may be called striking passages. Precision and a familiar simplicity are its leading characteristics; and we can imagine that a reader who should expect to meet with deep mystical truths and marvellous revelations, may, at first, as we have already hinted, be disappointed at finding himself engaged in perusing, it is true, a clear and dogmatic but, nevertheless, very simple exposition of the doctrines of the Blessed Trinity, the Incarnation, &c., and may almost be inclined to say, " I knew all this before; it is all very good, but there is nothing new, nothing which may not be gathered from theological treatises or even catechetical instructions."

Be it so; but did Marie Lataste know, could she have known, all that she states, and in the form that she states it? Implicitly, of course, she held these truths, but how could an ignorant peasant girl have drawn out in explicit terms, except by divine illumination, what she has committed to paper? That she was incapable of such a performance we have her own express declaration, and her genuine truthfulness cannot be questioned. But, moreover, any one who has become familiar with the amount of knowledge possessed by those poorer members of the Church whose life is one series of unbroken toil, and whose actual education has been limited to a short period of their early childhood, must know how utterly unable they would be to produce anything similar. We are far from meaning that the poor, so rich in faith, do not often possess a very large amount of infused knowledge of divine truths, much beyond what they have received in the form of direct instruction from books or teachers; but the knowledge of which we speak is the knowledge which can be scientifically produced, drawn out, and laid down; and to do this in the manner which Marie Lataste has done it, we may confidently assert would require on the part of a person entirely devoid of theological or, indeed, any literary education, a special illumination and gift from above. It is in the light of this consideration that these otherwise most edifying instructions—edifying to those who are not too proud to accept simple teaching, or, rather, we may say sublime doctrine conveyed in a simple form—must be received. And is it not marvellous to behold our Divine Lord thus stooping to instruct a little one of His flock? Is it for nothing that this spectacle has been presented to us? and is not this in itself a wonderful revelation,—a revelation, not designed to feed curiosity or nourish high thoughts, but to warm the heart, to enkindle love and gratitude, and inspire us with a great desire to obtain those lowly virtues of humility and simplicity which open the mind to the teachings of the Word?

The instructions which Marie Lataste committed to paper at the command of her director embrace the entire round of Catholic doctrine, so far as regards its leading points: first, dogma; then, morals; and finally, the spiritual life.* The chief heads of doctrine developed are:—God and creation; the general relations of God with men; Jesus Christ, His functions in the divine economy; the principal mysteries of

* The only change which M. Darbins allowed himself to make, when publishing her writings, was to transfer some portions to places where they would stand in better connection with the subjects preceding and following them, for Marie had not adopted any regular order. He also corrected all faults of orthography and removed a few stray Gascon idioms.

His Life ; the Blessed Virgin, her intercessory office, her mysteries ; the good angels ; the devils and their relations with men ; the sacerdotal ministry ; the Christian and his duties ; religion in general, and the great acts of religion : communion, confession, and prayer ; the law of probation and of mortification ; grace, its divisions and operations ; the theological and cardinal virtues ; the gifts of the Holy Spirit ; sins, their causes, their species ; the different relations between men, or the duties of different states in life ; religious vocation ; the last ends of man ; the past a figure of the future, or the allegorical explanation of certain facts in the Old Testament. Of course all these matters may be found fully explained in a number of works, but perhaps there never was written a treatise embracing the whole round of doctrine which more remarkably combined abundance, clearness, and conciseness ; in saying which we are giving not our own opinion, but, as will be hereafter seen, that of far more competent authorities.

Let us now imagine a selection made of the most intelligent and best instructed girl in any of our poor schools, able, like Marie, competently to read and write ; and let her be set down to compose a general treatise on the subjects which we have here stated. Let her have, moreover, a whole library of Christian instruction at her command (which certainly the poor peasant of Mimbaste had not),* so that her task should rather be that of simple compilation—what may we conjecture would be the result ? Rather may we not conceive that there would be none ; and that our pious

* We shall give elsewhere a list of the books of devotion possessed by Marie's family, with the addition of a few more which had been lent to her by M. Forbas, her first director.

but illiterate girl would, in all humility, lay down her pen, and declare herself unequal to a task for which her imperfect education had unfitted her? The other portion of Marie's works, as published by M. l'Abbé Pascal Darbins, nephew of her director, contains, as we have said, her letters, all, except seven of them, written before her entrance into the Congregation of the Sacred Heart. Some of these are doctrinal, the rest are what may be called biographical. The former, therefore, are the more immediate supplement to her works, while the latter serve to elucidate and complete her life. We have already given extracts from several of these letters and shall do so again, but, with the exception of any passage which it may suit our purpose to quote, we shall not introduce any portion of the writings, properly so called, for the reason we have alleged—namely, that to be duly valued they must be read in their entirety.

Besides answers to questions of her director, we find in her letters several specimens of our Lord's method of instruction which admit better of quotation. They may be compared to little sermons with which from time to time He favoured her. We will here insert one at length on the subject of solitude.

"Monsieur le Curé, he who addresses me has thus spoken of solitude : 'My daughter, I have chosen three solitudes for you ; and I have made them known to you by establishing you in them. The first is the dwelling-place of your family, situated in a little village, removed from the tumult of great cities, and hence a true solitude, since you live in it unknown and under the eye of God. The second solitude is your parish church, to which you come in order to separate yourself from all that is not God, to adore Him, to pray to

Him, to receive His graces and His gifts. The third solitude is your heart, an interior solitude, to which no one shall ever have access, if you preserve it wholly for your Saviour, who desires to be alone its possessor and its sovereign. The others are exterior solitudes; this one alone is interior, hidden, veiled from all eyes; it is also more perfect than the two former. Solitude of the heart may be had without the first solitude; without retiring into a desert, without being enclosed in a cloister, or abiding in some secluded spot. Solitude of heart may be had without being present in a holy place, or in the sacred sanctuary; but the first two solitudes may be had without possessing solitude of heart.

" 'Vainly, in fact, My daughter, might you shut yourself up night and day in My temples : unless you possessed solitude of heart, you would not be solitary; vainly might you withdraw into the recesses of a desert, far from men and from the whole world : unless you possessed solitude of heart, that is, if your heart were not separated from what takes place in the world, from its feastings, its pleasures, and its follies, if your heart were preoccupied with the things of earth which pass and rapidly vanish, you would not be solitary. Whereas if you lived in the world, and were mixed up in the affairs of human life, you might be, and would be, truly solitary if your heart were in the world as if absent from it ; because it would be completely detached from all and closely united to God.

" ' True solitude consists, then, in withdrawing from all that is on earth, from the world and from men, and drawing nigh to heaven and to God. You cannot of yourself acquire solitude of heart. It is a gift of God; it suffices, however, to beg it of God with a great desire to have it, in order to obtain and possess it. God never refuses it, for He ardently desires that all should pass their life in solitude of heart. Exterior solitudes,— cloisters, monasteries, deserts, the holy place,—are as the way which leads to solitude of heart. How many souls are there who would never have possessed solitude of heart if they had not sought it in exterior solitudes ! Nevertheless, since it may happen that a person may be unable to seek solitude of heart by means of exterior solitudes, God does not refuse it to such as find themselves thus circumstanced. Solitude of heart is a gift of God. God sends it in the manner that He pleases, and by the means which seem most efficacious to procure it—to wit, a great desire for this solitude, the constant efforts of a soul to abide in this solitude, detachment from the goods and from the turmoil of the world, fervent and continual prayer.

"'I have given you three solitudes ; the first has led you to the second. When any one is ignorant of the world, does not hear its conversation, is not disturbed by its feastings and amusements, then he knows God, hears His word, and lives in peace in His service. This soul knows God, and, in order to know Him better, frequents His temple and draws nigh to His altar, and so it comes into the second solitude which I have made known to you and which I have given you in the holy place : there the soul learns, by the reverence due to the Divine Majesty, to separate itself from all, to think only of that Majesty ; and, when this thought becomes the one thought of the soul, then the soul is truly solitary. This temporary and transient solitude of the heart leads on to that which is abiding, because the soul learns very quickly that if the church is the temple of God, and the place where His presence ought to be venerated and specially adored, the universe is also the magnificent temple which God has built for Himself with His own hands, and which everywhere manifests His power and His glory. This is why the soul, seeing itself surrounded by God on every side, no longer thinks of anything save Him, and lives entirely solitary in its heart. Have you not experienced this, My daughter?

"'A solitary soul has its eye constantly on itself, on its enemies, on God. It has its eye on itself : it is ever examining whether its life is a steady advance towards God ; whether it corresponds to the gifts of God, whether its fervour increases or relaxes ; it discerns the causes of any failings and their motives, and takes measures for removing them. It has its eye upon its enemies : they never take it by surprise. Solitude is to this soul like an elevated spot, whence it overlooks the whole neighbourhood. Solitude is to this soul like a wary spy, who warns it of all the movements, all the ambushes, all the preparations of the devil, the world, and the passions. And so to this soul victory is no arduous achievement. Its enemies, seeing themselves discovered, generally decline the combat and take to flight in shame and confusion. It has its eye on God, that it may execute His will in the smallest matters. God speaks to it, and, because it is solitary, it hears His voice, which penetrates into its heart. God bestows on it His graces, and, because it is solitary, it is ready to receive them, to profit by them, and to thank Him who confers them. God draws nigh to it, it receives Him eagerly and without delay, and between the Creator and the creature there is established an intimate familiarity, which constitutes the happiness of the soul, and which rejoices the heart of God, who is its father.

All the greatest saints of Heaven have lived in this solitude of heart. This solitude was their delight; therein they found strength and courage for the battles of life, consolation in their afflictions and tribulations, light in their labours and apostolate, shelter against all dangers, and a sure and certain ascent towards eternal felicity.

" ' Solitude of heart is a thing which pleases Me, and which I love above everything. Through all eternity I have reposed, I do repose, and shall for ever repose, in the bosom of My Father, separated from all, to live only of the life of My Father and to receive no other life but His life. Solitude of heart in the life of souls is an image of the everlasting solitude which I find in the bosom of God, because I am His Word; and this is why I so much love solitude of heart. As the Word of God made Man, I have, like you, My daughter, had three solitudes : the solitude of My dwelling at Nazareth ; the solitude of the world, which was the temple in which I adored God, My Father ; and the solitude of My Heart, in which, from the commencement of My life unto My last sigh upon the cross, I offered to Him the sacrifice of reparation for the sin of man. My entire life was a life in solitude. I was solitary, that is, isolated from men in My birth. I was solitary, that is, exiled and driven away by men in My flight into Egypt. I was solitary, that is, unknown to men, separated from all worldly things, in My hidden life at Nazareth. I was solitary in the midst of My Apostles, who did not understand the things of God, who forsook Me in the face of My enemies. I lived forty days in the solitude of the desert. I often retired into solitude to pay My homage to God My Father. When I looked upon mankind, laden with crimes and in revolt against

My Father, I found Myself solitary, that is, alone able to give adequate satisfaction to divine justice; the entire world was one immense solitude, and I was, as the prophet said,* the pelican of this desert.

" 'My daughter, love solitude of heart; suffer yourself to be led by My grace into this solitude; embellish it with all My virtues; render it more and more worthy to receive Me. It is there that I will come to instruct you, to manifest truth to you, to teach you to know God and what is of God; it is there that I will lavish on you the treasures of My love and of My tenderness; it is there that I will allow you to have a glimpse of the felicity of heaven, of which I will give you a foretaste. Solitude of heart will be for you the marvellous Ark of Noe, into which I would have you enter to save yourself from the stormy sea of the world. It is I who will guide this Ark, and it shall not rest on the mount of malediction and fear, but on that of benediction and charity.' " Our Lord referred to these three solitudes on another occasion, when he told her that He had chosen her sister Quitterie to represent His solitude in the world when engaged in His active labours; Marguerite to represent that of His home life at Nazareth; and herself to represent the most precious of the three, the solitude of His Heart.

She concludes with these words : " This, Monsieur le Curé, is what I heard. I beg you to believe that I am in no ways attached to my opinion. It seems to me that it was Jesus who addressed these words to me. It is at least some one who speaks in His Name. It will be easy for you to discern who it is who thus converses with me. I will submit myself, in all things and at all times, to your judgment and decisions." Such expres-

* Psalm ci. 7.

sions, which occur so frequently at the close of her letters, must not be taken as evidence of any substantial
doubt or misgiving, having its source in her own mind,
but simply as proofs of her entire freedom from all
attachment to her own judgment, one of the last re-
fuges of pride and self-love, and her complete abandonment to whatever God should be pleased to signify to
her, in the ordinary way, by the voice of His ministers.
Her directors were pleased to express doubts and hesita-
tions, and she plainly thought it her duty to adopt, so
far as she could, their attitude of mind.

But, not content with instructing Marie in the
mysteries of the faith and the ways of perfection, and
enlightening her on the duties belonging to all the
different states and relations of life, our Lord condescended even to train His docile disciple in the proper
control of her exterior movements, and in all that may
be included under the head of propriety or decorum of
behaviour. For, indeed, no outward movements, no
expression of the countenance, no attitude, no gesture,
especially if habitual, is matter of indifference. The
outward man typifies to a large extent the interior man;
at any rate it very commonly does so when the individual is freed from any motive for self-control. But
that motive is always present with the true Christian.
The Apostle suggests it when, after saying, "Let your
modesty be known to all men," he adds, "The Lord is
at hand."* Jesus told Marie that this propriety of behaviour was perfect among the perfect, and that He had
Himself set a perfect example of it when on earth,
because He was all-perfect. He taught her how, while
avoiding all affectation or constraint, to hold herself
upright, without that continual bending and reclining

* Phil. iv. 5.

which is an index of either feebleness, carelessness, or slothfulness. She was to avoid all lightness and levity of tone and manner, and especially everything like haughtiness or disdain in her countenance or her bearing, for these are signs of pride in the heart. She was to abstain from turning her head perpetually this way and that way ; she was not to laugh loud nor often ; she was not to look fixedly at any one, and her face was always to wear the expression of that modesty, mildness, and humility which is the token of a pure and virtuous heart. "Yes, My daughter," He said, "have always a countenance open, calm, full of kindness, gentleness, amenity, and which, by reflecting a frank and sincere piety, may gain all hearts and incline them to God."

Above all, it was in her words and conversation that she was to observe a becoming behaviour. The first condition was to speak little. "He who speaks little," said the Saviour, "is wise and prudent, and keeps his soul free from a thousand embarrassments. He who speaks little edifies by his modesty, preserves his personal dignity, and also continues more easily attached to God, because he practises detachment from self." The second condition, He told her, was to be careful, in conversation, to abstain from all raillery, disputes, contentions, detraction, calumny, falsehood ; worldly, idle, and altogether useless discourse ; eagerness, pretentiousness, captiousness, self-sufficiency and arrogance. The third condition was to speak always in a manner conformable to what is good, true, and just, with affability, modesty, gentleness, and charity. "Thus, My daughter," He said, "speak little ; yet never affect melancholy or excessive silence ; but look to your intentions, and never speak through self-love or to please the world.

If you are obliged to speak to any one, offer your words to God, and beseech Him to preserve you from sin. If you desire to speak for your own pleasure, hold your peace; if to complain, again be silent; silence is preferable, sometimes even obligatory. If you desire to speak in order to unburden your heart, let it be only with a select few, pious persons who love virtue: in short, always speak profitably and holily; thus shall you observe propriety of behaviour.

"Propriety as regards your neighbour," He added, "consists in rendering him all the duties of charity in your power when you are with him ; bearing with his faults, and pardoning all that is defective in him. Propriety demands that you should sacrifice your tastes, inclinations, and will, to follow the tastes, inclinations, and will of your neighbour in all that is not contrary to the will of God ; and this without contention, with kindness, and in a natural way ; and that you should forestall his wants and necessities, in order to do him service or to please him. Propriety of behaviour also requires that you should patiently endure all the infirmities of your neighbour, whether they be of the body, or the temper, of the mind or of the heart. Thus mutually to support and aid each other, My daughter, is to practise the highest and most perfect propriety of behaviour, because it is the fulfilling of My law."

Sometimes our Lord would address questions to her, in order to test her understanding of what He had taught her, in the same familiar way as one might do who was catechising the young or instructing a neophyte ; at other times, we find Him responding with the greatest sweetness and condescension to doubts, difficulties, or fears which had arisen in her mind. We will here give an instance of the manner in which He reassured her when pained by the apprehension lest she should be deceived, or be guilty of vanity. We again quote from one of her letters.

"Monsieur le Curé," she writes, "two things sadden and distress me considerably; the first is, the fear of being deceived; the second, the temptation to take a pride in what I experience and in what passes within me. Nevertheless, in the midst of my trouble and affliction, I am sustained by an invisible power which I cannot explain, and which I can call by no other name than the Saviour Jesus. And, in fact, when I am suffering from the fear of being deceived, I seem to see the Saviour Jesus coming to me and saying to me, 'My daughter, abandon yourself completely to God. Allow Him to do with you what He pleases. You will not be deluded, you will not be deceived, if you place your hope in Him.' At other times He adds, 'If you will not trust either Me or your own judgment, question your director; he has a special grace to enlighten you'

"In fine, He teaches me in what manner I am to reason with myself. 'My daughter,' He says, 'if the devil were deceiving you, if it were he who came to speak to you in order to lead you astray, he would forbid you to report his words to any one whomsoever, while I bid you to communicate Mine to your director. The devil, in fact, would teach you nothing but falsehood and lies, and, in order to prevail upon you more surely by preventing you from being undeceived, he would urge you to be silent. My word, on the contrary, is a word of truth : this is why I command you to communicate it to your director, that he may reassure you and confirm you in the truth which I teach you. The devil would, nevertheless, urge you to speak of the wonderful things which you see, and which are operated in you, because his greatest desire is to inflame souls with pride, whereas I enjoin you to speak of them solely to your director, in order to keep you perfectly humble. How can you dread being deceived? The tree is known by its fruits; if they are bad, the tree is bad. Satan will never inspire you with anything but evil; but I inspire what is good.'

"When I experience temptations to vanity and pride, when they are so violent that in the morning I fear not being able to hold out until evening without yielding to them, I seem to hear the voice of Jesus speaking thus to me, when I take refuge at the foot of His tabernacle to beg His aid: 'My daughter, why should you be proud? of yourself you are but nothingness and sin; all you may possess does not proceed from yourself, but from God. If you are but nothingness, can you glory in your nothingness? If you are only sin, can you pride yourself on sin? As being nothingness and sin, be assured that you deserve nothing but to be forgotten, hated, and regarded with horror by every creature.' Sometimes He says to me, 'Look upon yourself, My daughter, as the last of creatures, as the servant of all, as the one whom all the world has a right to command. Look upon God as your sovereign master.' Or He speaks thus to me : 'I will suppose, My daughter, that you are very rich, that you possess immense treasures. A poor man comes and knocks at your door, and, out of kindness, you bestow on him a considerable sum, which relieves him from his state of want. Another poor person comes, and you give him only an ordinary alms, so that he has to continue his beggar's life. Neither of these poor men had deserved anything more than had the other; you have given what you willed to give, and to whom you willed. Would he to whom you had given the large sum of money have reason to glory in the gift as if he had deserved it? No, My daughter. God acts in this wise: He gives to whom He pleases. All are poor before Him; He alone is truly rich, and no one must be proud on account of what God has given him.' On another occasion, He said to me, 'I suppose that some one gives you a magnificent book: would you not be very foolish if you were elated at the possession as though you had yourself composed it, while you had simply received it from another's hands? Still greater would be your folly if you were to pride yourself on the favours which I grant you. You do not merit them. I give them to you, because it pleases Me to do so, and without any merit on your part.'

"In conclusion, I will tell you what happened to me one day after holy communion. I was beseeching God to give me humility with a great desire to obtain it. I penetrated into my heart, where I found Jesus seated on His throne. I have already spoken to you by word of mouth or in writing of a deep abyss which I often perceive in my heart; at this moment it appeared more frightful than ever to me. Jesus took me by the hand and led me to the brink. I saw that round this abyss there were steps leading down to the depth below. These steps were about as distant from each other as those of a staircase. They were neither of stone nor of wood; they consisted merely of little iron bars about an inch in breadth and thickness; all the rest was an empty space, so that if you failed to place your foot on the bar, you must of necessity fall down into the abyss. Neither was there any handrail. The Lord said to me, 'Descend, My daughter.' I did not wish to disobey Him, but I clearly saw that I

F

should fall. So I took hold of Jesus's hand to support me, and then I descended fearlessly. After going down several of the steps, my two feet both slipped at the same time. How terrified I was! I clung with all my might to Jesus. with my two hands, exclaiming, 'Lord, hold me up, hold me up.' 'What would become of you, My daughter,' He said, 'if I were to abandon you?' 'Ah! Lord, I should be precipitated into the most terrible abyss.' Then the Saviour said to me, 'Let us return, My daughter; and understand that you can do nothing without Me; that without My aid you would every instant sink in the abyss. You can do nothing without Me: on what, then, can you value yourself?'

"This is what I experience, what I feel, what I hear It is a great consolation to me. You also will speak to me when you have passed your judgment on all, and I shall rely on your word as on the word of truth. I may fall into illusion, I may deceive myself as to what I experience, feel, or hear; but illusion is impossible with you; you are able to judge aright of what I communicate to you. You have the necessary graces for that purpose on account of your ministry. Aid me, enlighten me, show me the truth, show me the good way, show me the only true life; I desire to live by that life, to walk in that way, to embrace that truth. I desire to attach myself to truth, and never to abandon it; I desire to remain in the way which leads to God, and never to quit it; I desire to preserve the life which the Saviour Jesus has given me by His merits on Calvary, and never to let it go. O Life without which there is no life, be my life. O Way out of which there is no way which leads to God, be my way. O Truth

which art one and indivisible, be my repose in time
and in eternity."

We willingly quote these conclusions to her letter,
although they involve a repetition of the same or
similar ideas, because they serve to prove how much
dearer to her was truth than her own views, impressions,
or convictions; and how much more confidence she
placed in the judgment of her appointed guide than
in the evidence brought home to her own mind, strong
and clear as that was, in her visions and interior manifestations. For, although God knows how to give a
certainty surpassing reason and sense, nevertheless she
was bidden to refer all to her director; and she knew
also that it is the appointed way by which God leads
even those souls whom He wills to favour with supernatural illumination. In the last letter we have an
instance of the parabolic form in which our Lord often
instructed her by means of interior visions. We shall
have occasion to notice other instances when we come
to speak of some of the revelations made to her.

It will have been seen, by the specimens given, with
what great simplicity, familiarity, and patience Jesus
instructed this young soul. We seem to have here
the unveiled picture of what He is ready to do in the
soul of each of us, according to the measure of His
designs in our regard and our corresponding prepared-
ness; and the conclusion we are led to draw is that
simplicity and sincerity, which so eminently distinguished this poor peasant girl, are the best qualifica-
tions for learners in this divine school.

# CHAPTER VII.

BESIDES the close interrogations to which her new director and M. Dupérier subjected Marie, for the purpose of testing her spirit, M. Darbins also made her conduct and behaviour the object of his rigid scrutiny, knowing well that by this criterion everything else must be judged in order to prove its value. It is time that we should ourselves give a glance at the fruits of virtue which adorned this plant of grace, for of these we have only as yet incidentally spoken. We must therefore record a few examples of her goodness, collected after her death from the testimony of those who knew her. All concurred in saying that the whole parish was edified by her behaviour, and that the persuasion which her young friends entertained of her excellence, coupled with the charm of her angelic sweetness, gave her an influence with them which was quite irresistible. It is true that she did not mix much in their society, partly because her abode was in an isolated situation, being about a quarter of an hour's walk from the village, itself of a scattered description, but still more from her own natural as well as supernatural attraction for solitude. Nevertheless, although not by temperament of an expansive character, charity opened her heart and unloosed her tongue when it was needful or advisable; that is, when the profit, the edification, or consolation of her neighbour required it. And then she had such exquisite tact, such remarkable circumspection, and such delicate sympathy in dealing

with others, that nothing came amiss from Marie of
the Gran Cassou, as they often called her.

If her company was welcome to them, however, it
was not because she condescended to their tastes by
talking of anything or nothing, as girls, and, indeed,
their elders, often do, still less by joining in frivolous
gossip, but because she drew them up to her own more
exalted level and the higher interests which alone
occupied her mind. " We were obliged," they said,
" whether we would or no, always to converse about
God or pious things, but we lent ourselves readily to
her desire, so ingeniously did she contrive to lead the
conversation that way and to make it interesting."
And this Marie was able easily to do; for, when she
spoke on these subjects, she was speaking out of the
fulness of her heart and giving of her own overflowing
abundance. Perhaps it was by no means a disadvantage that the meetings of Marie and her friends were
rather rare than otherwise. Although it may be true,
in a general way, that frequent opportunities of intercourse are a help towards acquiring influence, yet are
there exceptions to the rule. Some influences are more
powerful from the very rareness, within certain limits,
of their exercise ; and this may be said to be especially
the case with those of the highest order : a peculiar
reverence attaching itself to those persons of eminent
virtue who keep themselves in a measure aloof and
maintain a kind of sacred isolation.

In Marie's case circumstances combined with her
temperament to restrict social intercourse. During the
week, she was engaged nearly all the day in the fields,
and on the Sundays the greater part was taken up by
the offices of the Church and her own additional private
devotions. Besides, Marie did not want to talk ; those

who do can always create opportunities; but it was
"the law of clemency" alone which, as it ruled, so also
unloosed, the tongue of this naturally silent maiden.
Accordingly, on the Sundays, what remained to her of
time not occupied in religious exercises she gave to
recreation and conversation with her young friends;
and from amongst them she singled out in preference
those who had made their first communion along with
her. It was at these seasons that she put in practice the lessons she had received from our Lord on
the manner in which we ought to sanctify the relations
of friendship, and the injunction He had given her to
edify her companions: an injunction which He had
enforced by a vision which she has described in one of
her letters to her director.

A few instances collected from the lips of her surviv-
ing friends—and as she died early, the greater number
lived to give oral testimony to her merits—will illustrate the discretion, and yet perfect frankness, with
which she knew how to administer advice and even
reproof. A young girl, whose family were very poor
and had to work hard to earn their livelihood, wearied
by a monotonous life which made her look to any
change as desirable, had resolved to accept a situation
as domestic servant at Dax; she hoped thus, as she said,
to make her own bread at less personal cost of fatigue.
It was a resolution in which personal inclinations alone
had been consulted. Marie, having heard of her deter-
mination, and dreading the dangers to which one so
inexperienced would be exposed in a town life, undertook to turn her from her purpose. Accordingly, having met her one day, she entered at once upon the
subject. "My dear friend," she said, "in a few days
you are going to do something which will distress me

greatly." "How is that?" answered the other: "God forbid, for I love you too much to wish to give you any pain." "I know you love me, and yet I repeat that you will give me much pain, and will also distress your mother, whom you likewise love." "Pray, explain yourself; I assure you that I would not do anything which would grieve either you or my poor mother." "You promise me this?" "Yes, I promise you." Then Marie acquainted her with what she had learned of her purpose, represented to her the need her mother had of her services, the embarrassments she would entail upon her, and the loneliness to which she would consign her. Turning next to more personal considerations, and bringing a few motives of self-interest to enforce her argument, she showed her how her expectations of being happier at Dax would in all likelihood be cruelly disappointed: she would probably have more work to do, and that under strict obedience to orders; meanwhile she must swallow all her troubles and griefs in silence, separated as she would be from those who cared for and sympathised with her; whereas now she had her mother and companions to console her. Did she reckon for nothing the sweetness of a home and the love of all her friends? "Believe me," she added, "you will do well to remain at Mimbaste; when you have much work to do and feel wearied, send me word; my mother will allow me to go and help you, and I shall do this with great pleasure." Marie gained her point; seldom it was that she failed. The words and arguments she employed may seem simple—so they were; their grace and influence came from the speaker; and besides, it was not mere advice which Marie proffered: that may often be cheaply given; it was the kind, self-sacrificing spirit, ever ready to manifest itself, which

lent to all she said a persuasive force difficult to resist.

Marie could discharge the office of fraternal correction with admirable candour and discretion. It is a
difficult office, as all know; and many find it much
easier to find fault with their neighbour to others, than
to offer the slightest remonstrance to himself. When
an attempt is made to discharge this duty, it is not unfrequently with accompaniments which mar its good
effect. Marie never shrank from the duty, and knew
how to perform it in a winning manner. One day, as
she was entering the church to assist at Vespers, she
met two young girls coming out in a hurried way,
laughing and talking together. Marie was deeply
pained at this act of irreverence, and, chancing soon
afterwards to encounter one of these giddy creatures,
she said to her, with a sweetness which she had herself
acquired by dint of doing violence to her natural disposition, "I love you very much, my dear N., and am
always happy to call to mind having had you for my
companion on the day of my first communion. I
should like to-day to give you a testimony of my affection, but I do not venture." "How so? you may rest
assured that I should receive it with gratitude." "I
fear lest this testimony of affection, as I regard it,
should not please you." "Don't be afraid of that; I
shall receive everything from you with pleasure." "If
this be so, then I will not lose so good an opportunity.
Do you remember what happened last Sunday just
before Vespers?" The culprit had forgotten, but, her
memory being aided by her charitable friend, she
readily acknowledged her fault. "I understand you,"
she said; "I disedified you, and certainly deserve
your reproofs. The thought did occur to me of making

my excuses to you about it, but no opportunity had
offered itself." "Nay," replied Marie, "you must not
regard what I say as a reproof, but, as you speak of
making excuses, it is the good God, and not I, who
ought to receive them : the church is not far off, shall
we go and offer them to Him ?" "Willingly ; but
since you have not chosen to reproach me, will you not
present my excuses to the good God ?" "Very well,"
replied Marie, smiling ; "and when I commit any
fault you will do the same for me." Marie's unfeigned
humility, which always made her place herself on a
level with the most imperfect, was one of the secrets of
her success in administering fraternal correction. She
gave it as one who felt she was as likely herself to need
it in her turn, or, as on the occasion of which we are
about to speak, as one who had often and more grievously sinned in the same way.

On another Sunday, after Vespers, several of the
young peasant girls had collected together and were
talking to Marie. One of them appearing particularly
joyous was questioned as to the cause. "Oh," she
replied, "my father had a lawsuit with a proprietor,
his neighbour ; if he had lost it we should have been
put to great straits, but happily our right prevailed, and
this is the reason why I am gayer than usual. I have
thanked our good God to-day, and have prayed Him to
prosper my family, to bless the harvest of our fields,
and to increase as much as possible our little possession
and our moderate fortune." While listening to this
candid avowal, Marie smiled, and at first said nothing.
The others were silent also. Perhaps they wished to
hear what she would say. To many it may appear
that there was nothing very wrong—certainly not consciously wrong—in the wish which had been expressed,

since it had been converted into a prayer. And are we not taught to pray in the Litany of the Saints that God "would vouchsafe to give and preserve the fruits of the earth"?* But Marie, whose eye was always fixed on the more perfect way, discerned the love of this world's goods and the ambition to rise which her young friend nursed in her heart. It was not mere gratitude for relief from anxiety and the simple desire to be prospered in their modest sphere which prompted the speech just uttered, or made the eyes of her who spoke dance with exultation. After a brief pause Marie said, "You would wish, then, my dear N., to become rich?" Receiving a reply in the affirmative, she added, "If by riches you could contribute more to the glory of God, and work more efficaciously for your sanctification, my desire would entirely agree with yours; but it is not always so; and we might often apply to ourselves those words of our Lord in the Gospel of to-day's Mass : 'You know not what you ask.'† As for me, I acknowledge in all sincerity that at one time of my life—and it is not so long ago—which I call the time of my illusions and of my vain dreamings, I desired to be rich, clever, well-informed, highly educated. I should have liked to possess more crown-pieces than I shall ever have pence, and to speak French better than I can speak Gascon. I longed for this to such a degree as to make me lose my appetite and my rest at night, and to make me dislike finding myself in the presence of any one whom I felt to be my superior. Truly, I did not know what it was I wished for. Thanks be to God, this did not last. I now only wish to be always a good Christian, and in my little retreat at the Gran Cassou to be

* "Ut fructus terræ dare et conservare digneris."
† Matt. xx. 22.

always your friend. N. will be in the same mind a week hence, will she not?" Marie's companion blushed, but the lesson had been so sweetly given, that it not only had not offended, it had worked its effect immediately. "A week hence!" she exclaimed; "that would be putting it off too long; it shall be at once. I see that I did not know what I was asking for. I don't want to lose either my appetite or my rest at night, and, still less, your friendship by becoming 'a great lady.'"

It will be observed that, while Marie candidly confessed her dreams of pride and vainglory, she did not make known, as we have seen her do to her director, the sublime aspirations which had replaced them; she had contented herself with saying, "Now I desire only to be a good Christian." The secret of her soul was for God alone, and for him who represented Him to her; to the rest of the world she disclosed nothing but what was simple and common. Simple and common, however, as what she said might seem to be, it came freighted with all the power which the abundant grace of the speaker imparted to it. Perhaps these conversions may appear to have been easily accomplished, even after making full allowance for the influence she exercised, but we must remember that these girls were not bad or ill-disposed but, at worst, only thoughtless or careless. Their hearts were yet fresh and tender, with the freshness and tenderness of youth, and, still more, by the yet unwasted effects of their first communion. But, if easy to turn to good, it by no means follows that these young women would have chosen ultimately what is good, had they not been blessed with a friend like Marie. Nay, many were already beginning to diverge in heart from the right way when Marie's winning voice recalled them. Two divergent lines may be very near at the point where they part, but soon they become very distant from each other. So it is with one who swerves ever so little from the right path : how soon has the poor soul travelled far out of hearing ! What an inappreciable blessing, then, was this poor girl to her young companions ; exercising as she did an apostolate which, by a rare gift, she knew how to render acceptable, and filling a mission which none but a companion could fill as well, but which companions so seldom fill at all !

Marie was in the habit, when she returned from her field labours, of collecting together some of the children who did not attend school, and who did not know how to read, in order to instruct them in the principal truths of the faith, and teach them by word of mouth the Little Catechism of the diocese. This was often tedious work. One of them in particular, a little boy, notwithstanding all the pains Marie took with him, knew no more at the end of a year than he did at the beginning ; he could scarcely repeat the " Our Father," or the " Hail Mary." " I must say," observed Elisabeth one day to her daughter, "that you must have a famous stock of patience to go on teaching that child ! " "O mother," rejoined Marie, " you needed pretty nearly as much with me. I am glad to be able now to make some reparation for my former untowardness by a little perseverance with this poor boy. By degrees you will see that, with the grace of God, he will arrive at knowing what is absolutely necessary ; he will make his first communion, and will not fail to pray for us."

Marie had always possessed a kind and feeling heart, and from her earliest childhood had ever shown great compassion for the afflicted. A little incident is recorded of her charity which took place at the time when she was making her first efforts to conquer her faults. To encourage her, her parents and their friends would reward her by giving her some little piece of money, which she used to treasure up carefully. Elisabeth, returning from Mass one day with her daughter, met a poor man who begged an alms. She had no money with her, and was obliged to turn away with regret and pursue her road; when Marie drew her little treasure from her pocket and, holding it out to her, said, "You have got nothing, mama? then give this for me." Her mother opened the purse but found no small coin in it. "There are no pence, my child," she said. "No matter," replied the little girl; "give him this piece, I shall soon have gained it again by my good conduct." "Well," replied her mother, "if this be the case, give it yourself; it will bring a blessing on your improvement, which is much to be desired." Marie quickly took a half-franc piece and slipped it into the beggar's hand, saying, "Pray the good God to make me better than I am," and, without waiting to be thanked, ran off to her mother with a joyous face, saying, "O mama, I shall certainly become better; the good God will repay me good measure for my little piece of money." Elisabeth had reason before long to note the fulfilment of this expectation.

If Marie was by nature kind, compassionate, and generous, much more did these good dispositions, under the influence of divine grace, grow, expand, and deepen. The love of Jesus, as it waxed stronger every day in her heart, also increased more and more her sympathy for His suffering members. She never let an occasion slip by of relieving them. One day, as she was bringing back her father's bullocks late in the afternoon, she fell in with a beggar who was with difficulty dragging

himself along. She inquired from whence he came.
"From Clermont," he replied—that was a neighbouring
village. " Have you had any dinner?" "No, I only
had a little *méture* (maize bread) in the morning, but I
hope some good soul at Mimbaste will give me a mouth-
ful of soup." "Yes, certainly you will get it. Come
along with me, and I will give you your dinner." Together they proceeded to Mimbaste and reached the
Gran Cassou. As soon as she had shut up the bullocks,
Marie went and asked her mother whether she had any
soup or broth. "You know very well," replied Elisabeth, " that I always put by some for you when you are
not at home in time to have your meal with us. You
will find your portion by the fire." "I am not asking
for myself," said Marie, " but for a poor man at the
door, who has only had a little *méture* this morning."
"Well, go and eat your own dinner, and I will make
him some good soup with what I have remaining."
" No, mother, as I invited him, I must wait upon him."
So she set to work, without thinking of her own dinner, prepared the soup, and took care to add the meat which had
been reserved for herself. The beggar, as may be imagined,
ate with a good appetite, and departed with thanks
and blessings. When he was gone, Marie took her portion of soup, but her dinner, it need hardly be said, did
not consume much time, since the best part had been
disposed of already. "Why don't you take your meat?"
asked her mother ; " it is there at the fire." " It is
not there now," replied Marie ; " the beggar has eaten
it for me. That poor creature only gets a little *méture*
every day ; so I pitied him, and gave him up my share.
It will do him good and me no harm. A good slice of
bread and a big apple which I am going to pick in the
garden will get me on very well to the evening."

Elisabeth could not find it in her heart to disapprove. She, too, was very charitable, and secretly admired the simplicity and the good grace with which her daughter denied herself to relieve the destitute.

The same charity which made Marie prompt to extend her hand to those in want, made her tongue ingenious in finding excuses for her neighbour's faults, —a charity more rare, perhaps, than the former. A man of some forty years of age had fallen dangerously ill in a village not far off. He had not approached the sacraments for a long time, and it was feared that he would die impenitent. Two or three young girls, friends of Marie, were talking about it to her one day. "He is an impious man," remarked one of them in a contemptuous tone; "he will die as he has lived." Marie Lataste quickly interposed. "Oh, we ought to pity him rather than despise him," she exclaimed. "If only he had had some of the graces which we have abused, he might very likely have been a great saint. Who knows? may be he was never properly instructed in his duties: perhaps he has had to struggle against terrible temptations, and may not be so guilty in the sight of God as he appears in those of men. We should do well to pray the good God to touch his heart, and grant him the grace of a true conversion. Possibly He is only waiting for the prayers of a few souls to sanctify his; let us not refuse them, and every evening let us at least say a *Memorare* to the Blessed Virgin for this intention." The proposal was welcomed, and the sick man soon evinced marks of the sincerest penitence, receiving the sacraments in a state of full consciousness and with much devotion.

But it was not by her companions and friends alone that Marie was regarded with so much esteem and even veneration. Her mere presence commanded respect among all the inhabitants of her native village; and her memory was still fresh amongst them when her life was first written by her director's nephew, the Abbé Pascal Darbins. This respect was not confined to her equals in station; the very *employés* at the tax-office used to receive her with a politeness such as they were not accustomed to display towards persons of her class, and would rise and uncover their heads as to a lady, when she went to pay what her parents owed. One of the friends of the receiving officer, who chanced to be present on an occasion of this sort, expressed some surprise, when she was gone, at the consideration shown by him to a poor peasant. "I can hardly say what it is I experience," replied the tax-collector, "but I never can see that girl without feeling myself a better man." A young man belonging to one of the most respectable families in the place believed that he could not do better than seek as his partner in life one who, if poor and humble in extraction, was so rich in virtue. Accordingly, meeting Marie one day, he accosted her, not without a certain degree of embarrassment, and, after some insignificant question as a preamble, at once broke through his shyness by plainly stating his object. "There is an obstacle in the way," she rejoined with much simplicity; "which is that I have formed exactly the contrary resolution." "What!" answered her chagrined suitor, "do you wish always to live an angelic life?" "Yes, yes," replied Marie, moving away; "you have guessed it: that is just what I wish—to be always angelic." An old man of the place, when questioned concerning his reminiscences of Marie, made this rejoinder :—"There is not a single young person about whom, right or wrong, people's tongues will not be busy; but never will you hear anything but praise of Marie Lataste, as regards her whole conduct from childhood upwards."

An instance of the effect equally produced by her presence on persons both of education and of spiritual discernment, may be recorded in conclusion. An ecclesiastic from the environs of Dax was one day sitting with the Curé of Mimbaste, who had been showing him some of the manuscripts entrusted to him by his penitent, and, in particular, pointing out a passage where she speaks of the dignity of the priesthood. At that moment there came a knock at the door of the presbytery. It was Marie Lataste herself; and the ecclesiastic begged M. Darbins to see her in his presence. Having bowed respectfully to the Curé and to his friend, she begged the former to have the kindness to go and visit a sick man whose name she gave. After replying very simply to a few questions addressed to her by her director, Marie again bowed and retired. She had certainly neither done nor said anything remarkable or extraordinary, yet this ecclesiastic declared that what he felt during that short conversation had never been effaced from his mind. "I saw in this young girl," he said, "the practical effect of the counsels which the Saviour had given her concerning her relations with priests. I discerned in her a reverence full of faith for him to whom she was speaking; and I may add that, while listening to the replies she made to her director, I had a vivid realisation of her colloquies with our Lord. It is a long time ago, and I never met Marie again, but the recollection of that countenance, beaming with angelic sweetness, is as fresh as if I had only just seen her."

# CHAPTER VIII.

### Marie's Visions of the Mother of God.

It is not within our purpose to give anything like a complete account of the visions with which Marie was favoured by our Lord. For a detailed narrative of them the reader is referred to her writings. Yet, as her instruction and training were partly conveyed and assisted by visions and symbolic representations, they cannot be passed over without some additional notice. We have already described those almost daily manifestations of His Sacred Humanity which our Lord made to His servant during a very considerable space of time. It would be impossible to relate her life without giving such an account; for these manifestations form the key and the clue to her history: without them, there is no history to tell. But the visions of which we here speak are further manifestations which our Lord condescended to make to her either for her instruction, consolation, or encouragement. A considerable number were parabolic in their character; and of these we shall say a few words by and by. For the present we shall confine our attention to visions of a more direct kind, and principally to those which relate to the Blessed Mother of God. The first, which we will give in detail, was most remarkable; we will relate it in Marie's own words.

"The Saviour Jesus," she writes, "had often spoken to me about Himself, but never had He as yet spoken about Mary. 'My daughter,' He said to me one day, 'do you desire to see My Mother?' 'Lord,' I replied,

'I have no desire of my own ; my will shall be Thy
will.   I desire to have no other will but Thine.'   Then
Jesus raised His eyes to heaven and cried; 'My
Mother, appear to My daughter ; I desire it, and, to
conform her will to Mine, she also desires it.   Do you
desire it, My daughter?'   'Yes, Lord.'   Then immediately I saw Mary, with the eyes of my soul, in front
of the altar, for I was in the church ; it was a Sunday
morning before Mass had begun.   I observed her
attentively.   Her countenance was brilliant as the
sun ; her hands shone like rays of the sun ; her robe
was white, sprinkled with stars ; a wide mantle of
flame-colour enveloped her shoulders, it was also sown
with stars.   Her hair flowed loose behind her, and over
her head was a veil of lace of most exquisite workmanship, while a crown of diamonds, of a purer and brighter
lustre than any of the heavenly luminaries, encircled
her brow.   This light with which Mary was invested
could be compared to no other light save that with
which Jesus shone.   The light of the sun would have
paled before it ; nevertheless, although my eyes cannot gaze on the sun, I could fix them on Mary, whose
splendour did not dazzle me to such a degree as to
prevent my contemplating her.   I gazed, then, on
Mary, and could not help gazing.   The sight of her
filled my soul with bliss.   When I had thus considered
her for some time, Mary took my two hands in hers ;
I rose without knowing whither I was going ; but I
had no fear, for my hands were in those of Mary, my
eyes were fixed on her eyes.   I regarded myself as a
child in its mother's arms, where no danger can reach
it.   We arrived at a magnificent temple paved with gold,
the columns whereof were very lofty, and the whole
interior was illuminated by thousands of lamps, all

lighted in honour of the Blessed Virgin. A countless multitude were singing her praises. She conducted me before a golden throne of exceeding magnitude which resembled an altar. 'That, my daughter,' she said, 'is the throne of the Godhead ; thence proceed all the effects of the justice of God.' Then she went to seat herself on a magnificent throne erected near to the first, and innumerable virgins, arrayed in white, came and ranged themselves around her. Their beauty was ravishing, yet was it much inferior to that of Mary. How poor and destitute I felt by comparison with all that I beheld! My miserable condition pierced and affected me so deeply that I began to weep. The holy Virgin then hid me under her mantle ; my tears ceased, and I saw the light which came from her pass through me, as the light of the day passes through glass. I was beside myself with joy.

" At that moment my bodily eyes were opened, and I saw the priest at the altar. I heard his voice distinctly saying these words : *Sanctus, sanctus, sanctus ;* and I felt penetrated throughout with the holiness of God. Again my eyes closed, and my ears heard nothing more, but I found myself still under Mary's mantle. The Blessed Virgin then rose, withdrew her mantle from me, approached the throne of the Divinity, and placed me in the hands of God. I had not seen God upon His throne even with the eyes of my soul, but as soon as Mary had placed me upon the throne on which He abides, I felt my soul all on fire with love, uniting itself to God in the Unity of the Blessed Trinity. God the Father blessed me, the Word of God placed His hand on my heart, and the Holy Spirit rested on my head like a refreshing dew, which made me live and die at the same time. I drew nearer and nearer to the Word of God, and through Him to God His Father. At last it seemed to me that I ended by reposing in the bosom of God the Father, that God the Son came to repose on my heart, and that the Holy Spirit presented to God the Father the Son reposing in me. Oh, moment of felicity, of joy, of indescribable transport ! Was this Heaven, and the bliss of Heaven, which I experienced at that moment ? Such happiness would have sufficed me for an eternity, and I would have accepted it of God for ever, if such had been His will. Mary came to draw me from this repose which I was enjoying in God ; she took me in her arms, and said to me, ' My daughter, live on earth thinking of Heaven; live on earth thinking of Jesus ; live on earth thinking of me.'

"At this moment Jesus descended from heaven to earth ; it was the moment of consecration. I descended along with Him. I prepared to go to holy communion. When I had the Saviour Jesus within me, I again seemed to be on the throne of God ; I again seemed to behold the Word of God reposing on my heart, and the Holy Spirit presenting me with Him to the Father. I thanked the Saviour Jesus for so many graces and so much goodness shown to me ; I thanked Mary also as well as I knew how, and retired." She goes on to describe how, during the whole of that day, she felt to be more in heaven than on earth. She almost seemed to possess no body, only her soul; the things around her were unnoticed ; she was, so to say, blind to them, and her eyes were open only to the marvels of heaven. No wonder she was in haste to return to Jesus, for it was in the church, as we have said, that she usually received these divine communications. She had no sooner placed herself in adoration before

the Saviour in His tabernacle than He came to instruct
her.  He told her that she had by means of His
Mother received the highest favours which God can
confer on a soul loved by Him ; and He proceeded to
explain to her that He had willed thereby to show her
how the relations of God with men subsist only by His
Mother and with His Mother.

After recording this magnificent vision, we cannot
omit to subjoin the remarkable communication made
by our Lord to His servant on the festival of the Immaculate Conception, while she was praying before the
altar of Mary.  It must be remembered that the date of
this communication, which was recorded in the manuscript placed in the hands of her director, preceded,
by several years, the elevation of Pius IX. to the chair
of Peter, and that Marie Lataste herself died in 1847,
seven years before the dogma of the Immaculate Conception was ruled by our Holy Father.  "I had paid
my homage," she writes, "to Mary, conceived without
sin ; I had congratulated our Lord Jesus Christ on
having so privileged a creature for His Mother; with
my whole heart I associated myself with the belief of
the Church, and united myself in spirit to all the faithful who on that day pay homage to Mary.  I had the
happiness of receiving communion.  When Jesus was
in my heart, He spoke thus to me : 'My daughter,
your homage has been acceptable to My Mother and
also to Me.  I am going to recompense your devotion
by telling you something which will give you pleasure.
The day is drawing nigh when heaven and earth will
unite together to accord to My Mother that which is
her due in respect of her highest prerogative.  Sin was
never in her, and her conception was pure and without
stain ; it was immaculate, as was the rest of her life.

It is My will that this truth should be proclaimed on earth, and acknowledged by all Christians. I have chosen to Myself a Pope, and I have inspired him with this resolution. He will ever have this thought in his mind from the time that he shall be Pope. He will collect together the Bishops of the whole world, that their voices may be heard proclaiming Mary Immaculate in her Conception, and the voices of all shall be united in his voice. His voice shall proclaim the belief to which the other voices have given testimony, and will resound throughout the entire world. Then, upon earth, nothing shall be wanting to My Mother's honour. The infernal powers and their adherents shall raise themselves up against this glory of Mary, but God will maintain it with all His might, and the powers of hell shall be thrust back into the abyss along with their partisans. My Mother shall appear to the world on a solid and immovable pedestal; her feet shall be of the purest gold, her hands like white molten wax, her countenance like the sun, her heart like a glowing furnace. A sword shall issue from her mouth which shall cast down her enemies and the enemies of those who have proclaimed her without stain. They of the East shall call her the Mystical Rose, and those of the New World the Strong Woman. She will bear upon her brow, written in characters of flame, "I am the City of the Lord, the Protector of the oppressed, the Consoler of the afflicted, the Rampart against foes." Now affliction shall come upon the earth, oppression shall reign in the city which I love, and in which I have left My Heart. She shall be in sorrow and desolation, surrounded by enemies on all sides, like a bird taken in a net. This city will seem to succumb during [three

years] * and a little longer after these three years.
But My Mother shall descend into the City; she will
take the hands of the old man seated on a throne, and
will say to him, "Behold the hour, arise : See thy enemies: I cause them to disappear one after another, and
they disappear for ever.   Thou hast rendered glory to
me in heaven and on earth, and I will render glory to
thee in heaven and on earth.   Look at men—they vene-
rate thy name, thy courage, thy power.   Thou shalt
live, and I will live with thee.   Old man, dry thy
tears ; I bless thee."   Peace shall return to the world,
Mary shall breathe upon the tempests and appease them;
her name shall be praised, blessed, and exalted for ever.
The captives shall acknowledge that to her they owe
their liberty; the exiled, restoration to their country;
the miserable, tranquillity and happiness.   Between her
and all her clients there shall be a mutual interchange
of prayers and graces, of love and affection ; and from
the East to the South, and from the North to the
West, all shall proclaim Mary conceived, without sin,
Mary Queen of earth and heaven.   Amen.' "

In regard to this prophecy, at once so striking and
so consolatory to us who live in the days of its partial
fulfilment, and who await the glorious issue which it
announces, we will hazard a few remarks.

From the terms employed—"three years and something more"—it might naturally have been concluded,
and, indeed, was by many concluded, that the persecution would not continue beyond three years and a-half,
or something, at least, short of a fourth full year;

* The words placed between brackets are omitted in the manuscript, but there is no vacant place left for them. The Abbé Darbins inserted them because they appear to be implied, and the
sense to require them.

and the frequent recurrence of this self-same period in connection with scourges, either recorded or foretold in Scripture, came to reinforce this view.   In Elias's time, for instance, the heavens were shut up and no rain fell for this space of time ; and, again, the persecution in the days of Antichrist is also to last during that same period of three years and a-half.   This is stated and re-stated in varying forms, sometimes in months, sometimes in days, sometimes as a time, times, and half a time.   Accordingly there seemed to be grounds for hoping that Rome might be delivered, the Pontiff set at liberty and restored to his rights, and the Church be freed from her oppressors, at the close of that period ; but that period has now gone by, and we are in the seventh year of the Holy Father's imprisonment and the Church's sufferings.   Must we say, therefore, that this prophecy, so accurately fulfilled up to a certain time, has failed of its accomplishment ?   This, we think, would be a hasty decision.   For, in the first place, the term of three years and something more may have been specified simply because that term is the space of time during which the great and final anti-Christian persecution is to last ; and what was meant to be indicated was that the present persecution would certainly endure as long as that of Antichrist, of which it was a foreshadowing, and (so to say) a threatening.   But, further, what seemed to be the natural, was by no means a necessary, conclusion.   What was positively asserted was that the Holy City should be encompassed by enemies for the space of three years ; but this was to be followed by an indefinite term, though apparently of brief duration.   Who knows but that the prolongation of this additional time, or its curtailment, may have been conditional—conditional on the fervent prayers of the faithful, and on the spirit of penance awakened in the hearts of the many whom God would recall to Him by His chastisements ?  St. Peter tells us that "the Lord delayeth not His promise, as some imagine, but dealeth patiently, . . . not willing that any should perish, but that all should return to penance." * It may be allowable, therefore, to look on that indefinite term as a reserved quantity, the duration of which is one of the secrets of God.  An analogous remark may be made with reference to the famous prediction of the Venerable Anna Maria Taigi, that the reign of the present Pope would exceed the years of Peter on the Pontifical throne, and something more.  That "something more " might in like manner have been supposed to be in length short of a year, but the event has proved otherwise.  Thanks be to God our Holy Pontiff still lives, and we hope and pray that he will live to behold the triumph which Marie Lataste foretold would be given to him by Mary.

We might add that the very terms of the prophecy are mysterious, and do not literally and explicitly speak of temporal restoration.  Our Lady's descent, her taking the hands of the Pontiff, her pointing to the gradual disappearance of his enemies, and her final blessing, may have other and deeper significations than we can divine.  Time will reveal these and solve the enigma.

We will, in conclusion, make one further observation, and it is this—that there is nothing less reliable in the interpretation of prophecy than dates.  Even in Scripture, where we know all was dictated by the Spirit of God, and nothing added thereto by the individual mind of the prophet, there is perhaps but

* 2 Peter iii. 9.

one date which was intended to be perfectly clear and devoid of ambiguity; and that is the date of the coming of the Messias, as announced to the prophet Daniel. How much more, then, is a feeling of confidence in what are supposed to be fixed dates to be discouraged in the case of private revelations, where we have no such security as regards the introduction of error, and equal reasons at least for not expecting that God would depart from His apparent rule of enveloping in mystery the precise times when His menaces or promises will have their complete fulfilment.*

To return to our more immediate subject. Marie records another beautiful vision of the Mother of God, vouchsafed to her by our Lord. This, however, was retrospective, and in the way of a picture. It occurred on the festival of the Annunciation, when, finding a difficulty in meditating on the subject of the feast, she threw herself on her knees before the Tabernacle, and besought Jesus to come to her aid, who speedily appeared to her, and said these words: "My daughter, you love Me to speak of My Mother, and I also love to speak of her. To enlighten you concerning the mystery of this day, I will take you with Me. Come, My daughter, follow Me." Marie proceeds to describe how, earth disappearing from her view, she was transported to an elevated plain or plateau, from which rose in succession nine degrees, or steps, one above the other. A multitude of youths in white garments descending to their knees, their arms being bare, and their beautiful long hair, divided on the forehead, flowing behind them, each having two outspread wings,

---

* On the subject of the conditional fulfilment of true prophecies, see Benedict XIV.'s "Treatise on Heroic Virtue" (Oratorian Translation), vol. iii. chap. viii.

occupied these successive stages, but on each ascending step the occupants shone with increased radiance. At the summit was a glorious throne, all light, prostrate before which were seven angels, like the rest in appearance, but more brilliant even than they. After this Jesus led her by the hand, and, quitting the plain, entered a lowly cell, where she saw a youthful maiden praying, with hands crossed on her bosom and eyes lifted up to heaven. Then Marie beheld enacted before her the scene recorded in the pages of Sacred Writ, when Gabriel came on his lofty embassage, and knelt before the humble Virgin, saluting her by those glorious titles which now are hers, and shall be hers for ever.

When this vision was over, and Marie once more found herself in her place in the church of Mimbaste, our Lord graciously proceeded to speak to her of the mystery of the feast, and of His Incarnation, which, after what she had witnessed, she would understand with greater facility. This instruction, which is related at length in the works of Marie Lataste, and is at once simple and profound, would be too long for insertion, as would also several others of much interest which He gave her on the subject of His Mother, His relations to her, and hers through Him to men. We shall limit ourselves to noticing cursorily some other visions of the Blessed Virgin with which Marie was favoured, prefacing them with a few remarks, extracted from her works, expressive of the sentiments which she entertained towards the sweet Mother of God. The love of Jesus and Mary was, we might almost say, identified in the affections of this favoured soul, so closely were the Mother and the Son united in her thoughts. " My soul," she writes, " overflows with joy when Jesus speaks to me of Himself, or manifests Himself to me; and my joy is no less when He speaks to me of His Mother, or when she visibly appears to me, or comes to speak to me herself.  When Jesus speaks to me of Mary, He speaks of Himself; when I see Mary, I see Jesus; when Mary converses with me, and causes me to hear her voice, it seems to me as if it were Jesus who is addressing me.  I make no distinction between the voice of Jesus and that of Mary. If my bodily eyes or the eyes of my soul were closed, and I were to hear Jesus or Mary speak, without seeing them, I should not know from which of them came the voice.  I have, however, remarked that the voice of Mary is invariably full of sweetness, kindness, tenderness, but that the voice of Jesus is at times severe, and has a tone of justice or of menace which I have never recognised in that of Mary.  The voice of Mary is always the same, of an inexpressible gentleness alike to the just and to sinners.  Why so ?  I know not; but I do know this, that Mary is the mother of the Son of God who died upon the cross, and that she is our mother.  Mary, mother of God, and my mother: this is Mary and her sweetness, Mary and her goodness, Mary and her tenderness, Mary and her compassion. O Mary, mother of Jesus and my mother, I love thee, I bless thee, I praise thee, I give myself to thee."

One Christmas Marie had several visions of the Blessed Virgin.  The first which she records took place before the midnight Mass, when she was making her meditation on the Birth of Jesus in the stable at Bethlehem before the altar of Mary, to which she had felt herself specially attracted; her usual attraction being, as we know, to the Tabernacle.  On this occasion she seems to have received a favour like that which was

granted to St. Anthony of Padua, and St. Stanislas
Kostka. She thus describes it :—"I had not addressed
myself to Jesus, I had had recourse to Mary. I had
forgotten the Saviour to think only of His Mother.
Nevertheless, this forgetfulness was not forgetfulness,
for, in addressing myself to Mary, I thought of Jesus
also. I only mean that my first glance this night had
been towards Mary, and that by Mary I desired to
reach Jesus. The altar of Mary was not lighted up,
but that did not matter to me. I saw Mary, if not
with the eyes of the body, at least with the eyes of my
soul ; I was with her and St. Joseph in the stable; and
along with her and St. Joseph I adored the Infant
Jesus. Soon the sight I had of Mary grew clearer and
more brilliant ; she became the light of her own altar,
which was not illuminated ; then she sweetly called me
to her. The Infant Jesus, wrapped in swaddling
clothes, was in her arms. I should have wished to
take Him into mine, press Him to my heart, and
caress Him, but I did not dare to make this request of
Mary ; however, she understood it, for, without ques-
tioning me, she placed her Divine Infant in my hands,
and then drew me nearer to her, as if to take me with
Jesus under her protection.

"The Infant Jesus was with me, but He was speech-
less. I looked at Him, then I looked at Mary ; I
embraced Jesus and I thanked Mary ; I desired to ask
some questions of Jesus, and I did not venture to
question Mary. Nevertheless, by degrees I grew
bolder, and I said to Mary, 'Holy Virgin, speak to me
of the Birth of the Saviour Jesus.' 'My daughter,'
replied Mary, 'I will satisfy your desire. My Son
Jesus, being an infant, does not speak. I will converse
with you in His place.'" Mary then proceeded to

instruct her how the Birth of her Divine Son was a
mystery accomplished by the will of the Blessed
Trinity, a will which in its triplicity was one will, and
reposed eternally in the bosom of the Godhead; that,
in like manner, there was a triple will accomplishing
this mystery on earth, the Will of God the Father, God
the Son, and God the Holy Ghost operating on earth
what had been decreed in heaven; the Will of God
the Son Incarnate, who was her son also; and her own
will. " This Birth," she said, " was operated in these
admirable relations between the Three Divine Persons
and me, the Mother of Jesus. The Three Divine
Persons gave my Son to the world; and I gave Him
to the Three Divine Persons. The Three Divine
Persons regarded me as the Mother of Jesus; and I
regarded myself as the lowly servant of the Three
Divine Persons. From this moment I felt myself
stronger, I felt within me the power of God Himself;
for Jesus was my Son, not only within me but without
me also, and He who commands in heaven and on
earth had become subject to me. I commanded Him;
He did my will as He did the will of His Father;
and thus, while the will of the Three Divine Persons
was the rule and motor of my will, my will was also
the rule and motor of the Divine Will of my Son."

We find Mary's lessons to Marie Lataste closely
resembling those of Jesus in their invariably practical
application. Accordingly, she does not leave the lesson
of the mystery to be implied, but explains it to her
simple client, as Jesus when on earth explained His
parables to His rude and uninformed disciples, even
when they seemed to bear their meaning on their very
surface. But the explanations of the Divine Word are
with power; we all need them, or we understand in an

unfruitful way. Mary, then, continued thus: "O my daughter, understand well the example which the Birth of Jesus presents to you. It·is an example of submission, an example of will executed and followed, an example of subordination; and this example comes from Heaven, comes from God. God willed, and I willed along with God. God the Father willed, and God the Son submitted to the will of His Father. God the Father and God the Son willed, and God the Holy Ghost willed with Them, and disposed the realisation and accomplishment of Their will. My will has ever been conformable to the will of God. God willed that His Son should become incarnate in me, and should be born on this day; and in all I conformed my will to the will of God. Forget not, my daughter, that the sin of man was opposition to the will of God; to repair this sin, submission to the will of God was needed. Behold the beginning of this submission in the Birth of my Son. Look further on, and you will find this submission in His Death. From Bethlehem to Calvary, all in Jesus, all in me united to Jesus, is submission to the will of God. Well, my daughter, be you also submissive to the will of God, let your will be always united to His and make one only will with His; remember the Birth of my Son, His submission and my submission; and, however hard to bear that may be which is required of you, reflect that your submission will augment your justice and unite you closer to Jesus and to His Mother."

On the feast of the Epiphany (during, apparently, the same Christmas season), she was favoured with another vision after receiving communion. "Having received Jesus into my heart," she writes, "I offered it to Him, with all I had and all I was, to acknowledge

Him as my King, my God, and my Saviour.   Then I
saw, not with the eyes of my body, but of my soul, a
young man, who seemed to me to be an angel; he
placed himself in adoration before the Tabernacle; then
he approached me, and said, 'Marie, follow me.'   I
rose and followed him.   We passed behind the altar.
There a wide-spreading country met my eyes, and in
the distance I descried a hill upon which a small town
was seated.   We walked very fast, and in a few minutes had reached the city.   We traversed it without
stopping, and directed our steps towards the foot of
the hill on the east side of the city.   We arrived at a
grotto hewn in the rock : ' Stop, Marie,' said my con-
ductor; ' this is the house of the Lord, and the place
where He was born for the salvation of men.'   This
grotto, which had served as a stable, was wide, spacious,
and covered with thatch.   It had been disposed as a
dwelling, and there, indeed, dwelt Jesus, Mary, and
Joseph.   The angel, addressing the Infant Jesus, said
to Him, ' Lord, Thou hast commanded me to bring
to Thee Thy servant Marie—here she is.'   Jesus, on
seeing me, smiled graciously, and then looked at His
Mother, who was holding His hand.   I prostrated
myself before Jesus, whom I recognised, as having
received Him in my arms on Christmas night.   I adored
Him anew, as my King, my God, and my Saviour.
He left Mary's hand and came to me.   I received Him
for some moments into my arms, and then gave Him
back to Mary ; after which I seated myself close to her
on a footstool which St. Joseph placed for me.   ' My
daughter,' then said to me the Mother of Jesus, ' never
lose sight of the grace granted to you this day.   God
has given you an angel, and this angel is the angel of
your salvation.   With him you have sought my Son

Jesus, you have been guided to this place which He inhabits, and I have permitted you to hold Him in your arms. Even so, my daughter, whenever you shall seek my Son with great desire, be sure that you will find Him. You will not find Him alone; you will always find me with Him. He will not give Himself to you; it is I who will give Him to you, who will consign Him to you, who will desire Him to go to you. He will not speak to you unless I tell Him to do so; but, if He does not speak to you, I will speak in His stead. God has given to my Son all power on earth and in heaven; but because I am His Mother, He wills not to exercise it save at my behest. Unite, then, always my name with the Name of my Son; seek me always in seeking Jesus; never separate us, and you will ever find us together, and we will give you a place in our family, and a share in our trials and sufferings upon earth, that one day we may draw you to ourselves to live with us in the presence of God!' "

This charming vision was followed by one of the Adoration of the Three Kings, who at this juncture arrived, and were ushered in by the angel; but we must refrain from quotations, adding, however, a passage from another part of Marie's works, where she is giving an account of our Lord's instruction concerning prayer. It forms a portion of what He said to her about praying to His Mother, which harmonises entirely with what Mary herself said concerning the maternal authority with which her Son, the God-Man, has been pleased to invest her for all eternity. This is a subject incomprehensible and a sort of scandal to those without, a scandal because incomprehensible. True and devout Catholics, however, instinctively understand it, and in proportion to their devotion and experimental realisation

of the mystery of the Incarnation will be their comprehension of Mary's position in the scheme of grace.
We seem to have a clue to the understanding of her
maternal prerogative in the words addressed by the
Mother of God to Marie Lataste regarding the power
imparted to her when He who commands in heaven and
on earth became incarnate in her. The will of the Three
Divine Persons, she said, ruled her will, and her will
ruled that of her Son. Nor let this seem strange. It
is part of the economy of grace that conformity with
God's will should give power with God. He does the
will of those who do His will. "Whosoever shall do
the will of My Father that is in heaven," Jesus told
His disciples, "he is My brother, and sister, and
mother,"—thus sharing in their measure the wonderful
prerogative which is Mary's in its fulness ; and if this
be true of every adopted child of grace who is obedient
to God, in how much sublimer a sense may we conceive
it to be true of His immaculate one, His own sinless,
peerless Mother, who gave to Him His human
nature !

While Jesus was speaking to Marie of prayer to His
Mother, it seemed to her as if a singular brilliancy
accompanied His words. After explaining how Mary
is the work and creature of God, but the highest,
the holiest, and the most perfect of His works, the
master-piece of His hands, He goes on to tell her how
it is the will of God that we should love and honour
His Mother. He bids Marie not only to pay her homage,
but to have recourse to her in all her temptations,
trials, and sufferings, "She will grant you," He continues, "help, grace, and consolation. I tell you this,
not to make you suppose that Mary is more powerful
than God, but to teach you that God wills not to grant

anything save through Mary. Behold the whole plan and economy of Providence concerning men.

"I am between God and men. No one can obtain anything from My Father unless he obtain it through Me. Now, I have placed My Mother between men and Me, and I grant nothing to men save by My Mother, and in consideration of her. Let the sinner address himself to Mary, let him obtain her protection, and he is forgiven. He who is at peace with Me is at peace also with My Father; in like manner he who possesses the friendship of My Mother possesses My friendship also. Ask of Mary all the graces which you need, and she will obtain them for you; recognising your unworthiness, address yourself to Mary, and Mary will pray for you. All the graces which God distributes are in Me as in an immense reservoir; I cause them to flow into Mary as into another reservoir; and you must go and draw them thence. A grace is asked for, My Father consents, I grant it, and Mary gives it. If you wish to be always received by Me, pray Mary to present you, or present yourself in the name of Mary, begging Me to receive you, not for your own merits, but in consideration of Mary. When you cannot come to Me, go to Mary; beseech her to intercede for you; I shall behold you with pleasure at her feet. Go to Mary in temptations, dangers, perils; by so doing you will be secure of victory. To be in the hands and under the protection of Mary is to be secure of your salvation."

The visions partially detailed above were by no means the only visions of the Mother of God with which Marie was favoured. During the same Christmas season to which we have alluded, she was guided by her angel, after the massacre of the Innocents, along the way by which the Holy Family had passed, to join

them in the desert. Here she was again permitted to
press the Infant Jesus to her heart, and Mary addressed to her a few sweet words of practical counsel;
telling her that, if she would establish the kingdom of
God in her heart, she must fly from the devil, the
world, and herself. She would then find herself in
a desert, but a desert not devoid of charms. She would
enjoy the consolations of God, figured by the fruit-
bearing and sheltering tree under which she was seated
with the Divine Child, with a spring of refreshing
water hard by to slake her thirst. "There," she said,
"you will find Jesus, and you will find me with Him."
When the revolution of the seasons brought round the
Mysteries of the Passion, Marie was led in spirit to
Calvary, where she saw her Crucified Lord, and the
Mother of Dolours at the foot of His Cross, and again
heard words of instruction from her lips, lessons of
patience and of the love of suffering. Again, during a
whole month of May, she had at different times the
privilege of hearing Mary's voice, and being taught
from her lips how she was the consolation of the
afflicted, the refuge of sinners, the help of the infirm,
the gate of heaven, the Virgin of virgins, and finally,
the Mother of all men. For all these instructions we
must be contented to refer our readers to Marie's works.
It would happen sometimes—we have already noticed
one occasion—that the Saviour would not Himself
speak to Marie, but would refer her to His Mother
that she might receive a lesson from her in His place.
At these, and other times, Marie perhaps only heard
her voice, but had no ocular vision; and she notices
besides, that, even when she heard no distinct voice,
she always carried away an indescribable sense of
happiness after addressing her who is the "cause of

our joy." "Never," she says, "did I leave the church without having offered a prayer before the image of Mary. I used to remain very long if my occupations allowed of it; I contented myself with saying one *Ave Maria* when I was pressed for time. Mary did not always manifest herself sensibly, but she always caused my soul to experience a certain impression of happiness, peace, and tranquillity, which I feel, but am unable to express."

---

# CHAPTER IX.

### JESUS INSTRUCTS MARIE IN PARABLES, AND SPEAKS TO HER OF FRANCE.

THE Saviour, as has been said, often instructed Marie by means of parables; these parables being acted out in vision before her, while she herself was called to bear a part in them. Every reader of the New Testament knows how frequently our Lord adopted the parabolic form of instruction, particularly at one stage of His ministry, and various reasons for this have been suggested, more than one of which, indeed, have Scriptural authority. Some of these reasons, at first sight, appear contradictory to each other. The most obvious one, for instance, would seem to be that these parables were intended to convey deep truths in a familiar way, and thus to make them easier of comprehension; but upon one occasion the inspired historian says that this mode was adopted in order that the hearers might *not* see or understand.* Nevertheless, it is clear that there

* Matt. xiii. 10-15. Mark iv. 33, 34.

is, and indeed could be, no real contradiction, for while parables served as a veil to those who were not worthy of more explicit teaching, they were a vehicle of truth to the faithful followers of Jesus, to whom He Himself explained them. The parabolic, allegoric, and emblematic form of instruction has also been often adopted by our Lord in His communications to favoured souls, especially where those souls were remarkable for a sweet, childlike simplicity; and—need we add?—such souls have always been specially dear to the great Lover of little children.

But concerning parables one general observation may be made. All instruction, all ideas, all truths, when conveyed in articulate language, are figuratively conveyed. To the sensible world, and the sensations which our physical frame receives therefrom, we must look for the primary source whence is derived every word we use, even such as relate to spiritual objects. It is true that in modern languages, which are conglomerations, formed out of the disjointed fragments of the more ancient tongues, this fact is much lost sight of, and the meaning of the words we use has become in a great measure conventional, the image underlying the terms being forgotten or overlooked; but this was not so, doubtless, in the early ages of humanity, when language, less flexible for the formation of phrases, must have had a deeper significance as regarded words and the imagery conveyed by them. Why this symbolic character of spoken language should exist we can readily understand from the necessary fact that all God's works must have a oneness which is the reflex of His own Unity. His ideas are Himself; and creation, whether material or spiritual, can only express His ideas because they can only express Himself, the inferior order being typical of the higher. Thus nature is one grand type; it is not merely that it may be made to furnish types, after the manner of similitudes, but it is all type. Hence also language is necessarily typical, and early instruction must necessarily be peculiarly typical.

Again, the whole history of the chosen people of God, the Israelites, was one continued type down to its minutest details ; not only typical as regarded the prefigured Messias, His office, sacrifice, &c., but typical also of the dealings of God with the souls of those in whom he sets up His kingdom, to wit, the spiritual Israel. It was to this mystical interpretation of events under the Old Law that our Lord, in His instructions to Marie Lataste, particularly drew her attention. "The Saviour Jesus has taught me everything," she says. "It is He who has manifested to my intelligence those admirable truths of the supernatural order with which it was so little acquainted ; it is He who, by means of images, figures, and comparisons, has ineffaceably engraven them on my mind. He said to me one day, 'My daughter, when I was on earth, I loved to speak in parables; I wish also to speak to you in that manner.' Now," she continues, "in the divers instructions which the Saviour gave me, He often showed me how the Old Testament was the figure of the New ; how the action of God on the Jewish people was the figure of His action on souls."

All the examples she gives of our Lord's teaching concerning the application of Scripture are of this character. We quote one taken from patriarchal times.

"My daughter," Jesus said to me one day, "it is related in the Sacred Books that Noe sent a dove out of the ark, wherein he was enclosed that he might not

perish in the deluge, for the purpose of ascertaining if
the waters had subsided, and that the dove returned to
the ark, bearing in her beak an olive branch.    This
dove is the figure of a solitary life.    It is not necessary,
in order to find solitude, to retire into convents or
cloisters ; it may be found in villages, in cities, and
even in the courts of kings ; and of all solitudes the
best, the most profitable, is interior solitude.    There
are souls which need exterior solitude in order to arrive
at interior ; but there are others who find themselves
as solitary in the midst of the greatest stir and tumult
as in the recesses of a desert.    The solitary soul takes
her delight in retirement, for there she finds God, and
God suffices her ; she unites herself to God, and this
union suffices her ; there nothing separates her from
God ; and this tranquillity is the sole object of her
desire.    To live for God, to suffer for God, to die for
God, and to repose in Him : behold the whole ambition
of this soul.    She is simple and innocent as a dove,
and leaves her heart quite open to God ; she gives it to
Him wholly.    She is timid and fearful as a dove, and
this fear makes her wise, and gives her the victory over
her enemies, because she does not expose herself to
dangers.    She fears the world ; she dares not rest her
feet upon it ; she returns to her solitude, bearing the
olive branch of her victory over the world, over her
enemies, over herself, and enjoys, in deep draughts, the
delicious sweetness of the love of God.    The worldly
do not understand the delights of solitude, and resemble
the raven sent out from the ark, who returns not.
Solitude is to them more than a mystery ; it is a
source of weariness, and they expend in the tumult
and agitations of earth their years and their life."

Our Lord thus compared the Temple of Solomon

to the soul in which grace dwells :—"My daughter, King Solomon, having caused a magnificent temple to be built to God, placed within it the Ark of the Covenant, and God testified in a sensible manner that He dwelt therein. This is why numerous victims were offered in it. This temple is the image of the soul which a man endeavours to adorn and embellish according to his means, by purifying it from all attachment and all affection to sin, that he may place therein the true Ark of the Covenant, which is the Son of God made Man, in the Eucharist. I prefer a pure heart to tabernacles of stone or of gilded wood, I establish My abode therein with pleasure ; and God, My Father, manifests in this heart His presence and Mine—for He is everywhere where I am—by the thoughts, desires, and works of Him in whom We come to dwell. Also, how many are the sacrifices offered to My Father by Him who receives Us and in whom We abide; sacrifices of the heart, sacrifices of the will, sacrifices of the passions, sacrifices of self-love! It is a victim which is immolating itself without cessation. How great is the beauty of this soul ! It far surpasses that of the Temple of Solomon, and so it must needs do. What will be the shame which one day will overwhelm those who shall discover the difference of their sentiments from those of the Jews ! These shall cover them with confusion and rise up to condemn them at the last day. Receive Me, then, often, and according to the counsel of your director. I shall be in you the true Ark of the Covenant between you and My Father, and nothing shall break this alliance, which shall endure for ever."

In the following we find a striking encouragement to prayer—not, we mean, such as is offered for our own personal needs, for none doubt the efficacy of petitions of this kind, however they may neglect to put it to the proof, but for some great general object, as, for instance, the triumph of the Church, the conversion of nations, and of our own country in particular, the evangelisation of the heathen, and the like. Many, perhaps, may have been tempted to feel that their own individual prayers offered for such ends—and how important it is that we all should offer them may be deduced from this fact alone, that they are one of the conditions prescribed by the Church for gaining a plenary indulgence—many, we say, may at times have been tempted to feel that their own individual petition is as a drop in the ocean, a kind of infinitesimal atom in the column of prayer which ascends to the throne of God. Such a feeling tends to chill fervour, and, indeed, is founded on a mistaken notion. "One day," writes Marie, " the Saviour Jesus spoke thus to me :—'My daughter, King Assuerus having resolved to destroy the nation of the Jews, Mardocheus counselled Esther, his niece and the consort of Assuerus, to beg that the Jewish people might be spared. She presented herself before the king, and, seized with fear, fainted away. The king at once lavished every attention and care upon her, and for a while she revived, but fell anew into a swoon. Then, moved with compassion, the king promised to grant her whatsoever she should ask. It was thus that Esther was able to save her people. My daughter, I say to you in truth that it is sometimes sufficient for one single soul to present itself before God in fear and trembling, and address to Him its supplications, to arrest His avenging arm already raised to smite a whole nation.'" And He then added an exhortation to her to pray for her country. " Pray, My daughter," He said, " pray much for France ; the number of its iniquities increases every day; pray for her, and disarm the anger of My Father. Unite yourself to the pious and holy souls who make their ceaseless supplications. If God watches over France and protects her, notwithstanding her iniquities, it is solely from regard to the numerous prayers which ascend before Him to appease Him."

This was not the only time that our Lord spoke to her about France and the destinies of her country. She had once a vision on the subject, which she relates in a letter to her director. "One day," she says, writing June 21st, 1842, "while I was working I felt in my heart a strong attraction which I could not resist, for I found it impossible to be at rest anywhere. I abandoned myself to this attraction, and then I seemed to find myself in a large square in Paris. In the middle of this square I saw a young man standing on a low pillar. He was clothed in a red garment; he had a diadem on his head, and in his hands he held a sheathed sword and a bow. His glances were like lightning, and his lips seemed ready to pour forth menaces. Over his head I saw inscribed, in characters of fire, 'The Destroying Angel.' At this sight, strange feelings of fear, grief, and compassion came over me, and I exclaimed several times, 'Lord, preserve Paris; save the King!' I remained a long time prostrate before God, uttering only groans and supplications."

Before long we shall find Marie taken to task about this vision, which was made matter of reproach to her, as was also a parabolic vision concerning her own future which she had related, and which was treated as a foolish delusion, mainly, however, with the view of trying her. Several of her visions were of the latter character; some pointing to her vocation to be a religious of the Sacred Heart, others designed to prepare her for sufferings to which we are about to allude.

Of the direct instructions given by our Lord to Marie, it would be impossible to give any adequate idea, so multifarious were they, descending to every practical detail of life, and expounding all the mysteries of the faith. We shall occasionally quote illustrative passages in the course of our narrative, but to judge them as a whole the reader must have recourse to her works.

Having, however, alluded to the exhortations she received on one occasion to pray for France, it may be well to give a few more extracts from other communications which our Lord made to His servant concerning her country. They are taken from a letter written to her director in November, 1843. This was five years, it will be remembered, before the dethronement of Louis Phillipe, an event certainly not generally anticipated at that period, notwithstanding the dissatisfaction prevalent in France, especially among certain classes.

"Here," she writes, "is what the Saviour Jesus said to me last Sunday after communion:—'My daughter, I am the Master of My Word; I say all that I will, when I will, and to whom I will, and no one has the right to question Me, saying, Wherefore, Lord, dost Thou speak in this wise? I know how to make all turn to My glory and the economy of My Providence, as for the entire world, so for each soul in particular. To-day I desire to speak to you of your country. Listen! The first king, the first sovereign, of France is I Myself. I am the Lord of all peoples, nations, kingdoms, empires, dominions; but I am specially the Master of France. I give her prosperity, greatness, power, above all other nations, when she is faithful in hearkening to My voice. I raise her princes above all other princes of the earth when they are faithful in hearkening to My voice. I have chosen France, to give her to My Church as her daughter of predilection. Scarcely had she bowed her head under My yoke, which is sweet and light, scarcely had she felt the Blood of My Heart fall upon her heart, to regenerate her, to strip her of her barbarism, and communicate to her of My gentleness and My charity, when she became the hope of My Pontiffs, and, soon after, their defence and their support. They gave her the well-merited title of Eldest Daughter of the Church.' The Saviour proceeded to say how He considered all that was done for His Church as done to Himself. If she is honoured, He is honoured in her; if persecuted, He is persecuted in her; if her blood flows, it is His Blood which issues from her veins. Now, as long as France defended and protected His Church, He blessed her, He blessed both her king and her people.

In reading the words addressed to Marie Lataste by our Lord in this 19th century concerning the position and vocation of France, as the first of Christian nations, the blessings she will bring down on herself by fulfilling this vocation, and the severe chastisement which her forgetfulness and betrayal of her charge will entail upon her, our thoughts recur to the close of the fifth century, when St. Remigius poured the regenerating waters on the head of Clovis, and on the heads of three thousand of his court and followers. On that Christmas Eve, Remigius thus addressed the Frankish monarch :—" Take notice, my child, that the kingdom of France is predestined by God for the defence of the Roman Church, which is the only true Church of Christ. This kingdom shall one day be great among the kingdoms of the earth; it shall embrace all the limits of the Roman Empire, and shall subject all other kingdoms to its own sceptre. It shall last until the end of time. It shall be victorious and prosperous as long as it shall remain faithful to the Holy Roman See, and not be guilty of any of those crimes which ruin nations; but it will be severely punished every time that it becomes unfaithful to its vocation." *

Our Lord continued:—"My generosity towards France is not exhausted. My hands are full of graces and benefits which I should desire to lavish on her. Why has it been needful, why is it still, and why shall it yet be needful, that they should wield the rod of justice? What a spirit of wild licence has replaced in her heart the only true liberty come down from Heaven, which is submission to the will of God! What a spirit of cold egotism has replaced in her heart the ardent spirit of charity descended from Heaven, which is the love of God and of neighbour! What a spirit of unjust intrigue and lying diplomacy has replaced that nobility of conduct and that rectitude both of speech and of action which once were directed by Truth, descended from Heaven, which is God Himself! I still see, and shall ever see, in the kingdom of France men submissive to My will, men inflamed with charity, men who are friends of truth; but at the present hour, My daughter, their number is small.

* This prophecy of St. Remigius was well known in mediæval times; and the yet unfulfilled promise of a great French king, who, before the end of the world, should attain the highest power, and reign over the whole Roman Empire, was current both in East and West.

France overturns the throne of her kings, banishes, recalls, and again banishes her monarchs; lets loose upon them the wind of revolutionary tempests, and makes them disappear like passengers in a vessel that is swallowed up in the depths of the ocean. Scarcely does there remain to them in this shipwreck a plank of safety to bring them to the shore. I have raised up kings for her, and she has chosen others at her own pleasure. Has she not seen, does she not see, that I make use of her self-will to punish her, and to force her to raise her eyes towards Me? Does she not now esteem the yoke of her king to be grievous and onerous? Does she not feel herself humiliated before the nations? Does she not see division in the minds of her people? She is not at rest. All is quiet on the surface; but all is murmuring, threatening, fermenting below, among her people, among those who are just raised above the populace, as also among the great. Injustice stalks about with head erect, and appears to be invested with authority; it meets with no obstacle, and acts as it lists. Impiety is preparing to raise its haughty head at a time which it believes to be not far distant, and which it desires to hasten on with all its might. But in truth, I say to you, impiety shall be cast down, its projects dissipated, its designs reduced to naught, at the very hour when it will believe that they are accomplished and firmly established for ever."

Words like these come fraught with singular consolation at the present moment, and are in complete accord with the expectation of holy souls, now that the crisis seems to be drawing near, and impiety is confidently making boast that it will utterly extirpate the religion of Christ. Our Lord thus continues:—"O France, France, how ingenious thou art both to irritate and to appease the justice of God! If thy crimes draw down upon thee the chastisements of Heaven, thy virtue of charity shall cry aloud to Heaven, 'Mercy, O Lord, pity!' To thee, O France, it will be given to behold the judgments of My irritated justice, at a time which shall be manifested to thee, and which thou shalt recognise without fear of error; but thou shalt know also the judgments of My compassion and of My mercy, and thou shalt say, 'Praise and thanksgiving, love and gratitude, to God for ever, throughout all ages and throughout eternity.' Yes, My daughter, at the breath which shall issue from My mouth, men—their thoughts, their projects, their works—shall vanish like smoke before the wind. What has been chosen shall be rejected, and what has been rejected shall be taken again. What has been loved and esteemed shall be hated and despised, and what has been despised and hated shall again be esteemed and loved. Sometimes an old tree has been felled in a forest, and nothing but the stump remains; but a sprout comes forth in the spring-time, it develops and grows with years, and it becomes at length a magnificent tree, the glory of the forest. Pray for France, My daughter; pray much, and never cease from praying."

# CHAPTER X.

WE have now given a general idea of the character of
our Lord's instructions and communications to Marie
Lataste; we shall have occasion to recur to them from
time to time, particularly when we come to notice the
changes that took place in His dealings with her.

Our Lord several times announced to Marie, under
the image of martyrdom, the sufferings that awaited
her. As she did not actually undergo a violent death,
but died after an illness involving great bodily suffering, there is something singularly consoling in our
Lord's mode of announcing to her the pains she would
have to endure, showing, as it does, that the love of
Jesus, and the desire to suffer for and in union with
Him, associate in a peculiar manner those who are thus
blessedly minded with the glorious army of martyrs.
He caused her one day to be in vision arrayed in a
robe dyed in His Blood. Thus clothed, and with a
veil of dazzling brilliance and a crown of flowers of
surpassing whiteness on her head, she remained the
whole day in the interior of her heart in company with
Jesus, the Blessed Virgin, and her guardian angel, in a
state of indescribable joy. On another occasion, being
assailed by a violent temptation, she took refuge in
spirit in the hall where Jesus was crowned with thorns.
When she beheld Him holding the reed in His hand
and mocked by the soldiers, the temptation vanished.
She continues thus: "The soldiers then turned to-

wards me, and, taking the reed from the hands of
Jesus, they presented it to me that I might strike Him
as they had done. I refused to do their will; immediately they began to blaspheme, and to insult me, because
I acknowledged Jesus as my God." She goes on to
narrate how she was threatened with death, denounced
to the governor, and, after being loaded with chains,
thrown into a dark dungeon, there to pass the night.
She did not know how she was set at liberty.

On a subsequent occasion Jesus seems to have furnished her with the interpretation of a portion of this
vision, while explaining to her another in which she
saw a deep dark ditch encircling her heart. This sight
saddened her. The Saviour said, "You are pained at
what you behold, My daughter. Here is the significa-
tion. For the space of a year you will be as one shut up
in a dungeon, where you will be made to undergo a thousand interrogations, and where menaces and promises
will be employed to shake your constancy. Tranquillise
yourself, however; your pains and tribulations shall be
alleviated by the sweetness and power of My grace."
We shall see presently the probable interpretation of
these words in the mental anguish which she had to
endure from the trial to which it was thought proper to
subject her.

Another time she had a vision of a person representing herself, but dressed as a religious, who was subjected to an interrogatory such as Christians under
Pagan persecutions were called to endure, and are still
in our day frequently enduring in heathen lands. She
followed her to the place of execution. "This, then,"
she said to herself, "is what awaits me." She adds,
however, that she did not see by what kind of death
this representative of herself died. She then returned

into her heart to Jesus. "He seemed contented," she says, "and so was I."

It is evident, however, that, notwithstanding these visions of martyrdom, and although our Lord Himself once told her that she should mingle her blood with His, she did not thence conclude that she was literally to shed her blood as a martyr.* The following words, which immediately succeed her account of the vision to which we have just alluded, prove this unmistakably. "I have often," she says, "had exterior signs and, as it were, predictions of considerable sufferings which await me during the life I have to pass on earth. What will these sufferings be? Of what nature will my martyrdom be? It matters little to me. I know that it was by suffering and by His painful Death on Calvary that the Saviour Jesus redeemed the world and entered into His glory; I know that whoever would be His disciple must walk in His steps, and not reject what He voluntarily accepted. And the sight of my Saviour will support me, fortify me, and make me love tribulation, pains, and tears. I will not myself refuse the bitter chalice, and I will say at the height of my torments, 'My sweet Saviour, may Thy will be done,

---

* Even if she had so understood our Lord's words, this need present no difficulty. St. John of the Cross says in his "Ascent of Mount Carmel," where he is treating of the words of God being true in a spiritual sense : "Let us suppose a man longing for martyrdom, to whom God shall say, 'Thou shalt be a martyr.' Upon this such an one feels great interior consolation, and hopes of being a martyr. Still he does not die a martyr's death, and yet the promise is fulfilled. But why is the promise not literally performed? Because God keeps it in the highest and substantial sense, bestowing on that soul the essential love and reward of a martyr, making it a martyr of love, granting to it a prolonged martyrdom of suffering, the continuance of which is more painful than death." —Lewis's Translation, vol. i. p. 141.

not mine. Thou offerest me this chalice, I accept it to please Thee and to testify to Thee how much I love Thee.'" The letter from which we have quoted these words was written on the 30th of April 1842. The vision had neither alarmed nor grieved her, as we have seen. Jesus was contented, and so was she.

Another vision, however, which she had later, and of which she gives an account in a letter dated June 16th, 1842, would seem to have produced a more disturbing effect on her. She was in the church, praying before our Lady's altar, when she saw a figure draw near. Fearing illusion, she paid no attention to this apparition, and prayed our Lord not to permit her to be deceived, humbling herself before Him as unworthy of every grace and favour, and imploring His compassion and mercy. The person, however, did not disappear; on the contrary, he approached and delivered to her a piece of white paper. She then ventured to inquire who he was. "Read the paper I have given you," he said, "and return it to me." Then she read these words: "'I am the angel of the Lord, and I execute His commands. He has sent me to you to apprise you that you will have to pass through severe trials, and will have to endure much suffering, possibly very soon." Marie gave him back the paper, and begged to know when these trials and sufferings were to begin. The angel told her that he would not fix the time, but that he warned her beforehand in order that she might prepare herself, and that her pains might be the lighter when they came because she would have fortified herself against them. "That I may aid you to bear them," he added, "with still more patience, I assure you that they will obtain for you grace and mercy from God. Then the angel prostrated himself before the altar of Mary, his face all glowing with devotion, and presently disappeared.

A few days after this vision, Marie fell into a state of deep despondency. Questioned by our Lord, she replied that she was discontented and afflicted without knowing why. "My daughter," Jesus said to her, "know that the heart of man cannot be happy and contented upon earth. It will never enjoy true felicity except in heaven. Verily, I say to you, you will never be happy so long as you abide on earth. You will suffer much. I warn you of this beforehand; prepare yourself. Embrace My cross with courage; be a faithful lover of the cross. Could you refuse suffering when I have suffered so much for you? Could you refuse suffering when you see My Mother so afflicted as she beheld Me expiring upon the cross? You are a daughter of Adam; you have sinned; you ought to suffer; suffering is the punishment of sin. Accept it, then, in the spirit of mortification, in the spirit of penance; in all things submit yourself to God, His will shall be manifested to you by your director. Do whatsoever he tells you, whatever pain it may cause you. Do nothing save by his order or his permission. Communicate only as often as he allows you. Remain in the world, if he bids you do so. Prepare yourself to depart when he shall give you leave. Abandon yourself to God; God will dispose all things for His greater glory and your salvation. Abandon yourself to your director; I will manifest to you My will by his. Be not occupied with yourself, your thoughts, your opinions; sacrifice all to please Me, sacrifice all for My will. Now, you will do My will, and be pleasing to Me, and follow on My steps, if you hearken to your director. He is, in your regard, the instrument which I use to guide you, to try you, to make you suffer when I please, in order to increase your merits and completely break your own will." He added words of encouragement, telling her that He would console her and send His angel to support her, and bade her love suffering, uniting her pains to His. " Let your life be, as Mine was," He said, " a perpetual sacrifice to My Father. You have suffered little hitherto; the days of tribulation are to come. They are before you ; do not reject them."

Another day, when she was weeping, He came to console her, saying, " Take courage, My daughter ; the heavens are about to be shrouded for you with the clouds of tribulation and suffering. You are not as yet in the state in which I desire you to be, in order to draw you into the companionship of My chosen souls. I wish to make you pass through the refining furnace of affliction. Always follow the counsels of your director; he will advise you what you are to do. When your lips have tasted of My chalice of bitterness, you must drain it all to the dregs. My daughter, martyrdom awaits you. You will die far from your country ; your death will be one of cruel suffering, yet nevertheless full of sweetness. It will be terrible ; but your heart will remain calm and tranquil. I do not tell you what will be the manner of your death, nor of what nature your martyrdom will be ; but verily it will be a true martyrdom." The words which she had heard from the angel and from our Lord, she owns, presented themselves often to her mind, and sometimes she experienced much dread at the thought of the dungeon in which she was to be confined, and of the torments of her death. Yet these considerations, she said, were profitable to her, because they helped to detach her from every earthly affection, and to make her desire God alone. She relates another vision during which she was led to a spot where she witnessed Jesus hanging on His cross, who thus addressed her : "Come, Marie, and see the state in which My love for you has placed Me. See how I suffer, and yet you would suffer nothing for Me, My daughter ! " "I cannot say," she exclaims, " what I felt at that moment ; I would have wished to suffer in my body and in my soul all the torments which Jesus endured. I cast myself at His feet, and said, ' Lord, I embrace Thy cross, I fasten myself to it, I desire nothing but it ; cause me to suffer whatsoever Thou pleasest. Let suffering enwrap my very life,* let pain be the pillow of my head, and tribulation the clothing of my person.'" "My daughter," said the Saviour, "you desire, then, to live for Me ? " "Yes, Lord, for ever ! " "Will you always thus bear witness to Me ? " " Yes, Lord, I will witness even with my blood, if Thou shalt ask it of me." " Do you, then, hope to suffer all this in your own strength ? " " No, Lord, I can do nothing without Thee ; but with Thee I will brave the fury of all the demons in hell ; with Thee I will set at naught the barbarity of the most ferocious and cruel executioners." Marie adds, " It seems to me at this moment that I am ready for everything ; that I fear nothing. I have a hunger and thirst for sufferings and tribulations. Will they come ? of this I am ignorant. If none come to me, my suffering will then be not to suffer, and my martyrdom not to be martyred. May the will of God be done in all and everywhere."

Thus had Jesus brought His servant gradually to a complete preparation of will to embrace the cross in

* Literally. " Let suffering be the *bark* of my life—Que la souffrance soit l'*écorce* de ma vie."

whatever form He should please to present it to her. Doubtless, in His wisdom and love, He has His own hidden ways of preparing each one of us for His designs in our regard, if only we yield ourselves to His teaching. In Marie Lataste's case, we behold the process, as it were, made patent and sensible, and may see reason to think (as has been already observed in regard to other points) that in causing a minute record of His dealings with this favoured soul to be published to the world, our Lord desired that we should learn this consolatory lesson.

We should gather from these different communications on the subject of Marie's future trials that they were to be mainly of two kinds : the first to be of a spiritual nature, and inflicted by those who had authority over her. Subsequent events, at least, would seem to favour this interpretation. The dungeon in which she was to be enclosed for a year was, of course, figurative. The second trial seems to have been that of a very painful death, accompanied by such sufferings as gave it a title, when voluntarily accepted, to be viewed as a species of martyrdom. And that she did accept these sufferings voluntarily is plain from the passages just quoted. We may conceive, indeed, that our Lord's object in announcing them to her was not merely to fortify her and prepare her for them, but thereby to increase the merit of her sacrifice.

The first trial, however, which awaited her came, not from her directors, but from Jesus Himself ; a trial, nevertheless, out of which He compassionately willed to extract all the bitterness which might otherwise have been its attendant, by Himself warning her of the change about to take place. Towards the close of the year 1842 the Saviour apprised her of the coming privation of His sensible presence, which she had enjoyed for three years. "My daughter," He said to her, "do you remember the affliction you experienced when I hid Myself for a time from your eyes after having manifested Myself to you? You must now be possessed of more fortitude, vigour, and energy. I mean no longer to treat you like a child. I mean no longer to give you milk for your nourishment, but strong and solid food. Soon you will no more see Me, but you will continue to hear My voice and My words; after a little while you will not even hear Me any longer, and then again you will see and hear Me once more." * Marie observes with much simplicity, when relating this communication, " Jesus said that by this time I must no longer be like a child, but indeed I was so still, and cried a great deal when He told me I should cease to see Him."

Our Lord, however, had pity on her. He came and consoled her with these words of kindness: "My daughter, do not weep, dry your tears and be comforted; you will no longer see Me in a sensible form, but I shall be really present in the Tabernacle, on the Altar, and also in your heart. You can pay Me your homage there, and I shall accept it with as much pleasure as heretofore, for I shall still love you, and shall always love you, although you may no longer receive sensible marks of My love by a visible manifestation of Myself. I shall witness your groans, your prayers, and your

---

* Marie appears to have understood this last promise as only to be realised at her departure from this world; for at the close of the letter she says that when the time shall come that she shall no longer hear the voice of Jesus, she will consider it as the announcement of her approaching death, since He had assured her that after a little while she should hear Him again, and behold Him face to face.

petitions.    I will be your help, your support, and
your stay.    Have confidence, My daughter; always
obey your directors, practise submission, offer yourself
to God every day; imitate My actions with increasing
fidelity, and I will give you graces more precious than
those which you have received.    My daughter, I bless
you."    As He said these words, she beheld Him raise
His hand over her head, and she felt as it were floods
of grace and of happiness inundate her soul, freeing it
from all distress and disquietude, fortifying it as though
with a shield that was intimately one with herself.

Nevertheless, for some days after Jesus had withdrawn
Himself, although her heart was free from sorrow, she
felt herself like one in a strange land, and bewildered
by a totally new mode of life.    And what a change it
was to cease to behold Him as her familiar friend and
teacher!    Still she heard Him, and, though she did
not enjoy His sensible presence, she had the sweetness
of His grace, and "reposed," as she says, "with delight
in the immensity of God."    The words of Jesus, however, had no longer in their tone, expression, or even
in their import, the same tender sweetness, but the
effect they produced upon her and worked in her was
most remarkable.    "His words," she said, "consoled,
supported, strengthened, and defended me.    His voice
still instructed me, but this instruction more often concerned the defence of my life than the education of
my soul."    By defence, as is evident from the context
(to which we are about to refer), she meant the vindication of her assertions with regard to her religious call,
and the like.    So far from having lost by the subtraction of the sensible presence of Jesus, she states
that she had gained in firmness, courage, and, above
all, in light.    She had more insight into divine truths;

and it was at this time also that she began to receive additional light for the benefit of others, frequently accompanied with the gift of reading their thoughts and knowing the state of their minds. Her mode of prayer likewise underwent a change, corresponding to her change of state. We have seen her pass through several progressive stages, in which she was gradually taught by our Lord to make less use of discourse and imagination than when He first called her to the practice of meditation. She was now advanced to prayer of a more contemplative order; but, as we shall refer to this subject more fully further on, we shall content ourselves with quoting here a few words written in the letter from which we have been giving extracts, and which is dated June 24th, 1843. "Rising in the morning, I offer to God my day, my actions, all that I have, and all that I am. I hold myself each morning in readiness to resist the trials which may arise. I make my meditation, in which I listen to the voice of Jesus."—We may observe here the diminution of mental action, characteristic of the approach to the state of passive contemplation.—"I keep myself always in the presence of God; from time to time in the course of the day I pay Him my duties of adoration and love; I keep myself united to Him. I address my prayers to God, and I do so, it appears to me, with more calmness and freedom; I might say, with more fervour. I raise myself towards God, and *lose myself in His immensity.*" This last expression she uses more than once, as best describing that kind of prayer which takes place in a region indescribable by human language, and inscrutable by the discursive understanding.

# CHAPTER XI.

## Fresh Lights and the Beginning of Trials.

ALLUSION has been made to the changes which took place in Marie Lataste, upon her entering into the new state described in the foregoing chapter, and, in particular, to the increase of light which she began about this time to receive, not for herself alone, but for the benefit and guidance of others. We find traces of this even in letters written in the year 1842 ; and it would appear that, on one occasion at least, whether with the view of proving her, or from a real desire to ascertain her opinion, M. Dupérier himself was among those who consulted her. It will be remembered that by his advice M. Darbins had subjected Marie to a very long and severe scrutiny, and had allowed him a sight of her manuscripts. M. Dupérier himself also, we are told, questioned her separately; but as, in the letter from which we are about to quote, she speaks of not having the honour of knowing him save by the praises she had heard of his virtues and merits, its date must be referred to some time previous to that interview, which seems to have been in January 1843.*

* If this date be correct, that which is assigned to this letter of May 2, 1843, can hardly be so. There are other reasons which make it improbable that this date is the true one, since, as we shall find, it was just about that time that M. Dupérier was on the eve of subjecting Marie to a severe trial, with which such an application would have been inconsistent. In the impossibility of reconciling the assigned dates of the letters referring to M. Dupérier's communications to Marie on his own behalf, we have omitted them. The matter is of no practical importance, but, if we may hazard a conjecture, we would suggest that the letter quoted above was written in May 1842. Internal evidence marks it as written when the days are long.

What was the subject of M. Dupérier's application
to Marie of which we are about to speak, does not
appear. From her letter we learn that he had expressed
a desire, through the Curé of Mimbaste, that she
would pray for him to Jesus and communicate the reply
to him. The subjoined extract from her letter to
M. Dupérier will show how she acquitted herself of her
commission:—" The day following that on which your
desire was expressed, I awoke, contrary to my usual
habit, at day-break. I felt myself well rested from the
previous day's fatigue. I got up, thinking that I
should thus have a very favourable time for making
my meditation. I transported myself, as is my custom,
into the presence of the Blessed Sacrament, and, after
having devoutly contemplated the sufferings of His
Passion, I thus addressed our Lord : ' My Saviour,
Thou knowest the commission which my director has
given me to Thee. I do not know what prayer I
ought to address to Thee ; but do Thou who knowest
the state and the needs of every soul, tell me what will
be most suitable for this priest in whose behalf I have
recourse to Thee. Pardon my boldness in making this
request ; I should never have done such a thing of my
own accord, but Thou hast enjoined me to be always
obedient in all and for all. Lord, it is to obey Thee
that I speak thus. I do not ask this of myself or for
myself, but through Thy merits and for Thy great
glory ; and I will continue to ask Thee until Thou hast
granted my prayer.'

" The Saviour Jesus hearkened to me with kindness.
I was kneeling before Him, and He spoke thus to me :
' My daughter, you will say to him who has asked you
to pray for him—this is what God Almighty, who
regulates all by His providence, says to him.' "—Here

she interrupts her narrative to observe that a fear came over her at that moment, founded on the sense of her unworthiness to be the reporter of the words of God to His minister, and a misgiving lest her memory might betray her, and that she might mix something of her own therewith; but the Saviour at once re-assured her, and then continued—"Behold what saith the Almighty Lord, who governs all things by His providence: 'Be of good heart, faithful servant, cast your eyes on Me who am your model, and see what I should do in your place. Obey your bishop's voice perfectly as My voice.' My daughter," added the Saviour, "the obedience of this priest will meet its reward. Let him not act as others have acted whom he knows; they had better have obeyed without resistance; they would thus have spared themselves many troubles. He is revolving a number of thoughts in his mind; let him not disquiet himself, but listen to My voice in the depths of his heart. Let him consult on the subject which occupies him, and which I need not mention to you, one grown old in the priesthood, who has experience and an upright judgment; let him divest himself wholly of his own judgment, and submit to the decision made known to him. In acting thus, he will walk in the footsteps of his Saviour, who was subject to Mary and Joseph, and even to the secular powers, and to the soldiers who crucified Him. He who obeys can console himself by saying, 'I am doing the will of my superiors, and consequently that of God.' Let this priest be thus subject to the will of his bishop, and I will cause him to gather a rose from a thorn-bush. Let him, in the office he fills at the seminary, be full of vigilance, firmness, and gentleness. Let his vigilance prevent abuses, his firmness banish them, and his gentleness gain him the affection of all his pupils. Let him have a great devotion to My Mother, and let him inspire therewith all who approach him. If in the course of his life he finds himself assailed by the contradictions of men, whoever they may be, let him recall to mind the recommendation I have to-day transmitted to him by My little servant Marie." Our Lord also assured Marie that the person in whose behalf she applied was amongst His well-beloved ones, and lauded his humility in having solicited her prayers, and, through her intervention, the grace of an answer from Him.

If M. Dupérier had not made known to Marie, as it seems almost certain he had not, the precise subject upon which he desired light and guidance, there was enough in her answer to satisfy him of the reality of the supernatural communications of which she believed herself the recipient. Perhaps it was with this view chiefly that he asked her to make the application. Apparently he was desirous, as regarded himself, to have more direct personal illumination; and certainly Marie desired it for him, if only from the sense of her own unworthiness to be the intermediary. For we find her soon afterwards, in a letter to her director, telling him that she had prostrated herself at the feet of Jesus, begging Him to tell her why He would not reply to her petitions on M. Dupérier's behalf, and that our Lord had said, " My daughter, tell this priest not to afflict himself, for I love him." Not contented with this answer, Marie continued her instances to obtain one of a more favourable character, and to receive the assurance that He would answer M. Dupérier personally, instead of through her means.

Our Lord's reply is remarkable. He gave it, He said, because she insisted so much, and desired her to report it to the priest in question. "My son," He said, "marvel not if I have not satisfied your desire. It is not that I am unwilling to teach you for your own good and that of others; you would be the first who, sincerely desiring to be instructed in the knowledge of the truth, should not have received the necessary lights; but I had My designs in not instructing you in the way you desire. I do not instruct all in the same manner. If I have never instructed you sensibly, as I have Marie, it is because there is a great difference between you and her. I require more of him who has received more. I have illuminated your mind, I have enriched it with science, I have rendered it capable of profound and serious reflection. I had placed Marie in a condition where it was impossible for her to receive instruction, and where her mind must have remained unfitted for much reflection; her education, by human means, could not have been such as to qualify and enlighten her sufficiently for the designs I had formed in her regard: this is why I have Myself become her preceptor." Blessed ignorance and incapacity! we are disposed to exclaim, which, when accompanied with simplicity and humility, could obtain for a soul a teaching which the loftiest intellects might well envy it. "For you, My son," our Lord continues, "do not expect all from God; avail yourself of what He has given, apply your mind actively in His presence, and He will act in you, by suggesting to your mind such thoughts and reflections as are needful for you in the situation in which you are placed. In truth, I say to you, ask Me all the questions you please: I will answer them all, but in the manner which I see fitting. When you have received My answer, and light arises in your mind, consult your director and act as he shall tell you.

K

Seek always, O My son, the instruction which you
require ; you will find it, according to those words of
the Gospel : 'Ask, and you shall receive ; seek, and you
shall find ; knock, and it shall be opened to you.'"

It would seem that M. Dupérier acquiesced, for we
find Marie, in another letter to her director, which, in
all probability, refers to what we have been speaking of,
repeating to him the words which, she said, the Saviour
had addressed to the ecclesiastic in question. This
ecclesiastic was undoubtedly M. Dupérier. Jesus tells
him that He is pleased with his submission in doing
His will and obeying His directions, as also with his
humility and charity ; and our Lord proceeds to give
Him further words of encouragement and advice.*
"Advance," He says, "more and more, My son, in that
filial love which you have for the best of fathers. Be
of good heart, and fortify yourself to support the
troubles and afflictions which you may have to encounter
in the course of your life. Trials are but for a season,
and they purchase an immense weight of glory for him
who endures them with patience. Do not suffer yourself to be disquieted by the smoke exhaled from the
hearts of the wicked. I will rise up against them, and
with one breath of My mouth will scatter them. Do
not attach yourself to earthly greatness. What is it in
comparison with the greatness of him who belongs to
Me, or with the sweetness of My love ? Is not My love
like to exquisite honey which ravishes the heart of him
who tastes it ? The speech of man is as a light feather

---

* If we are correct in considering this letter as referring to the
subject on which M. Dupérier had consulted Marie—and there
seems every reason to do so—its date of Nov. 13, 1842, would
corroborate our opinion that the former letter belonged also to
that year. '

carried away by the wind, but My will abides stable
and firm in the heart of him who fears Me.   My son,
raise, strengthen, perfect the spiritual edifice of your
sanctification, in order that He who laid its first founda-
tions may complete it by crowning it.   My son, adorn,
prepare, perfume well your house, for I have determined
to abide in it eternally.   My son, what are your
thoughts, your desires, your affections?   Trust in Me,
I will not forsake you.   I know all that passes within
you ; and your sentiments and your prayers do not find
Me indifferent.   My son, although you are still on
earth, place all your affections in Heaven.   My son, it
is a mark of the love I bear you that I am pleased to
speak these words to you to-day.   I finish with those
which I once addressed to My disciples :  ' Watch and
pray, that you enter not into temptation.' "

A letter of Marie's, written a few days later to her
director, is in reply to another application, on the part
of an ecclesiastic, whose name, however, does not
appear.   It forewarns him of sufferings, and contains
also promises of support and consoling encouragements.
To these is added an exhortation to pray for France,
which we here insert as a supplement to what has been
already noticed of the same kind.   "My son," said the
Saviour, whose message Marie is conveying, "pray for
France.   I have already said, and I love to repeat it,
that if the strokes of My Father's justice have not yet
fallen on her, it is Mary, the Queen of Heaven, who
has withheld them.   Satan roars from the depths of
Hell against a kingdom which, in truth, has dealt him
rude blows ; he is convulsed with rage when he beholds
the good done in that country ; he directs all his efforts
to augment the evil and to provoke still more the
Divine vengeance.   But a chain which he cannot break

holds him captive; for My Mother has a special right over France, which is consecrated to her, and, in virtue of this right, she arrests the vengeful arm of God, and pours upon it the benedictions of Heaven, that it may produce good more abundantly. This is why I cease not to warn, in order to avert unspeakable calamities. O France! thy glory shall spread afar; thy children shall go forth beyond the vast expanse of ocean, and those who know thee only by name shall pray for thy preservation and prosperity."

Our Lord also bade him, whenever he celebrated Mass, to pray for the welfare and conservation of France. Marie, after delivering her message, adds these words of her own : "M. le Curé, I know not into whose hands this letter may one day fall, but, since there is in it mention of France, I will permit myself to add what follows : In the last letter which I addressed to you, I only heard the words which I reported, that is to say, I did not receive within myself any interior illumination; whereas, when the Saviour Jesus addressed to me the words I have reported in this letter, there appeared within me, as it were, a spiritual and heavenly light. I saw clearly and distinctly, unless it were an illusion, what I may thus express: There is in France much good and also much evil. If the good were proportional to the bad we should not have so much reason to dread the strokes of God's justice, because it would be as much appeased by the good as provoked by the evil committed. Now it is not so ; the good is less than the evil, and is not sufficient to turn away the vengeance of God. More good is needed. Happily, the Blessed Virgin intercedes for us and prevents the justice of God from falling on our heads. But Mary desires us to implore her assist-

ance.   She places herself between God and us, and
awaits our prayers and supplications.   Her heart is full
of kindness and tenderness.   One single word addressed
to Mary obtains for us immeasurable graces.   God will
allow Himself to be appeased if we have recourse to
Mary.   Mary begs for our prayers, so great is her will
and desire to come to our aid.   We ought also to have
recourse to Mary, because it is the will of God and
the means of rendering Him favourable to us."

Whoever this ecclesiastic may be of whom Marie
speaks in this letter, it is evident, from what has been
stated, that several communications upon matters personal to himself had taken place between M. Dupérier
and her previously to what we are now about to narrate.   He had also, as we have seen, interrogated her
closely, but had detected nothing to excite suspicion.
M. Darbins, on his part, had enjoyed still ampler
opportunities of testing the spirit operating in his
penitent.   Until he was satisfied on this head he had
refused to entertain the subject of her vocation, but we
have reason to believe that every day had only served
to confirm him in a favourable opinion respecting her
state.   However, he withheld his decision on a subject
of so much importance, and, while bidding her reveal
frankly everything that passed within her, he had
taught her to be doubly cautious and fearful lest she
should be the victim of illusion.   We have seen how
she thought herself bound to accept the attitude of
doubt and hesitation assumed by her directors, so far as
her judgment was concerned ; the assurance she experienced while Jesus was speaking with her in no way interfering with this habitual deference to their opinion.
Yet they had never hitherto taxed her with delusion ;
still less had they hinted any suspicion of a design

on her part to delude others. Indeed her director's
command to write down all the communications of a
supernatural kind which she had received, or should
receive, was evidence enough that M. Darbins was not
disposed to regard her as either a visionary or an
impostor.

The scrutiny to which M. Darbins had during these
two years subjected her conduct had also been most
satisfactory in its results. The life, behaviour, and
conversation of Marie Lataste were irreproachable, nay,
they were edifying in the highest degree, while her
reserve, her modesty, her simplicity, her candour, and
her humility were all so many guarantees of the absence
of any evil spiritual influence. Nevertheless, M. Darbins's cautious friend was not yet fully satisfied, and
had resolved to put her spirit to a very severe test.
Marie was about to enter now into the figurative
dungeon, and to undergo the torturing ordeal of which
she had been forewarned. In the month of February,
1843, she heard, as she believed, from the lips of our
Lord, a parable, of which we will give the substance,
premising that Jesus at this time had ceased to render
Himself visible :—" A king, visiting his dominions,
found in the desert a plant, which he recognised to be
an olive-tree of an excellent species. He had it transplanted into his garden, and gave it into the care of one
of his esquires. The esquire cultivated it; he pulled
up the weeds which might injure it, dressed it with
good manure, and poured over it pure water. The
other esquires laughed at him, assuring him that he was
mistaken in the nature of the plant, but, like a faithful
servant, he none the less obeyed his master, whose
opinion, moreover, he shared. By his orders he removed the young olive-tree into a more fertile garden,

and put it in a golden cage in order to keep people
from examining it too closely, or tarnishing its beauty
by touching it.  Many persons, however, imprudently
drew near ; they were dazzled by its splendour and in-
toxicated, as it were, by the strength of its perfume ;
and they paid the price of their temerity with their
lives.  The olive-tree grew and spread ; its flowers
gave forth a sweet and delicious odour, its abundant
fruits yielded an exquisite oil, and its roots, which
spread themselves through the whole garden, seemed
to enrich its soil and improve the other flowers."  In
reporting this parable to her spiritual father, who,
it will be remembered, had laid on her an obedience to
relate to him every communication of which she
believed herself to be the recipient, Marie had said in
conclusion, "You will think what you please of this ;
I am completely indifferent about it, as about all else.
I desire God alone, I attach myself to God alone, Him
only do I wish to possess."  M. Darbins, as usual,
consulted M. Dupérier, and in the following June this
ecclesiastic addressed a letter to the Curé of Mimbaste,
accompanied with a request that he would acquaint
his penitent with its contents and closely observe the
impression which they produced upon her.  In the
letter he expressed himself in these terms : " After
maturely reflecting upon all that you have said of
Marie Lataste ; after reading her writings and conversing with her myself two or three times, I can entertain
no doubt but that this poor girl is either a visionary to
whom no attention ought to be paid, or a person who
seeks to deceive us.  You desire to know my judgment
with regard to her ; and she desires also to know it.
Such, then, is my judgment ; will you please to read it
to her.  Now, I base my view on the minute details

which I meet with in her writings; on the parable of
the king, the esquire, and the olive-tree, which seems to
me a pure invention of her own; on the falseness of
the prophecy about Paris; on her vocation, which has
its source simply in her own imagination, excited by
long night-watchings; on her proposed departure and
admission into the Sacré Cœur, which are things
incapable of realisation." This letter, accordingly,
M. Darbins read to Marie. When he had arrived at
the close of the first paragraph, where M. Dupérier
suggested that she might be an impostor, an expression
of sadness passed over her features, and tears flowed
from her eyes. "Why do you weep, my daughter?"
asked her director. "I weep, sir," she replied, "because I must weep. You know that I am not easily
moved to tears; but how could I now restrain them?"
The Curé encouraged her by some words of kindness;
indeed, he was probably not a little pained at the
office laid upon him. "Ah, sir," she said, "it is not
you who afflict me, neither is it the judgment of
M. Dupérier which makes me shed tears; if I weep, it
is on account of myself. I must, indeed, be a great
sinner since I am supposed to be such a cheat as to
desire to deceive two priests who have always shown
the greatest interest in me, and who have invariably
treated me with the utmost charity. If this be the
judgment which M. Dupérier has formed of me, I must
have deserved it, not by my lies and deceits,—for
I assure you I have never wished either to deceive or
to lie,—but on account of my sins, which must have
provoked God against me. I am a great sinner; this
is why I weep." "Compose yourself," said the Abbé
Darbins; "God sees the dispositions of your heart,

He will accept them; be calm and abide in submission to His will."

In the course of the following week he advised her to reply in writing to the contents of M. Dupérier's letter. She had not waited for this advice to cast herself at the feet of Jesus, and pour out her heart before Him who was her constant refuge. "Lord," she had said, "I do not know what turn things are about to take, but, whatever may happen, I place all my trust in Thee." Jesus then told her that she would have to undergo other trials equally painful, but assured her that He would ever be with her to enable her to come out of them victorious. Then one by one He took up and refuted the objections brought against her; and she was thus supplied with the materials for the letter which she was now enjoined by her director to write. She had only to commit to paper the words of her Divine Master. Of this letter we give the summary.

To the first objection, the minuteness of the details in her writings, our Lord replies that there is nothing minute or small in the breathings of the Spirit of God. He blows where He wills, when He wills, and whatsoever He wills; and that which seems to all appearance small has often most important effects. He says the same of the words which He dictated to her. He then expounds the parable which she was accused of having drawn out of her own imagination. He who had judged her had erred in attributing it to her invention, but he had been right in three things : that is, in supposing that by the king God was signified; by the esquire, her director; and by the olive-tree, herself. The other esquires, who laughed at the care bestowed upon it by the king's esquire, believing him to be mistaken in the nature of the plant, were those who,

having heard of her and her writings and the confidence
reposed in her by her director, blamed or ridiculed the
zeal and charity which he had manifested in her favour.
He need not, said our Lord, tell her who those were
who would touch the plant and to whom the odour of
its perfume would prove pernicious and even fatal.
Later this would be seen. Of these some were near her,
some would be at a distance; some there would be
during her lifetime, others after her death. Plainly
our Lord alluded to what is the invariable accompani-
ment of all His supernatural manifestations whether in
His saints or in other ways. To many such manifestations are but the savour of death. This result was first
announced by the aged Simeon, in the Person of the
Infant Saint of saints, when he took Him in his arms
and said, "Behold, this Child is set for the fall and for
the resurrection of many in Israel."* So it is also, in
a measure, with His servants. Contact with what is holy,
and with the supernatural, produces evil effects, instead
of the good for which it was designed, on rebellious
and incredulous hearts.

As regarded the prophecy concerning Paris, our Lord
first asks, "Was this a prophecy?" It was couched in
the form of a menace. She had, in consequence, prostrated herself before God, praying with tears that this
judgment might be turned away. But, granting it was
a prophecy, who does not know that there are prophecies which are conditional, especially such as announce the chastisements of God's justice? And here
we cannot help observing that, were it not that we must
credit M. Dupérier with the simple desire of trying
Marie Lataste's spirit of humility, this objection,
grounded on the non-accomplishment of the prophecy

* Luke ii. 34.

concerning Paris, must be considered as most unreasonable and futile. No time had been marked for its
fulfilment, and not four months had elapsed since it
had been uttered. There are still current, at this day,
many prophecies, uttered by persons of great reputed
sanctity, threatening the destruction of Paris, and no
one thinks of charging those persons with illusion,
because this judgment is, as yet, withheld. Besides,
prayer and penance may avert the fulfilment, not of a
menace only, but of a positive prediction. Jonas was
commissioned to go through the streets of Ninive and
proclaim its destruction at the end of forty days. Yet
Ninive was not destroyed. Was Jonas, therefore, an
impostor and a false prophet?

To proceed : our Lord then adverts to the accusation
brought against Marie, on account of her alleged call
to religion, of being merely under the influence of a
heated imagination, the effect of want of sleep. Our
Lord denies the fact, and says that she takes enough
repose to provide for the health of her body, over which
He watches as well as over that of her soul. This,
He adds, is the argument of one who has no true
reason to allege. "Have they not," He continues,
"sufficiently tried your vocation? and have they not
always found you submissive, docile, patient? What
more do they want?" He goes on to ask why her
departure and admission into the Sacré Cœur should
be incapable of realisation? Had she not the power
which others had of walking and going whither God
bade her; and, if any danger threatened, was He not
there to protect her? But they asserted that she could
not possibly be admitted into the Convent of the Sacré
Cœur. And why not? Had He not said that the
Bishop of Aire would request her admission, and that

he would not be refused? And had He not said, besides, that if that prelate should be unwilling to interest himself in her favour—which in point of fact, we shall find, proved to be the case—it would in no way be necessary that he should do so, for that He Himself would provide for her a sure entrance into the retreat He destined for her. "You are poor, it is true," He added, "but I am the riches of the Sacré Cœur. The faithful souls who there dedicate themselves to honour My Divine Heart, knowing My will, as I shall make it known to them, will not reject you." He, moreover, encouraged her by telling her that strength would be manifested in her weakness, wisdom in her folly, and truth in her visions. "The words which you hear," He said, "are not of you; they belong to Me; you only write them down. You are nothing, you can do nothing of yourself; but I am all, I can do all, I regulate all, I take care of all; and the greatest as well as the smallest things enter into the economy of My wisdom, My providence, and My mercy. Let them examine everything attentively in your writings and in your vocation; let them seek in them for deception and falsehood, and they will find only truth. But let them not attempt to scrutinise the designs of My Providence; never will they succeed in that. No one will know why I address Myself to you; no one will know why I hold converse with you in the wisdom, depth, suavity, and perfection of My word; no one will know why I call you to the Convent of the Sacré Cœur at Paris, and not to the Convent of the Ursulines at Aire, or any other which it has not pleased Me to choose for you. I do all this because I will to do it, and no one has the right to ask My reason for this My will."

Such was the reply which Marie faithfully transmitted. Nothing, indeed, is more remarkable than her care to report every communication of which she was the recipient, whether it seemed to contain censure of others—and those, too, persons for whom she had the profoundest reverence—or vindication and even praise of herself, for whom she entertained the profoundest contempt. This candour, frankness, and fidelity, and the self-abnegation which made her on these occasions speak of herself as if she were another person, whose abasement or exaltation equally concerned her not, are most remarkable, and, we may add, are also among the surest guarantees of her truthfulness, and of the genuineness of her visions and revelations. Her fidelity in repeating what might expose her to be taxed with pride appears still more strongly in other letters to which we shall hereafter have to allude. If it cost her anything to record the testimonies of our Lord in her favour, this does not appear; nothing is shown but the completest indifference, coupled with the most earnest desire to transmit accurately every single word.

We are disposed to think, however, that she so intimately realised what our Lord had told her as to her being nothing, and able to do nothing of herself, her office being merely to write down what He was pleased to dictate, that the notion of apparent self-exaltation in what she was commissioned to repeat was not at all prominent in her mind. She regarded herself as a mere instrument, like the pen in her own hand, only that, as a living and rational soul possessed of free will, she could freely acquiesce and co-operate in what God, the Supreme Lord of all, willed to do through her rather than through others far more worthy. For our Lord had taught her to feel that,

if she, a poor, humble girl, had been selected for this
office, it was not because of any merit of her own, but
through an exercise of that Sovereign Will which owes
no account of Its reasons to any one, and which is
often pleased to choose the most incompetent and
lowly agents for the execution of Its purposes. She
had, therefore, no reason to glory.

This complete spoliation of self and the simplicity
which is its result are rare to find, but, without
attempting to scrutinise what, as our Lord gave Marie
to understand, is a mystery of His electing grace, we
may at least perceive a certain fitness in such persons
to be the recipients of peculiar favours. They take
nothing to themselves; they leave to God all His
glory, of which we know He is jealous, and which
He has declared He will not give to another. It is
perilous in this our mortal and probationary state, all
filled as we are with infirmity, and still retaining the
roots of corruption in our old nature, which we bear
about with us, to be called to manifest God's glory in
any special way. The saints in Heaven manifest it and
rejoice in it; they are all permeated with it and radiant
with it, and they glory in the possession of it; but
this is because they are now in a state wherein it is
impossible for them to refer it to themselves as its
source. A saint in Heaven may praise himself; for
in so doing he is praising God's gifts in him, he is
praising God who is glorified in His saints. The only
sinless creature, the Immaculate Mother of God, while
still on earth, could in this spirit exclaim, " My soul
doth magnify the Lord, and He that is mighty hath
done to me great things ; and behold, from henceforth
all generations shall call me blessed ;" but to us, poor
sons of Eve, it is dangerous for the most part to have

to speak of ourselves, or to be the recipients of exceptional favours.   In such cases simplicity and humility are the only safeguards.

———◆———

# CHAPTER XII.

### MARIE IS ADVANCED TO A HIGHER STATE.

WE have said that Marie told her director that since the subtraction of the sensible presence of Jesus, although she still heard His voice, it had no longer the same tones of familiar tenderness as when He used to appear to her; that now He more often spoke in the grave and earnest manner of one who defends the cause of another, His instructions being directed to this object rather than, as heretofore, to her spiritual education.   His aim (she says) seemed to be to come to her help, at moments when she was most severely tried, by advocating the truth of the relations which subsisted between Himself and her.   "It was at those times," writing to her director, she adds, "that He inspired me with answers to all the difficulties which M. Dupérier addressed to me through you.   His voice tells me, not only of what passes in myself, but also of what passes in the minds of others.   It is that voice which has often told me your thoughts, those of M. Dupérier, and also of the Bishop, as you may have perceived by the replies which I have made."   Marie was here evidently appealing to the unquestionable experience of her director.   Of the freedom with which she expressed herself, after receiving these divine com-

munications with regard to others, the following may
be taken as a specimen :—"One day," she writes, in
November 1843, "I heard our Lord pronounce these
words with inexpressible benignity : 'O Abbé Dupérier,
what are your thoughts ?  I know your heart, I have
penetrated to the very depths of your soul, I know
your most secret thoughts.  I have considered and
examined your conduct, I have weighed your actions,
the good, the indifferent, and the bad, in the scales of
My justice.  You have an ardent and a sincere love for
God, a profound humility, and a rare and high degree
of purity of heart.  Your knowledge of the science of
salvation is great, and your lights are extensive.  You
observe the law after a perfect manner, and do not fail
in any of your duties.  Your heart expands before Me
with confidence and simplicity, your spirit rises towards
God with fervour, you banish from your thoughts, not
only what is bad, but also all which is vain and useless.  Nevertheless, because you are a man, all sorts of
thoughts form themselves within you, but you are careful to stifle all that would be evil as soon as you perceive them, and grace comes to your aid to help you in
this work.  The offering of yourself which you make each
day to God is very pleasing to Him.  My son, receive
the testimony which I award you ; it is full of truth.' "

We should gather from what our Lord says at
different times of M. Dupérier, that he was a fervent
and devoted priest ; and we should also gather that he
had an active intellect, apt at times, by its very activity,
to cause him trouble.  The thoughts he revolved in his
mind are often alluded to, and we have reason to conclude that in his situation, as head of the Dax seminary,
he was not without his trials and perplexities.  Such a
state of mind, however inculpable in the person suffer-

ing from it, is nevertheless unfavourable to the perception of the more delicate touches of grace, and to that illumination, almost resembling intuition, which more tranquil and childlike souls may enjoy. Marie's position in life rendered her exempt, of course, from those responsible cares which tried the ecclesiastic; still it would appear that her disposition also was remarkably favourable to the simple reception of God's Word, however communicated. There may be Marthas, troubled and careful about many things, even in the humblest spheres, but Marie, like her holy namesake, the glorious Magdalen, had chosen the better part. She truly sat at Jesus's feet; she received as in a clear unruffled glass the image presented to her contemplation, and not a ripple on the surface intervened to break its integrity; and when we say that such was her disposition, it must be remembered that it had become what it was chiefly through the influence of grace, for her young heart, before it yielded itself captive to divine love, had been enthralled by selfish ambition and embittered by ungratified aspirations, but, when she gave herself up to God, she gave herself with all that truthfulness and self-abandonment which distinguished her; for Marie never had a divided heart. It was all for the world before it was all for Jesus.

To return to her account of the communication she had received on the subject of M. Dupérier. Our Lord, after a few more words of exhortation to further progress, proceeded thus to address him : "Now, My son, let us speak a while of the object of My solicitude and of your care, My little servant Marie. What do you think of her? Do you believe that she is but a poor girl, deceived and deluded by the devil? Is she a visionary? Has she an arrogant spirit, which in its

L

pride seeks for self-display ?  Do you really hold her
to be full of extravagant notions ?  Is Marie a girl who
has always lies upon her lips, and deceit in her heart?
Does Marie resemble some persons of her sex who, in
spite of their ignorance, flatter themselves that they
know everything ?  Men have said to each other, ' Let
us keep silence, and try Marie in the most sensitive
quarter; let us feign to despise what she sees, what she
hears, what she experiences within herself; let us, in
appearance at least, pay no regard to these things, and
observe how she will behave.  Will she be as indifferent
as ever ?' "  Certainly, it would be difficult to conceive
how Marie, so humble and submissive as she had ever
proved, and still continued to prove, herself to her
spiritual guides, could have resolved of her own accord
to pen these lines, and thus as good as show her directors that she completely saw through their manœuvres.

"Yes," our Lord continues, "let us keep silence.
But cannot I make known all to her, if so it pleases
Me, and show how I make light of the designs of mortal
men?  Cannot I acquaint her with your secret intentions, so that, sustained by My grace, what you esteem
to be strong trials shall to her be only harmless amuse-
ment, and an assured proof of the weakness of man
when he would strive to contend with the wisdom of
God ?  Have I not said that Marie would not be the
dupe of the conduct adopted towards her, and do you
think that she does not perceive the judgment formed
of her ?  Say nothing to her if you will; if it so pleases
Me, I will tell her more than you would ever be able
to tell her.  She will elude your sagacity with her
frank simplicity.  I have inspired her with a horror
of dissimulation.  Faithful to My teaching, what she
has said once she will repeat a second time, and a

third, and as often as may be necessary. You will never tire out her patience; she will always get the better of you. Put her to the proof in every way, seek out any new way, and endeavour if you can to match your trials with her courage. My son, be not negligent, and take care of My little servant Marie." All this Marie wrote down and sent to her director with the utmost composure, making no comment save the following :—" The Saviour Jesus pronounced these words in a tone full of gentleness, but at the same time of great majesty."

This may serve as a specimen of what she meant when she said that our Lord's instructions were now rather an advocacy and a pleading of her cause as regarded His relations with her. Their purpose seemed to be at one and the same time to vindicate her from the accusations of her superiors, and to fortify her to endure and persevere. But the time was now come when our Lord in speaking to her soul often forebore the use of words, while producing effects in it transcending those of articulated language. There are several letters of hers, written in the month of August of this year (1843), which give an account of this change in her state, and of the corresponding change in her manner of prayer. Instead of words which addressed themselves to the ear, and, by this channel, to the understanding, her intellect appeared now to be directly illuminated by a bright and supernatural light, which made her at once understand and taste the sublimest truths, and in a special manner initiated her into the secrets of the Mystery of the Cross. It was beyond her power, however, to convey to another what had thus been communicated to her, except in a very insufficient degree, and, when pressed on the subject by

her director, she confessed, after making her best efforts
to obey him, that words were inadequate for the purpose, since "it is impossible," she says, "to express a
teaching received in the splendours of a light emanating
from the Cross, by conventional signs taken from the
language of man and called speech." We can gather
enough, however, from what she says to infer that the
state to which she was raised was one of very exalted
contemplation. Nevertheless, although of so intellectual
a character, it was not unassisted by the imaginative
faculty, through which it had pleased our Lord to convey so much instruction to this simple soul.

We will give a description of her state in her own
words. "It seems to me," she writes, "that my soul
has entered on a new life, in the centre of light and
of interior and spiritual knowledge. This marvellous
centre appears to me like an apartment which is neither
large nor small; it is closed, but not by any wall, for
all therein is spiritual. This new apartment into which
my soul retires the Saviour Jesus has taught me to call
the 'Admirable Tabernacle.' I perceive within it a
great Cross from twelve to fifteen feet high, the Christ
upon it being of the natural size. It rests on a beautiful
pedestal, which seems to be of marble as well as the
Cross, and which, nevertheless, is not, because all there
is spiritual. There is in this Admirable Tabernacle, as
it were, a living and luminous atmosphere of knowledge
and of sentiments drawing the soul to God. It is impossible to enter without being all penetrated therewith.
Now, I have clearly discerned that these lights, communications, and sentiments proceed from the Cross of
the Admirable Tabernacle, as from an inexhaustible
source. I cannot always penetrate at pleasure nor
remain as long as I please in the Admirable Taber-

nacle, but I am sometimes permitted to enter, and to taste and receive the instructions given therein, but without words. This is one of the most signal favours which the Saviour Jesus can grant me. He grants it to me in order to give me more force and vigour to operate what is good; for I feel this force and vigour penetrating and encompassing me within and without in such a manner that nothing afterwards can deprive me of them. You will with difficulty understand what I mean by instructions without words; what I mean, Sir, is, that in the Admirable Tabernacle my soul sees things so clearly, whether with regard to God, Jesus Christ, and Mary, or as respects myself and religious matters, that it is instructed as if by means of language. Sometimes it sees without comprehending, but it tastes with sweetness the astonishing mysteries presented to it. At other times, an invisible power hinders me from entering into the Admirable Tabernacle, or compels me to leave it as soon as I have entered."

She seems to have been drawn at this time chiefly to the contemplation of the Passion, to which she had always had a great attraction. Her director begged her to give him some account of the lights she now received on this subject, and, after again alleging her great difficulty in relating in words what had been communicated mainly in the character of light, she endeavoured, as she invariably did, to obey him so far as she was able. Several of her letters are occupied with this attempt, and embrace three views of the Passion: Jesus on the Cross to make us understand the greatness and enormity of sin; Jesus on the Cross as the model to us of all virtues; Jesus on the Cross manifesting the justice and the mercy of His Father. She is evidently

labouring throughout against an insurmountable difficulty, for, her perception of these truths and mysteries
not being received in the way of meditation, they were
seen by her in a manner altogether independent of
human discourse; yet, when she has to give an account
of them in words, they must of necessity appear simply
in the garb of a discursive meditation. " It was not
an articulated word that I heard," she says, " but I
understood better than if I had been listening to the
most learned man and the most eloquent preacher. It
was a word without a voice, and a voice without a
word; and I have no word to express this voice, nor
voice to express this word. I saw, I heard, I understood ; I should endeavour in vain to recall it, I could
not do so. It was more powerful, more tender, more
sensible, more sweet, more painful, more sad, more
intelligible, more impressive to me than anything in
the world. It is now so deeply graven in my heart
that I find myself unable to give it external utterance
in writing or in speech." She then bursts forth in a
succession of ejaculations: " O Jesus on the Cross,
salvation of my soul ! O Cross of Jesus, salvation of
the world ! O Jesus on the Cross, God dying for my
sins ! O Cross of Jesus, deliverance from my iniquities !
O Jesus on the Cross, Repairer of the injury done to
God ! O Cross of Jesus, splendid and glorious pledge
of the forgiveness of God the Father ! O Jesus on the
Cross, Liberator of the human race ! O Cross of Jesus,
buckler against Satan, the world, and our passions !
O Jesus on the Cross, felicity in our sufferings and
troubles ! O Cross of Jesus, rainbow of the compassion
of God ! O Jesus on the Cross, it is my sins which
have caused Thy death ! O Cross of Jesus, it is my
sins which have reddened thee with the Blood of my

Saviour! O Jesus on the Cross, let me be ever near to Thee, with Thee, in Thee! O Cross of Jesus, may I embrace thee for ever, and die pressing thee to my heart!"

Again and again she alludes to her inability to convey what she has heard or, rather, experienced, for she hears neither voice nor word, yet sees and comprehends the things which are presented to her, and would wish for ever to see them and repose her mind upon them. Speaking of Jesus on the Cross as the model of all virtues, a subject which detained her for several days in this mystical chamber, she says, "It is impossible for me to endeavour to express to you what I have experienced regarding the love of Jesus Christ for His Father; a love which makes Him assume a body and a soul like to ours, to live a life like to ours, and which makes Him die upon the Cross to offer to God a sacrifice worthy of Him; or regarding the entire and perfect submission of the Saviour Jesus to the will of His Father, through which He sacrifices His own will to do that of His Father, or His infinite desire for the reparation of His Father's glory, or His abandonment and unlimited confidence in God His Father, into whose hands He commits His Soul when dying. It is impossible for me to endeavour to express to you what I have seen of the love of Jesus Christ for all men, for His executioners, for me, and to show you the picture of light which formed itself round that word, which I saw in characters of fire in the Heart of Jesus—'I thirst.' It was the thirst for our salvation, for the salvation of poor sinners, with which He was devoured. He would have wished to be able to say to all what He said to the good thief: 'To-day thou shalt be with Me in Paradise.' That was the desire of His Heart,

an immeasurable desire, which He manifested in that
word of a God dying for the redemption of men—'I
thirst.' Vainly should I endeavour to express the
humility of Jesus on the Cross, of that God, sovereignly
great and exalted, abased amidst sufferings and death.
Vainly should I try to express His obedience to His
executioners, His patience, which prevented Him from
complaining, His meekness, which made Him in His
sufferings the Lamb of God who taketh away the sins
of the world." Each of these virtues of Jesus on the
Cross kept her a day in prayer before Him. "That,"
she says, "is all I can say. If I wish to write, my
pen stops, my tongue remains dumb." And what, after
all, could she say? What words could she use which
saints had not used long before, and holy men and
women without number? What she could not express,
and what they could not express, was what these
things—so poorly represented in words—were in experimental reality to her and to them. What a con-
trast Marie Lataste evidently felt to exist between the
terms she had to use in order to convey those things
which she had seen and experienced and the characters
of fire in which they had been, as it were, branded into
her soul!

Every one knows the difference between understanding the meaning of words and realising their full
significance; and this, which is true even of natural
things, is far more true in the case of divine verities,
whether brought home to us in the way of reflection or
suddenly flashing upon us in the pages of Sacred Scripture. The same expression is a mere truism to one
man and a burning truth to another; nay more, to the
same man its import will suddenly burst upon him or
will expand and deepen in his mind after a manner

quite impossible for him to convey to others. For, when he comes to speak of this truth, he can but use the words he used before, so that, if others catch a glimpse of what he has so profoundly realised, it is from some mysterious hidden influence, which we all acknowledge to exist, not from any employment of new expressions. Now, if this be true where there is no question of special manifestations to favoured souls, how much more so must it be in such exceptional cases! *

When Marie had proceeded to the contemplation of the Cross of Jesus as manifesting the justice of His Father, the knowledge of which is the terror of the impenitent, she was led on almost immediately, as was with her the usual order, to the practical, rather than to the speculative, view of the mystery. The justice of God, manifested by the satisfaction which it needed of a God Incarnate dying on the Cross, blazed only for one moment before her eyes. " I suppose," she adds, " because it is an unfathomable mystery, I was not

---

* Père Surin, in his *Catéchisme Spirituel* (t. ii. c. vii.), when treating of those who have been the recipients of sublime interior lights, asks this question: "How is it that these persons, with such great lights, do not express themselves better than others, when they speak of our mysteries?" To which he replies, "It is because they have no words corresponding to their sentiments. They resemble people who have returned from a distant land, where they have seen rare things of which they preserve a very perfect knowledge, and which, nevertheless, they cannot make others clearly understand, because they have no expressions fitted to convey what they have seen. This powerlessness to find expressions is much more sensible in supernatural things, of which it is said (2 Cor. xii. 4) that 'it is not granted to man to utter' them. Hence St. Teresa, when, out of obedience to her confessors, she wrote down what took place in her interior, continually complained of not being able to say what she wished, because she lacked words to render her thoughts and sentiments."

permitted to dwell upon it." For three days, however, she was called to contemplate the terror which the sight of Jesus Crucified ought to cause to the impenitent and hardened sinner. Out of obedience she endeavours to relate what she saw and felt, but she again declares that all she could do was to show her good-will, for that she could not describe the sentiments of her heart during those hours of intimate communication with Jesus. "It is," she says, "the secret of the King, which I cannot unveil."

After this she was shown how the mercy of God was manifested by Jesus on the Cross, His loving-kindness in the chastisements which He sends us and the pains we endure, and how we enjoy thereby a participation in the sufferings of Jesus, in union with which they sanctify us, and expiate for our sins. She was also shown the mercy of God in bestowing on us the bliss of Heaven, purchased for us by Jesus, who by His Cross delivered us from the bondage of Satan and made us the children of God. "O Cross of Jesus," she exclaims, "mystery in time, mystery in eternity, life of our life, death of our death! O Jesus on the Cross, let my soul be consumed in loving Thee! O Cross of Jesus, may I bear thee on my shoulders, not for a moment, like the Cyrenian, but for my whole life, all my days; and let me, with thee, present myself to God to ask of Him mercy for all eternity!"

She was also shown in the Admirable Tabernacle the sufferings of Jesus in Body and Soul; and of all the pains which He endured in His most holy Body, inscrutable as they were, nothing seemed to her comparable to the thirst which devoured Him. Her heart was quite broken at the sight, and she seemed to be herself enduring a thousand deaths, knowing that

Jesus was innocent, and she, for whom He was enduring these sufferings, a miserable sinner. At this moment the light round the Crucifix became more brilliant than ever. The Body of Jesus appeared to her as an immense illimitable ocean, whence flowed forth into all times, past, present, and to come, upon the trials, evils, pains, and afflictions which men endure, a new fecundity, a divine virtue, changing these tribulations into eternal joy, these evils into everlasting good, these trials into a never-ending rest. At the same time she beheld this ocean the recipient of all the woes and pains of humanity, which rushed in upon Jesus to overwhelm Him, and of sufferings, greater far than would have sufficed to crush the whole human race ; but He was God, and His divine strength could contain and support all these evils in the Body and Soul which He had assumed. Then she heard the voice of Jesus, or, rather, she understood without His speaking what she endeavours to the best of her ability to put into words :
" I am the King of sorrows, the Master of suffering, the Dispenser of tribulations. I have won My crown upon the Cross, My dominion by My Death, and My authority by My Resurrection. Those who would be crowned with Me must bear My crown of thorns ; those who would reign with Me must die the death which I destine for them each day of their life ; those who would share in My authority will receive it only by the painful way of tribulations. It is I who send to each his trials, who regulate their length as well as their intensity, and who give to all the example of the glory of Paradise won by conquest. I needed not suffering for Myself. It is out of love for men that I suffered. All men have sinned ; they ought to suffer in order to expiate their sins, suffer in union with My

sufferings, suffer out of gratitude for what I have endured for them." But we must forbear making further quotations and, as before, refer the reader to Marie's writings.

---

# CHAPTER XIII.

### PRAYER AND COMMUNION.

WHEN Marie was advanced to the higher spiritual state described in the foregoing chapter, she was led to follow a different method in her mode of prayer. What had hitherto been profitable to her was no longer seasonable. A cursory allusion to this ultimate change was made when we enumerated the progressive stages of meditation which were taught her by our Lord. Her prayer now consisted in a simple elevation of her soul to God, to whom she united herself as her principle and her end; her whole occupation being to keep herself in this state of union with Him, to repose tranquilly in His Infinite Being, and to receive the different operations of His grace. To this we may add that, although she continued to acquit herself of her obligatory vocal prayers, vocal prayer had, nevertheless, become very fatiguing to her, sometimes even when she only formed the words in her heart without pronouncing them with her lips. She commonly, therefore, offered all her petitions to the Lord, and expressed all her sentiments, in a tacit manner.

When first she entered on this last state of prayer,

into which she had not had any previous initiation from our Lord, as was the case in the three previous stages, she was a little uneasy, not understanding the meaning or cause of what she experienced. She thus relates what took place in her, and the answer and instruction which she received on the subject from Jesus, to whom, as ever, she brought all her doubts and difficulties. "The state" (she writes in August, 1843), "in which I had found myself for some time past caused me some disquiet. During my prayers, during Mass, and at my communions, I was, so to say, without any sentiment. I was completely absorbed by an ineffable sweetness which filled my whole soul, and hindered me from reading as well as from praying, compelling me to follow the attraction of this sweetness. I spoke of it to the Saviour Jesus, and said to Him, 'Lord, I know not what it is I feel, nor in what state I am; do Thou, who knowest, deign to enlighten me, instruct me, and teach me in what manner I ought to act.' 'My dear daughter,' the Saviour Jesus replied, 'yes, I know you, I know what you experience, I know what you are. You are still but an apprentice, a young novice, who as yet are ignorant of how you ought to conduct yourself in the new way into which it is My will to make you enter. This sweetness which fills your soul and, like a gentle slumber, sets it to sleep that it may repose in God, while your body remains without motion and your heart without action, under the weight of this beatitude which penetrates while it unites you to Me, is a grace which it pleases Me to grant to you, and which, far from saddening you or causing you trouble, ought to excite your liveliest gratitude towards your Saviour. Taste this sweetness whenever you experience it; follow the attraction which it gives you, and which has produced it.'"

Our Lord then proceeded to speak to her about prayer, which had already been the subject of one of His previous instructions. Prayer being an elevation of the soul to God, whereby it offers to Him its homage and begs for His grace, it must be an act. When, therefore, she shall find herself devoid of all sentiments and attraction, He bids her seek to move herself thereto by some devout book or pious thought. But if she found herself unable to read or fix her mind on any good thought, and that this attraction supervened, although unaccompanied by any sensible feelings or thoughts, she was to remain in this state, which was a very perfect degree of prayer, more or less perfect according as the degree of repose was more or less perfect. It was similar to the state of the blessed in Heaven, who repose in the contemplation and love of God. "Now, My daughter," He continued, "you must increase and grow in the new way, of which you have entered only on the first degree. Arm yourself, then, with vigilance and humility; wanting these, you will sink instead of rise, and will come to resemble those souls which, after having soared as eagles up to heaven, fall down to earth, becoming like to the meanest animals. Be vigilant and be humble: vigilant, in order to advance; humble, in order to abide in the friendship of God and in truth, which will tell you that in yourself you are nothing. Be circumspect also, that you may not allow yourself to be seduced or led away to vain, useless, or evil things; for it is only holy things which lead to God." He then told her that this way was not only an unknown way, but also more perilous than the other ways; perilous, because it was possible to make deplorable falls therein, consequently the soul must be on its guard that its repose might be only in God and on God. This way is an unknown way, because God alone can give the knowledge of it. It is impossible for the soul by itself to discover it, or to walk in it, unenlightened and unguided by the Holy Spirit. Now the Holy Spirit only shows it to, and leads into it, certain privileged souls. "Since this way has been opened before you, My daughter," He added, "follow with humility and circumspection the attraction which draws you to it. I will sustain and enlighten you; when you are in need of My help, call Me, and I will hasten to you. Whether it be during holy Mass, or after communion, during prayer or meditation, always follow the attraction which may be given to you; but follow it in the manner I have taught you, that is to say, occupying yourself with God and with what belongs to God, and reposing in Him. If you do this be at rest, for you will be acting aright. My daughter, seek in all your actions rather to do God's will than your own. Seek rather the good pleasure of God than your own pleasure. Let Him lead you by this way or by that way, what matters it to you, provided you are doing His will? O Marie, My dear daughter, you are little on earth, but I will give you an exalted place in My kingdom. Communicate all that passes within you to your director, and follow his advice in everything. Whatsoever you may experience tell him all, and then remain calm and tranquil."

We will now give a few further details extracted from one of her letters written, a little later, in reply to some inquiries of her director. "You oblige me," she writes, "to tell you what I experience in my meditations at present. I own that this is very difficult. I will strive, however, to obey you, and will do my best. When I wish to pray [mentally], I do not propose to myself any subject beforehand, I do not make use of any book; nothing of this kind would suit the attraction which I experience on each occasion; and thus, so far from being useful to me, this selection or preparation would prove a burden or an irksome hindrance to me. I place myself, then, in prayer with the sole disposition to receive the attraction which shall be given me. Sometimes I immediately feel myself drawn to seek God, and I seek Him with docility and humility. At other times this attraction delays coming; I then repose myself in the Bosom of God, humbling and annihilating myself in the presence of His infinite holiness, I a poor creature, a sinner, and prone to evil. God allows Himself to be sought for a longer or a shorter time, and I remain always in a state of submission even though He should not permit me to find Him. But no; sooner or later, He comes, and says to my soul, 'Seek Me,' and then I seek and find Him. God, in fact, never resists a full and entire submission to His divine will."

She then goes on to describe, with her usual briefness and simplicity, the different ways in which God communicates Himself to the soul. One is by His simple presence, and then the soul sensibly experiences this presence, reposing in it, and following the attraction conformable to this communication. Another mode of communication, she says, is by an influx of His gifts of grace. The soul feels to be flooded with them; they fill the heart, and penetrate the whole body as if coursing with the blood. It is a kind of spiritual inebriation. All sufferings of whatever kind vanish,

or the soul, at least, is insensible to them through the
joy which replenishes it.  Sometimes, again, God communicates Himself in the way of light and illumination, manifesting to the soul divine views which are,
so to say, beatific in their character ; or He speaks to it
through the thoughts which He inspires or the words
which He causes it to hear.  But God has a yet more
intimate and perfect way of communicating Himself to
the soul, and that is by causing it to penetrate into
His Heart.  Marie draws a great distinction between
the Bosom and the Heart of God.  In a previous letter,
when giving her director an account of lights she had
received in prayer, she had mentioned to him three
several communications made to her in the Bosom of
God, and in that letter she also refers to the difference
which she understood to exist between the Admirable
Tabernacle, the Bosom of God, and the Heart of God ;
a difference to which, she said, she had alluded on a
former occasion.  In the present letter she describes, so
far as she is able, what she intends by the Heart of
God.  " The communications," she says, " which God
makes to a soul in His Heart are the most intimate,
the most exalted, the most perfect.  It is there, in
effect, that the soul finds the point of reunion of all
the perfections of God ; there it receives into itself the
sweetest impressions, and is altogether penetrated by
them.  There it sees and contemplates the divine perfections in all their splendour, seized with wonder,
admiration, and love.  The Heart of God is the source
whence spring all graces.  The Heart of God is the
plentitude of all goods, and the soul which penetrates
into this Heart possesses them to such a degree that it
seems to hold them in common with God.  It is there
that He discovers to it the reality of His substance, of

M

which He calls it to a participation in order to make it one with Himself. In fine, it is there that between the soul and God, the creature and the Creator, the finite and the Infinite, the most marvellous, the most admirable, and the sublimest conceivable intercourse takes place. There God speaks a language unintelligible to men; there the soul speaks to God in a language of which it has no longer the intelligence when it has ceased to speak, and which it will only find again in Heaven to possess it for ever. This language is hidden, interior, mysterious; it is in the form of a song, and yet it is not a song. For this language the sound neither of voice nor of words is needed. The soul instantly understands this language, yet not by a real and reasonable comprehension, but by the sweet and delightful sentiment and impression produced within it. O ineffable bliss of the communications of the soul with God in the Heart of God, that is, in His Eternal Word! Language inarticulate, silent and mysterious conversations through the Eternal Unction of the Divinity, that is, through the Holy Spirit! O Sir, I believe that this must be Heaven. O God, Trinity and Unity! O God of my soul, God full of mercy, God full of tenderness, God full of love, God most admirable, God thrice holy, may I love Thee for ever!"

Another letter, written a few days later, is devoted to this same subject, being an attempt to give an idea, however inadequate, of what she understands by the Heart of God. The state of grace gives a soul access to the Bosom of God, but to live in His Heart, she says, requires a far higher perfection. She did not, she adds, by any means receive similar communications in all her meditations. The privilege was even rare, owing to her unworthiness; and, if she enjoyed it at all, she owed it entirely to the infinite goodness and compassion with which the Saviour Jesus had treated her.

In speaking of the Heart of God, Marie makes this observation : "It is not necessary that I should say that I understand nothing material by the Heart of God. God is a spirit, and all is spirit in Him." She has, in fact, as appears to us, endeavoured in her own way to convey an idea of her various states, which other mystics have rendered differently by referring what she treats as more intimate regions, as it were, in God, to the soul itself. Every one at all conversant, even in the most general way, with mystical theology, will be familiar with the distinction between the exterior and interior regions of the soul, or the inferior and superior, for both images have the same meaning. Moreover, mystical writers recognise, in this interior region of the soul, a more intimate portion, called sometimes the centre of the soul, where the most noble and sublime operations of grace take place and where true wisdom resides. "It is in this most intimate portion," writes Surin in his "Catéchisme Spirituel," * "that the soul enters into a sacred intercourse with the Three Divine Persons. It is there, says St. Teresa, that great secrets are learned through the communication which the soul enjoys, sometimes with One, sometimes with Another, of these Adorable Persons. It is there that it distinguishes Each from the Other with great clearness, and that different impressions are received, now from the Father, of whose power it is sensible, now from the Son, whose wisdom it experiences within itself, or again from the Holy Spirit, of whose sweetness it tastes. There, in fine, the soul receives and possesses all the

* Tom. ii. chap. iv.

good things which it pleases Each of the Divine Persons to pour into its depths."

Again, Surin thus defines the distinction to be made between the depth of the soul and its more intimate centre :—"The depth of the soul is that region where the soul resides tranquilly when it reposes in God ; it is there that most of the operations of grace terminate, and from whence also they pour themselves forth on the faculties. . . . We must not, however, confound the depth of the soul with the more intimate portion, which is deeper and more imperceptible, and which serves as the secret cabinet of the Heavenly Spouse.   St. Teresa, in her 'Interior Castle,' represents it as the centre, so to say, of man.   It is the abode of the Three Divine Persons, when they deign to dwell with us in a special manner, according to what is said in the Gospel : 'We will come to him, and will make Our abode with him.' " *

Surin further illustrates what he has been stating by comparing the soul to a globe.   " The intimate portion will be in the centre, where the fire of divine love is enkindled.   Going from the centre to the circumference, you will meet first with what we have called the depth, then with the intellectual faculties, next with the senses, and finally with the body.   The divine operations which take place in the interior preserve this order in their progress : they first make impression on the depth, whence they pass to the faculties, from the faculties to the senses, and sometimes even to the body."

Now may it not be that what Marie describes as the Bosom of God, in which the soul enjoys repose, is no other than this interior region, called by mystics the depth, while the Heart of God corresponds with the

* John xiv. 23.

centre, in which ineffable communications take place between the soul and the Three Adorable Persons of the Blessed Trinity? The expressions she uses certainly tend to suggest this idea, although, owing to her ignorance of the terms of mystical theology, she uses language at variance with that which is usually employed. We have seen that she speaks of her admission into the region called by her the Heart of God as comparatively a rare privilege; but, whether or no Marie was introduced into this inner chamber of the Heavenly Spouse, where the spiritual espousals are described as taking place, it is evident that, in speaking of more interior regions in God, she is alluding to those high progressive states of union with God which are generally indicated by the image of different abodes, or apartments, in the soul itself. Her testimony, however, devoid as it is of all science or art, is all the more valuable, as proving that nothing was borrowed or unconsciously adopted from the working of the imagination on acquired knowledge.

After speaking of the high privileges she had enjoyed in spite of her unworthiness, and through the pure compassion of her Lord, she concludes with a remark which is characteristic of her dominant feeling, that of a holy indifference to everything. "Whatever communications I receive," she says, "they are not the less agreeable to my heart, or less profitable to my soul. It is occupied with but one engrossing thought, to follow with entire submission the attraction presented to it, recognising that it deserves nothing on the part of God. In following that attraction my soul finds God, and, finding God, it finds grace and happiness. I am attached to nothing; I desire only the perfect accomplishment of the will of God. All else is indifferent to me, even what interests me most." Marie Lataste truly describes herself in these few words. We have just said that she had a holy indifference to everything, but this, by her own confession, must admit of one exception, for she had a passionate desire to conform herself, and to be conformed, to the will of God. If she ever expresses an ardent desire, it will be observed that it has this end and object. This is her peculiar attraction, her special devotion.

Saints, considered in one point of view, are similar to each other. They all love God above all things with an intense love, and His Holy Will, which is Himself. They all manifest those virtues which are the fruits of God's grace, and tread in the same Divine footsteps, following their Master and Model; they are all devout to the Passion of Jesus; their hearts are all drawn to Him in the Adorable Sacrament of His Love; they all desire that Supersubstantial Bread and nourishment of their souls; they all love Mary, the great Mother of God and their mother, with the tenderest love; and many more things might we say of these resemblances. Nevertheless, they undoubtedly differ also: they differ in the prominence of certain virtues; they differ in the variety of their attractions; and this causes a diversity in appearance like that of the varied hues in nature. Pure white, it is said, renders perfectly all the luminous rays of the sun, but that every variety of colour is the result of partial reflection. Thus, to carry on the comparison, we may say that Mary, who super-eminently reflects the image of her Son, is like the white light; so adorned is she with every grace that we cannot single out one perfection as being more prominent than another, or as imparting its colouring to the picture we present to ourselves of her: not so with the saints, or with those saintly personages to whom we venture in familiar parlance to give the name of saints.

For instance, we are naturally led to compare with each other two saintly women of our own day, not only because they both belonged to the humbler classes of life, received singular divine favours, and were taken away in their youth, but because both were drawn by a special and engrossing devotion to the Tabernacle where the God-Man abides, the Prisoner of Love. The life of each was at the foot of that Tabernacle; nevertheless, there is a distinctive difference between the two; they are like and unlike; their respective physiognomies impress us differently. We may surmise that this proceeds, not entirely, by any means, from difference in natural character, although their natural characters had points of difference, but from a certain diversity in their attraction, which at first sight appears, and in one sense was, the same. Marie Eustelle Harpain, the seamstress of Saint-Pallais, would seem to have been attracted to a hunger for the Divine Manna of our souls, and to have received from Its participation a sensible sweetness and support, which made her break forth in the most passionate expressions of longing for the communication of Jesus in His Sacrament, so that she fainted and was ready to die when more than a day passed without receiving Him; and thus we are led to view her as one called of God to manifest in herself a love which should excite in others a great desire for that Bread of Life, and an appreciation of the need in which we stand of Its fortifying and vivifying effect. Marie Lataste, like Marie Eustelle Harpain, was a lover of Jesus in His Adorable Sacrament, and we cannot doubt that she, too, longed for that food of her soul, when not permitted to receive it, though—at least, while living in the world—she did not communicate daily, nor do we hear of that sinking of the frame during the intervals from which Marie Eustelle suffered. If those languors of love affected her she is silent concerning them, but of one thing she is not silent, and that would suffice to account for her silence concerning what she may have experienced from any spiritual deprivation : she is for ever speaking of the Holy Will of her God—" My meat is to do His Will." It is this special attraction, above all, to which she seems called to witness; so that, if one was styled the Angel of the Eucharist, the other might be styled the Adorer of the Holy Will of God ; not as if Marie Eustelle Harpain was not also most conformed to the Divine Will, or as if Marie Lataste was not a most devoted lover of Jesus in His Adorable Sacrament, nevertheless, the same love which consumed each of them had a special manifestation in their several cases.

What Marie Eustelle experienced physically, when not receiving the Bread of Life daily, was, we need scarcely say, an exceptional phenomenon, one which need not have taken place in another who yet loved with equal fervour. It pleased Jesus to exhibit thus, as it were, in a palpable manner, as He has been pleased to do miraculously in other cases,* what He is to us, and to prove sensibly that, as He says in the Gospel,† His Flesh is meat indeed, and His Blood is drink indeed. That Marie Lataste received Him sacramentally with ineffable spiritual joy there is no question. How often do we find her saying, " I had the happiness

---

* Witness the examples of holy persons living for years without any other nourishment than the Blessed Eucharist. This was the case with the Addolorata in the Tyrol, and, we believe, is that of Louise Lateau.

† John vi. 56.

that day of communicating;" and it was on these occasions that she was favoured with some of her most beautiful visions of the Sacred Humanity. That she, whose life was spent in desire, when not in reality at the foot of the Tabernacle, would also, while submitting herself without remonstrance to her spiritual guide, have wished to receive Jesus more frequently in communion, there can likewise be no doubt. Indeed, some incidental remarks of her own testify to such a desire, and we may gather the same from our Lord's own words to her on several occasions; as, for instance, when He said to her, "If, My daughter, you cannot receive Me sacramentally as often as you would desire, who can hinder you from receiving Me spiritually?" And, in fact, our Lord seems to have specially made up to her in these spiritual communions for not receiving Him more often sacramentally. Marie, herself, says that she regarded it as a peculiar favour on the part of our Lord, that He should have directed her to communicate spiritually several times during the day.

"How often, Lord," she asked Him, "dost Thou desire that I should receive Thee by spiritual communion?" Jesus replied, "My daughter, you will communicate spiritually on rising in the morning, and then after your morning prayer, as you are in the habit of doing; you will also communicate again twice during the day, and, finally, after your evening prayers. I desire to enter you heart five times a day by spiritual communion." Marie then inquired what preparation was requisite for these communions, and our Lord told her that the preparation needed was not difficult; that it was not necessary to make all the acts appertaining to sacramental communion. "Present yourself," He said, "in spirit before My Tabernacle, and say to Me,

'Lord Jesus, come down into my heart.' That is enough. But in each spiritual communion you should always propose an end to yourself; such, for example, as to obtain some grace or particular virtue. You can also communicate spiritually for the intention which I suggested to you for your sacramental communions, namely, that of obtaining from God, My Father, by My merits and by the communion you are making, the necessary graces to know and perfectly fulfil His holy will. Though you should never have any other intention but this, it would always be agreeable to Me." It then occurred to Marie to ask how she should behave in regard to these spiritual communions on the days when she should have the happiness of communicating sacramentally; and our Lord told her that she would please Him by communicating spiritually, even on those days, in the manner which He had pointed out. " You cannot," He added, " receive too often within you the virtue and grace of the Sacrament of My Love." That our Lord attached particular importance to this recommendation, which is suitable for all Christians, whether their spiritual state may or may not warrant frequent sacramental communion, is proved by what she subjoins. " My intention," she says to her director, " was to tell you this by word of mouth ; but the Saviour Jesus bade me give it you in writing."

Before leaving this subject, it may be well to add a few passages from the instructions given to Marie by our Lord with reference to communion, and detailed in her writings. Speaking of one of her communions made on Palm Sunday, and of her meditation on the words, " Daughter of Sion, behold thy King cometh to thee, meek,"* she says that after receiving our Lord

* Zach. ix. 9; Matt. xxi. 5.

she seemed to hear a voice in her heart saying, " Rejoice, daughter of Sion, thy King is come to dwell in thy heart." These words filled her with indescribable joy, and she soon became aware that the voice which uttered them was that of Jesus. He said to her, " My daughter, it is thus I address Myself to souls well-disposed who receive Me in Holy Communion. Happy the souls who communicate; more happy those who communicate often ; but happier still those who communicate daily. Holy communion is the greatest action which it is in the power of man to perform ; because it is that which honours Me the most, is the most pleasing to God, and the most profitable to man." Jesus proceeds to demonstrate each of these assertions in a beautiful passage, which it were a pity to curtail, but which our space forbids us to insert at length.

Elsewhere he speaks to Marie of three different communions ; the sacrilegious, the tepid, and the fervent. After dwelling briefly on the horrors of the first, of which on another occasion He gave her a symbolical vision, He goes on to speak of tepid communion, and says, " There are numbers of persons who, after so many communions, have still the same faults, the same imperfections. They do not pay any attention to such small things ; satisfied with their manner of life, they never dream of becoming better. When they receive communion they amuse their minds with reciting prayers with some sensible devotion ; but they do not dive into their hearts, they do not search its folds, they do not apply themselves to purify their souls from affection to venial sin. It is as though they said to Me, ' Lord, I love Thee ; but although such and such a thing may be displeasing to Thee, it is only a trifle, and so I shall continue to do it.' I do not with pleasure go into such hearts; I should wish their principal devotion to be a resolution to avoid all that may be displeasing to Me. It is true that venial sin does not render their communion sacrilegious; but it causes Me not to communicate Myself to them fully; I do not bestow upon them My graces in such great abundance. They go to communion in order to preserve themselves from mortal sin, and they receive therein sufficient grace for that purpose." He then describes fervent communion as that which is made without affection to venial sin, and with a sincere desire to advance in perfection. The fervent soul communicates in order to obtain fresh graces, and increase more and more in the love of God, and in the accomplishment of the Divine will; to honour the greatness and infinite perfections of God, and to testify to Him its love. "To persons thus communicating," our Lord adds, "I give abundant graces."

It may be observed that in the above definition no mention is made of sensible fervour, although there is a certain allusion to it as existing very commonly in the communions of tepid Christians. This is encouraging to those who, while recognising in themselves substantially the intentions here enumerated, may be depressed by the absence of those ardent feelings which are described by so many holy souls as accompanying their communions. Not that we should cease to desire to be participants of this fervour, but we may gather from our Lord's words that its absence need not cause alarm, or lead any soul to fear that it communicates too often. The devil would be very glad that such a conclusion should be drawn.

For the rest, as regards the frequency of communion, our Lord refers persons to the judgment of their spiritual director, adding, however, some advice for the director himself. While enjoining prudence, and saying that he must avoid alike too great facility in this matter, and too much rigour, He says that He would more readily forgive an error on the side of indulgence, "for," He adds, "even as it is impossible to go near to the fire without being warmed, so also is it impossible to approach Me, who am all fire, in the Sacrament of My Love, without having fervour more or less rekindled. How shall weakness sustain itself, if it does not go and draw from the very source of strength? How shall he who is nothing but sin live in justice if he does not use the remedy against sin? A director who makes persons communicate often does more good than another who is backward in allowing communion." He proceeds to give some practical directions to confessors to aid their discrimination as to allowing more or less frequency of communion.

Another day He indicated to Marie what were the requisite dispositions for frequent communion. In order that a communion should be good, it was necessary that the recipient should be exempt from mortal sin, and from attachment to it; but this state did not qualify a person to be a frequent communicant. There ought to be further a freedom from venial sin, that is, from all such as is deliberate, and from attachment to sins of this kind. So long as there is attachment to venial sin, the soul is not in the way of perfection, and runs the risk at any moment of lapsing into mortal sin. In order to be a weekly communicant, a person must not be attached to venial sin. Such dispositions are pretty common, and are within the reach of all, even of those who are living in the world. More perfect dispositions are needed for those who would communicate also two or three times in the course of the week; they must, moreover, not be attached to their imperfections or lesser faults, and must be endeavouring to purify their hearts from these also, and from all attachment to them. For daily communion still more perfect dispositions are requisite ; a greater purity and detachment from self, from one's own will and desires, a closer union with God, and a sincere desire to do all things in order to please Him. Our Lord added, " Endeavour more and more to acquire these necessary dispositions for frequent communion. Be not discouraged, My daughter, but rather humble yourself, and abandon yourself to the mercy of God. Above all, have a great desire to communicate often. If you desire ardently to do so, God will have more regard to your desire than to your dispositions, and He will permit you to communicate more frequently. Draw near with confidence to this Sacred Banquet, feed with avidity on this Bread of Angels, strive to become like them by purity, obedience, humility, and charity, and often repeat those words of the centurion : 'Lord, I am not worthy that Thou shouldest enter under my roof,' that is, into my heart. Then add, with faith and confidence in the mercy of God, 'Lord, speak the word only, and my soul shall be healed.' "

---

# CHAPTER XIV.

### MARIE IS REASSURED BY HER DIRECTORS, AND COMFORTED IN HER ANXIETIES BY OUR LORD.

WHILE Marie was steadily advancing in the path of perfection, and daily receiving fresh proofs of her Lord's tender care, the Abbé Darbins and M. Dupérier were

continuing their study of her manuscripts.    As they
read, their wonder and admiration increased.    Where
could an ignorant and illiterate peasant girl have
attained the knowledge requisite for placing on paper
such a compendium of dogmatic, moral, and mystical
theology?    Whence had the light come?    and how had
she found words to express what had thus in some way
been manifested to her?    Whence indeed?    As they
asked themselves this question, there seemed but one
reply : The finger of God is here.    On the other hand,
they had failed, notwithstanding the severest scrutiny,
in detecting in Marie the least sign of illusion.    The
candour, straightforwardness, and simplicity with which
she had related all that had taken place in her soul,
and, above all, her humble and unquestioning submission to the judgment and commands of her spiritual
superiors, and her entire abandonment to the divine
will, appeared to them, and justly so, as the surest
tokens of the principles which actuated her, and of the
spirit which was guiding her.

They thought it good, therefore, now to reassure
her.    M. Darbins, after administering this comfort to
his penitent, expressed his wish that she should give
him her own opinion concerning her writings.    She
was to tell him frankly what she herself thought of
them.    She at once obeyed, and expressed herself with
a holy liberty.    Never, certainly, was any one freer
from human respect than was Marie.    If she had
hitherto acquiesced in all which M. Darbins and M.
Dupérier had been pleased to manifest in the way of
doubt and mistrust, it was from a genuine and heartfelt reverence for the judgment of those whom God
had placed over her and invested with His authority.
She was not merely silenced, she submitted her own

opinion to theirs. Now it was otherwise ; and we find her replying thus to her director :—"I am going to speak to you with the sincerity and frankness which you know I always do. I have never concealed anything from you ; I have never disguised my sentiments. I should be ashamed to lie or deceive ; God forbids this ; and the gratitude I owe you for the interest you take in me makes it my duty to speak to you always with an open heart. You reassured and tranquillised me when you told me that you thought that all which I had experienced comes from God. As for myself, that was indeed my conviction from the beginning, that is, at the time you arrived at Mimbaste. Later, seeing that you doubted, I doubted with you, and, to avoid being led astray, I have faithfully told you all that passed within me ; I have never hidden anything from you. My misgivings very much increased when I saw that M. Dupérier doubted as well as yourself. Oh ! with what suffering and pain was my soul tortured then, above all, when he entertained more than doubts, and thought that I deceived you, and that all my words were lies. My affliction was very great, because I thought that I must be a very wretched sinner, since I could be supposed capable of such behaviour. The Saviour Jesus consoled me after this severe trial, and light has seemed since to return by degrees to my mind.

"These, then, are the reflections which occurred naturally to me with regard to the words which I heard and repeated in writing. Nevertheless, I did not dwell on these reflections ; I awaited your decision. While I was in the sad perplexity which you know of, and was vainly seeking to know the truth from the lips of men, I never ceased addressing myself to God to beg Him to

enlighten me, or to enlighten him who directed me.
God, no doubt, came to my help, since my thoughts on
this subject have been conformable with your decision.
I considered the instructions which I had received, in
their principle, in their end, in themselves. Under all
these points of view I clearly perceived that they could
proceed only from God. From my infancy I have been
taught that there was a God, that I must attach myself
to Him, that I must adore Him, love Him, and serve
Him. Now, in seeking God and in loving Him, I
have experienced all that I have stated in my papers
and in my letters. In order not to continue to experience it, I must separate myself from God. It is
from Him, then, that all has proceeded. Never will I
separate myself from Him, unless this God who was
made known to me in my childhood, and in whom I
have experienced all that I have related, be not the
true God, but is rejected by the Church. I would then
refuse Him all my adorations, and would regard all that
He has told me as needing, in order to my belief in it,
to be-modified by my belief in the teachings of the
Church. I desire to follow the mind of the Church in
all things. But I know very well that there is no
other God save the God of my heart, the God whom I
know, whom I feel, and whom I love with my whole
soul. It is He who has taught me all, it is He who is
the principle of all which I have committed to you, it
is from Him that I received it. These writings, then,
must be good, as is all which comes from God."

Marie reasoned well, and, we think, could not have
better expressed that conviction and inward certainty
against which all argument is powerless, and at the
same time its compatibility with a perfect submission
to the judgment of the Church, as represented by her

N

lawful superiors. Humility renders such an attitude
of mind possible; to the proud natural intellect of
man it will be utterly unintelligible. But what she
must have endured during such a conflict may be more
easily imagined than described. Her soul had been
placed in the dungeon which had been figuratively
presented to her in vision. She continues: "If I
consider them [the instructions she had received] in
their end, I still say that they come from God, because
the end of these writings is good; it would not be so if
they came from the devil. What, in fact, is the object
of the writings which I have committed to you? The
glory of God, the salvation of my soul, and the salvation of the souls of my brethren. Indeed everything
therein speaks of giving glory to God and submitting
to His will; everything leads souls to Him, attaches
them to Him, and engages them to love and serve
Him faithfully.

"Finally, consider the writings in themselves. Is it
not true that they conduce to the practice of good, and
of perfect good? Is it not true that they draw the soul
to God, and inspire a hatred of sin? Now, can the
devil ever produce works of that kind? We judge a
tree from its fruits, the Saviour Jesus said, and a bad
tree cannot produce bad fruits. How, then, could the
devil have suggested to me things so good and so
agreeable to God? It is thus, Sir, that I reasoned,
almost without perceiving that I was doing so; and
this reasoning did me good. But as soon as I became
aware of the reflections which my mind was making, I
turned it away to other subjects, in order to conform
myself in all things to the will of the Saviour Jesus,
who has constituted you as my judge and father. I re-
nounced my own views in order to defer entirely to you."

Thus did Marie Lataste recover her perfect calm with respect to the supernatural communications of which she had been the recipient. Our Lord had secretly reassured her, and now she was openly reassured by her director. Hitherto M. Darbins had communicated the manuscript which she had given him, only to M. Dupérier, but he considered that it was now fitting that he should show it to Mgr. Lanneluc, the Bishop of Aire. The impression which it produced on the mind of this good prelate was extremely favourable. Having fixed his residence at the Great Seminary of Dax, for the convenience of his pastoral rounds in that portion of his diocese, he gave up all his leisure moments to the perusal of the papers. He now commissioned M. Dupérier, in concert with some other ecclesiastics belonging to the seminary, to examine Marie Lataste's works, and the result was their united report that they contained nothing contrary to faith and that they were calculated to do great good to souls.

It was natural that this inquiry, which brought the subject to the knowledge of several individuals, should lead to a certain publicity, however little intended. The reputation of the poor peasant girl began to spread, and the consequence was that a number of persons applied to her, through M. Darbins, for light in their spiritual difficulties or for advice concerning the salvation of their souls. Marie in all simplicity had recourse to the Saviour for her replies, which she transmitted to her director. We have seen how our Lord had prepared her for this new office by the illumination which for some time past He had been giving her respecting the spiritual state of other souls. He often even communicated to her what was passing in their minds; an instance of which we have seen in a letter already

quoted, in which she shows that our Lord had manifested to her all that M. Dupérier thought, suspected,
or planned with reference to herself. Had discretion
allowed of their publication, we are assured that there
are other letters, besides those which have been inserted
in her life and works, which prove her possession of
this gift of reading the secret thoughts of others.

When this new favour, however, was first conferred
it had alarmed her. Always absorbed in the one desire
to do the will of God with all perfection, the fear of
being led to pass rash judgments on others, or to feel
censorious in their regard, or in some way to offend
against charity or humility, rendered her uneasy. The
fear of illusion also would sometimes assail her, when
she saw herself commissioned to instruct those who
were her own appointed guides. As usual, she betook
herself to Jesus, and thus addressed Him: "Saviour
Jesus, vouchsafe, I pray Thee, to enlighten me; teach
me how to behave, and how to accept this knowledge
and these divine lights which my mind receives regarding persons and their actions. My heart is consumed
with the desire of Thy glory; my soul burns with love
for Thee and for my brethren. Lord, how ought I to
conduct myself, experiencing what I do? Thus far
Thou hast had the goodness to instruct me; leave me,
then, not in ignorance as to this matter, and I will
testify my gratitude by a greater love and a blinder
obedience." The Saviour replied, "My daughter, you
know that I am acquainted with the lights which are
manifested to you." "Yea, Lord, I believe that Thou
knowest them better than I do myself." "These lights
do not diminish or weaken, do they, the love which you
have for God and for your neighbour?" "No, Lord."
"Well, My daughter, whatever these lights may show

you, refuse them not, whether they enlighten you
respecting profane or sacred things, the religious condition, the virtues or the vices, of governments and
peoples, of nations in general or of individuals in particular; even when they disclose to you the dispositions,
the sentiments, and the secret designs of persons who
are known to you, and with whom you have intimate
relations, do not reject them, but use much discretion.
Nothing can be hidden from God; He knows the depths
of all hearts; and therefore, when He wills and judges
it fitting, He can impart the knowledge thereof to whom
He pleases.    Accordingly, when God shall manifest to
you the interior state of a person, and you see him such
as he is, do not imagine that in thus seeing him you
are rashly judging him.    There is a great difference
between rash judgments and these kinds of light or
knowledge which are imparted to you."    Our Lord
then pointed out to her the evil source and principle of
rash judgments, proceeding as they do from pride and
jealousy, and their pernicious fruits in the contempt
and exposure of our neighbour; whereas the lights
which she received had their source and principle in
God, and for their effect His glory and the salvation of
souls.

He then gave her some practical directions for the
examination of these lights.    She was to note whether
they excited in her mind any prejudice against the
person whom they concerned, or diminished the love
which she owed him; if so, she was to reject such lights.
But if they produced in her heart a charitable compassion, joined with a sincere desire for God's glory,
then she was to accept them whatever they might be.
She was on no account, however, to impart to any one,
without His command or permission, what had been

made known to her concerning individuals. Moreover, He told her, as He did also on many other occasions, that he had great designs regarding her. "You must have a large heart," He said "in order that it may contain all that I desire to enclose within it; a strong and firm mind, that it may preserve the due balance which wisdom, prudence, moderation, and discretion prescribe. Establish yourself in a profound humility; but do not let this humility make you timid, or lead you to conceal that in your life which it is My pleasure should be made known. Let your humility consist in your sentiments rather than in your acts, strengthening you in the performance of those things which otherwise might have been the most likely to tempt you to vanity. Arm yourself with courage; let a holy intrepidity enable you to surmount all that might involve peril to your life, excite feelings of repugnance in your heart, or be irksome to your mind, when it is a question of fulfilling My will. Ever place in Me all your confidence, and await patiently God's own time."

These words were consoling and sustaining to the spirit of Marie Lataste in more ways than one. They removed anxiety and doubt, and they encouraged her to bear the distressing opposition she had to encounter in the affair of her vocation to the Congregation of the Sacred Heart, of which we shall give some details in the following chapter.

# CHAPTER XV.

MARIE had never ceased reporting to M. Darbins what our Lord continued to manifest to her on the subject of her vocation; and ever since he had come to take the charge of the parish of Mimbaste, she had persisted in saying that God called her to be a religious of the Sacré Cœur. But he had taken very little notice, or, at least, had appeared in the first instance to attach slight importance to the communication. Subsequently what he had said was discouraging; and, indeed, humanly speaking, there appeared to be great difficulties in the way. But M. Dupérier went still further, and insisted that the thing was out of the question and impossible. It could not be. But Marie knew that nothing was impossible to God. If God willed it, it could and would be. What were difficulties to Him? Perhaps M. Dupérier reasoned in a reverse order: As a matter of fact, the project was incapable of realisation, therefore it was not to be supposed that God willed it. Were not the arrangements of His Providence one of the marks we have, in any given circumstance, to direct us to the knowledge of His will in our regard? He may even send a desire, and a very strong one, and since this comes from Him, it is, in one sense, a call; but He may merely wish to furnish the occasion of merit to a soul thus called, without intending its realisation.

Whether or no M. Dupérier thus reasoned, he set

himself steadily against Marie's alleged call. He judged the difficulties in the way to be insurmountable, difficulties which were, however, magnified by some false impressions prevalent as to the organisation of the Sacré Cœur. Marie's family had imposed great sacrifices on itself to raise the sum required for her sister Quitterie when, fourteen years before, she had become a Sister of Charity. It was erroneously believed that a similar dowry, probably a much more considerable one, would be expected as a condition for admission into the Sacré Cœur. In justice to Marie's parents, it should be said that they did not shrink from any necessary outlay in behalf of their youngest daughter, in case she persevered in her desire. Her mother, indeed, was resolved, in that event, to use every endeavour to collect what was required for her reception as a choir nun, being averse to the idea of her entering only as a lay-sister, and thus being a servant rather than a member of the Community.* Marie relates how her mother said to her one day, "My daughter, we will give you a thousand crowns to take to the Sacré Cœur, and a thousand francs for your journey, your equipment, and your maintenance until your reception." This was, indeed, a generous offer on the part of an afflicted parent, who was thus willing to impoverish herself in order to facilitate what would deprive her of a child who was the solace and consolation of her declining years. Marie felt this deeply, and immediately replied, "Mother, you will give me less

* The nuns of the Sacré Cœur were not classed according to the fortune which they brought. The postulant's degree of education determined her position. If deficient in that respect, she was ranked among the Sœurs Coadjutrices, or Assistant Sisters, but these were by no means regarded as servants, and the other nuns often even took a share in their labours.

than that, and nevertheless they will receive me at the Sacré Cœur. I will tell them, and besides they will know, that I am poor, and they will not refuse me entrance." "No, my daughter," rejoined the mother ; "however much we may be straitened in means by furnishing this portion, we will bear it courageously, thinking that thereby we have secured your not being the servant of the rest in the convent." Marie's thoughts were different. "I did not desire to embrace the religious life," she writes to M. Darbins, "for the purpose of living more at my ease, but that I might do the will of Jesus. What does it matter to me that I should be the servant of all, if such be the will of Jesus ? Oh, that I may not fly from the Cross, in leaving the world, but fasten myself to it with Jesus for my whole life !" Her heart, however, was heavy within her. She hoped that she did not love her parents too much, but she could not help feeling pained at the sorrow she was inflicting on them, and at the straits to which her family would be reduced by their endeavours to provide her with a portion. On this head, however, Jesus reassured her, telling her that she would be received at the convent from a motive of charity, not of interest. Consoled with regard to this point, the only anxiety which still troubled her, was that, knowing the tenderness of her parents, and the grief which parting with her would cause them, she dreaded lest she should fail in any way in that disengagement of heart which a spouse of Jesus ought to have. Jesus again comforted her, and to her humble inquiries replied, "My daughter, I love your submission to My will, and I also love your affection for your family. God and your family may both be loved, provided the love of your kindred does not make you forget what is owed to God." He also

sent her a vision, in which her father, her mother, and
her sister Marguerite were introduced, and Marie heard
the Saviour address them in words calculated to tranquillise and console them; doubtless meaning her to
understand thereby that such were the thoughts and
feelings which He would secretly and efficaciously
breathe into their hearts.

But besides the difficulties connected with Marie's
family and the portion, other objections were raised by
her directors. Communications were not so easy in those
days; there was no railway, so that, to reach the noviciate of Paris, this young woman of but twenty-two years
of age, who had never left her native village, would have
to make a long journey alone and unprotected. And
what was she to do without friends, without recommendations, when she reached the great city? and how
could she expect, unless the Bishop of the diocese
would second her application, which it seems he was
not prepared to do, that she would be received at the
Sacré Cœur? Accordingly, both M. Darbins and
M. Dupérier, although they must day by day have
been becoming more convinced of the truth of her
interior call, recoiled from the apparent obstacles
in the way of its realisation, and persisted in seeking
further delays, alleging that they must be more fully
satisfied as to her vocation before they could sanction
her departure. Meanwhile Marie continued to be inwardly pressed upon the subject, Jesus was constantly
speaking to her of His purpose; and the parable He
had shown her of the King and the Olive-tree, which
was carefully cultivated and transferred to the shelter
of a golden cage—a parable which she was accused
of having invented—was intended, we may suppose,
to bring the matter afresh before the minds of her

directors, and urge it upon their consideration ; for Jesus, as we know, bade her always faithfully report all the communications which He made to her.

We cannot be surprised that, as days sped on, Marie, in spite of her entire submission to her superiors, and her confidence that her Lord would know how to bring about His designs in His own good time, should feel distressed and harassed by these delays.    Ever since she had attained her nineteenth year, Jesus had made known to her that her life would be a short one ; and she was now twenty-two.    In December, 1843, we find her mentioning this revelation to M. Darbins.    The Saviour Jesus, she told him, had made her a promise with which she had not hitherto acquainted him.    It was one day after communion when our Lord warned her that she should die young, and bade her, therefore, labour diligently to lay up merits for eternity.    She had felt very desirous to know the exact time of her death, but made an inward sacrifice of her anxiety for more precise information and abstained from asking Him any question.    Nevertheless she said to herself, "Suppose it were this very year that I am to die !" Then Jesus replied to her thought, and said, "No, My daughter, you will not die this year, you will live through next year, and will even see the whole of your twenty-fifth year ; but you will die before you have completed your twenty-sixth."    He then exhorted her to prepare herself for death by uniting herself more and more to God, and detaching herself more and more from creatures.    After that, He had asked her whether she regretted dying so young.    "Ah, Lord," she replied, "how could I regret death ?  Hast Thou not told me that death is a good thing, for that after death a soul offends God no more, but loves Him perfectly and is united to Him for ever? If so, how could I regret death?" and, in fact, she tells her director that the prospect of death, so far from saddening her, filled her with joy, made her bear the severest trials with patience, and disengaged her heart from all, even from those who were most dear to her. She loved her family, as He well knew, but she could bid them adieu that very hour without shedding a tear. Happy, indeed, would she be to fly from the tabernacles of sinners, to go and be with God ; and often did she adopt the Psalmist's words and lament the length of her sojourning, her soul groaning within her at having to dwell so long in the tents of Cedar. She hoped, therefore, that the Saviour's promise would be fulfilled, yet, if it was God's will to prolong her trials and sufferings, she would only say, " Thy will, not mine, be done." If it was sweet to die, it was sweeter still to do the will of God.

Marie, however, allowed herself lovingly to complain to Jesus of the straits in which she was placed, between her longing to accomplish her vocation, and the obedience she owed to those who opposed it. " O Jesus, my amiable Saviour," she exclaimed, " have compassion on me. O my tender Father, suffer me to pour forth my heart in the bosom of Thy mercy with the confidence and simplicity of a child. Thou alone, O my God, knowest all that I feel within me, all that I experience. Lord, do not take what I am about to say as the murmur of a rebellious heart, but as the complaint of a child who makes a loving appeal to its father. Wherefore, my sweet Saviour, dost Thou cause me to feel all these things, things which sometimes are so extraordinary and surprising that they occasion me terrible trials and every kind of humiliation? To please and obey Thee I have always sacrificed everything ; I have always consented, for the love of Thee, to pass in the eyes of men as one foolish and demented, and never to take offence at their opinion of what I said to them. But how long, Lord, wilt Thou leave me in my present condition? I am as one without life, and yet I find not death. I languish like a plant that is withering up, but still remains where it is. When shall I see, Lord, the fulfilment of Thy promises? When wilt Thou show Thyself as my God, my protector, and my defender? Oh, let me never be deceived in the hope I have placed in Thee! Yes, my Saviour and my God, I hope in Thee, I hope in Thy mercy, I hope in Thy love and Thy charity, I hope in Thy Divine providence, I hope in Thy strength and Thy support, I hope in Thy words, and in Thy promises, I hope because Thou hast bidden and commanded me to hope. Yes, I hope in Thee, and my hope shall not be confounded. Nevertheless, happen what may, I will never cease saying to Thee, ' Lord Jesus, Thy will, not mine, be done.' "

She had no sooner pronounced these words than she was filled with such abundance of grace, that she became, as it were, immovable and deprived of all sensation. Then Jesus addressed words of consolation to her, bidding her not to fear, but to rely upon Him in all things. "Your affairs," He said, "are Mine much more then they are yours. I can easily make them turn to My glory. For, if you are ignorant of the thoughts of men, I know them, and I penetrate to the depths of their hearts. Among men there are some who appreciate those things which I am operating in you; others are content with admiring; and some, again, disdain and despise them. Let men think as they will; you are what you are, and, in the day of light, that which I am working through you will appear in its reality.

Let them act according to their fancy; it is not you
who will have to render an account to Me of their
actions." Then He reiterated His command to her
always faithfully to report His words and her own
sentiments ; whether what He said was for or against
her, and whatever might be the judgment she might
naturally have formed of it, all was to be repeated
without exception. She was to conceal nothing; and,
with all her woman's weakness, she was to show herself
stronger and more courageous than men.

Marie was much consoled and strengthened; nevertheless, her position continued to be very trying to her.
She was like one dragged violently in two opposite
directions. On the one hand was the irresistible
attraction she experienced, and on the other were the
fears which the constant representations and observations made to her by those who were her spiritual
guides could not fail to inspire. In this perplexity she
again took to sounding her heart, and examining all
her sentiments in the presence of God, with simplicity
and sincerity. No, she could not be deceived as to the
force and reality of the attraction which was drawing
her to the Sacré Cœur. She felt that it had entire
possession of her soul, and that it was impossible for
her to struggle against it. However, to put an end to
all doubt, she had recourse again to the Saviour.
"Lord Jesus," she said, "is Thy will absolute, and
dost Thou really call me to become a religious at the
Sacré Cœur ?" The Saviour answered in words to
which she was desired to listen attentively. They
were designed for her pastor, and Marie was, of course,
bound to repeat them, at whatever cost to her humility.
The words contained a high commendation of this
favoured soul, together with an emphatic declaration

of the great work which He purposed to effect by her means, making her the spiritual mother and teacher of sinners, and the light of the ignorant, both in her own country and in distant lands. He ended by saying, " She is on the point of entering into the profound retreat which I destine for her. Permit her to depart, and you will do what is agreeable to Me."

This was not the only time that Marie was commissioned to repeat words of this character spoken of herself, and much more besides, which would have sounded like the wildest self-laudation in the ears of any one who could have suspected the truthfulness of the poor girl, or questioned the lowly estimation in which she held herself. Possibly M. Dupérier was sometimes a little staggered, and feared, at least, that an excited imagination had some share in the matter. This he might conceive to be possible without throwing any doubt on the reality of the supernatural state to which she was raised. At any rate, we have every reason to believe that of the two he was much the more difficult to satisfy. But then M. Darbins, as Marie's confessor and immediate director, enjoyed opportunities for acquiring a more perfect and intimate knowledge of her soul, which M. Dupérier did not possess. Still the opinion of this eminent ecclesiastic would naturally have great weight with him.

Soon after the communication we have just recorded, Jesus again spoke to Marie. He told her that He was the Increated Wisdom, and that His words were not casual words, thrown to the winds. He was going now to speak to her of what concerned her salvation and His own glory. "Tell your director," He said, "who is in a certain state of indecision respecting the reality and truth of your vocation, that I desire to reassure him, and you also, by imparting to you both My own immovable certainty. Now, I declare to him, and I declare also to you, that your vocation is truly such as you have announced to him. The time which I have fixed, with an absolute will, for the accomplishment of My designs regarding you is when you have entered on your twenty-fourth year. Up to that time My will is not absolute; I abandon it to the will of your director. But when you have reached your twenty-fourth year, My will shall then be absolute; and nothing ought, nor shall anything be able, to detain you. When I will with an absolute will, I speak as a master, and make Myself obeyed by all hearts." He explained also to Marie how His judgments and decisions often seemed to be abandoned to the will of men, so that, if they were regarded in a merely human way, He appeared liable to change; but this was not so. "These," He said, "are trials which God sends to His servants to test their faith and their fidelity. Obedience and submission to the judgments of God obtain judgments of mercy; the want of faith and of submission draws down judgments of justice. So that in God there is no change even where the execution of His expressed will is conditional on the will of man. In God there is 'no change nor shadow of alteration.' All," He added, "is foreseen by My Father; nothing is new to Him."

In retailing this communication to her director, Marie added no comment or solicitation of her own. So far from this, she said, "Act in what concerns me as you shall judge fitting. I am ready and disposed for all, with the grace of God and the help of your prayers. Above all, never fear distressing me or giving me pain in anything or on account of anything."

M. Darbins, as usual, consulted M. Dupérier, but he was at this time apparently still labouring under the impressions of which the parable of the King and the Olive-tree had been the origin, or which, at any rate, had furnished the occasion for his putting Marie to the test, in order thereby to satisfy his own misgivings, or, at least, to prove more thoroughly the genuineness of her revelations.   He would naturally, therefore, waive for the present the consideration of a vocation in the way of which he, moreover, believed that he saw too many hindrances.   A subsequent letter of Marie's, to which we have already referred, and in which she showed her knowledge of what was passing in his mind, probably had a powerful effect in clearing away his remaining doubts.   The two priests, accordingly, agreed that the time had come for reassuring her mind.   It was about a couple of months later, in the beginning of the year 1844, that we find M. Darbins requesting Marie to tell him her views concerning her vocation.   Thus authorised to speak out her full mind, she wrote with firmness and decision.   This had now become her duty, since the same spirit of obedience which had hitherto restrained her now bade her express herself without reserve.

"You desire," she says, "to know what I think about my vocation.   My vocation is to become a religious at the Sacré Cœur.   This vocation is not from myself; if it were so, it would be no vocation.   He who has held converse with me in the depth of His infinite wisdom, with all His ineffable gentleness, sweetness, and holiness, He it is who calls me to the Congregation instituted in honour of His Sacred Heart.   I am called, and it is towards this kind of life that I feel drawn.   I am not acquainted with it either in the

o

general or in detail; it suffices me to know that it is
the Congregation of the Sacred Heart of Jesus. I desire
to live therein as in my God and Saviour, and to be
united to Him ever more and more closely in all the fulness of love. This is my motive for desiring to be a
religious; and it is also the motive for which I am
called by the Saviour.

"It is, therefore, neither from vanity nor ambition,
nor from the hope of leading a pleasant, comfortable,
and easy life. No, Sir; God knows my sentiments;
they are free from all personal attachment. Trials
await me there as here. I shall suffer much; I know
this, for Jesus has told me so; but I fear neither
labours, nor humiliations, nor contradictions, nor
sufferings, nor trials of any kind, be they what they
may. I fear neither prisons, nor chains, nor death.
My ambition is martyrdom, and I shall not be disappointed, for I shall endure a true martyrdom. Let
me be praised or blamed, despised or esteemed, honoured
or insulted, all is alike indifferent to me; I desire to
render perpetual homage to God by living in the profoundest humiliation of soul, because I am nothing but
sin, and God is sovereign perfection. I would willingly strip myself of everything; I love poverty, and
should be content to beg my daily bread. If from the
depth of misery I were to be raised to the highest
worldly greatness, wealth, and glory, it would not affect
me; and again, if from this height of riches and honour
I were to be plunged into the extremest indigence, it
would not make me lose my calmness and tranquillity.
I desire only one thing—to love Jesus, to love Him
above all, to love Him always, to love Him without
ceasing. Jesus is everything to me, He is my support,
my strength, my vigour, my life; without Him all is
as nothing to me, I do not live, I abide in death.

Now, that I may attach myself more and more to Him, that I may be one with Him, I must follow the attraction which He has given me. He calls me, and I ought to fly to the retreat to which I am summoned by His will. I feel very strongly that I shall not be able to keep myself in peace situated as I am now, resisting the attraction which He sends me. The life I am living is not life, neither is it death, it is an agony more terrible than death.

"If such be my vocation, I think that I ought to follow it, and go whither God calls me. I ought to follow it, and that as soon as possible ; and this brings me to speak of my departure. What is there to delay it ? It must be either the necessity of testing me, or your desire to exercise my obedience, or the fear of my encountering dangers on the road or difficulties as to my admission at the Sacré Cœur. Now, Sir, have I not been sufficiently tested for more than two years? Have I not been subjected to the most searching and distressing trials ? No one is better able to judge of this than yourself ; and these trials must, doubtless, have clearly proved to you the solidity of my vocation. I have not a word to say against your desire to test my obedience ; it was only right and prudent in you to prove it. But in what have I disobeyed you since I have been under your direction ? As for obedience, I shall also have to pay it elsewhere. I do not desire to be a religious in order to do my own will, but to do that of Jesus, which will be manifested to me by my superiors. If it be urged that so long as I do the will of my director I cannot go wrong, I admit this to be true in the ordinary ways of life and in common things ; but in the extraordinary state in which I find myself, without any merit on my part, but solely from the will of Jesus—when I see things in the brightness

of the light which God imparts to me—when I clearly
discern that my conscience is interested in the matter—
I believe that it becomes my duty to follow this light.
Let it be proved to me that I deceive myself, that I
am in error, that this light is only darkness, I will
then submit; I am submissive now, and my obedience
will ever be discreet and reasonable.   But, Sir, if you
have recognised the intervention of God in my writings,
why should you not do so also as regards my vocation
and my departure?   Or rather, why should those who
guide you refuse to recognise it, and pertinaciously
continue to persuade you not to let me go?   You are
bound to use prudence in your dealings with those who
are under your direction, but they also are bound to
use a corresponding prudence in their relations with
their director.   When the case is only between you and
me I ought in everything to submit to you; but having
to deal both with Jesus and with you, does not prudence bid me attend both to your words and to His?"
This whole passage is very remarkable, particularly
when we consider by whom it was written.   It contains
strong expressions as regards the rights of the conscience,
and might serve to convince those who believe, or affect
to believe, that the influence of the priest and the
authority of confessors and directors tend to enslave
the free-will and the judgment, that such ideas are
utterly groundless.

Marie continues, "Ah, do not think, Sir, that this
opinion is the mere result of natural feeling, or that it
is dictated by self-love.   It is stronger than myself, it
is in me, and I know not how, or, rather, I do know: it
is in me by the power of the word of Jesus, who
operates all that He pleases.   I write these lines, as I
write all the rest, because you bid me do so; and I

write it as my mind, enlightened by Jesus, dictates it
to me. Now, to sum up all in one word : if God has
given me a vocation, it was not in order that it should
remain without effect. I can well understand that you
have fears for me, and that others have still greater
than you have, on account of my making this journey
at my age ; they dread the risks to which I may be
exposed. Ah, Sir, I can here assure you that, with
God's grace, I would die a thousand times rather than
ever be guilty of anything that was evil either in
words, acts, looks, or thoughts. Life is nothing to
me ; the state of grace is everything to me ; to this I
would sacrifice my life and all that I have dearest in
the world. Besides, I shall know how to mistrust
myself and to hope in God. He will be my support
and my defender. He watches over me ; who, then,
shall seek to injure me ?

"In fine, Sir, the difficulties in the way of my
admission ought not to detain me, or cause my
departure to be deferred ; they will always remain the
same. You know how Jesus has shown to me that He
will remove them all. I confide in His word, and I
desire to abandon myself to Him. You will not, I am
sure, oppose my departure, and you will pray that the
purposes of God with regard to me may be accomplished. God knows, Sir, the reliance I place in you,
the respect, the esteem, the veneration which I entertain for you. I have spoken to you in this letter with
confidence, and I have done so only because such was
your command. Let me place myself on my knees
before you to entreat your pardon ; if there has been
anything in my letters which might offend you, it will
have been truly against my intention. Allow me also
to beg you, for the love of God, to tell me if you

sanction my departure. Oh, how happy I should be if I had your assent joined to that of Jesus! Oh, speak, my father, and let your word be a word of blessing and of conformity with that of Jesus. In the meantime I submit myself in all to you, and renew the expression of my most respectful sentiments."

Long as it is, we have thought it well to give this letter at length. The reader could hardly otherwise have appreciated Marie Lataste's character or the strength of the grace that was urging her. It throws a light upon the excruciating pain of her position, and reveals to us what her obedience must have cost her. Her writings show how high was her estimation of the priestly character and of the sacred claims of the guides whom God has appointed to lead, to instruct, and to judge us; but, in thus placing His authority in their hands, He does not for a moment abdicate His right of speaking immediately to our souls, and, in speaking thus, of conveying at times a certainty transcending all reason. Usually, however, He bids those whom He thus enlightens with an extraordinary communication of His grace to abide nevertheless by the decision of the authority which He has set over them. Many saints have been severely tried in this way. Still, even in these cases, the authority of directors has its limits, as Jesus has more than once signified when they have ventured to lay on souls injunctions which He Himself disapproved.

The contest in Marie's mind between the expressed will of her Lord and the opposition of her director, whom, as we have seen, she knew to be acting from deference to another, rather than from his own free judgment, was becoming very critical. We are not called upon to imagine what her course would have been had she arrived at her twenty-fourth year without obtaining M. Darbins' permission; nor can we imagine that our Lord would have allowed her to be placed in so cruel a dilemma. She continued to submit so long as His will remained conditional; and she had evidently an assurance that when it became absolute, and even sooner, her director's will would coincide with that of our Lord. But she no longer wavered as to the genuineness of her own convictions, or doubted as to what might be their source. There was no attempt now, as heretofore, to place herself in that attitude of hesitation which was felt or assumed by her directors, or to remain in suspense as to whether duty called her to follow her vocation without delay, even as once she had thought herself 'bound to doubt, or, at least, to try to doubt, whether the voice which she internally heard was that of Jesus. The time was past, not because Marie had come to prefer her own judgment to that of her superiors, but because the Holy Ghost can make Himself unmistakably heard by the souls which on every title are peculiarly His own.

Marie, however, was to be spared the necessity of deciding between two apparently conflicting duties. God, after trying them to the utmost, is sure eventually to make the path sufficiently plain before those who have unreservedly committed themselves to His leadings. In Marie's case every difficulty was now to be speedily removed. We have reason to conclude that this letter had a powerful effect on M. Darbins' mind, if it did not lead him to an immediate decision. At any rate his consent was not long delayed, although two letters from which we are about to quote seem to have preceded the expression of his full acquiescence, which to all appearance was at last conceded in the commencement of the ensuing month of February.

# CHAPTER XVI.

## MARIE DEPARTS FOR PARIS WITH THE ACQUIESCENCE OF HER DIRECTORS.

MARIE's letter which was given in the last chapter seems to have elicited a final objection, or, at least, the representation of a difficulty from M. Darbins. We have already intimated that the Bishop of the diocese was not disposed to take any active part in furnishing Marie with a recommendation to facilitate her reception at the Sacré Cœur. What his reasons may have been we do not know. Perhaps, like her two directors, he saw great obstacles in the way, and would have been glad that this holy girl might be induced to content herself with entering some convent nearer at hand in his own diocese. Marie, writing to M. Darbins on the 22d of January, observes that he appeared to have understood that the execution of her project depended entirely on the patronage which the Bishop of Aire might be willing to accord her, but that this was not the case, and she proceeds to explain to him how she has understood, and still understands, the manner in which her vocation is to be accomplished.

"It is not he" (the Bishop), she says, "but you, M. le Curé, who are charged with my vocation; all that lies with him is to be its protector. With his powerful patronage, I know that my admission into the Sacré Cœur would encounter no difficulty. But his patronage is not the only means by which my entrance can be facilitated. Neither, indeed, is it an absolute necessity that the Bishop should interest himself in the matter, for he is not my director. Should he grant me his protection, he will do what will be pleasing to the Saviour Jesus; but he can refuse it me; he is perfectly free to do so. The realisation of my vocation does not depend on him; it depends on you. You are the spiritual father of my soul; it is you who will have to present or recommend me to the ladies of the Sacré Cœur; and on your recommendation I shall be received."

M. Darbins does not seem to have insisted any further on this point, but a letter of Marie's, dated the 28th of January, shows that he had not yet given his formal consent to her departure. This letter, as containing an account of the sentiments of her family, will interest the reader. M. Darbins had asked her to inform him how they stood affected in the matter of her vocation. After telling him that, two years before, she had communicated to her family the design she entertained of corresponding with the call she had received by becoming a religious at the Sacré Cœur, she continues, "You know, Sir, how happy I reckon myself for having been born of such good and kind parents as mine are, you know their affection for me, and how they are pleased, along with my sister Marguerite, to make me the special object of their love. Ah, Sir, I perceive well, and I have often perceived, that my departure will sadden my family just because they love me too dearly. But I can assure you that they will offer no opposition to the accomplishment of my vocation. I have heard my father, mother, and sister talking over the loss they were to suffer, and exclaim, 'God's will be done!' I have also heard them say, 'We might be the cause of Marie's unhappiness by opposing her departure; let her follow her vocation, since God calls her, and be happy.' These words penetrated my heart, and I thank God for inspiring my father, mother, and sister with such sentiments.

"For this year past, my father has often inquired when I proposed to carry out my intention. Perhaps you will think this strange. Oh, do not imagine that he is in a hurry to get rid of me. No, Sir; such are not his feelings. But, seeing me going on living at Mimbaste, he has feared that I might not correspond to my vocation, or that some word of his may have too much impressed me, and induced me to delay the entire consecration of myself to God. I have tranquillised him by telling him that I was awaiting your decision, and that I should go as soon as you gave me permission, after having sufficiently examined my vocation. My father loves me dearly, but he does not love me for himself; he loves me for God and for myself. He prefers the good pleasure of God and the happiness of his daughter to his own pleasure and his own happiness. I cannot better make you understand the love of my father for his children than by telling you that he cannot bear to be absent from his home for one whole day and night, because, he says, it would deprive him for too long a time of the pleasure of seeing Marguerite and Marie. How many parties of pleasure has he refused for that reason! His pleasure, his happiness, his satisfaction, his consolation here below, is to see his children and be with them. How he does love us! I could never explain how much. But his love is generous, disinterested; above all, it is Christian. He suffers from the thought of parting with me, because I am his child; but he makes an offering to God of his sorrow with full submission of heart.

"My mother is more demonstrative in her grief, but so she is in her resignation; it is she especially who often exclaims, when· by herself, ' My God, may Thy will be done !' My sister Marguerite loves me with the tenderest love; but I need not tell you this. You know what care she took of me when I was young, when I was wilful; you know how my sufferings pained her at the time that my soul was harassed with scruples; you know how she strives in every circumstance to please me, and how united her heart is to mine. Her love will not be less pure than that of my father and mother, and I know her well enough to affirm that she, too, will faithfully join in saying, ' My God, Thy will be done.' My family would wish to know the time of my going, in order that they may prepare the things which I am to take with me. They would insist on stripping themselves of all they have to provide me with a suitable portion, and I have much trouble in persuading them that I shall not require any. They have often said to me, ' Supposing we had nothing left, we should still have the protection of God; He would not forsake us.' Ah, how much many persons of my age who, like me, have received a call from God have to suffer from their relations, and how I bless God for the good dispositions of mine !

" As for me, I have been for a long time fixed in mind regarding my vocation. My resolution is taken ; and it is all the stronger because it is not founded on persuasion, but on the most perfect conviction that such is the will of God. No one knows better than I do myself what passes within me. Also every argument, every representation addressed to me, every trial to which I may be subjected, will be useless ; nothing will shake me, and people lose their time in putting me to the proof. The strongest trials will find my strength still greater, because it is not through caprice or from any human motive that I wish to be a religious of the Sacred Heart, but solely to follow the will of God. Yes, Sir, I am still prepared to suffer everything, so great is my conviction, and so great is the strength and vigour which it imparts to me; but, however immovable I may be in my resolution, I am not attached to it in such wise as not to know how to endure generously any delay you may please to impose. The Saviour Jesus has promised me that this delay shall not be prolonged beyond my four-and-twentieth year. I shall wait and persevere, not in my own strength, but by the strength and grace of the Saviour Jesus. I shall wait, but my expectation will be realised before that date. It will be realised even long before; I have this hope, nay, almost certainty, in my heart, being convinced that you will be unable to find any reasons for detaining me."

M. Darbins must have been struck with the decisive tone of this letter, so different from those which some time back she was accustomed to write on this subject, or, rather, with the altered state of mind which this change implied. Although the same respect, humility, and submission were evinced, she had evidently no doubts now, nor did she, as we have already pointed out, any longer subject her vocation to the judgment of her directors. The Saviour had bidden her wait until her twenty-fourth year, and she obeyed with resignation.

No one, we think, can help giving a passing tribute of admiration to the good family of Marie Lataste, who behaved with such touching generosity and truly Christian disengagement of heart under circumstances most trying to their natural feelings. Marie was clearly, we will not say the favourite daughter, for Marguerite, as their child, was equally beloved by her parents, but she was the treasure of the whole family; for, as she herself confesses, the affections of father, mother, and sister centered peculiarly in her. From the moment Marie had received this call to a religious life, foreseeing that one day she would have to inflict on the hearts of her parents a most poignant sorrow, she had habitually foreborne making any expressive demonstration of affection towards them. She had never been lavish of those caresses which, if they do not increase love, foster its tenderness, and had limited herself in this respect to what could not be omitted without suggesting coldness or indifference of heart. We will quote what she herself says on the subject. It is contained in a letter written, the previous year, in reply to some inquires of her director as to a certain sadness which he thought he remarked in her. Everything, we see, even to the very expression of the countenance, or to her general bearing, which might well be the harmless result of natural temperament, was made the subject of criticism and examination. Nevertheless Marie, with her usual humility, thanks M. Darbins for the untiring interest he manifests in the welfare of her soul, an interest which covered her with confusion, feeling herself, as she did, so great a sinner.

She proceeds to explain to him that she is not really sad or melancholy, but that she had always been of a grave and serious turn. In her childhood, she had, it is true, felt mortified and saddened at the thought that the absence of lively and engaging qualities, such as she remarked in others, made her unable to gain the world's esteem. Jesus, however, had taught her to despise the praise which natural advantages procure, and to prefer humility and simplicity to every brilliant endowment. Although as yet she had not attained to this humility or simplicity, nevertheless she desired to do so with all her heart; and, perhaps, as long as she should have to seek the acquirement of these virtues, she might have a pre-occupied air, which was not sadness though it might bear that appearance. She adds that her mother and sister had often been distressed at her not talking a little more, and the knowledge that they were thus distressed was painful to her. She adds that she knows not why, but when she was with her mother and sister she felt a great difficulty in expressing herself, and often lacked words. With strangers she had more facility and fluency, and when explaining the Catechism always found abundance to say, and was never embarrassed in the slightest degree.

There were other reasons besides, which, she suggests, might make her appear melancholy. Amongst these was her intense desire for growing union with God, and the feeling that she was out of her place; her Lord having given her a vocation which she was unable to realise. The secret of her inner life also, which she discovered to him alone, was another cause, perhaps, of her apparent reserve; she could not speak of that which formed her almost exclusive interior occupation. Moreover, her inward concentration did, she confessed, proceed at times from a sense of abandonment, weakness, languor, and her exposure to temptation from her spiritual enemies; but none of these trials, she could assure him, disturbed the peace and serenity of the superior region of her soul. "I repose," she says, "without disquietude in the will of God, my Heavenly Father."

It is thus that Marie exculpates herself from the charge of melancholy, which, wilfully indulged, is a moral fault, and, even where not so, is at best a great spiritual disadvantage to the soul naturally subject to its attacks, and still more to its habitual presence. "What you have remarked in me," she concludes, "is not, then, genuine sadness. Neither is there anything in it to create uneasiness in my mother or the rest of my family. They are not the least surprised at seeing me thus grave and reserved, so long as a smile comes to my lips when I speak or am spoken to. I have never accustomed any one to see in me that demonstrative joyousness observable in others. I limit myself to smiling quietly, without affectation or stiffness, and showing a cheerful face to all. I take care not to display too much affection to my parents, in order to avoid attaching their hearts too closely to me. I kiss my mother every day, that she may not doubt my love, but I do not make myself like a slave with her. This would hamper me greatly in the future, as it also would at present. Nevertheless, if she had not the company of my sister, I would devote all my attention to her; but you will remember what the Saviour Jesus said to me on this point."

Marie is, doubtless, here alluding to the instruction she had received with reference to her own vocation and that of her sisters, Quitterie and Marguerite, which she had reported to him in a letter written a very short time previous. The three sisters were to imitate in the character of their lives the three different lives which He had Himself led : His public life among men, whom He instructed and healed of their diseases ; His hidden life at Nazareth with His Mother and St. Joseph, to whom He was subject ; and His intimate life with His Heavenly Father. He had cast His eyes on Quitterie that she might follow His steps in His public life, succouring the bodily infirmities of men and often procuring spiritual aid also for the infirmities of their souls.

Marguerite was chosen to imitate Him in His hidden
life at Nazareth; she was to remain with her father
and mother, to watch over them, take care of them,
and obey them. But Marie He had selected to imitate
Him in His intimate life with His Father in Heaven.
His will was ever conjoined to that of His Father; He
never sought His own glory; He sacrificed Himself to
this will every moment of His life for the redemption
of men; He awaited in everything His Father's hour.
She, too, in imitation of Him, was to have no other will
but that of His Father. She was to sacrifice herself at
every instant, in order to expiate her own sins and
obtain mercy for others. She was to wait with submission for His hour, and He would glorify her in
Heaven. This life was the highest of the three, as we
have also seen Him tell her when speaking to her of
His three solitudes. It was of a character, however,
which implied, if need were, the forsaking of her earthly
parents and the severing of every human relationship;
hence the necessity of that reserve which she had practised in her intercourse with her family.

A letter of hers dated the 8th of February, 1844, and
written, therefore, eleven days after her reply concerning
the sentiments of her family, which we have quoted at
length, is the first in which we find proof that M.
Darbins had at last yielded his consent to her departure.
The letter in question regarded the disposal of the
papers which she had written. She had besought our
Lord to let her know His will in this matter. Jesus
replied that her director already knew that these instructions were intended, not simply for her own profit, but
for that of many. He desired, therefore, that he should
take great care of them; their publication at the proper
time was to be left to his discretion; but, as soon as

this was resolved upon, he was to apprise the Bishop of the diocese, to whom our Lord specially recommended the work whenever it should be undertaken. It was His will that it should have the approbation of her Bishop attached to it. If any one should ask her why she had written, and why the Lord had sanctioned her acting in this wise, she was to reply that His purposes were secret and unknown, and that He had desired to exercise her in obedience, self-abnegation, and humility. Her papers and letters were to be printed separately, and her name was to be affixed to them. Her director was also to furnish the necessary documents for writing her life, which was to be illustrated by reference to the writings and letters. After giving these directions our Lord had added, "My daughter, in speaking thus to you, I know that what I say will not wound your modesty, because My word is Light, and consequently it reveals to you that of yourself you are nothing, and that you have received all from Me; that what has been created has not made itself, but that all comes from the Creator; it shows you that your writings do not contain your own words, or your own knowledge, but Mine."

On the 21st of February we find her handing over her papers to her director. She reminds him that they are her own property, which she was free either to give or to retain. Such being the case, she constituted him, not only the guardian of them, but the possessor, to make such use of them as he should judge proper, as of a thing entirely belonging to him. These papers were her sole earthly property, and it was a pleasure to her to give him the only thing which she had at her disposal. "Oh, that I could, indeed, present you," she exclaims, "with something which might recompense

P

you for all your benefits to me! But if I cannot, God
will do so for me, and this consoles me."

All obstacles being now removed to the accomplishment of her vocation, whether arising from consideration
for the needs of her family or from regard to the opposition of her directors, Marie's heart was full of joy.
True, others might still apprehend dangers for her, such
as she might encounter on the journey or on her arrival
in the great city; or again they might anticipate
difficulties in the way of her reception at the Sacré
Cœur; but all these were as nothing in the holy girl's
estimation. "Our Divine Master," she writes, "will
take me under His protection, He will lead me, He will
guide me, and I shall behold the fulfilment of His
promises. I have this assurance in my heart, and my
heart will not be deceived; for He has spoken these
words to me:" "My daughter, fear not, I will not
forsake you; I promise you this, and I say it to you
in very truth."

Nothing, therefore, alarmed her; she knew she might
meet with humiliations, but these would only furnish
her with an opportunity of imitating her Lord and of
exercising the virtue of humility. "Oh, what joy and
content do I experience!" she exclaims. "How happy
my heart is! It has made all kinds of sacrifices, and
now only awaits the moment for making a true oblation
of itself. Yes, it is with joy that I shall take up the
Cross of the Saviour. It is with joy that I shall look
upon myself as an exile upon earth. It is with joy
that I shall raise my eyes to heaven, to gaze on my
true country there. The Cross shall become the portion of my inheritance, my riches, and my consolation.
I shall regard all the ties which bind me to earth as
broken by my separation from my family. I shall

remember no longer save in God that I have a father on earth, a mother, and two sisters, whom I have abandoned into the hands of Providence. I will lift up my eyes to the Lord, and will say within my soul, 'Behold my Father;' to Mary, and say, 'Behold my Mother;' I will look on creatures, and say, 'Behold my brethren and my sisters.'"

Nothing now delayed her journey except the necessary preparation of her clothes. On the 15th of April she was able to announce to M. Darbins that her departure was fixed for the 21st of the same month. Before leaving Mimbaste, she desired to thank him for his unwearied charity and kindness, which she does in the most grateful terms, and to entreat his pardon for all the trouble and anxiety which she may have caused him. She begs him also to convey the same to him who had conjointly directed her, not feeling herself worthy personally to address him. To both was she deeply indebted for their good and charitable counsels, and for the patience with which they had guided her. She ended by beseeching him to remember her daily as a poor sinner before God, and by bidding him adieu until they should meet in a blessed eternity. Not contented, however, with expressing these sentiments in her letter, she begged, before leaving, to see him once more as her confessor, and receive from him a last parting benediction.

The day for bidding her family farewell was now come. She was to walk to Dax, and thence proceed the next day by the public conveyance to Bordeaux. Her poor father had insisted on her taking with her the five hundred francs which he had laid by for her journey and expenses in Paris, and her mother, on her part, constrained her to accept the best linen she

possessed. All exerted themselves to the utmost, as
though they were forwarding an object of great personal satisfaction rather than one which involved so
heavy a loss. Such were the generosity and piety of
this simple and virtuous family.

According to the directions which Marie had received
from our Lord, few persons had been apprised of her
approaching departure. She was thus spared many
profitless comments and lamentations; and, indeed,
the family parting was sufficiently painful without any
additional distressing adieux.

Her mother's infirmity disabled her for accompanying
Marie any part of the road. She had, therefore, to
embrace her child for the last time under the roof
which had sheltered them during so many years.
François Lataste, Marguerite, and one who had been
an intimate friend of Marie's from her childhood, walked
with her some little distance on her way. But they
must separate at last. It was a trying moment. The
sobs of her old father which, with all his self-control,
he could not repress, and the sight of the tears on her
sister's face could not but excite the deepest emotion in
Marie's loving heart. She too wept; but no feebleness
was displayed on the part of any; no agony of grief
was indulged. The sorrow of both father and sister
was calm and gentle, and such as became a Christian
family which had found its support in a strong faith
and in perfect submission to the will of God.

Victoire, the young friend, went a little further.
Thus all the ties were not snapt at the same instant,
and the two companions had, doubtless, also special
communications to make at this final interview. We
may guess the nature of them, but all we know is that
this short time was not spent, as so many parting

moments are, in the expression of regrets on the one side and of friendly consolation on the other. It was no common leave-taking. Victoire had been selected alone of all Marie's friends to receive her last farewell; it was because she was like-minded with her holy companion, and because words of mutual encouragement were alone likely to be uttered on so solemn, we may almost say so sacred, an occasion.

When Victoire had left her, Marie felt, as she says, that she was alone in the world, without either relatives or friends. Henceforth she looked upon herself as a stranger here below, and threw herself with utter abandonment into the arms of a merciful God.

---

## CHAPTER XVII.

### Marie's Reception at the Sacré Cœur.

Few of Marie's letters remain from the date of her leaving Mimbaste, and, no doubt, she wrote but few. A different phase of life had begun for her when once she had entered the Sacré Cœur, and the gate of the golden cage, figured to her in the parabolic vision which had been the cause of so much reproach, had closed upon her. The world was henceforth shut out from her, and she was shut in from the world, in that place of refuge and retreat wherein her Spouse had designed to harbour and conceal her. And, truly, she was there concealed even from those around her. Her companions could not but see and be edified by her virtues, but her previous life, with all its wonderful revelations and the prodigies of grace of which she had been the recipient, were entirely unknown to them until after her death ; for to her superior alone did she ever confide the secret of her soul. From the world without she had altogether disappeared. To her former director at Mimbaste, who had no longer her spiritual charge, she wrote but few letters. They were but six in number, and were dictated by a feeling of gratitude, and by a desire to fulfil the promise she had given him. They include an account of her journey to Paris, her reception at the Convent of the Sacré Cœur, and her entrance into the noviciate at Conflans. The last, written from Conflans, is a letter conveying her good wishes for the new year. These, with two to M. Dupérier, one to Victoire, and two to members of her family, complete her biographical remains. For her convent life, during the short period it lasted, we are, therefore, almost entirely thrown on the reminiscences of her sisters and superiors in religion. Some of these—indeed, we might say all, considering the person to whom they relate—are of much interest.

Nothing in the least remarkable occurred on Marie's journey to the French capital, but her simple and pious comments impart a certain charm to her account of it, as given in her letters to M. Darbins, which otherwise it would not possess. When she reached Dax, she paid a farewell visit to M. Dupérier, and slept at the house of a friend. The next morning she went to the seven o'clock Mass, and at ten took her place in the *diligence*. A gentleman got in after Marie ; she did not look to see whether he was old or young, but read her book. He was similarly engaged for some time, and proved a very quiet and inoffensive companion. After a while there was a little conversation between them. He told her he was a Captain, and had seen thirty years of service. With her usual *naïveté* Marie says, " I perceived from what he said that he had not formed a bad opinion of me. I replied to his questions frankly, giving such answers as occurred to me." Until they reached Mont-de-Marsan, they continued to talk at intervals. " He must have had," she says, "more respect and esteem for me than I deserved, for he was very civil and full of attentions, and, when he alighted at Mont-de-Marsan, he wished me '*bon voyage*' with much politeness." Poor Marie wondered, doubtless, at receiving so much consideration, but there was something in her bearing, simple as it was, which, as we have already noticed, often constrained those who saw her, to treat her as one of a superior rank.

She was now the sole occupant of the vehicle, and she truly enjoyed her solitude. She sang Psalms with all her might, well persuaded that she was unheard, which in a rattling French *diligence* she probably was. However, her comfort was broken in upon, after two hours, by the entrance of a couple of passengers. This time she was not so fortunate. One of them was a young man whose appearance and manner impressed her very unfavourably. Nevertheless she felt no anxiety on the subject ; she confided in God, and read as long as the light permitted. Her two travelling companions remained silent. When darkness, however, set in, the young man availed himself of the obscurity to be jocose and attempt a little freedom, putting his hand upon her knee. She vigorously pushed it away, bidding him in a tone of grave displeasure to keep quiet. He never stirred again, and got down at the next stage. Another took his place who was " reserved and civil." " Do not think," she said, " that this journey produced any disturbance in my mind. I tell you in all sincerity, and to the glory of God, that I found myself among these passengers as if they had not been there. My heart enjoyed a profound peace, and I felt the grace of God inundating my soul. I owed these favours to the fervent prayers which have been addressed to God in my behalf." She did not reach Bordeaux until four o'clock in the morning, but the *conducteur* of the *diligence* had the kindness to take her to an hotel, where, as she writes, " I am at this moment, very quiet, in an excellent apartment."

She can have taken little rest on arrival, for we find her visiting the Cathedral at an early hour that same morning. A young girl showed her the way; and Marie, after remunerating, dismissed her, wishing to remain some time before the Blessed Sacrament. She heard several Masses, after which she set out on her return to the hotel, but found that she had forgotten the way. Poor Marie, it would seem, had not even noticed the name of the house at which she had passed the night, and the problem was how to find it. Happily, however, she recollected the names of some of the streets through which she had passed, for she says, " I asked for the Rue Maucret, but no one knew it ; the Rue du Chapelet, but they could not tell me where it was. Then I inquired for the Rue Sainte Catherine, and all did their best to point out the way to it. At last, by dint of searching, I got back to Madame Bardeux's Hôtel." She had found time, however, to look, meanwhile, into another church in the immediate neighbourhood.

She would willingly have postponed her departure until the 25th of the month, in order to enjoy the advantage of travelling in company with some nuns

who were on their way from Bayonne to Paris, but she
was told that she might reckon herself fortunate in
being able to secure a place in the *diligence* the next
morning, so that it would be wise not to run any risk.
Travellers were more numerous just then than were
available places. So she acquiesced. "God," she adds,
"has protected me as far as Bordeaux ; He will take
the same care of me to Paris." The postilion, whom
she had not omitted to fee, had promised to let her
know when the conveyance was about to start, and she
was in the *diligence* by ten o'clock. This was on the
23d, and her next letter, written from Paris on the
25th, reports her safe arrival on that same day, after a
long but uneventful journey. God had provided her
with as good a companion as the Religious would have
been. "I had the company," she says, "of a lady who
was on her way to Paris. I sat opposite to her, so that
we were able to converse during the journey. She
was very kind, and, indeed, played quite a mother's part
by me."

Marie, as soon as she reached Paris, went straight to
the Enfants Trouvés in the Rue d'Enfer. Her sister,
Quitterie, who, as already noticed, had been a Sister of
Charity for some fourteen years, was there, and had
been apprised only a few days previously of Marie's
projected journey, and of her object in making it.
This news had taken her completely by surprise. She
had left her youngest sister quite a child, and knew
nothing whatsoever of the prodigies of grace of which
her soul had since been the theatre. We have seen,
indeed, that the members of her own family, with whom
she had resided up to this day, knew as little of these
as did the absent sister ; while what the family did
know of Marie's long cherished desire to enter the

Congregation of the Sacred Heart, and of the proofs she had given of a true vocation, had certainly not formed the subject of any communication on their part. Probably, indeed, letters had been both scarce and scanty between Quitterie and those to whom she had bid a long adieu when she left her home to become a daughter of St. Vincent. It can be no matter of wonder, then, if, judging merely from reason and natural prudence, she should have considered the step which her sister was taking to be both hazardous and imprudent. To come off by herself to Paris without friends or recommendations in order to beg admission into a Community where she would indubitably meet with a refusal—who could do otherwise than disapprove such indiscretion? Since such had been pretty much the view which M. Dupérier and M. Darbins had taken for two years, notwithstanding all they knew of Marie's holiness and supernatural state, Quitterie, who knew nothing whatsoever about her, cannot be blamed for regarding the matter in a similar light, and even for being displeased with her sister. And displeased she certainly showed herself, good religious as she was—and Quitterie was an admirable religious—so that poor Marie, after all the trials she had undergone, had to encounter this far from agreeable reception, and, instead of being welcomed with joy, to meet with reproofs and reproaches. She listened to and accepted all with that imperturbable serenity with which we can readily credit her.

But it must not be inferred that Quitterie did not behave kindly to her sister. Far from it; Marie was most hospitably entertained at the Enfants Trouvés, and received every attention, not only from Quitterie, but from her sisters in religion. Indeed, if she had pleased, Marie could have remained with them permanently; for the Superioress said to her, " If you cannot be admitted at the Sacré Cœur, do not distress yourself, mademoiselle; St. Vincent de Paul will take you under his protection, and will contrive to find you a place in his family." Marie thanked her cordially, but told her that, much as she loved and venerated St. Vincent, and notwithstanding the additional attraction she might have found in the kindness she had received from his daughters, God willed that she should belong to the Congregation of the Sacred Heart; and she added, " I shall not be refused." Of this she was well persuaded; nor did she waver in her conviction, although the first step she took had no encouraging result.

She possessed one letter of recommendation; it was addressed by M. Dupérier and the Curé of Mimbaste to the Abbé Dupanloup, whose zeal and charitable labours had already begun to make his name well known throughout France. The two priests had united in begging him to interest himself in the reception of Marie Lataste at the Sacré Cœur. To all appearance they could not have done better; for, although neither of them was personally known to the future Bishop of Orleans, they felt sure that a heart so full of charity as he had proved himself to possess, would not be less ready on that account to further any good and kind work that might be brought under his notice. But he was not the instrument chosen by God for the accomplishment of His purposes regarding Marie Lataste. Circumstances which, in ordinary way of speaking, are called accidental, interfered to prevent her from gaining access to him. He was at that time Superior of the Little Seminary of St. Nicholas, and Marie, hearing that he admitted persons to audience twice a week, on Tuesdays and Saturdays, hastened to present in person the letter with which she had been provided. She made two attempts to see him, but without effect; for on both days, just as she hoped that her turn had come, the Abbé Dupanloup was called away on some pressing business, so that those who were waiting to speak to him had to be dismissed. .

The porter, observing Marie's disappointment on the second occasion, asked her whether she would like to see the Director of the Seminary. Concluding, as she says, that he also must be a great person, and wearied with waiting for M. Dupanloup, she replied in the affirmative. The interview was not at all encouraging. The Director looked surprised at what she told him, and even a good deal embarrassed, but all he replied was, that M. l'Abbé Dupanloup had a great deal of business on his hands, and would not be able to give any attention to her affair. She had better go and speak to the Ladies of the Sacré Cœur, although he doubted very much their consenting to receive her. Marie answered that, such being the case, she did not wish to add to the occupations either of the Abbé Dupanloup or of himself, and that she relied on Divine Providence to take care of her. They parted very civilly, and Marie went her way.

Far from being disheartened by these unsuccessful attempts, our persevering applicant proceeded straight to the Convent of the Sacré Cœur, according to the advice which the Director of the Seminary had given her, thinking very little of the doubt he had expressed. She asked to see the Superioress, the Mère Eugenie de Grammont, but was informed that she was ill. Her assistant, the Mère du Boisbaudry, however, received her, and Marie spoke to her with great confidence and openness, giving a short account of her life, and explaining how she was situated.   Mme. du Boisbaudry inquired her age, asked how long it was since she had known her vocation, and whether she had good health. She then remarked that it was scarcely to be expected that at her age she would be able to fit herself for educating others, since she would first have to be educated herself; she, therefore, suggested that it might be better for her to enter some other Congregation. There was, as we have already observed, so much simple dignity in the manners of this illiterate peasant girl, that even those who were made aware of her humble condition were disposed to treat her as if appertaining to a higher class.   This was perhaps the reason why the Mère du Boisbaudry does not seem to have thought of proposing to her the inferior situation of Sister Coadjutrix.*

"Ah, madame," rejoined Marie Lataste, "I would prefer to be a lay sister, or servant, in your house, to being a nun in any other convent."   Mme. du Boisbaudry then told her that all were alike Religious at the Sacré Cœur, but that those who had education were employed in instructing youth, while the others were occupied in the domestic work of the house.   Observing that the petitioner had made up her mind to enter the Sacré Cœur, she went on to say that she could not at once give a decisive answer, but that Marie might write to her director and beg him to send in writing his opinion of her, for that this was an indispensable step to her admission, and she must, besides, address herself to one of the Fathers of the Company of Jesus, that he

---

* The Sœurs Coadjutrices, or Assistant Sisters, bear the usual appellation of Lay Sisters in the convents of the Congregation Order in this country.

might examine her vocation. She mentioned several, but specified in particular the Père Cagnard, who was Confessor Extraordinary to their Congregation.

Marie was much touched by this lady's kindness; and, indeed, the Mère du Boisbaudry was so kind and gentle with her, that she left the Convent quite contented and even joyful. " I hope," she writes to M. Darbins, " that all is going on well, and will turn to the glory of God and the welfare of my soul." She then requests him not to delay sending the required information, and meanwhile not to be uneasy on her account, for, while awaiting her reception at the Sacré Cœur, she finds plenty of occupation at the *Crèche*, of which her sister had the charge. On her return to the Enfants Trouvés, after her interview with the Mère du Boisbaudry, full of hopes as she was, and well satisfied with her prospects, she had not met with approval from Quitterie, who would have had her go back and try once more to see the Abbé Dupanloup. Marie, as usual, said nothing to justify her own opinion or to excuse herself, but she lost none of her confidence in the mercy of God.

The next morning she went to see Père Cagnard, Quitterie accompanying her, although she had not approved of the step which her sister was taking. Marie had written to the Father to prepare him for her visit, and she gives the substance of her letter in one addressed to M. Darbins. It was simple, humble, frank, and to the point. Père Cagnard had received it only a very little while before the writer made her appearance, but, being a man of great experience and spiritual discernment, he felt at once that the case about to be submitted to him was of an extraordinary character. He was raising his heart to God to obtain the necessary light, when Marie arrived. A short interview served

to confirm his first impression. She answered his
questions with a combination of simplicity and deep
conviction, which assured him that he was conversing
with a highly privileged and favoured soul, in whom all
had been marvellous, from her conversion at the time of
her first communion down to the present hour. He
therefore did not hesitate to give her a letter to the Mère
du Boisbaudry, in which he acquainted her with the
favourable opinion he had formed of the young person
who had come to consult him.

In a subsequent interview with Marie, he questioned
her still more particularly, and everything which he
heard only served to increase his admiration and his
interest about her. It was probably during this interview that Marie communicated to him the words which
she had heard our Lord address to himself, to the Archbishop of Paris, and to the Superioress of the Sacré
Cœur. Père Cagnard requested her to put them down
in writing, and he afterwards showed the paper to Mme.
de Barat, the Superioress, who was as much struck by
them as he had himself been. It was while Marie was
engaged in praying that all the obstacles standing in
the way of her admission might be removed, that this
manifestation was vouchsafed to her, no doubt for her
encouragement and consolation. We will content ourselves with quoting the remarkable menace addressed
by our Lord to the city of Paris, when commending
Marie to the Archbishop's protection amidst the dangers which, alone and unprotected, she might encounter
in that sink of iniquity. "O Paris," He said, "exe-
crable city, for a long time thou hast merited My
indignation, and, if I have not poured upon thee the
floods of My anger, it is an effect of My mercy. I
have held back My avenging arm, ready to fall heavily

upon thee, I have spared the countless multitude of sinners, in order not to strike the just. Thy inhabitants will one day curse thee, because thou wilt have saturated them with thy pestiferous air, and those whom thou hast harboured will hurl maledictions at thee, because they will have found death in thy bosom."* These words are rendered the more remarkable when it is considered that the person to whom they were addressed was to die a martyr to his charity in one of those revolutionary outbreaks of which Paris has been so often the scene in these latter days, and that the occasion did not appear in itself to call for so solemn a threat ; which, however, modern prophecy continues still to echo.

Provided with Père Cagnard's letter, Marie and her sister Quitterie went the next day to the Sacré Cœur, where they met with a most cordial reception from the Mère du Boisbaudry, who agreed to communicate the Father's letter to Mme. de Grammont, who, as we have said, was the Superioress of the Paris house, Mme. de Barat being the Superioress-General. She promised also to let Marie have an answer the next day. On the morrow, accordingly, she had a letter summoning her to the Sacré Cœur. She was intro-

* This passage has been omitted in the latest editions of Marie Lataste's Life and Works. If the omission be not accidental, it may be owing to the fact that no application was ever made, or required to be made, for the favour and protection of the Archbishop. But we do not see that such application was necessarily implied in our Lord's revelation, any more than by the words which Marie, in vision, heard Him address to her family He meant to declare that they were ever to be really uttered. Might not these words (as we have already suggested) have been simply designed to console her by intimating the sentiments which He would breathe into their hearts ; while by His address to the Archbishop He might intend to assure her that the highest protection, if needed, should not fail her? The hearts of all are in His hands, and He sways them to His purposes.

duced this time into a more private room, where
Mme. du Boisbaudry had an intimate conversation with
her. Marie, whose lips were always sealed concerning
her spiritual experiences in the case of nearest relatives,
dearest friends, and the world in general, was, on the
other hand, very frank and open with such as stood in
the position of her spiritual superiors, and on the
present occasion she responded fully to the questions
addressed to her respecting her past life. She was
dismissed with a favourable answer. "Return to Père
Cagnard," said Mme. du Boisbaudry, "and tell him
that Mme. de Grammont, the Superioress, desires to
receive you." Père Cagnard, when this message was
delivered to him, rejoined that such also was his desire.
"I was sent," writes Marie, "for a final interview with
Père Cagnard, in order that he might again examine
me, and to beg him to aid me with all the credit he possessed at Conflans." The Father asked, in conclusion,
whether she had anything to add; to which she replied
that she had not, save that she would be very submissive and very obedient, and that, since he was
pleased to interest himself in her behalf, she would
take care to give him no cause to regret having done so.
Père Cagnard willingly undertook the office. He went
to Conflans, and laid the whole matter before the
Superioress, who took the same view as he had himself
taken, recognising the finger of God in all that the
Father communicated to her respecting the Divine
dealings with this favoured soul. Both were fully confirmed in their opinion by the Curé of Mimbaste's
letter, which, according to Marie's request, was sent to
her without delay.

On the 10th of May, Marie went to the house of the
Jesuits to hear what reply had been received from the

Q

Superioress, and, to her inexpressible joy, learned that
the Mère de Barat had consented to receive her into the
Congregation of the Sacré Cœur. As Marie already
knew that the Mère de Grammont did not see any
obstacle to her reception, she now considered that her
entrance into the Sacré Cœur was secured to her.
" Bless Divine Providence, sir, which has so sensibly
protected me ; " it is thus she writes to the Curé of
Mimbaste. "I had thrown myself into Its arms with
the confidence of a child, and It has manifested to me
the goodness and tenderness of a mother; It has led
me by the hand, and I may say that It alone has done
all, by enlightening the minds of some, and inclining
the hearts of others in my favour. Pray for me, that
I may cleave to the will of God, and that He may grant
me the grace of fulfilling it in the most perfect manner
possible."

We need scarcely tell the reader, who by this time
is well acquainted with Marie's habits and tastes, that
during her fortnight's stay at the Enfants Trouvés she
made small acquaintance with Paris, where all must
have been so new and striking to a country girl. In
fact she saw nothing of it, and, as she writes to her
former director, had nothing to tell about it. " Paris,"
she says, " was to me just as Mimbaste. However, I
visited the Church of Notre Dame des Victoires, and
the church in which the relics of St. Vincent de Paul
repose. I also assisted once at Holy Mass in the chapel
of the Ladies of the Visitation, which is close to their
house." It was no feeling of curiosity, we well know,
which attracted the steps of Marie Lataste to those holy
places. She looked on the visible world, as it were,
with closed eyes. Neither Bordeaux nor Paris had
power to draw her for one moment from the solitude of

heart to which her Lord had called her, and she was
now, by her entrance into the retreat which Jesus had
provided to shelter and hide her during the remainder
of her short sojourn on earth, to plunge still more profoundly into its sanctifying depths. The world had
truly become to her the desert where the Lord had
spoken to her heart; but the house of His own Sacred
Heart was to be to her henceforth the hole in the clefts
of the rock where His dove was to abide, according to
the promise which He had made her, and which has
been already recorded.

On the 15th of May, 1844, which in that year was
the vigil of the Ascension, Marie bade her grateful
adieux to the Community of St Vincent de Paul,
where during her short stay she had given nothing but
edification by her virtues, her modesty, and continual
recollection; and, in particular, her whole air, penetrated, as it were, with the sense of the presence of
God, when kneeling before the Blessed Sacrament,
whither, when she had a few minutes' leisure, she
was always attracted, remained ineffaceably impressed
on their memory. Accompanied by Quitterie, she took
her way to the Rue de Varennes, where her sister, after
consigning her into the hands of the family which had
adopted her, bade her what must have been a last
farewell on earth, but not a sad one—of that we
may be sure. Were they not both travelling the same
road ?

# CHAPTER XVIII.

## RECOLLECTIONS OF MARIE AS A POSTULANT DURING HER STAY IN PARIS.

THE olive-tree was at last transplanted into the new garden and enclosed in the golden cage. Moreover, the veil, foretold in the parable, was thrown over it. The King desired to have His chosen plant all to Himself; it was not to be too closely viewed. Hence, in the mysterious designs of His providence, He has not permitted many details of the three years which Marie spent in the Sacré Cœur to be preserved. Not so many as we certainly should have wished, for no record of them was kept; those which have survived have been gleaned from the reminiscences of two of her superiors, and of the Assistant Sisters, who were brought into more immediate relation with her. We have no longer Marie's own letters, in which she furnished an unconscious portrait of her soul. Three or four short ones are all that remain to us, nearly all probably that she ever wrote; and from one of them we gather that our Lord henceforward led her by a new way, new to her, because more common and simple.

But what a change! Looking at all from a merely natural point of view, and from what our human feelings would suggest, we cannot but feel that it involved a trial. After the exceptional privileges which she had enjoyed, and the magnificent promises which had been made to her by the Saviour's own lips—after seeing herself surrounded by esteem, respect, and even veneration—after exercising an influence, not bounded by her own homely circle, but extending to men of position, erudition, and even sacerdotal dignity—after thus living, as we may say, amidst supernatural splendours and natural honours—to find herself hidden away and buried in a sort of total oblivion; to have to bestow all her time, all her strength, and expend all the zeal which consumed her heart, upon the lowest and meanest employments; to have to live in a state of still more profound self-annihilation as respected her intellect, putting by all the sublime lights and heavenly science which she had received as a scholar of the Divine Master Himself; to be, in short, like every mere ordinary novice, who has to learn, to submit, and to obey—did this involve no trial? If it did not, then, indeed, it must be confessed that Marie had arrived at a very exalted degree of perfection. But, even granting that it were so—and this is only to grant what we have ample reason to believe—we must remember that nature is not destroyed by grace, although ruled and controlled by it; it still continues to prefer in its inferior region what is conformable to it. Who, for instance, could say that Marie must not, so far as nature was concerned, have felt the eclipse of the supernatural light which had formerly filled her whole being, as it were, with indescribable gladness?* True, all regrets, all desires, all natural inclinations were by her always plunged into the absorbing ocean of the Divine Will, which she was ever adoring; nevertheless, we know that such an act may be perfect and yet, unless

* Although it seems to be true, speaking generally, that there was a cessation of her former visions and revelations, yet several circumstances combine to show that allowance must be made for exceptional occasions, as will appear in the course of the narrative. We have, however, her own authority for asserting that the way by which she was henceforth led was new.

God be pleased to order it otherwise, may be accompanied with suffering of a most excruciating kind. The Prayer in the Garden is sufficient to teach us this. Therefore it is that we say that for nature such a life as Marie was now called to lead was, under one point of view, a long and obscure martyrdom; and that all who reflect on her antecedent existence cannot but feel how much energy of purpose and heroic virtue was needed to enable her to enter heartily and persevere unrelaxingly in this way of self-renunciation and abnegation.

But all this is perfectly compatible with the joy beyond expression with which she entered the haven where she would be, and, what was more, where she knew that Jesus would have her to be; not merely a joy attendant on the fulfilment of her long-cherished desires, but an abiding joy, which never left her. Trials she knew she was to have, she had often said so; she was never to be without them; but these were to be the instruments of her entire conformation to the Divine Will, her complete purification from every spot of imperfection; and even as the holy souls in Purgatory endure willingly and patiently those pains which are fitting them for union with their Only Good, and would not withdraw themselves, if they could, one moment before the process is accomplished, so it was with Marie. There was but one thing which she had felt most acutely, the thwarting of her vocation, although even to this trial we have seen her humbly submitting; she had felt it most acutely on account of that filial fear which was always a remarkable feature in her character. She feared losing the friendship of her Saviour in the midst of a world which the devil has sown with traps and pit-falls, as St. Anthony the Hermit once beheld

it in vision ; and so she had longed for the golden cage
and its veil, she had longed to find herself the companion for the rest of her days of those whose only
wish and occupation it was to adore the Heart of Jesus,
that Heart so loving and so little loved.

As we have so few letters of hers now to refer to,
and these very brief, we must seek the interpretation of
her most intimate sentiments chiefly in her outward
conduct and in the effect which it produced on others.
From the very first, Marie's object appeared to be to
efface herself : no other term would sufficiently express
our meaning.  She looked upon herself, and wished
others to look upon her, as the least among the members of the family devoted to the Sacred Heart which
had admitted her to their fellowship.  As yet, of
course, she was but a postulant, and was given in
·charge on her arrival to a young novice, a Sister
Coadjutrix, whose name was Adèle Sisteau.  Her
testimony as to the impression produced upon her by
the new-comer has been preserved in a letter of hers.
Sœur Sisteau was a novice of six months' standing
when Marie Lataste entered the Sacré Cœur.  Marie
was dressed, when she arrived, in what we may suppose
was her best gown, provided by the care of her mother,
who, it will be remembered, was determined that her
daughter should make a good appearance.  This gown
was of silk, with what Sœur Sisteau calls "*volants.*"
Everything connected with dress finds a name at once
in France, but, as fashions change very rapidly, our
readers will excuse us if we cannot accurately describe
these appendages, which so much impressed Sœur
Sisteau and led her to think that Marie was a lady and
intended for a choir nun.  What, then, was her surprise
when, at recreation time, she saw her take her place

among the sisters who belonged to the second class!
But still greater was her astonishment when the Mère
du Boisbaudry said to her, "My sister, as you are now
becoming an old novice, you will to-morrow morning
take our sister Lataste with you to help to sweep out
the class-rooms; you will show her how to do it,
keeping silence."

This word "silence" was not lost on Marie, whose
whole mind was intent on learning the rule, down to
its least minutiæ. Indeed, in this respect of devotion
to the smallest items of the rule, she reminds us often
of St. Aloysius Gonzaga, and of his punctual imitator,
the Blessed John Berchmans. On the morrow Sœur
Sisteau had to give the required instructions to her
assistant. This cost her an effort; and, what with the
recollection of the silk dress, with its trimmings, and
the air of simple dignity which pervaded Marie's every
movement, whether attired in silk or stuff, the young
novice, it is evident, would gladly have exchanged
places with her at that moment. "She appeared to
me," she writes, "so very superior to myself in
position." However, she was soon set at her ease by
the genuine humility and modesty of her companion,
who would not touch a bench or a chair without
direction. She inquired whether she was to do this
or that, and moved the furniture with the greatest care
in order not to make a noise; whatever question she
asked, it was always in a low voice and with a corresponding lowliness of manner; and this behaviour,
Sœur Sisteau tells us, was not limited to the first day,
but continued as long as they were associated together.
" I was only in company with her," she says, " when
we were sweeping the class-rooms; during the rest of
the day I would watch my opportunity to see her pass

along, for my own edification." At recreation, also, she used to try and sit near her in order to catch some edifying remark from her lips, but Marie never addressed her, the rule on these occasions being that the conversation should be general, not private between next neighbours; so that Sœur Sisteau, not thinking it well to question her, failed of extracting any word proportioned to the idea which she had formed of her.

Immediately after her arrival the first communion of the pupils took place; and in the afternoon there was a procession to the chapel of the Children of Mary, which was in the garden. Marie Lataste was placed in the line on the right, while Sœur Sisteau was in the corresponding situation on the left, so that she had the opportunity of observing her. She looked repeatedly, and always saw Marie with her eyes cast down. It caused a little surprise to the young novice that she was never able to catch the new-comer in the act of bestowing a single glance on the garden, alleys, or green lawn, through which the procession wound, and which she had as yet scarcely seen. But Marie's world was within.

Arrived at the chapel, every one proceeded to station herself so as conveniently to hear the sermon which was to precede the act of consecration to the Blessed Virgin. Sœur Sisteau drew near to Marie to advise her to secure a good place, but she, casting a rapid look on the chapel, perceived that it was too small to contain them all, so, thanking the Sister respectfully, she gave her to understand that she was very well where she was; and there she knelt down on one side of the walk, under the trees facing the chapel, where she remained in a state of deep recollection, not seeking either to see or to hear anything.

These may seem trifles, but trifles often reveal the character more surely than do greater things. Anyhow, Marie Lataste's behaviour on this occasion gave much edification, not to Sœur Sisteau alone, who was naturally led to observe her, but to others also. "I saw her," said one of the Religious, "immovable, with her face all radiant, her eyes calmly fixed in the direction of the chapel; she seemed as one ravished in God." This Religious was so deeply affected at the sight, that she declared that long afterwards, if she passed that tree, which recalled what she had witnessed there, she experienced an indefinable emotion. Another Sister who remarked her spoke in a similar manner; but they did not know what we have since learned from a Jesuit Father, and also from one of her superiors who had the direction of her, that Jesus deigned on that occasion to manifest Himself to His faithful disciple, filling her with light and with the consolations of His love. The Jesuit Father who revealed this circumstance after the holy girl's death happening to be at Conflans at a time when Marie was suffering from interior trials, she was recommended to consult him. The Father having asked her whether our Lord had appeared to her since she had entered the Congregation of the Sacred Heart, she mentioned that particular occasion to him. This priest was struck by the perfect simplicity with which she manifested the state of her soul and replied to his questions; it might have been supposed that she was speaking of some other person, and it was evident that all she sought was to be enlightened by one who was the minister of Jesus Christ.

But it was not only when engaged in some act of devotion that Marie's appearance and demeanour attracted notice. On the very day of her reception in the Rue de

Varennes, when the Mother Superior, accompanied by
her assistant and the mistress of novices at Conflans,
who happened just then to be at the Paris house, was
going with her to the chapel, one of the Sisters who
saw her pass was struck with the air of purity and recollection in the countenance of this young woman, as
yet unknown to her, which riveted her attention. She
afterwards said that she had never seen any one who so
strongly reminded her of portraits of our Blessed Lady.
A few days subsequently, the Mère du Boisbaudry took
Marie to help this same Sister at some needlework
which had to be finished without delay. The Sister,'
who for some reason of convenience was stationed at
the end of a narrow passage, endeavoured to make room
for her new companion. Marie, however, would not
allow her to put herself out of the way, but, taking a
chair, placed it in the corner of the landing on a neighbouring staircase. Here she remained employed on
the work allotted to her for several hours, but it was
observed that during the whole time she never once
raised her eyes. It was sufficient, however, to look at
her to perceive that the occupation on which her hands
were so assiduously engaged was not the object which
engrossed her thoughts.

That there was something very striking in Marie
Lataste's appearance and manners will have abundantly
appeared from much that we have hitherto said.
Besides the edification which is the usual attendant on
the words and behaviour of holy persons, she created a
certain impression of being superior to her class in life,
which, considering her antecedents, is not a little remarkable. For what were those antecedents? She had
kept cattle and sheep on the wild pastures round her
native village; that village being a scattered hamlet in

one of the most secluded districts of France. Of education she had received a very moderate proportion. It was merely such as sufficed to enable her to fill her very humble sphere, and the everyday toil which was her lot precluded her from giving much time to what is called improvement of mind. Improvement of mind, however, is, as we know, the main source of refinement of bearing; for although the conventional manners of what goes by the name of good society may be acquired by imitation, genuine politeness has its root in the true education of mind and heart, and is fostered by association with those who have themselves received the same mental culture. The absence of such culture has for its usual result, in a greater or less degree, a certain deficiency in outward grace.

Whether Marie was endowed with much or any personal beauty we are not told; we may presume, therefore, that she did not rise above the average in point of good looks; but we frequently hear of the simple, unassuming dignity of her appearance, and of the deference which this innate nobility won for her from all classes. Who was her instructor? Her natural disposition had been in childhood proud and discontented. Conscious of her ignorance and worldly disadvantages, she had been habitually sullen and reserved; and the continued indulgence of such a temper is sure to find its reflection in an unattractive exterior. Who was it that set before her, and taught her to copy, a model precisely the reverse of all this? The reader already knows. It was Jesus Himself. Marie repeatedly described herself as an ignorant girl, who knew only how to read, write, and use her needle. All that she knew beyond this the Saviour Jesus had taught her. He had even, it will be remembered, deigned to instruct her how to regulate her external bearing; not merely her tongue, but her very gestures, and the expression of her countenance. He had taught it, however, not as a worldly instructor teaches, who aims simply at giving to his pupil a pleasing deportment. He had taught her to cultivate the virtues from which perfect modesty of exterior springs, while at the same time He instructed her in that exterior modesty itself, because, besides the edification it produces, it reacts, as we all know, on the interior, when practised with a simple and virtuous intention. Hence we may with confidence refer even the superior manners which distinguished Marie Lataste to the training she had received in the highest of schools. We may say, indeed, that she was the very workmanship of Jesus, evidencing what He can and will do with us if we place ourselves in His hands like the clay in that of the potter.

From the moment she entered the convent Marie's whole attention, as we have noticed, was given to learning the rules, but this without either stiffness or over-eagerness. The rule has always been an object of much devotion to saintly souls, because they have regarded it, not only as the means of practising obed-ience and the renunciation of all self-will and private choice, but as the mould in which is to be formed the special perfection which God expects from them, inas-. much as it embodies and reflects the spirit of the institute to which He has called them. With Marie, therefore, this study of the rule was an exercise of piety, performed with a calm recollection, which, to those who had the opportunities of observing her most closely, gave her the appearance of one who had already been many months in religion. The ease with which, when the rule did not enjoin silence, she would converse with

those who addressed her, and the absence of that constraint which almost inevitably attaches to beginners,
but which perhaps results in no small degree from a
consciousness of being observed, helped to create this
impression ; for Marie, in fact, walked purely in the
presence of God, and if the eye of her superiors were
remembered, it was only because they represented Him
and were invested with His authority.  Whoever works
simply for God is sure to work without embarrassment
or after-thought, and to enjoy a tranquillity which
comes, not from self-reliance, and a sense of security
against failure, but from the consciousness of acting
under the eye of an all-seeing and infinitely loving
Father.

As allusion has been made once or twice to Marie
Lataste's *trousseau,* which her good mother had been
so anxious to provide of the best quality, and which
appears even to have been unnecessarily good, we may
point out a slight circumstance which, we think, tends
to illustrate that complete freedom from every secondary
view which continually attracts our attention in what
is recorded of this holy girl.  Left to her own choice,
she would, we may be sure, have presented herself, on
entering the doors of the Sacré Cœur as plainly dressed
as might be : this would have been most consonant to
her own feelings, her love of poverty, and her humility.
But her mother had given her a handsome silk gown,
and expected her, possibly had asked her, to wear it on
this occasion.  Marie accordingly put it on without
comment, and appeared thus attired, as we have seen.
But, having performed this piece of filial complaisance,
she handed over her clothes to the Superior of the house,
and, after quietly answering every question connected
with the different articles which the Sister in charge of

the wardrobe thought good to put to her, replied, when she was asked what her wishes were in regard to them, " Do with them what you please." She had worn them, and now gave them away, with the same simplicity and disengagement both of heart and manner.

Marie remained only about three weeks in the Rue de Varennes. She was then removed to Conflans, at which place was the principal noviciate of the Congregation.

———◆———

# CHAPTER XIX.

## MARIE AT CONFLANS.

ALTHOUGH Marie had made so short a stay in the Rue de Varennes, nevertheless she left a profound impression of her high sanctity on the Community. Nuns may be allowed to be good judges in this matter. They are not easily deceived by counterfeits; and by counterfeits we do not mean hypocrisy or conscious assumption of piety to which the interior in no way corresponds. They have been themselves subjected to a spiritual training of so searching a nature, that their perceptions of any want of reality must needs be very delicate. To be called " quite a saint" by admiring friends in the world is a tribute cheaply won, though seldom deserved, but for Religious to esteem a person to be, if not a saint, at least journeying fast on the road of perfection, is a weighty testimony in her favour. They know the real thing when they see it, and are not deceived by superficiality. They judge less severely than seculars the sins and infirmities which they discern, for, indeed, their hearts are too full of humility and love to judge any one; but they see with incomparably more clearness, and if, when not required by the charge they hold, they are willingly blind to faults, to goodness they are never blind. To discern what is good is, in fact, a much higher gift than to perceive what is evil.

Marie Lataste's character, then, was patent at once to the inmates of the Paris house. Her least and simplest words seemed to carry with them an influence of grace. We have mentioned, at the close of the last chapter, how she replied to the Sister in charge of the wardrobe. There was not much in the words she used, neither did the giving up the ownership of her clothes imply much sacrifice, situated as she was; nevertheless there was such a heartfelt tone of detachment in her manner of saying them, that the Sister was deeply impressed. From that moment, and for so long as she had the opportunity, she took the new postulant as her model, and watched her constantly with that view, and especially as regarded her fidelity in observing the rule, which, as we have said, was as remarkable as it must be rare in one to whom it is quite new; for Marie's exactness would have been worthy of notice and commendation even in one who had long practised it. The other point in her behaviour which excited universal admiration in the Community was her extraordinary absorption when in prayer before the Blessed Sacrament, her whole countenance and attitude at such times being suggestive of one to whom the Majesty of God is revealing Itself. If we add to this the sweetness, gentleness, lowliness which breathed in every word and action of this holy girl, we shall not wonder that the fragrance of her virtues long hung about the house which had been blessed by her presence for these twenty days.

On arriving at Conflans, Marie was confided to the Mère Mathilde Garabis, the Assistant General. This is how that religious later reported her first impressions of the new postulant:—" Her air of candour, peace, and modesty struck me at once. Nevertheless, her countenance bore the traces of interior sufferings courageously endured ; one might have supposed her to be thirty years of age, and she was but twenty-two. There was truly in her whole person and manners something which appeared superior to her condition." Mme. Garabis had the charge of the Assistant Sisters, and was in the habit of speaking privately to each of them every week. Marie Lataste opened her heart to her with the fullest confidence. The Mère Garabis heard her with secret admiration of the wonderful dealings of God with souls, but at the same time she felt fearful at having to direct one who had been led by such extraordinary ways, in which illusion is so apt to mingle with reality. Accordingly, she consulted the Reverend Mother General on the subject ; who wished her to continue her office of direction, giving her, however, a few counsels to aid her in discharging it.

The Mère Garabis, notwithstanding her cautious dread of illusion, saw nothing in Marie to raise any suspicion of this kind. All that she told her of the communications which our Lord had vouchsafed to make to her bore the impress of the good Spirit. The Mother's usual plan was to listen in silence to what was told her, inwardly noting the tact or discretion evinced by Marie in her disclosures. Occasionally she would express some doubt or disapprobation of what she said ; this occurred not unfrequently in their earliest conversations, and Marie always humbly submitted, never persisting in her own view, even where it must have

R

been most dear to her.   Her sweetness, her evenness of
temper, and the cordial charity which the slightest
occasions were sure to elicit, soon won for her the
affection both of the choir nuns and of her own immediate companions, the Assistant Sisters ; but there was,
over and above all this, what we may call a sort of halo
of sanctity investing her, felt by all, but not susceptible
of being described, which added veneration to the love
which she inspired.

The humble Sister was, however, quite unaware of the
sentiments entertained towards her, and imputed the
behaviour of those around her to their exceeding charity,
which only served to humiliate her in her own eyes, as
we learn from the letter which she addressed from
Conflans to the Curé of Mimbaste.   "I am happy and
contented," she writes; "that is all I find to say to
you.   I am alike confused at the kindness with which
I am treated and the charity with which my continual
failings—involuntary ones, however—in practising the
rule are endured.   Ah ! Sir, I wish to be very docile,
very obedient, and to testify my gratitude to God and
to my Superiors by the most entire submission.   I will
submit my will to that of God; He shall do with me
what He pleases ; He is my father and my mother, and
I pray Him to treat me as a thing that belongs to Him.
I hope to be penetrated more and more with the spirit
of the sublime and holy state which I desire to embrace,
in order that I may accomplish all its duties.   Pray for
me that I may become a religious agreeable to the
Sacred Heart of Jesus."

The failings with which she reproached herself, and
which she owns were involuntary, arose merely from
her as yet imperfect acquaintance with all the details
of the rule, and she never had to be told of a fault of

this kind more than once. Thus, for instance, when first Marie came to Conflans, a Sister, observing that, instead of getting into bed at the sound of the bell, she remained on her knees praying, asked her whether she had received permission to do this, as otherwise it was not allowable for her to prolong her devotions in that manner. She accepted the monition thankfully, and punctually attended to it ever after.

If surprised into committing some fault of inadvertence, Marie never lost her beautiful tranquillity. To what we call fussiness she was a perfect stranger. No matter what blunder she made, she was in no way discomposed. One day she unconsciously intruded herself on a gathering of the Community, to which postulants were not in the habit of being admitted. It was believed by those who related this circumstance that she had owned that she felt specially moved to do so. She had been guilty of some trifling mistake or awkwardness in acquitting herself of her employment, and desired to accuse herself of it before the Community and entreat their pardon. All secretly admired the grace and simplicity with which she performed this little act, the presiding Superior perhaps no less than the rest, though she profited by the opportunity to administer a sharp reproof to her for having come without permission. At the next recreation Marie made her appearance with as sweet and cheerful a countenance as if nothing had occurred to ruffle her, and, indeed, she was not ruffled; she might be humbled, but she was glad to be humbled, and consequently did not experience any disturbance of mind or discomposure; such feelings being almost always symptomatic of some remaining self-love and the excitement which is its result. "Oh, how good it is," she wrote, "to taste of humiliations; how exquisite is their flavour! Without desiring them, without seeking them, thank God, I often meet with them; and they are so much the more delicious as they are the less voluntary."

Another little instance is recorded of Marie's imperturbable composure, which is the more remarkable considering her natural silence, reserve, and repugnance to put herself forward or produce herself in any way. She used to be admitted to the evening meetings of the Assistant Sisters, which were presided over by one of the Assistant Generals, when it was customary for some book to be read. It came into the mind of the presiding nun to question her, after the lecture was finished, upon the subject of which it had treated. Marie replied with the utmost ease and calmness, and her remarks were so full of deep and practical piety that all went away astonished, and many imagined that she must previously have belonged to some other religious Congregation, or she could not otherwise have acquired so much spiritual knowledge. They did not know that Marie had been trained in a higher school.

Marie Lataste seemed to have nothing to acquire as regards modesty of demeanour. It will be remembered that she had learned its rules from the Saviour's own lips, and it may be added that they were precisely similar to those enjoined in the Congregation of the Sacred Heart. She practised them without constraint, as one already familiar with them, and into no inadvertence regarding them was she ever betrayed. She never raised her eyes needlessly, and several Sisters afterwards testified that they could not say what was the colour of them. Here, as in the observance of the rule, there was no stiffness, no preciseness. Her religious habits seemed formed and perfected before she came, so easily did they sit upon her.

Sœur Sisteau, whose association with Marie in the Rue de Varennes we have mentioned, gives an instance of the punctuality, ease, and modesty with which she evinced her fidelity to the rule. It was one of those chance incidents which, perhaps, best illustrate perfection of conduct, because accidental occurrences take by surprise and have a tendency to throw us off our guard, if we are as yet only scholars learning our parts. " I remained," says Sœur Sisteau, " but a short time in the Rue de Varennes after Marie Lataste's arrival, for I was sent to the Pensionnat of Conflans. Marie was soon after transferred to the Noviciate in that house, of which I was not aware." This might easily be, for the Sacré Cœur had three distinct establishments at Conflans : the Noviciate, a Pensionnat, or Boarding-school, and an Orphanage. There was, however, an interior communication, and for certain operations, such, for instance, as the washing, the choir novices used to join the Assistant Sisters and help them in the work. It was on an occasion of this kind that Sœur Sisteau encountered Marie, when she came one day with another sister to help in washing the clothes of the Noviciate house, which was done in the Pensionnat. A feeling of joy and happiness took possession of Sœur Sisteau at the sight of an acquaintance who had so much edified her. She eagerly advanced, and embraced her, adding words of kind inquiry. Marie answered only by a sweet and amiable smile, but was not surprised into speaking one word, not even so much as a monosyllable. "I knew," says Sœur Sisteau, "from the expression of her face, and of all her movements, that she was pleased to see me, but that she had no permission to converse, and she said not a single word to me. I was very desirous to have news of my mother and sisters in the Rue de Varennes, but I saw that her modesty and fidelity to the rule would not permit her to reply; so I made the sacrifice, hoping that I should have the happiness of meeting her another time, but I never saw her again."

All felt the same attraction towards her. They loved to catch if it were but a sight of her, especially when she was either praying or doing some work in the chapel. "I see her yet," writes Sister Agnes Vernay, "scrubbing the vestibule with gown tucked up and so recollected an air that, as I passed, I would linger and hide myself to watch her; but, indeed, so absorbed did she seem in God that she had probably not observed me. Ah! I shall never forget the expression of her face; there was something seraphic in it."

Marie never spoke to any one except the Mère Garabis, who directed her, of the favours she had received or of those she still continued to receive. Nevertheless, the superiors had a general acquaintance with the fact that she had hitherto been led by extraordinary ways, and accordingly watched her attentively. Marie on her part lived a life of such complete abandonment to Jesus, seeking on all occasions to testify to Him how entire and disinterested was the oblation which she had made of herself, that it would indeed have been surprising if her exterior conduct had furnished no evidence of what passed in her interior. She lived, it is true, the common life of the Assistant Sisters at the Sacré Cœur, but few, it may be surmised, led a life of such close union with Jesus as she did, and the effects of this could not fail to be felt by all who approached her. For herself, she never was happier than when she was in perfect solitude, although she accepted with entire indifference every successive office in which she was employed. Once, when engaged in dressmaking, at which she was very expert, but which kept her in a room by herself for a great part of the day, one of her companions asked her whether she did not feel wearied at spending most of the day so completely shut up and occupied with such commonplace work. She replied, " No, Sister Procule, I am never happier than when I find myself, by being alone, in the company of our Lord." To live was, for her, to think of Jesus, to converse with Jesus, to contemplate Jesus, to separate herself from all that she might give herself completely to Him, to forget all in order to remember Him alone and other things only for Him. This state of mind explains that calmness and imperturbability which an engrossing affection, banishing multiplicity, has always a tendency to produce; how much more when the love which thus unites all the faculties of the soul in one aim and one desire is divine love !

No wonder that it was when she was kneeling before the Tabernacle that the absorbing influence of this love was specially revealed. As at Varennes, so at Conflans, it could not fail to rivet attention. Kneeling unsupported, with her hands joined, she seemed lost to earth in the contemplation of the things of Heaven ; and, in the absence of an express signal to summon her away, she more than once forgot herself, from having taken no account of time. This was the only fault, if such it can be styled, for which she incurred a reprimand more than once ; but Mme. Garabis made the most of it, for, in order to exercise and try her virtue, it was necessary to be closely on the watch for opportunities, so difficult was it, as her directress

avowed, to find anything to reprehend in one so
perfect.

A few more reminiscences, referable to this period,
of those slight touches of character which speak so
strongly, may here be added. The following is an
extract from a letter of Madame Adèle Lefebre :—
"I passed several months," she writes, "at the Sacré
Cœur at Conflans with Marie Lataste, but I was not
brought in connection with her very frequently; here,
however, are some circumstances which recur to my
memory very clearly. I had charge of the wardrobe.
One day I gave Sister Marie some stockings to darn;
she performed her task, but it was far from being well
done. I pointed this out to her, but did so consider-
ately. She perceived this, and requested me not to
fear reproving her as she deserved, begging me as a
favour not to spare her. I felt that I had to do with
a soul greedy of humiliations. Another time she
came to ask me for some shoes in place of those she
was wearing. They were much needed, for it was win-
ter. I gave her what I had. The shoes were far from
being new, but she said they were good, and thanked
me. Soon after, I observed that she walked with them
down at the heel. I inquired the reason. 'They are
rather short,' she replied ; 'however, they answer very
well. I draw up the heel, when going to receive Communion, and that is sufficient.'" Immediately after her
arrival Marie was put in charge of the Refectory, and
attended punctually to the slightest directions. She
had been shown where everything stood, and, if any of
the nuns or Assistant Sisters happened to make use
of any article, she was always there to put it back into
its place. Some one having expressed some surprise
at her extreme exactness, she answered simply, "I have

been told that this cup or this water-jug was to stand here." *I have been told*—that was always sufficient for Marie. But not only did she perform what she had been enjoined to do—this is the lowest degree of obedience—but she performed every direction that was given her as coming from superiors who spoke with our Lord's authority; that, too, with a worship and a love which sublimated the meanest and most trifling acts of service. Nothing, in fact, was to her either small or trifling; she did not pass the slightest judgment on anything so as to estimate its intrinsic worth or importance, or exercise her mind on the subject in any way, save to do what she was bid in the most perfect manner.

Another Sister testifies that, not satisfied with mortifying her own will, by the closest practice of the virtue of obedience, she was also ingenious in intermingling, as the opportunity offered, other acts of mortification. Everything which could in the least degree savour, however innocently—as most persons would have deemed it—of personal delicacy and niceness, was sedulously avoided. If, for instance, she had been given a clean cap, it was noticed that she would find some excuse for exchanging it with the Sister who looked after the poultry-yard, whose caps were naturally by no means the freshest. The Refectory furnished her with many opportunities for practising these small mortifications; small as regards their subject-matter, but, from their very smallness, wanting in that grandeur which renders great mortifications at times even attractive to self-love, and compatible, therefore, with deficiency in humility and in purity of intention. The constant practice of these unobtrusive mortifications is free from this danger, and, doubtless, highly meritorious

in the sight of Him who looks with so much favour on
what is little and lowly in the eyes of men, and, above
all, in the eyes of those who practise them. Marie was
also observed, when attending to the Refectory, to
reserve for herself fragments or portions of what could
not be served up to the rest, often contenting herself
with what would even have been reckoned repulsive.
If this did not escape notice, it was because those
around her were moved to scrutinise her least actions,
from the veneration which she unconsciously inspired,
but they were intended for God's eye alone; for Him
who was the Lord of her heart, and to whom, as she
considered no sacrifice too great for Him, so neither
did she reckon any too small to offer.

Such was Marie as a postulant, and the whole Community at Conflans soon learned to share the opinion of
the Mère Angélique du Boisbaudry, who, after seeing
her for only those few days at Varennes, said to the
nuns of the Sacré Cœur when she was leaving them,
"It is a saint who is going to the Noviciate at Conflans." Later, when sent to Conflans for the direction
of the novices, amongst whom Marie had by this time
been admitted, the Mère du Boisbaudry had full opportunity for noting the daily advance of this holy girl in
virtue and merits; so that one day, when her sister
Elisa came to the Convent to pay her a visit, she could
not resist pointing out to her Marie Lataste, who was
at work in a corner, and saying, "Do you see that little
novice there? she will one day be a great saint."

# CHAPTER XX.

## MARIE A NOVICE.

THE edification which Marie gave, and her wonderful fidelity in practising the rule, induced her superiors to curtail the usual length of the postulancy in her case, and to allow of her taking the religious habit at Christmas. The 27th of December was chosen for the ceremony, which thus gave her, as her special patron in religion, the Beloved Disciple, who reclined on Jesus's bosom, and was favoured with the most intimate knowledge of the secrets of His Divine Heart. On that day, so long desired, Marie's soul was filled with overflowing joy. "How good is our God!" she writes to the Curé of Mimbaste. "Eternal glory, love, and thanksgiving be rendered to Him for all the benefits with which He has overwhelmed me, and still continues to overwhelm me. Love Him, thank Him for me; my heart suffices not for this, nor would the longest and most fervent life suffice; but, with the help of Thy grace, my God, I will devote eternity to doing so."

She is writing on the 2d of January, 1845, only six days after receiving the habit, and with her heart still full of the consolation with which the attainment of this, its sole desire, had replenished it. She had reached the centre to which grace had been attracting her for so many years, and her soul was at rest; for spiritual desires, being inspired by Him who can give what He promises, have not to encounter, when realised, the disappointment, disenchantment, or satiety which follows the attainment of earthly wishes. So Marie Lataste was happy, supremely happy, yet she was not egotistical in her happiness, and, after this first outbreak of joy, she has words of sympathy for those whom she had left behind : for her former director, who had been recently indisposed, and whose fatigues at Christmas time she bears in mind, though she is sure that he has willingly accepted them for the salvation of souls, and to win hearts to the Saviour Jesus; and for the dear inhabitants of her native village, of whose good dispositions she is rejoiced to hear. " If only," she adds, " you could succeed in banishing human respect from that parish, how much more abundant still would be your harvest ! Human respect, the spirit of the world—it infects even little secluded Mimbaste ; for it is the enemy of the Spirit of Jesus, and wherever there are human hearts which He claims as His temples and tabernacles, there also—in the village as in the city—is the spirit of the world sure to be found contending with Him for their possession." And so Marie dreads it, as a more subtle foe, and one more difficult to vanquish, than even the flesh and the devil ; the foe against which Jesus, before His Passion, offered a special prayer, when pouring forth all the love of His Soul in supplication to His Heavenly Father for His elect in all ages.

Marie has also respectful and grateful homage to offer to the " very worthy and venerable M. Dupérier," begging the Curé to tell him that she was happy and contented, loving her vocation more and more in proportion as she came to know it better. In a former letter she had recommended herself to his prayers, and assured them both that she never forgot either of them a single day before God. And then she returns to speak of her own happiness. " How goodly a thing it is," she says, " to live in community, where there is but one heart and one soul, all united in the one desire to love God, and serve Him faithfully; where we have good examples continually before our eyes, and hear the words of fire which proceed from the mouths of our most worthy mothers; where everything, in fine, even to our very recreations, is calculated to enkindle and maintain fervour! As a young novice, I aspire with the sincerest desires of my heart after religious perfection. I am as yet very far removed from it, but no matter; with the aid of grace, I do not despair of attaining to it, and our Lord will certainly not refuse me His grace. For, indeed, He has not led me here merely to cover me with a veil and a mantle, but that I may practise virtue more perfectly. I remember well His exhortations, and also yours. I will attend to them to the best of my ability, and to this end I recommend myself to your powerful prayers. I must now conclude and leave you, but every day we meet in the adorable and most sweet Heart of Jesus."

Marie's sentiments on entering her noviciate are also consigned to paper in a list of resolutions which she wrote upon the occasion. These resolutions, while not prescribing for herself anything out of the common way of life, prove the perfection of sanctity to which she aspired in every action. She ended with these words:— "My God, I desire to act thus, not from fear of punishment, or of Hell, or of Purgatory, or for the sake of my own interests, but for the love of Thee and of Thy glory alone." From the time she began to be an actual member of the Congregation of the Sacred Heart fresh graces were poured in rich abundance into Marie's soul; she seemed to live permanently in the company of the Saviour Jesus, of which her countenance gave expressive indication by its recollectedness and the heavenly joy which irradiated it. No one could help remarking this; nothing, however, was externally manifested by her in regard to the extraordinary favours of which she was the recipient. The Mère Garabis alone was admitted to the secret of what passed within her soul; to every one else she was silent; and her sole object seemed to be to escape notice and to be forgotten. To Mme. Garabis, then, we are indebted for what we know on this subject; and from her account we gather that Marie was favoured at different times with supernatural manifestations.

While she was yet a postulant, a soul in Purgatory, a religious of the Sacré Cœur, appeared to her. The Mère Garabis, when Marie related the circumstance to her, affected doubt, and told her that her imagination must have deceived her. " Marie," she says, " did not add a single word in order to convince me of what she had stated. ' But what,' I asked, ' was the person like whom you fancy you saw ?' She then described her with such accuracy of detail, as regarded features, manner, and the whole exterior, that I perfectly recognised one of our sisters, who had lived a most edifying life, and had died in the odour of sanctity a few months before the arrival of Sister Marie. I refrained, however, from naming her. ' But,' I continued, ' did this soul ask for prayers ?' ' This,' replied Marie, ' is what she said to me : I am one who is called here the Mère Eulalie de Bouchaud ' (this was the nun I had recognised); ' God in His goodness sends me to you, Marie; you can by your prayers diminish my sufferings and shorten their duration. I do not yet enjoy eternal beatitude ; first, on account of certain negligences regarding the love of God, which is a great calamity for a soul, especially for a religious ; secondly, on account of the stiffness and dryness of my behaviour to certain persons, by which charity was wounded.'" The Mère Garabis did not remember the third cause with sufficient clearness to be able to repeat it. The suffering which seemed to consume this soul came almost exclusively from the intense desire to go and unite herself to God. "I knew," added Sister Lataste, "that this soul received great assistance from the Archangel St. Michael, and she gave me to understand that the high degree of glory and the exalted place to which she was to be raised in Heaven, demanded a perfect purification."

"Marie," continues Mère Garabis, "begged me, in the name of the Mère Eulalie de Bouchaud, to set the Sisters to observe strict silence and the most perfect charity during ten days. I did so, without telling them the motive of this injunction. At the end of five or six days—I think it was—this Mother again appeared to the good Sister, when she was at Communion. This time she was resplendent with the glory of the Blessed, and thanked Marie; who has often said to me since, 'Oh, how beloved of God is this soul! How high must be her place in Heaven!'" It may interest the reader to know that among the papers left by the Mère Eulalie was found a protestation, in the form of a vow, by which she engaged herself to aspire in all things after the highest perfection, to walk continually in the presence of God, and never to act save from a motive of pure love. This promise, while it marked the generosity of the heart from which it proceeded, indicated also the eminent sanctity to which our Lord had called her. It may thus serve to account for the rigorous expiation exacted of one apparently so faultless. Where much is given, much is required; and it must also be remembered that, while a vow adds greatly to the merit of those acts of virtue which are its object, it also renders the faults committed against them more serious.

The knowledge of future events, and of other things of which she would naturally have been ignorant, was communicated at times to Marie; but Mme. Garabis adds that it was only by our Lord's express injunction that she revealed them even to her. In this manner the Mère Garabis was made acquainted with several circumstances relating to houses or persons belonging to the Society which subsequent events verified. Marie foretold to this Mother her promotion to the office of Superior. One day she wrote her a note containing this intimation. "My worthy Mother," she said, "forgive me if I venture on too great a freedom. To-day at Mass, at the moment of Communion, it seemed to me that our Lord, looking benignantly upon me, said, 'What would you wish Me to give to the Mère Mathilde ?' Ah ! my heart expanded with joy. For an instant I hesitated as to what I ought to ask; then I said, 'Lord, Thou art never sufficiently loved : give her charity;' for this appeared to me the best of things. Then He added, 'and *discernment*, for she will need that.'" At the close of the year 1845, the Mère Garabis was, in fact, made Superioress of the house of Kintzheim, in Alsace, where there was a noviciate ; the necessity, therefore, of making a wise choice, and of forming the subjects committed to her charge, explained the peculiar need in her case of the possession of discernment. Marie Lataste also told her that she would be sent out of France to found a new house of the Sacré Cœur, destined to produce rich fruits for the glory of God and the salvation of souls ; and that the Adorable Sacrament of the Altar would be specially honoured there. Ten years later this prediction received its accomplishment.

To the same nun we are indebted for the following instance of Marie's prophetic gift. Towards the close of the year 1844, the Mother General of the Congregation, Mme. Barat, then aged sixty-five, went to Rome, and, on the road, was taken ill at Aix. The news received of her at Conflans gave serious alarm to the Community, and the Mother Superior urged all to pray fervently for her recovery. "Sister Marie," says the Mère Garabis, "came to speak to me after making a visit to the Blessed Sacrament, and told me, on the part of our Lord, that I was not to feel any more apprehension, for that our Reverend Mother had many years yet to labour for the glory of the Sacred Heart. Mme. Garabis asked Marie, in reply, whether she called five or six years many years. The age of the invalid, no doubt, appeared to render a very prolonged term of life unlikely in her case; but Marie reiterated her assertion in its positive, not comparative, sense. "No, my mother," she said; "reckon on some twenty years."

The Abbé Pascal Darbins, in his fourth edition of the "Life and Writings of Marie Lataste," observes that he had inserted this prophecy in his manuscript copy, in order that later no suspicion might arise that it was subsequently added. At the beginning of May, 1865, when it was question of a second edition of Marie Lataste's works, he hesitated whether he should allow it to appear, the Mère de Barat being still alive. It was upon reflection judged expedient to keep it back awhile, lest it should produce a painful effect upon the religious family which she had so long ruled and to which she was very dear. At that time there were no

S

symptoms to indicate the near approach of death.
After a long period of suffering the Reverend Mother
had rallied, and regained a considerable degree of
strength. She had accordingly resumed her ordinary
occupations with marvellous activity, when, on the
morning of Monday, the 22d of May, after attending
Mass, she had an apoplectic seizure, and expired on the
Thursday following, which was the festival of the
Ascension, in the calm and peace of the Blessed.
She had directed the Congregation for sixty-three
years, and her death at the time announced by Marie
Lataste has served to confirm the truth of her prediction. We are told that other instances might be
alleged of her prophetic spirit, and of the special lights
she received and was commissioned to impart to some
of the mothers, but that they related to subjects of too
intimate and private a nature for publication.

From all these examples it is clear that, if our Lord
had withdrawn His habitual sensible communications
from His servant, He frequently spoke to her with un-
mistakable clearness. As regards the manner of these
communications we are left to conjecture. From something, however, which the Mère Garabis related, it would
seem that Marie was still occasionally favoured with
the sight of His Divine Countenance. One day she
showed Marie a very good painting on canvass of our
Lord, with this inscription under it : "True portrait of
Jesus." It was probably a copy of the likeness ascribed
to Him by a tradition of more or less authority, and
known to most of us. "Here," said the Mother, "is a
true portrait of our Saviour ; since you see Him"—it
may be observed that she does not say since you *have
seen* Him—"you will recognise the resemblance."
"S'ster Lataste," adds the Mère Garabis, "looked at

the portrait, but made no response; from which I understood that she did not venture to tell me that this was no likeness of Him who manifested Himself to her. Her silence, then, failing to satisfy me, I asked her to describe to me our Adorable Master. She gave me no details as respected His features, but what she did say made so deep an impression upon me that my soul was quite penetrated by it. I should have wished to pass the rest of the day and night at the foot of the Tabernacle, where I could taste more perfectly the presence of Jesus Christ in the Sacrament of His love."

The Mère Garabis tells us that Marie had arrived at a most sublime degree of prayer, but that, " nevertheless, she used to listen attentively to the lessons given on the subject to the novices, and endeavoured, although in vain, to follow each day the points proposed for their meditation." Perhaps this is one of the most perfect acts of humility which could be recorded, far surpassing all that could be practised of an external kind, however mortifying. For one who could fly and soar into pure spiritual heights or, rather, who was borne thither without effort, to consent, nay, to strive, to keep herself down and creep along, so to say, in leading-strings, like the veriest beginner, was no ordinary sacrifice. But Jesus, who exalts the humble, and will never be outdone in generosity, rewarded her for these struggles to keep in the lowest place, by rendering His divine presence more sensible to her amidst her occupations. It is hardly necessary to say that in her exact observance of the rule she continued to be a model to the novices, as she had been to all even as a postulant. She always manifested much pleasure in the explanations given of it by the mistress of novices; and the Mère Garabis says, "I used purposely to insist strongly on the spirit of humility and simplicity which it requires of us, and on the perils which beset an exceptional way. Like a docile child, she would afterwards come and promise me to neglect nothing in order fully to enter on the path traced out for her."

She was ever the first to take her place at the common exercises, and even at the prayers offered at five o'clock in the morning, and that, too, after her health had begun to fail so much that she might fairly have been dispensed from making this exertion. In everything she endeavoured completely to assimilate herself to the rest; but, do what she would, in this she could not succeed, since she was always distinguished for the perfection with which she followed the smallest details prescribed by the rule. A remark of one of the Sisters who lived with her at Conflans well describes her. "Sister Lataste did everything like the rest, and no one did anything like her." This fidelity in the practice of obedience and conformity to rule, at every instant and under every circumstance, is perhaps the most perfect engine for breaking self-will and immolating nature. The old Adam is suffocated under such a process. Marie was aware of this, and, although she may be said to have passed through a trying noviciate in the world, before entering on that of the religious life, which one might believe had left in her few movements of self-love to combat, she thus expresses herself to M. Dupérier in a letter written in November, 1846, as to the power of the rule and its efficaciousness as an instrument of mortification when strictly observed: —" At the Sacré Cœur the rule is not very austere, because strength is needed in order to labour for the glory of God; but it none the less puts nature to death by crucifying self-love, when it is carefully observed in every point." And, as we have just remarked, Marie entered her noviciate by no means unproved and untried in the ways of self-abnegation and renunciation of her own will. "Nearly three years of trials," she wrote to the Mère Garabis in the early days of her noviciate, "have taught me more than would ten years of study. I have come to understand what man is and what God is. Alas! however learned, however holy, a man may be, he is still always a man, and Thou, O my God, art always God and infinitely exalted above all that is great!" To know this truth experimentally, as did Marie, and not in words only, implies no small advance in the ways of perfection; for, as the author of the "Spiritual Combat" so truly observes, "all our force for conquering the enemy springs from a diffidence of ourselves and a confidence in God:" nay, it is something to be aware that we as yet lack that knowledge; for who is to obtain these necessary weapons if he is not even conscious that he does not possess them?

Zeal for the glory of God filled the heart of Marie before her entrance into religion, a zeal which never fails to be the companion of conformity to His blessed Will; for we know that God's glory is especially dear to Him. Accordingly, the adorers of His Holy Will ever burn with a desire to contribute to that glory, and, unable to increase the sum of its infinite perfection and fulness, they long to add to it accidentally. Nowhere is the glory of God exhibited with so much splendour as in the salvation of the souls which He has redeemed through His ineffable charity. To save souls, then, becomes, as it were, the passion of the Saints. By her

admission into the Congregation of the Sacred Heart,
Marie's duties of charity towards the souls for whose
salvation the Heart of our Redeemer thirsted were
necessarily increased, and so also was her zeal, in like
proportion.   Our Lord, soon after she had assumed the
habit, called her to exercise it specially in favour of
certain souls, for whom He desired her to pray and
suffer; and one time in particular she felt herself urged
to offer herself as a victim for the conversion of an
illustrious person—we are not told who this individual
was—on whose head she beheld the justice of God
about to fall heavily.   She begged permission of her
superior to do this, but for several days her request met
with a refusal : at last she was allowed to carry out her
wish, with the expressly annexed condition that no
change was to be made in the order of her occupations.

It would be impossible to describe the sufferings to
which, from that moment, this holy girl became a
prey : she herself could find no other name for them
than the "just anger of God;" for well she knew that
what she endured was a supernatural, not a natural
malady.   For more than three weeks, her stomach
could bear no solid food whatever.   An inward fire
seemed to consume her, to which an occasional glass of
water was the only partial palliative she could receive.
Nevertheless, she continued to discharge the minutest
duties of her employment with the same assiduity as
ever.   Her superior, however, seeing her enduring
tortures which could only be compared to what we
conceive of the pains of Purgatory, bade her pray for
their cessation.   Marie obeyed, and immediately she
was restored to her usual state of health, her countenance regaining its habitual calm serenity.   The Saviour
also filled her soul with interior sweetness, and pro-

mised her that the sinner who had been the object of her generous self-sacrifice should not die under the displeasure of God. We are told that what had been revealed to Marie was a few years later unmistakably accomplished. The Abbé Darbins adds that we may be permitted to hope that the lessons of adversity were not thrown away upon him, and that religion, called in to bless his last moments, found in his heart that deep contrition which the Father of Mercies never rejects. Who was this illustrious personage? The language used would lead us to infer that we are expected to divine his name. Was it Louis Philippe?

Sister Lataste continued, as heretofore, to receive lights as to the spiritual needs of some of her sisters; but she communicated them only to the Superior who directed her; and the latter had occasion often to remark how, with the accuracy of discernment which had been supernaturally imparted to her, was mingled a sweet and delicate charity, which knew how to bring forward the good qualities of those to whose faults or deficiences she had to allude in acquitting herself of the commission she had received. This charity which led her on all occasions to excuse the faults of others when she could not ignore or veil them, her patience, gentleness, and kindness to every one, gave her an irresistible ascendancy over all who approached her. And then her very looks preached, and exercised a silent apostleship. Of this we have already spoken; suffice it, therefore, to add here the following testimony as to the salutary influence of her very looks on all who were nearly associated with her.

Long after Marie had left Conflans, the Sister who had shared the office of portress with her used to speak with admiration of this gift which she possessed.

"There was in her whole person," she said, "a something I could not account for, which drew me towards God." This gift, in a certain measure, almost always attends eminent sanctity, and it is not so much a gift, perhaps, as the necessary splendour of a soul in which the new life in Christ is developed in all its beauty, and would be visible to all were it not veiled by the fleshly tabernacle. It pleases God, however, usually to permit some of its rays to permeate the vessel in which they are contained; not so much for the glory of His saints on earth, for that glory is reserved for a future state, as for the spiritual benefit of others. The edification produced by every word, every look, and every gesture of a saint could not be effected by any imitation, however close, if such were possible, because the cause is, not natural, but supernatural. The holy person from whom this influence radiates is commonly unconscious of it; but not always. Thus we read of the Saint of Alvernia, the preacher of poverty, the great St. Francis of Assisi, inviting one of his religious to go and preach with him in the city. They made a silent round of the place, and then returned to their convent. "But, Father," said his companion, "are we not going to preach?" "We have done so already," replied the saint. The mere sight of them, as they passed, had been a very sufficient sermon.

# CHAPTER XXI.

## MARIE IS SENT TO RENNIS.

TOWARDS the close of the year 1845, Marie fell ill. Medical advice had to be called in, and the doctors were of opinion that change of air, coupled with a more active life, would be conducive to her recovery and to the removal of the general debility which affected her. Now, it so happened that at this very time the Sacré Cœur was about to found a branch establishment in the capital of Brittany, and it was decided that Marie Lataste should accompany the little colony. She received this decision as the expression of the will of God, submitting joyfully, notwithstanding her attachment to the Noviciate at Conflans and to the mothers and sisters to whom she must bid adieu.

Being still a novice, she was, as is the custom, the virtual possessor of that *trousseau* to which allusion has already been made as being far more handsome than could have been expected for a person in her humble class of life. It was, therefore, to go with her · to Rennes. The Mère Adèle Lefebvre, who had the care of the wardrobe, tells us that Marie came to her and urgently begged that only a few ordinary things might be packed up for her. "I fancied," says that religious, "from her wishing for so few, and those the commonest clothes, that she had some particular reason for this selection ; such as the expectation of returning soon to Conflans." But any such idea was far from Marie's thoughts. It was her love of holy poverty which made her eager to rid herself of her good clothes, and desirous at a new place to pass for a very poor girl, who had brought little with her into religion. It can be no question, at least, that such was her motive. Her predilection for what was common and worn in the way of dress had been frequently remarked. On the day when she was clothed with the religious habit, her things were new, as they are on such occasions, and she was observed at recreation time to eye with complacency the Sister who had charge of the poultry yard, and who, owing to her employment, was always the shabbiest in her dress. So absorbed was she in this contemplation that one of her companions laughed at her for being so taken up with this subject that she could attend to nothing else. Marie, in reply, quoted a passage of the rule which had just been read out in the Refectory. "Every one ought to rejoice in the Lord with a holy joy when she receives at the distribution that which is meanest and coarsest." The expression of her countenance, as she said these words, evinced the holy envy which she experienced at the sight of her, who bore most patently of all the livery of poverty, and she ever cherished a kind of preference for this Sister on account of the humble nature of her office. She was observed also to show special gratitude when some half-worn-out garment was bestowed on her, and was dextrous in exchanging or passing on to others what was allotted to her of a better character, and in divesting herself of everything which was not quite indispensable.

The same spirit of poverty made her careful and economical to the greatest degree of all that was intrusted to her; and she humbly repaired and made amends for the slightest faults she might have committed, or thought she had committed, against this virtuc. We may add that it is a rare virtue even amongst those to whom one would have supposed an early life of indigence would have taught it only on the score of prudence. Wastefulness, indeed, is seldom noticed as a fault unless it arrives at some considerable degree; and this for want of the proper conviction that whatever we have, be it little or much, is not our own, that we have been intrusted with it, and must give an account of it. Yet how remarkable are those words of our Lord just after He had worked the miracle of the multiplication of the loaves: "Gather up the fragments that remain, lest they be lost." *

The religious set off for Rennes on the 4th of May, under the leadership of the Mère de Charbonnel. She was Assistant General, and one of the oldest in the Congregation. This venerable mother had founded a house at Laval some years earlier; here she and her sisters halted, and the two days which they spent there were rendered very agreeable by the many interesting circumstances which she was able to relate, and which were recalled to her mind by her presence at the scene of her former labours. Every one was anxious to join the happy circle—all but Marie, who, without affecting either singularity or indifference, was able to keep herself aloof. To be effaced and left out, so to say, was her constant ambition, if such a word can be applied to a desire so opposite in character to what the word imports. Her extreme fatigue furnished an available pretext ; nevertheless, her exhaustion, which was very real, did not prevent her helping the Sisters in getting forward their work, in order to enable them to take part in the additional recreations of which this visit was the occasion.

* John vi. 12.

"I observed her, without her perceiving that I did so," says the Mère de Lemps, who was the Superior at Laval at that time, "and I saw that she profited by every moment she had at her free disposal to go to the chapel; and, when there, her appearance impressed me as that of an angel in adoration before the Blessed Sacrament. I was struck with the modesty, recollection, and peace which shone upon her sweet and virginal countenance; there was something intellectual and distinguished in her look, which led me to suppose that her humility had induced her to choose the lowest and obscurest rank. I confess that I should have been very glad to keep her at Laval, but I abstained from expressing the desire, in order not to rob the infant community to which she was to belong." The similarity of the testimony given to Marie Lataste's virtues by all the nuns from whose letters or oral depositions we have quoted, must be evident to everyone; and, when it is remembered that these were collected many years after the death of the holy girl, from persons of all ages and classes, most of whom were at that time dispersed in different convents of the Institute, their witness is rendered all the more weighty, as each of them speaks independently of the others, thus giving a force to their collective attestation which it would otherwise lack.

The travellers arrived at Rennes on the Saturday, the 9th of May, and took possession of the little property of Begasson which was to be their abode. It was situated at a very short distance from the town, but was quite rural in its aspect. In front of the house was a small plantation of plane-trees and limes, and their little demesne comprised, moreover, an avenue of chesnut-trees of almost secular growth, and a good-sized piece of pasture ground, intersected with those thick hedges which in Brittany and parts of Normandy remind an English visitor of his native land. All this was very pretty and pleasant, but the house was by no means in keeping with its surroundings; in fact, it was in a somewhat ruinous condition. The ground-floor was left in its primitive state, the ground being literally the floor. Neither did the building make up in size for its deficiency in comfort. It was small, and, although the most urgent repairs had been effected before the arrival of the nuns, so as to render the tenement just habitable, much remained to be done, and a number of workmen were still engaged about the premises, the noise of whose labours was likely to disturb the silence and peace of the house for several months to come.

Marie nevertheless was charmed. She who had never given a look at the wonders of the great cities through which she had passed—not even at those of the splendid capital of France—allowed her eye to rest with pleasure on scenes which recalled those in which she had spent her early years. But if the freshness of the pure country air and the spectacle of nature reminded her agreeably of her home among the Pyrenean solitudes, much more was she delighted to meet again, in the good Breton peasantry, with a genuine and uncontaminated faith which brought back to her memory that of her devout and simple compatriots of the Landes. The marks of devotion to the Blessed Mother of God which she observed among the workmen frequenting the house were a real joy to her heart. "I am very much pleased with this country," she writes to her father on the 12th of July. "These good people are truly devout; I have observed several men wearing the scapular."

To the hitherto calm and retired life which Marie had led at the Noviciate at Conflans had now succeeded one of great and multiplied activity, which would have been a source of much distraction to a soul less firmly anchored in the deep waters of peace, the peace of God which passeth all understanding. The Community was at first composed of only seven persons, four of whom belonged to the Assistant class. Upon these sisters almost all the domestic labours devolved; and these labours were rendered much more heavy by the embarrassments and privations which are inseparable from a new foundation, where everything has to be begun. The choir nuns could lend no help, for their time was fully occupied with educational duties; the eagerness of families to send their children having induced them to receive a certain number of pupils, notwithstanding the unprepared condition of their establishment. It may easily be imagined, under such circumstances, that every one had enough and more than enough on her hands. When Marie, however, wrote to her father in July, the Community had been increased in number to ten.

The care of the Infirmary and Refectory were given to Sister Lataste, but this was not all; she was moreover portress at certain hours of the day, and had to look after the lights. She accepted cheerfully, nay, joyfully, this large share of work, which there is every reason to believe proved too severe a burden for her failing health; but there was a great deal of work to be done by very few hands, and active employment had been recommended by the doctors for Marie's case. Anyhow, she managed to find in her spirit of self-devotion strength to perform it all, and even often to aid her sisters in their departments. As infirmarian she was frequently brought into contact with the pupils, and as portress with persons from without, which multiplied her opportunities of showing charity to her neighbour and doing something for the glory of God. She never, however, put herself forward, but behaved always with a wonderful tact, prudence, and modesty, knowing well that, although she was not intrusted with the direct charge of souls, the Apostleship of example belonged to all; and, indeed, the veneration which she inspired rendered the influence she thus exerted peculiarly efficacious.

The pupils were so much impressed by her sweetness and kindness that they were delighted when they had an opportunity of seeing and speaking to her; and her devoted care and attention to any whom sickness brought into the Infirmary attached them to her in a special manner. Again, we find the same remark made by these young creatures which we so frequently meet with, that the very sight of her inclined them to what was good and enkindled their piety. Often would they be heard to exclaim, " Oh, how good, how gentle Sister Lataste is ! we like so much to be with her; she is a saint ! "

The relatives of the pupils, and other secular persons in the town and neighbourhood, used to try and see her at the door, for during a portion of the day, as has been observed, she acted as portress, and would sometimes make requests which they knew could not be granted, and which were only a pretext on their part in order to have some conversation with her, hear her gracious replies, and see her modest and winning countenance. Hers seemed a divine modesty rather than a mere natural bashfulness, and a little girl, with the true instinct which innocent childhood often displays, appeared to perceive this. She was niece to the Superioress, and took every opportunity which offered to go to the convent and visit her aunt, because she knew she should then also get a sight of Marie, and perhaps say a few words to her, and, better still, hear her say a few; for the child was strangely attracted to the holy novice. Going home one day, she told her young companions that she had seen a religious who was like what she fancied the Blessed Virgin in Heaven to be. Nor had she been the only one to remark in Marie's modesty, humility, and purity of expression a resemblance to the type we all conceive in our minds of the Holy Virgin of Nazareth. What wonder! since Marie had the tenderest devotion to the Blessed Mother of God, whose voice she had heard and whose countenance she had beheld in vision, and whom she made the continual object of her imitation.

As there was no sister in the little community in the first instance who was fitted to fill the place of cook, the Mère de Charbonnel engaged a person from Rennes, who had been strongly recommended by one of the nuns in whose family she had once lived. Madeleine Daligaut (for such was her name) was a good woman, but unused to Convent ways; a circumstance which would have made it not so easy to get on comfortably with her had not Marie known how to smooth over every difficulty. The cook was aware of this herself, especially after she had joined the Congregation, which she eventually did. This is the testimony she gave respecting Marie:—"I lived four months with this good sister; our intercourse was pretty frequent, but our relations were more external than intimate, for I was not admitted to the exercises of the Community. I used to go out and execute commissions, and also acted as cook, Sister Lataste being portress and infirmarian, and also having the care of the refectory, we were often together; but no difficulty ever arose between her and me, although with anyone else I might have given rise to something of the kind ; for, being only a secular, I was almost wholly ignorant of the ways of a religious community. I never saw her sweetness or patience fail. After making long rounds marketing, I sometimes came in feeling greatly in need of rest, and I showed that it was a trouble to me to have to go marketing, and then have to go and look after my ovens and get the meal ready. Sister Marie would smile, and say these words to me which were often on her lips: 'Let us work all our life long; we shall have all Eternity for repose.' I told her one day that I was thinking of looking out for a situation, for that I neither felt any attraction nor had I the courage to embrace a life of self-sacrifice and abnegation like that of the Sacré Cœur. 'Go, go,' she replied ; 'but you will be like the birds : you will fly away for a short time, and then you will return to drop once more into the Sacré Cœur.' Her prevision proved correct, for the sight of the virtues of this good sister gradually dissipated my repugnance and inclined my heart towards this vocation, which at that time had no attractions for me. In 1847, I presented myself to be admitted into the society as an Assistant Sister."

Marie Lataste, she tells us, knew how to conceal from the eyes of others the amount of fatigue she underwent. She had every day to fill a certain number of pails with water from the well ; this must have been a heavy labour to her, but she never made a complaint. "One day," says Madeleine, "I offered to help her, she accepted my assistance with perfect simplicity, thanking me for my kindness." Although so forgetful

T

of herself, no service rendered to her, however trifling, was unappreciated or passed unnoticed. "In the kitchen," continues Madeleine, "she made much of the least trouble which I took, 'Madeleine,' she would say to me, 'you leave me nothing to do. Your soup plates, your dishes, are all arranged in order; I have only to carry the things in.'"

We add the testimony of another sister, which contains some account of the inconveniences connected with the domestic arrangements, and of the trouble thereby entailed on Marie, as well as other trials to which she was subjected at this time. "I had been scarcely eighteen months a novice," writes Etiennette Chateigné, Sister Assistant at Poitiers, "when I was sent to Rennes. I could not describe the impression produced on me by the fervour, regularity, modesty, simplicity, and equable temper of Sister Marie Lataste, as also by her boundless devotion to the Society and zeal for the salvation of souls. The work had to be done by the Assistant Sisters—one of us was already laid up—and in every foundation there is always much toil and a great deal of poverty. Though Sister Marie was already in a suffering state of health, she got through more work than all the rest put together; she filled the offices of infirmarian to the Community and to the boarders, of refectarian, and sub-portress; and she also looked after the lamps. These employments furnished matter to her for many sacrifices and frequent humiliations, of which our Lord was not sparing to her, and which she bore with an incomparable sweetness. There was no regular kitchen; meals were prepared at a common fire-place, and the Infirmarian was obliged to make use of the same grate for her *tisanes;* on these occasions she knew how to wait with patience, and yet to do all in an orderly way, without ever uttering a word that could wound charity. She loved this virtue dearly; and we often heard her exclaim, 'Oh, how lovely is charity!' But, above all, she gave proof of this in her behaviour; for, ever forgetful of herself, to others she was full of delicate consideration, and obliging attention.

"While she waited on the refectory, she had in all weathers to cross a yard, carrying the dishes, no easy matter to this good sister, who had little strength, and was, besides, encumbered with thick heavy sabots; but she never complained, putting on her lumbering wooden shoes even when she could scarcely drag herself along, that she might practise obedience and mortification. Notwithstanding her many occupations, she was always first at the exercises of the Community, including the morning devotions, and this at a time when her sufferings had become very great. Neither did she ever fail at recreation. One day, when our worthy Superior was engaged in the reception-room, I began saying that it was very tiresome that our mother should be there just at that time. Sister Lataste immediately answered, 'It is a happiness to have this little sacrifice to offer to our Lord.' In the midst of her work, and suffering constantly as she did, you might always see her calm, modest, kindly, and recollected. Gentleness appeared her distinguishing virtue; she conquered all hearts.

"They were not less touched by her fervour and love of God. No sooner had she a free moment, in the little room where she had to attend when acting as portress, than she would kneel down against the wall, at the place where the Tabernacle was, on the other side (for the chapel adjoined this apartment), and there she adored her God. Alluding to this, I said to her, 'O my sister, you are a spoilt child of our Lord's; you are always near the Blessed Sacrament.' 'My sister,' she replied, 'I take what is given to me.'" Little did her companion then know how much was hidden under these simple words! She continues, "It was, doubtless, from these frequent communications with the Divine Heart that she drew that strength of soul and that deep humility which she so often evidenced. But, new as I was to the religious life, I was struck, on the one hand, with the harsh treatment she received from superiors: reprimands were not spared her; it would have seemed as if she could never do anything well; and, on the other hand, with her being always the first to accuse and condemn herself, and that with such ease, simplicity, and perfect sweetness! No matter how much she was reproved, she never had a word of excuse to offer; nothing could move her from that gentle and modest peace which was the fruit of the dominion over self which she had acquired. Our Lord, who, doubtless, had very special designs with regard to her, also permitted her confessor to lead her by hard and rough ways. She used often to say to us, 'My sisters, you must seek only God in the confessional, for you will find nothing else there.' Her confessor, however, had so high an opinion of her that, after she was dead, he said to Sister Etiennette, 'Let us try and imitate Sister Marie; she was a saint!'"

We have seen how greedy of sufferings Marie was while still living in the world. Her long and fervent meditations on the Passion could not fail of producing this love of mortification; and when our Lord sends this love He means to content it in some form. In giving an account of her interior dispositions to the

Mère Garabis, after entering on her noviciate, she spoke thus of this inward longing of her soul : "I cannot satisfy the intense desire which I feel to consume myself for my God. Must I respond so ill to all the love which He deigns to show to His weak creature? Ah, if people did but know the good which comes to a soul from the love of the cross and of humiliation! Our Lord has vouchsafed to teach me this; but how little, alas! have I profited by His divine lessons." She was to have her wish ; and her martyrdom was to be none the less real for being slow and, in great part, hidden. It was her own desire that so it should be. All was thus for Jesus alone. Nevertheless, if she hid her sufferings, she could not, and did not, endeavour to hide her value of them. It was seen in the pleasure with which she would welcome the smallest privation or disappointment, as we have just had occasion to observe when the absence of their mother from recreation time caused some trifling vexation to the rest.

What Sister Etiennette Chateigné said with regard to the severity of superiors was perfectly true. God permitted Marie to pass successively under the direction of several who all tried her sharply, because each was anxious thoroughly to prove the spirit of one who had been led by such unusual ways. But not an excuse or complaint ever passed her lips ; and it was only on her death-bed that she confessed to one of the nuns who attended her, how much she suffered when she was transferred from the hands of her to whom, on arriving at Conflans, she had given her confidence, to the direction of an old and experienced mother who omitted nothing to exercise her virtue. This was, of course, the Mère de Charbonnel. "They believed," she gently said, "that I was a proud creature; I spent many very trying moments; but our Lord permitted this, and my superior acted for my good." It is well to add that this same mother who treated Marie so severely, inwardly recognised her merit; for later she used to quote her example to others. Her object had been to convince herself that the sister was not under the influence of imagination excited by self-love, but that what passed within her was truly from God. The confessor had acted in the same spirit; leading her soul by the way of a pure and naked faith, a way hard to nature, and, therefore, calculated to search and try whoever is restricted to it.

The Mère de Keroüartz, who succeeded the Mère de Charbonnel as Superioress of the house at Rennes, knew that Sister Lataste had received special and supernatural favours, and she also knew that it was Marie's wish to remain unknown. "What I ask of the good God," she had said to her, "is to be forgotten of men after death, as during my life." The Mère de Keroüartz resolved to second this aspiration by leaving her in the routine of religious life, without giving her any opportunity of alluding to the past. Marie's sentiments on this subject are expressed in a letter to M. Dupérier from which we have already quoted. "You wish," she writes, "to ask me several questions. Ah, I guess what you desire to know. It will suffice to tell you that God has led me by the hand in all circumstances. I have placed all my hope in Him, and it has not been deceived. You know how He opened to me an entrance into the Sacré Cœur. I have nothing more to add on this subject. I am here in the place of my soul's repose and tranquillity in that Heart, so loving, of the Saviour Jesus. He conducts me by a way which He has indicated to me, and which I shall never leave. To lead a humble, hidden, obscure, unknown life, to live for God in Jesus Christ,—this is what has been designed for me, and it suffices me. There are troubles everywhere, sufferings everywhere; but God has had regard to my good will, and He has changed the thorns into flowers. It matters little that I should describe to you all the happiness which I taste in my new life, for I can say all in one word: my heart is happy; it regrets nothing, and desires nothing but what it possesses. I am happy; I have found, and I every day find, happiness at the foot of the Cross and in the Adorable Heart of Jesus. I am happy, and my happiness is that of every soul which lives in religion,—Jesus and the Cross of Jesus (you will understand me) : that is enough for me; all the rest is little in my eyes; all the rest, indeed, is nothing to me."

In the same letter she gives M. Dupérier a list of her many employments, which are sufficient, including pious exercises, to occupy her from half-past four in the morning to half-past nine at night; and she also tells him that he is evidently ignorant of the constitution of the Sacré Cœur, which makes no distinction between its members, the Choir Nuns and the Assistant Sisters, save that the former are employed in education and the latter in domestic work. This difference, she says, is purely exterior, for all live according to the same rule, and form but one heart and soul in the Adorable Heart of Jesus. They all labour for the same end, the glory of the Sacred Heart of Jesus; and she who best knows the Heart of our Lord, and she who lives the most holily, is the one who works the most efficaciously to fulfil the object of her vocation.

Such, amidst her distracting occupations, was the

imperturbable calm of Marie's soul, which had found its
centre of repose in the Adorable Will of God and in
the fulfilment of her vocation, which was the expression
of that will. This, in fact, is the only centre of perfect
repose for every soul. All repose short of that enjoyed
in our centre is but partial, temporary, and liable to be
disturbed. Even very pious souls experience this
disturbance at times, because few abide so fixedly in
their centre, and persons of much virtue will either
fail under unexpected trials of their patience, or will be
harassed occasionally by the mere press of a work
which gives no reprieve; for this continual strain on
strength, nerves, and attention has an irritating effect,
of which it is difficult for the best never to betray
tokens in their manner, if not in words. We have seen
the testimony of Madeleine Daligaut, the cook, given
after she had joined the Congregation and had become
one of the Assistant Sisters at Angoulême, that she
never saw the patience and sweetness of Marie Lataste
fail her.

This same sister relates a noticeable instance of her
long-suffering charity. A beggar presented himself at
the door, and the sister gave him, in accordance with
the orders she had received, five centimes. "What is
that?" asked the man contemptuously, and in a rough
and almost threatening tone. Sister Lataste, without
making a remark, went to the Superioress and got her
to double the sum; but this bold beggar was not satisfied, and repeated what he had said before. With the
same patience Marie went back a second time. Madeleine, who had noted the man's bad countenance, was
looking on all the while, ready to interpose if it should
be necessary. She believed that Marie went to and
fro at least five or six times, although on each

occasion she had to mount a staircase, and her state of health rendered the effort peculiarly exhausting to her. At last, when the man had succeeded in extracting fifty centimes; he said, "It was well worth your while, to be sure, to go backwards and forwards so often; you ought to have given it me at once." Marie only smiled, and said, "Come, are you satisfied now?"

This reads very much like a passage out of a saint's life; saints have done, and still do, these strange things. The world, of course, has nothing but censure for what it regards as acts of foolish leniency or weak indulgence; and even we ourselves may have to remember that St. Thomas of Villanova, for instance, was a great saint, not to blame him for indiscriminate bountifulness when we find it related of him that, feeding, as it was his custom, five hundred poor people daily at his door, and a poor man on one occasion having returned surreptitiously to get his portion twice over, he ordered his servants to overlook the fraud, and let the poor man enjoy his double meal. Again; there is our good King Edward, who bade the servant boy who was robbing him, and who, supposing the king to be asleep, came back to help himself a second time, take care lest Hugoline, the Keeper of the Privy Purse, should catch him, for he would have him severely flogged. However, it may be frankly owned that such acts would change their character if performed by mere ordinary Christians. A literal imitation of these exuberances of charity, in which it is the privilege of saints to indulge, could not be recommended as a general rule of conduct; but one lesson, at least, we may gather from such narratives as these—that it is according to the spirit of true charity not to be rigid or exacting, especially in the case of Christ's poor.

Another instance of Marie's charity, which is also related by Madeleine the cook, will commend itself to all. A suspicion arose in the mind of the sister who managed the provision department that the baker was not furnishing his stipulated quantity of bread. Marie thought it was quite correct, but the sister, who had got puzzled in her accounts, persevered in her opinion, even after making Marie repeat the process of weighing the loaves ten times over. This process was a very troublesome one, for the nuns had no scales; the substitute being a large stone which they slipped along a lever placed on their shoulders. Marie, much distressed at the suspicion cast on the man's honesty, begged the Superioress to let her weigh the bread daily; and this she did with the help of Madeleine for a whole month. The result was a complete exoneration of the baker, whose reputation would have been much damaged by such an imputation.

She was as ingenious in justifying others as she was ever slow to say a word in self-defence. For example, the nun who superintended the health of the Community, the "Maitresse de Santé," complained one day to Marie that a sister who had been ordered a particular medicine was very careless about taking it at the appointed hours. "Oh, how she edifies me by forgetting herself in that way!" was Marie's spontaneous exclamation; "as for me, I only think too much of what I need." True indeed; she thought of it, but this was from the spirit of obedience and of mortification; and never, as we shall find, was she known to fail in taking everything prescribed by the doctor, notwithstanding any disgust she might experience.

We will add one further testimony to the calmness and serenity of Marie under her manifold sufferings, rendered by a sister of many years' standing, who came to Rennes at that time and shared with her for three months the office of portress. " She was already very ill," says this sister ; "and I cannot describe the impression I received of her saintliness. All in her breathed the love of our Lord, and her humility enhanced in my eyes the perfection I observed in her behaviour. I was more than once struck with the depth of her reflections on the things of God, and I felt instinctively drawn towards her. My soul experienced a sense of repose and edification, particularly when she spoke to me of the value of sufferings, which she so well knew. The symptoms of several maladies manifested themselves in her frail body, and yet there was always a smile of content and peace on her lips. I regarded it as a precious favour to be allowed to converse with this excellent sister, who seemed to live only in the supernatural, completely abstracted from herself and her sufferings. I left her fortified in spirit and filled with the desire to imitate her."

It remains for us to contemplate that picture of sweet conformity to God's will which she was to present in her last and most painful malady, before departing from this vale of tears to enjoy the rich reward which we have every reason to believe awaited her at the hands of her Saviour and Judge.

# CHAPTER XXII.

## Marie's Last Illness and Death.

From the month of September, 1846, Marie's health
began to decline more and more rapidly. As long,
however, as she could actually perform her allotted
duties, feeble and suffering as she was, she kept on;
bearing all in silence and with the most perfect patience.
But at last her weakness became so excessive, that she
broke down with exhaustion. She had plainly become
unequal to further exertion, and was accordingly placed
in medical hands. The poor sufferer, however, was to
derive no relief from this well-meant proceeding. The
doctor did not understand her malady, but, of course, he
must prescribe something. A substantial diet, joined
with moderate exercise, he hoped would restore her
strength. He ordered her three or four meals a day;
these meals consisting of beef with oil sauce. Poor
Marie! this was worse to her, and probably also for
her, than the most rigid fast would have been. The
cook several times offered to vary the repulsive dish by
a different seasoning, or to prepare something else for
her, but Marie would not consent. "It is the doctor's
orders," she replied; "we must not make any change."
And so she continued to swallow as much as she could
of cold beef and oil several times a day, notwithstanding
the disgust she felt for such a dish. She had also
a great loathing for a medicine which had been prescribed, and which she was to take every few hours.
She used to conquer her repugnance by saying, "It is
for God I take this."

It can scarcely surprise us to learn that this regimen was quite unsuccessful either in curing her or in restoring any of her lost strength. On the contrary, she became so enfeebled as to be hardly able to drag herself along, while a general swelling of her limbs seemed to threaten the approach of dropsy. The plan of exercise combined with abundant nourishment had clearly failed, and must be relinquished. So it would seem that the good doctor thought it well to try the exactly opposite system, and now prescribed complete rest in bed and a very spare diet. She accepted the new *régime* with the same readiness and cheerfulness as she had submitted to the former; and it was only in her last moments that her Superior learned from her own lips all that she had endured in consequence of the varying medical treatment to which she had been subjected. She then said with all simplicity that so long as she had an exceeding repugnance to food, the doctor had made her eat four or five times a day, and that afterwards, when she felt a great need of nourishment, he had let her nearly die of hunger.

This remark, we need hardly say, was made without the slightest bitterness of feeling; on the contrary, she recognised in the method pursued towards her a special appointment of God; as she did also on another occasion when she confessed that whatever her superiors had at any time done to procure her some alleviation had invariably aggravated her sufferings. With Marie, whatever might be the result of that which her superiors ordered, it was always good. She regarded them as God's representatives, the interpreters to her of the Divine Will; and His Will must always be good. Thus she could not do otherwise than take in good part all they said and all they enjoined; and she knew how to instil into others similar sentiments, as well as to discourage the opposite. Never, indeed, did she set herself up as the censurer of the words or actions of others; and, if any expression of the kind was inadvertently uttered before her, her silence and modest reserve administered a salutary admonition. After she had taken to her bed, a young novice was entrusted with one of the functions which Marie had previously discharged. "Having no acquaintance," she says, "with this kind of work, I was much puzzled, and used to go to her room to seek the instruction which I needed. She explained everything with sweetness and unfailing patience, although the pains she suffered were already very acute; and as I sometimes allowed myself to be disheartened at the sight of difficulties, she would encourage me, saying, with that calmness and kindness which lent so much force to all her words, 'My sister, be well assured that one can do everything which superiors command.'"

Much as she suffered, the rest and rigid abstinence which had been prescribed appear at first to have had a more beneficial effect on Marie than had the generous diet and exercise. She seemed to rally a little, and after Easter was able to get up for part of the day. It was during this month of April that she received a letter from M. Dupérier transmitting to her questions from several persons who sought light and guidance from her counsels. He also desired to know what were at present her own interior dispositions. Marie's humility and her strong desire to remain forgotten and unknown were alarmed by this letter. She took it to her superior, and begged to be allowed to destroy it and keep silence. With such force and vivacity did she express the apprehensions aroused within her, that the

Mère de Keroüartz was quite surprised; she thought it well, however, to advise her to answer the letter with simplicity, and also to say what were her interior dispositions. Marie, as usual, gave up her own view. She wrote to M. Dupérier a week after the receipt of his letter; and as her reply is short, and is, moreover, the last letter of hers which remains to us, we give it in its entirety.

" MUCH HONOURED SIR,

" You express a desire to know if it would be contrary to our rules to receive a letter like the one you have addressed to me, and others of the same character. I have spoken on the subject to my very worthy mother superioress. She told me in reply that there was nothing in this opposed to the spirit of our rules, and that it may even furnish us with opportunities to fulfil a duty of our vocation, which is to contribute, by the prayers asked of us, to the good works done or undertaken by others for the glory of God and the salvation of souls. But she gave me to understand at the same time that letters of mere personal gratification were contrary to the spirit of our Congregation. She was so good as to say that she would unite her prayers to yours.

" In order to answer every point in your letter, permit me to add that our Lord has changed nothing in respect of His goodness towards me, although His mode of dealing with me has altered. There is no longer anything either doubtful or of the sensible order; the way in which He leads me is a simple and common way, wherein I enjoy the deepest peace. I will pray for you with all my heart. There is nothing else which I can do. I thank you for the interest you feel in my family, and I beg you to receive the assurance of the profound respect with which I am,

"Much honoured sir,

"Your very humble servant,

"Sister Marie Lataste, Novice of the Sacré Cœur."

This letter is valuable, not only as being the last we have from her pen—one, and one only, written later to her sister Marguerite, not having been found—but because it contains an explicit assertion that our Lord no longer manifested Himself to her in any way recognisable by the senses.

Spring was now come, bringing softer air and, as it was hoped, a beginning of convalescence to the sufferer. She would sometimes sit in the garden for a while, and it might be observed that her eyes frequently rested on the budding flowers. She loved to "consider" them, speaking as they do, by their wonderful texture and delicate hues, of the loveliness of Him who made them, and who is Himself Infinite Beauty. For if His goodness, and greatness, and power are shown forth in all His works, flowers seem designed chiefly to manifest His beauty. The pupils knew her love for them, and, glad to catch a sight of her once more, would gather some to carry to her, and ask her prayers. Marie received them with a smile, never failing to speak a few words expressive of her gratitude to the Creator of so many wonders, and these devout ejaculations always had the effect of refreshing the faith and piety of these good children. Etiennette Chateigné, whose testimony has already been quoted, found her one day seated in the garden and contemplating the flowers which were blooming at her feet. "How pretty they are!" said Marie. "Yes," replied her former associate, "but you ought to beg our Lord, who is so good, to cure you; then you could come and help us : see, how much we have to do !" "Whatever God wills," rejoined Marie; "nothing but what He wills. When death comes, we shall be so glad to have suffered something for Him." The work of life was over for Marie Lataste, that is, the active work ; for the passive work of endurance was still unfinished, and that work is the hardest. But she welcomed each in its turn.

That Marie's pleasure in flowers and the spectacle of nature was wholly referred to God, is proved by a slight remark she made to a postulant who gave her the support of her arm the last time she attempted to walk a few steps in the garden. The young girl noticed the freshness and purity of the air, and said how delicious it was to breathe it, and scent its fragrance. "That is sensuality," replied Marie ; thus showing that she refused to herself everything which came in the form of sensible gratification, however innocent.

The moment was now approaching when she was to consummate by a most painful death her long martyrdom of suffering, of which none will know the full measure until they behold the glorious crown and palm which they were preparing for her. On Sunday, the 9th of May, she was pretty well, well enough, at least, to receive her Lord at the community Mass, and even to assist at the Mass which followed. Nor was her fatigue sufficient to interfere with her sitting in the garden, during the remainder of the morning, close to the chapel whither she hoped to return for Vespers. The sisters who had seen her that day, often recalled her peculiar air of recollectedness and peace, remarkable even in one whose face habitually wore a calm and interior expression. The pupils sought some pre-

U

text to draw near occasionally, a flower to present being the common excuse ; and the smile with which she repaid them, and the few gracious words she uttered, alike bespoke the close union of her soul with God.

At half-past twelve she left the garden, and entered a small room on the ground-floor, where she was to partake of some dinner. She felt an extreme disinclination to eat, but, faithful to the end in combating all her repugnances, she compelled herself to swallow a few morsels. The effort had evidently cost her much, for, looking up in the face of her superior, who was present, she said, but still with an accent of submission, "My mother, I cannot." The Mère de Keroüartz knew well that inability alone would have extracted the words "I cannot" from the lips of Marie Lataste ; so she reassured her, and bade her not put any force upon herself. Presently she left her to go and preside at the recreation. Marie pressed the young girl who attended on her to go also. "It is so long, Louise," she said, " since you have been there : it will do you good : I can remain by myself." But Louise would not go, and well it was that she refused, for very shortly Marie was seized with those acute pains in her interior which were to reduce her to the last extremity in the course of a few hours.

She returned to her room, but with great difficulty, and the effort was followed by a paroxysm so violent that her companion believed that she must be in the agonies of death. In the midst of her excruciating sufferings, Marie's chief thought was for the trouble and fatigue which she was causing to her attendant. As soon as the Mère de Keroüartz could be apprised, she hastened to Marie's room ; medical advice was promptly called in, and her danger declared to be imminent.

Marie's life had been a preparation for death, and her pure soul was entirely disengaged from earth. The Superioress knew this, and could, therefore, without fear and without preamble, tell her that she was about to receive the Last Sacraments and pronounce her vows. For several months the period of her noviciate had been completed, and her profession had been delayed only because it had been hoped she would regain her strength sufficiently to make the customary retreat preceding religious consecration. Ardently as Marie desired to complete her union with her Heavenly Spouse, she had said nothing about the delay; she judged herself unworthy of so high an honour, and abandoned the matter, as all else, to the judgment of others. Her joy and gratitude at this announcement were, therefore, great. Earth had still a happiness reserved for her, the prelude to the bliss of Heaven.

The cell of the dying girl was small, only seven feet long by five and a-half in breadth; yet it was the most suitable that could be found in the house : a fact from which its deficiency of accommodation as of other comforts may be inferred. Hither our Lord was borne to her in Viaticum. It would be impossible to describe the heavenly joy which illuminated Marie's countenance as He entered, yet so great was her weakness that it was doubted whether she would be able to pronounce the formula of her vows; it was even considered a question whether it might not be wise first to administer Extreme Unction. But Marie, collecting all her remaining energy, and taking in her hand the blessed candle, asked pardon of all the community for the bad example she believed she had given, adding, "I have committed many faults, but I have always done all that I could." Wonderful avowal, and dictated, doubtless, at that supreme moment by the Spirit of Truth to one who had never been known to justify or exculpate herself. But she is departing now, and, even as the Apostle was inspired to say, " I have fought the good fight, I have kept the faith," so, we may believe, was this lowly servant of God inwardly moved to bear this testimony to herself: "I have done all that I could." She then pronounced in a clear and distinct voice her sacred engagements, after which Communion was given to her.

The nuns, gathered round her bed, were then to witness a scene surprising in itself, considering the utter extenuation of the dying girl, and the more so because it was quite foreign to her ordinary custom to give external expression to her inmost sentiments. By nature not demonstrative, grace had taught her still greater reserve, but she was about to depart, and the usual motives for concealment no longer existed; or, perhaps, the truer reason may be found in her obedience to a movement of the Spirit of God, who would thus at the last manifest and glorify the treasures of grace which He had bestowed on this favoured soul, and which she had ever laboured to hide. After she had received our Lord, Marie burst forth in aspirations of most ardent love, which she interspersed with passages from the Psalms and others borrowed from the writings of saints. "Is any happiness like to mine?" she exclaimed. "I am all Jesus Christ's . . . and for ever. I have never loved any but Him. . . . O Beauty, always ancient and always new!" These words of St. Augustine she repeated several times, without adding those which follow them, and which were not applicable to herself.

The chaplain, M. l'Abbé Lemot, fearing that she might sink from exhaustion, advised her to moderate her transports. She ceased immediately. This temporary silence was, however, only a tribute to the virtue of obedience. She would make this act of submission, but there was One within her stronger than all, who would be obeyed. For, after this brief pause, she recommenced, and with much energy said, "No, no, do not fear, this does not fatigue me; it is not I who speak, it is God who speaks in me, and I cannot hold my peace;" and she then resumed her ardent ejaculations. For a few instants, as they watched, they beheld her, as it were, absorbed and lost in God; her eyes were raised, and fixed as on some glorious object above her, while slowly and at intervals she uttered these words: "O Divinity! . . . O Trinity! . . . O Unity! . . . O Jesus!" Three of the nuns who were present thought they heard her add, "I behold you," which led them to believe that it was given her to fathom something of the deep mystery of the Ever-Blessed Trinity. Be this as it may, her whole act of thanksgiving was like an ecstasy of love. "How happy one is," she exclaimed, "to have loved God from one's youth! . . . I am all Jesus Christ's. O yes, my God, I am indeed all Thine for ever. I have always been Thine with my whole heart, and now I am about to die all Thine. . . . Oh, what a happiness! To die a spouse of the Sacred Heart! What a favour! I did not deserve it . . . but, my God, Thou knowest that I have never willed anything save Thy will in all things. Yes, I am all Thine, all Thine, my Jesus;" and she would repeat those words, "all Thine," over and over again with an indescribable accent of tenderness. Then once more she would exclaim, "O Beauty ever ancient and ever new! As the thirsty hart pants after the living waters, so does my soul sigh for Thee, O Jesus! Oh, come, then, and take my soul. . . . This is the foretaste of Heaven."

Her face meanwhile was all beaming, and they who witnessed this scene, and knew how great was her state of exhaustion, could entertain no doubt but that the strength communicated to her was supernatural. No wonder, therefore, that not only were they deeply affected by what they saw, but that they gazed on her with a kind of religious awe and veneration, as on one who seemed already to enjoy the intimate vision of God. Her paroxysms of pain returned at intervals, during which she endured excruciating torture. The doctors in attendance testified to the intensity of her sufferings, which, they said, were such as would ordinarily have a fatal conclusion within five or six hours; yet, in the case of this weak girl, who seemed to hang to life by so frail a thread, they were prolonged beyond double that time : a circumstance which reminded the Religious that Marie, to whom Jesus had made known that she was to die a death of exceeding agony, a true martyrdom, had repeatedly begged them to pray for her that her patience might not fail. Nor did it fail for one moment, and the sole complaint she uttered, if complaint it could be called, during the most violent attacks which now rapidly succeeded each other, was "O my mother, how I suffer!" or, "Ah, how much one must suffer in order to die!" but she would add immediately, "I am the spouse of the Crucified Jesus." When the sisters saw her about to swoon away from excess of pain, they would rub her temples with eau-de-Cologne, or cause her to inhale it; once or twice she asked for it, but so accustomed was she never to seek any relief or alleviation, that she accused herself of sensuality for making this request. "I must be mortified very much," she said, "to expiate all this." Being asked if it grieved her to die, she replied, "To live or to die is the same to me;" so entirely was every desire, even that of going to be eternally united to God, absorbed and engulfed in His Holy Will.

She sometimes lost her consciousness, but she never lost her self-possession or wandered in mind; the moment she revived, she was completely herself, and would speak, not only calmly, but cheerfully. She would even indulge in some gentle pleasantry, as other holy souls have on similar occasions been known to do. On coming out of a fearful crisis, she said, smiling, "Now that I have made my vows, I have a notion that I shall not die; but I shall have made them all the same. However, if I do get over this, I shall be a sort of contraband religious." Occasionally this idea that she might recover would flash across her mind, and cause her some momentary apprehensions; for, though perfectly conformed to God's will whether to live or die, her spirit sighed after union with her Lord. To depart and be with Jesus! Once she called to the Superioress, in a tone of some dismay, "My mother, do you think my Saviour is going to play me a trick?" "How so?" "Perhaps I am not going to die." Another time, when recovering from one of her paroxysms, she said to her, "I frightened you a good deal; you thought I was dying; but no, He does not wish to take me yet." Her calmness, however, was never for one moment disturbed. She said, it is true, to the Mère de Keroüartz, "You will keep the devil away from me; will you not?" but the enemy of her soul was never suffered to approach it, or so much as to ruffle its surface. Thus was verified what she once heard her guardian angel say in reply to the evil one, who was claiming her as his prey : "Her death will put you to flight."

Towards ten o'clock in the evening, her sufferings having somewhat abated, the chaplain withdrew, believing that she would live through the night. This priest had not witnessed the death of any of the Religious since his arrival; Marie being the first whom he had assisted on her death-bed. Filled with admiration, he repeatedly exclaimed, "It is very beautiful. It is most consoling to see such deaths. If this is the way people die at the Sacré Cœur, it is well worth the trouble of living there !" Marie's respite was very short. Presently the spasms returned with increased violence, and every moment, it was expected, would be her last. These cruel tortures, convulsing her whole frame, would produce at times a change in her features ; but the habitual serenity of expression returned immediately afterwards. She might be heard, indeed, after the sharpest pains exclaiming, " Oh, how sweet is death ! My heart is bursting in twain with love." While making these exclamations her countenance assumed a look of heavenly joy impossible to describe. Her excruciating pains would occasionally, as she lay in a half-unconscious state, extract a groan. The Superior, fearing that she would be heard by the pupils, whose dormitory was quite close, and knowing how powerful over Marie were the claims of obedience, said to her, "My little sister, do not cry out; you will awaken our Lord's children, who are now taking their rest." Although the dying girl at that moment gave no signs of consciousness, her moaning ceased at once, and she never uttered another complaint.

One of the nuns who was in attendance on Marie, being alone with her for a few minutes, confided to her some commissions for Heaven. Marie replied to all with perfect clearness. It was in the intimacy of this last interview that she made that acknowledgment of what she had interiorly suffered, to which we have alluded. God inspired her, no doubt, to do so, that we might not remain in ignorance of what His servant had endured, according to the prediction He had made to her. The sisters who were allowed to sit up with Marie Lataste during this last night she spent on earth, regarded it as a very great privilege, and seventeen years later every particular of her death-bed was still fresh in their memory, as were also the impressions it had made upon them.

What remains to be told we cannot convey better than by quoting the Mère de Kerouartz's account of the closing scene, written on the 18th of May, 1864. "To-day is the anniversary of the death of our good sister Lataste, and the thought of her has never left me; every instant of the night I seemed to be once more near her; I seemed to be present again during those touching and consoling hours of agony, and of feelings on my part which I could not express, and which I have never again experienced, although I have assisted under like circumstances many of ours, whose end has been very edifying. The account that was given in 1847 presents a faithful picture of what occurred. The heavenly transports of this dear sister when dying have been recorded, but it must not be forgotten that she was closing her life by a death of violent pain, the terrible crisis of which lasted much longer than the intervals of calm. This serves only to place in a stronger light her perfect self-possession.

"Filled with a lively sense of the sanctity of a soul whose heroic virtue was now more clearly unveiled to my view, I felt myself moved to ask her forgiveness for all that I might have made her suffer, and I begged her prayers for our Reverend Mother General, for our whole society, and for myself. To the first part of what I said Marie answered by an expressive look of manifest surprise. She appeared, in her deep humility, to be saying to me, 'Why do you say that?' She then promised that she would not forget me, but, when she was in Heaven, would keep in remembrance those who had so loaded her with benefits on earth. As the end drew nearer, Sister Lataste entered again into that state of deep and tranquil recollection which had become, as it were, natural to her. We spoke to her of Heaven, towards which she seemed to be so rapidly going; but we did not feel any necessity, as is usually done in the case of the dying, to suggest that recourse to God and those ejaculations the object of which is to re-animate their courage, their confidence, and their faith. How exhort to patience one who was giving us the most sublime example of it? All were sensible how close was her union with our Lord; her love for Him had made itself manifest in every way.

"Towards four o'clock in the morning her eyes wore an expression which I have still before me; she seemed to be seeking something; she no longer spoke, but her whole appearance betokened that her thoughts were fixed on God. I endeavoured to catch her meaning. In order to explain what occurred, I must observe that the room in which we were was overshadowed by great trees, and all know how in the spring time of the year the awakening of nature at that early hour has a peculiar charm which transports and elevates the soul towards the Creator of all things. A number of birds of various kinds were filling the air with their songs and together forming a concert of enchanting melody. Recalling what we had been saying of the happiness of praising the Lord for all eternity, it came into my mind to address these words to our good Sister: 'You are listening to the birds who are commencing their lauds to God?' She answered by a sweet smile; there was something indescribable in the look she gave me. I had understood her. If I have cited this circumstance, trifling in itself, it is because it was to us a fresh proof of the purity and simplicity of this privileged soul. This loving habit of recognising her Divine Master even in a flower, and in nature generally, did not abandon her at this last and awful passage from time to eternity, and when she might be said scarcely to touch the earth. And, in fact, almost immediately afterwards she kissed her crucifix and expired; heaven, as we felt fully persuaded, opened to receive her, and she exchanged the bitterness of exile for the joys of home. It was the 10th of May, 1847."

The Abbé Lemot, who arrived early, was quite disappointed at not having witnessed Marie's admirable end; such sights are the consolation of Christ's ministers, called, as they so often are, to behold far other scenes at the bedside of the dying. Going up to the little cell, he there found Louise, who, having failed in obtaining permission to pass the night with Marie, had now hastened to the room in which she lay, and was already invoking her intercession; so deep was the general impression of her sanctity. The worthy priest was himself so convinced of the eminence of Marie's virtues, that he began at once to remind the postulant of them, and to exhort her to imitate this chosen soul, that she might one day share the happiness which she was enjoying.

There was something remarkable in the profound and, as it were, heavenly calm which seemed to fill the whole house after Marie had breathed her last. This sentiment, indeed, prevailed over the universal regret for her loss. All pressed into the room to behold her. There she lay, with an angelic expression of innocence on her countenance, which not only had lost all trace of the cruel sufferings she had endured, but was not even overspread with the pallor of death. Those, indeed, who laid her out for burial affirmed that her limbs had retained all their flexibility. To look at her, you might have supposed that she was taking a refreshing sleep. Yes, and truly it was so ; the mortal remains bearing witness to her being in the enjoyment of that blessed rest of the just which the Church implores for each of her children when she says, "Requiescat in pace."

The Superioress, the Mère de Keroüartz, from whose account of Marie Lataste's death we have just quoted, judged it well, on account of the smallness of the cell in which she lay, to have her transported to her own, which was larger and of easier access. She observes that by nature she felt a certain distressing repugnance to approaching the bodies of the dead, but in this instance she experienced nothing of the kind, and had no such feeling to overcome, although a mere screen separated the funeral couch from the other part of the room, in which she continued to pursue her usual occupations ; nay, she even lay down to take some rest for a few hours on her bed, which directly faced that on which Marie was lying. Others, who more or less shared the usual feelings of this Religious about the dead, attested that these had been entirely replaced by the thought of the bliss which their sister, the faithful spouse of Jesus Crucified, was already tasting, and the desire that they too might die a similar death. With the young pupils it was the same; the virtues of Marie were the one subject of conversation amongst them, and they all rejoiced that they had now a new and powerful intercessor in Heaven. Far from feeling the shrinking natural to their age at the sight of the dead, they vied with each other in begging for the favour to go and pray awhile before those blessed remains, on which a ray of Heaven's own peace seemed to rest.

A miracle of grace was at that time worked in the soul of one of these young girls. She had given a great deal of trouble to the nuns of the Sacré Cœur, as she had also at home to her own family. Hitherto she had responded but little to the care bestowed upon her. On one occasion, however, when sickness confined her to the infirmary, she learned at least to appreciate Marie Lataste. The virtues which particularly struck this wilful girl, were her great humility, her tender devotion to the Sacred Heart of Jesus, her exceeding gentleness, and her angelic candour. But though she retained both gratitude and love, and, above all, a deep veneration for Marie, nevertheless her indocile heart had not yet responded to the touch of grace. The last time she saw Marie alive was one day when, accidentally meeting her, she said, "My good sister, you suffer much; do you not?" "No, indeed, Mademoiselle," was Marie's reply; "for I am very glad to suffer what I do suffer. Soon, I hope, I am going to see my Jesus. It is very sweet to die when one has left all for God, and when one loves Him alone." These words made a great impression on her to whom they were spoken, and caused her to reflect. "I should have wished," she says, "like this saintly sister, to be wholly God's." That kind of aspiration has been made by many who have nevertheless died unconverted; the moment, however, of true conversion was not far off in the case of this young girl. She begged the Reverend Mother, as a great favour, to be allowed to go and see the dear sister whom she had loved lying on her bed of death. She felt a strange attraction; a great grace was awaiting her. "I can see her yet," she writes years afterwards, when she was married and the mother of a family,—"I can see her yet on her bed of rest, surrounded with flowers, her hands joined, her face beaming with happiness. It would be difficult to say what I then experienced. These are things which are felt but cannot well be described. At the moment I seemed to have a kind of foretaste of Heaven. I seemed to see her with Jesus in an ecstasy of love, interceding for me who, regarding her as a saint, was praying to her. I no longer clung to anything on earth; I was ready to make every sacrifice. From that day, you must remember,"—she is addressing Mme. de Keroüartz,—"I made great efforts to overcome myself, and I obtained, by the intercession of this dear sister, grace to conquer myself. It is to her I owe my conversion."

We must add that, although this young girl felt attracted towards the chamber of death, she had a great fear of dead bodies, and entered the room with closed eyes and trembling all over; after a brief prayer she opened them, and cast a look on Marie. From that instant she remained (as those present have described) for a long time immovable, all absorbed in meditation,

and apparently paying no attention to anything which
was passing around her.   Faithful to the divine call,
she finished the devotions of the Month of May with
touching piety, and gave the most humble and sincere
testimonies of repentance; and very soon she came to
be pointed out in the school as a model of virtue, for
the transformation that had taken place in her was as
durable as it was complete.

Long after Marie Lataste's mortal remains had been
laid in the ground, her memory was still living among
the Community.   " I wish to become a Sister Lataste "
were words often repeated; and they were not mere
words, for her example continued to act powerfully in
the way of encouragement to the practice of the virtues
of a true religious.   A very young sister who was
languishing with a chest complaint, being observed one
day to be particularly calm and cheerful, it was hoped
that this was a sign of amelioration.   She confessed,
however, that it was not so.   "To become a Sister
Lataste," she said, " one must bear one's cross joyfully.
Oh, if I could die like her!"   The resolutions which
Marie had consigned to paper (as already noticed) were
occasionally read to the Assistant Sisters to animate
and renew in them the spirit of their vocation.   They
all recognised in those simple rules which she had laid
down for her own guidance the marks of consummate
virtue, such as they are depicted in St. Aloysius
Gonzaga and other youthful Saints who have accomplished a long career in a brief space of time.   The
weak ones sometimes asked themselves if it were possible for them ever to approach the perfection of such a
model, but all liked to speak of her and to recall those
instances of her sanctity which had fallen severally
under their notice.

Her example acted even on those who had never known her, from witnessing the effect it had produced upon those who had enjoyed this advantage. Mme. Marie Passedouet, a Religious of the Sacré Cœur, relates, in a letter written from the Rue de Varenne, how, when she became a postulant at the house at Rennes, she was struck with the mutual charity evinced by the sisters. She remarked upon this to the Mère de Vaux, who replied that all wished to become Sisters Lataste. "But I do not know that sister," rejoined the postulant. "I well believe that," said the mother, "since she has been dead these three years." "This sister was very holy, then?" "Yes, she left us great examples of humility; her love for the hidden life and her purity of intention were remarkable, as well as her self-devotion; and yet she was only a novice." The postulant avowed that these words increased her desire to give herself to God, and confirmed her in her resolution to make this consecration of herself at the Sacré Cœur, since it could train up saints. From that moment some lingering prejudices which had been instilled into her mind against the Congregation vanished. In the course of the following year, this same sister, when giving a report to Mme. de Keroüartz of the children entrusted to her care, complained, a little too bitterly perhaps, of one among them, adding, "What a difference between her and Amélie D——!" that was the young girl who had been converted at the time of Marie Lataste's death. "If you were as humble as was the Sister Lataste," answered the Mère de Keroüartz, "you would make of Gabrielle what she made of Amélie, who, three years ago, was ten times more unmanageable than she of whom you complain." The sister observed that it needed all her reliance on the word of her respected mother to believe that Amélie whom she beheld so pious, so courteous, so modest, so devotedly kind to her companions, could ever have been so troublesome. She added that she had seen her perform acts of virtue from which she herself might possibly have recoiled, although she had already entered on the religious life.

The examples of eminent holiness which Marie Lataste had given to the Community must certainly have been very striking to produce so abiding an impression, particularly when it is remembered that the Religious during this first year of their foundation had their time so much occupied with work, owing to their limited number, that they could see very little of each other, and had scarcely leisure enough to become mutually acquainted. An ancient Religious, who was sent to Rennes three years after Marie's death, mentions that she constantly heard the sisters, at their recreation hour, recalling all the particulars of her last moments. "I attributed this, I must allow," she continues, "to a pious enthusiasm, which with time would evaporate. Time, however, has advanced, and yet the impression, instead of fading away, vindicates by its endurance what is said in Holy Scripture, that the memory of the just is eternal."

On the 19th of May the Superioress received a letter from M. Dupérier, of which the greater portion is here quoted, as it serves to prove that ecclesiastic's firm persuasion of the sanctity of her whom once he had treated as a visionary. "Madam," he writes, "I have heard to-day of the loss you have sustained in the death of one of your sisters, Marie Lataste. I know not whether, on this occasion, to offer you my condolence or to congratulate you upon having another protectress in

x

Heaven. For I entertain the strongest conviction that she was a saint. I had been acquainted with her for two or three years before she entered the noviciate of the Sacré Cœur. She was always a pattern of virtue in her parish. Although she had never received any education, and had never been to school, having merely received a little instruction from her mother, whose own knowledge was very limited, she nevertheless wrote with clearness and precision, and in a manner that was truly astonishing, a number of things upon religion, devotion, and the mystical life. These writings were submitted to my examination, and I obtained the opinion of others regarding them; all who read them thought them wonderful. They contained some predictions, and, amongst them, one which seemed to announce her early death. . . . I should feel extremely obliged to you, Madam, if you would have the goodness to give me some particulars concerning the close of this young sister's life, and the reputation in which she was held, both at the noviciate house and also in your house at Rennes. You may depend on my making no use of this information further than you may be pleased to sanction. The day may come when, along with the documents we already possess, it may help to promote the glory of God and the edification of souls. I am, with the profoundest respect, &c., (Signed) Dupérier, Professor of Theology at the Seminary of Dax."

Such, then, was the life and such the death of this humble sister. God hearkened to her prayer and to the internal desire of her heart, inspired, doubtless, by Himself, to remain hidden during her life. But it is the firm conviction of those who know what that life was, and who, besides, are well acquainted with the works she has left, that the day is not far distant when

the promise which she heard from the lips of the
Saviour will receive its full accomplishment: "I will
render your name famous among those who have been
devout to the Sacrament of My Love;" and again,
"All that I have said to you shall be published throughout the whole world, and shall be profitable to many."
But it seems to have entered into the designs of God
that, in order to the accomplishment of these promises,
which have already begun to receive their fulfilment,
Marie should be like a light hidden under a bushel
during her lifetime. We may perceive one possible
reason for this dispensation regarding her. For, supposing that her great and exceptional gifts had been
better known, and she had in consequence been made
a choir nun, receiving the additional cultivation which
would have fitted her for that position, and which she
was well able to acquire, it would have been impossible
not to recognise in her one of the most remarkable
Religious whom the Sacré Cœur had ever possessed.
But then, the suspicious and incredulous—and they
abound even among good people—would probably have
been tempted to attribute her writings to her natural
powers; and, if they had not actually believed, in the
face of contrary evidence, that they had been penned after
she had profited by the literary culture bestowed upon
her at the convent, they would, at least, have surmised
that subsequently to her entrance into religion she had
retouched and perfected them. Now, as we have seen,
Marie remained illiterate to the last; she was also
moved, before she left her distant home, to divest herself entirely of her right over her own productions, and
to commit them to the keeping of one whose testimony
was incontrovertible as to their genuineness. The
nuns of the Sacré Cœur never saw her works until

after her death ; and, with the exception of her superiors, none assuredly so much as knew that she had
ever written a line. She would have been the last to
tell them, and superiors were led to adopt a system towards her which kept her in the mortified and humble
sphere in which it was her own cherished desire to
remain.

This hidden character of her life accompanied her to
the grave ; and, strange to say, the precise spot where
she was interred is not known. Only a few days after
her death, the Superioress inquired whether a cross
had been placed upon her tomb, with the customary
inscription. This had not been done ; and, desirous
of repairing the omission without delay, she had the
keeper of the cemetery questioned on the subject. He
replied that, several burials having taken place the same
day, he could not furnish any precise information. No
doubt, so short a space of time having elapsed, it would
have been quite possible to ascertain the exact locality ;
and it may appear surprising that the Mère de Keroüartz abstained from taking any further steps to discover
it. The reason which she afterwards alleged was that,
having recalled to mind that Marie had often said that
she begged God to keep her hidden in death as in life,
she believed that she saw in these circumstances the
fulfilment of that prayer, and a sign that God willed
to accomplish it through these means.

This neglect on the part of the Mère de Keroüartz,
however good the motive, is much to be regretted ; and
especially has it been lamented by those—and, we are
assured, they are not few in number—who, having
been moved to invoke the humble peasant of Mimbaste,
believe that they have obtained signal graces through
her intercession. We are led, therefore, to cherish the

hope that one day our Divine Lord will hearken to the prayers of His suppliants, and make known to them the spot in which the precious remains of His faithful disciple have been deposited. Meanwhile the Religious of the Sacré Cœur have transformed the little cell where Marie completed the sacrifice of her pure soul, into an oratory dedicated to the Heart of Jesus. Hither many ecclesiastics, as well as lay persons, come from time to time to pray; and hither also the nuns themselves often repair for pious meditation—thanking God for the example He had been pleased to give them in their departed sister, and begging Him to grant them the courage and the grace to emulate her virtues.

## CHAPTER XXIII.

### THE WRITINGS OF MARIE LATASTE.

IN the course of this narrative, continual allusions have been made to the writings of Marie Lataste, and frequent extracts have been given from them. The reader is already acquainted with all the circumstances under which they were penned, and their consignment by Marie into the hands of her director, the Curé of Mimbaste, when she repaired to Paris to seek admission into the convent of the Sacré Cœur. After her departure, he consulted M. Dupérier, who shared his admiration of these writings, and they agreed together in judging that it would be desirable to publish them for the sake of the spiritual benefit which it might be anticipated they would produce. This anticipation was

not grounded solely upon the value which they themselves set upon the writings.   The manuscript had
been confidentially shown, in whole or in part, to
various persons, and discretion alone has restrained the
editor of her works from recording several examples of
their remarkable effect.   One, however, was related by
M. Pascal Darbins in the earliest edition.   The Curé
had shown the first sheets of Marie's manuscript to a
distinguished magistrate of the town of Dax, for which
he testified his gratitude in a letter, adding these
noticeable words :—"The perusal has done me more
good than I could tell you.   I can, however, give you
some idea of it.   God has preserved to me the life of
my daughter, who has been so dangerously ill ; such
would have been my grief in losing her that I certainly
should not have survived her.   Now, since reading
these papers, I am prepared for any sacrifice.   I should
have the courage to bear all, and to say to God, Thy
will be done.   I should even willingly make the sacrifice of my life, and die contented."

Mgr. Lanneluc, the Bishop of Aire, being consulted on
the subject of the publication, judged it desirable to
defer it, and it was in consequence postponed.   In the
meantime the Curé of Mimbaste was transferred to the
parish of Saint-Paul-lès-Dax, in the town of Dax, where
his duties were necessarily much more onerous than they
had been in the little village of Mimbaste.   The preparation of Marie Lataste's works necessitated the
expenditure of some time and trouble ; not that it was
contemplated to make the slightest alteration in the text,
beyond the correction of some faults of orthography and
the removal of a few Gascon idioms, but they were written
without any method or plan, according as memory recalled to her the words and instructions of the Saviour,

and several who were well qualified to judge, being consulted on the point, were all of opinion that it was most desirable to classify and arrange in a certain order the different subjects treated of before proceeding to print. Marie herself seems to have expected something of the kind; at any rate, her own observations tended entirely to remove any scruple that might have been entertained as to making such a revision.

"I have written," she said, "as things occurred to my mind. What I know is, that the Saviour Jesus from the beginning promised to instruct me in the true science—the science of salvation. There ought, then, to be in what I have written, in obedience to my director and to the Saviour Jesus, wherewithal to satisfy the desire of any mind intent on salvation, and of any soul aspiring to God. It will be easy to supply what may be wanting; it will be easy especially to arrange my writings in such a manner as to fit them to be communicated to the faithful and to be profitable to them." Our Lord, she added, told her that He had inspired her director to require her to write them, desiring that later they should be placed in the hands of those who were devout to His Sacred Heart. They were to be all, therefore, carefully preserved, but He reminded her that she was to regard herself simply as an instrument, since of herself she was utterly ignorant. He also bade her give them up to her director, who would keep them by him till the time should have arrived for making them known.

It was clear, therefore, that a certain obligation had been laid upon M. Darbins respecting the papers which Marie had bequeathed to him when she bade adieu to the world. Accordingly, it was natural for him to seek the best advice and assistance in fulfilling this duty;

and it is believed that, had M. Dupérier lived, he
would have been the person selected to edit the writings, but he died in 1848, only a year after Marie.
The task of arrangement was then entrusted to the
Abbé Pascal Darbins, nephew of the Curé of Saint
Paul, and the first edition was published in 1862, with
the formal approbation of Mgr. Épivent, the then Bishop
of Aire.  The work had been prepared under the eye of
Marie's director, and no changes, however trifling, were
made without the consent and authorisation of him
who was most deeply sensible of the responsibility of
the undertaking, and better acquainted than any one
else could be with her mind and wishes.  These
changes, in fact, were very slight, as we have already
stated, and no omission was permitted, save of a few
passages containing obvious repetitions.

Some critical spirits might find fault with the course
pursued, and, indeed, as the Abbé tells us, persons did
raise objections.  They said, How is it, if it be true
that our Lord instructed Marie Lataste in this marvellous way, that He did not at the same time impart to
her the necessary knowledge for expressing herself in a
thoroughly correct manner, so as not to require the intervention of others for making known these extraordinary conversations? and further still: Why did He
not follow the order which was afterwards judged to be
the more suitable, or, at least, some kind of order?
Why, finally, was not the text preserved just as Marie
wrote it, with all its defects of spelling and its Gascon-
isms?  The answer to these difficulties, the Abbé
suggests, was furnished beforehand, and recorded by
Marie in her correspondence.  Our Lord, she relates,
said to her one day, " If anyone should ask you why
you have written thus, and why I have allowed you to

do so, reply that My designs are hidden and secret; that I desired to exercise your obedience, your perfect abnegation, and humility." Here is a satisfactory answer to the first difficulty. It is in accordance with the dealings of God even with those who were divinely commissioned to announce His word. It did not please the Lord to impart a polished style even to His Apostles and Evangelists; and we cannot, therefore, wonder that Marie Lataste should not have been supernaturally taught to write irreproachable nineteenth-century French. Indeed, in such a case, there would not have been wanting persons who on that very account would have seen reason for suspecting that the writings were not purely her own.

As for the second objection, it may be gathered from Marie Lataste's own statements that our Lord made His communications to her at different times, according as her spiritual progress, her needs, or casual circumstances required. He began by instructing her how to correct what was defective in her, proceeding afterwards to reveal to her the secrets of divine science and wisdom. This, surely, was to follow a plan, the plan best suited for training the soul under His guidance. But Marie herself, in relating our Lord's communications to her, drew upon her memory, aided supernaturally, as we have seen, and reported them as they successively recurred to her mind; most of her letters being written to supply omissions or furnish additional particulars.

Finally, in reply to the inquiry why the works were not published precisely as Marie had grouped them in her manuscripts, the Abbé quotes, in justification of himself and his advisers, her own written authorisation. She states that our Lord on one occasion thus addressed her:—" Your director will arrange your works as he shall judge proper, if he shall have the time, in order to their being printed; if not, he will do it by the hand of another." We have already quoted a remark of her own to the same effect. All this is sufficient to prove that Marie Lataste's director had full powers to make the specified changes. It may, of course, be a matter of opinion which of the two arrangements was most advisable; some persons might have preferred the un-classified form, in which Marie simply reported what she had heard, but those competent authorities who were consulted were all in favour of a methodical arrangement, such as was in fact adopted, believing that it would be the most satisfactory to the generality of readers.

The works were preceded by her Life, in conformity with the desire which she, by divine dictation, had manifested. "Your director," the Saviour Jesus had said to her, "will furnish the necessary documents for writing your life, and he who shall be selected to write it shall at the same time avail himself of your papers and letters, which are to be carefully preserved." These directions were strictly followed, and in the earliest edition the Life contained numerous quotations from the works and letters; and it was certainly well, notwithstanding the repetitions thus entailed, that this should be done, at least in the first instance. The Life of Marie Lataste is utterly incomplete without continual references to our Lord's conversations with her and to the visions with which she was favoured. Such references, however, have been, as far as was possible, curtailed in the last two editions.*

In the year 1866 the third edition was published;

---

* In the last two editions, the Life, as also the letters connected with it and necessary for its illustration, has been detached from

and Pièrre Darbins, the revered Curé of Saint Paul-
lès-Dax, whose health was failing, handed over to his
nephew, Pascal Darbins, together with a written attestation, the manuscripts left him by Marie. In the
following year the holy man departed this life, to the
great regret of all who knew him, and of his bishop in
particular. The Abbé Pascal, previously to publishing
the third edition, had the manuscripts carefully collated
with what had been printed, and for this purpose submitted them, with the approval of his bishop, to the
examination of several Fathers of the Company of
Jesus. The most sceptical mind could therefore entertain no doubt as to the genuineness and authenticity of the documents or as to their faithful reproduc-
tion.

We may therefore leave this subject, and proceed to
give a few examples of the high testimony rendered to
their value by various persons well qualified to judge ;
and this, not as respects their substance alone, but their
form and expression also. We have seen what was the
opinion of her director and of M. Dupérier, and how
great was their surprise at finding truths of so exalted
an order, couched in language at once simple and
forcible, which at times even rose to eloquence, flowing
from the pen of an illiterate peasant girl, and not even
written in the tongue with which she was most familiar,
her Gascon *patois*. They rightly judged that it would
have been impossible for a country-girl, left to her own
natural resources, to have produced anything similar,
and Marie had not even, as we have said received the
usual education of village children ; neither could she
have derived it from books, for the few she possessed

the works. The execution was entrusted to a Religious of the
Sacré Cœur, the sister of a learned Jesuit.

were of an ordinary character.*    Besides, what *literary* use can any uneducated person make of a book ?

The same opinion we find recorded by the Abbé Pascal Darbins, the editor of the works; and when, from discussing their style, he proceeds to speak of their substance, he expresses his amazement at the sublimity and depth of the truths developed and explained by one who had never learned anything but the simple catechism in which youth is instructed in the chief articles of the faith.   " How sublime are her views,"

* The books possessed by Marie's family, which she therefore had always at hand, consisted of a small volume of "Meditations for each day in Lent;" "Think Well On't ;" "Visits to the Blessed Sacrament;" "The Way of the Cross ;" " The Month of Mary ;" "The Angel our Guide in the Christian Life ;" "a Paroissien ;" and another book styled "Prayers and Divers Instructions."

The following books had been lent her by her first director M. Forbas, and returned to him on his leaving Mimbaste :—"An Abridgement of Saint's Lives," in one volume ; " The Introduction to a Devout Life," by St. Francis of Sales ; "The Imitation of the Blessed Virgin ;" "The Golden Book;" "A Paraphrase of the *Salve Regina;*" "A Picture of Penance ;" " The True Belief of the Church ;" "Tho Spiritual Combat;" "Lives of Fathers of the Desert," by Michel Ange Marin, of the Order of Minims; some volumes of "The Life of the People of God ; " a historic treatise on Providence; and two volumes of P. Bourdaloue's Sermons.

M. Forbas also lent her the Old and New Testament, but it incidentally appears from a passage in her Life (page 66), that she afterwards possessed a Bible of her own.

Her new director, the Abbé Darbins, does not appear to have lent her any books ; and those which M. Forbas afforded her the opportunity of reading were returned before the command to write had been given to her, or could possibly have been anticipated by her.   Besides, being mainly books of piety and simple instruction, intermixed with a few historical works, they were not of such a character as would have enabled her, had she possessed them for reference, to write with their help the complete treatise of doctrine and morality which she produced.   But on this subject sufficient has already been said in Chapter VI.

he exclaims, "regarding the power, wisdom, mercy, justice, and holiness of God! She speaks of the mysteries of the Trinity, of the Incarnation, and Redemption with a depth of thought and of knowledge equal, as respects the substance, to that of the great Doctors of the Church. She proposes the most difficult questions, that of predestination, for instance, and suggests replies with a clearness and a simplicity which bring them within the reach of the least developed intellects. Within the limits of a few pages she has summed up the most important points of all that the best theologians have written on the subjects of grace, the virtues, and sin. All is set down with the order, method, and precision of an accomplished scholar."

The dogmatic accuracy of Marie's writings is one of their most remarkable and marvellous features. There are, however, here and there some inexact expressions open to adverse criticism, or which have been considered so by certain critics. An eminent theologian furnished some notes, which have been appended in the fourth edition to the questionable passages, rectifying them or explaining them by her own statements in other parts of her works. Most of these corrections had been already given by P. Toulemont in an article inserted in a well-known religious periodical,* when reviewing the first edition. After summing them up he justly observes that this very limited number of doubtful expressions is scattered over a voluminous body of instruction, the accuracy of which is irreproachable; and that, moreover, most of the difficulties they present are indefinitely diminished or altogether disappear when the doctrine is examined in its

* "Études Religieuses, Historiques, et Littéraires," par des Pères de la Compagnie de Jésus. No. 7. 1863.

entirety. He adds " There is little rashness in affirming
that Marie Lataste's *thought* has never been erroneous;
it is rather the expression, as Mgr. the Bishop of Aire
observes, which has been wanting in exactness." Of
course, as P. Toulemont remarks, inexact expressions
could never have been dictated by our Lord, but Marie
had taken care, from the very outset, to state that she
was unable to represent in words all that she had heard.
Elsewhere she says, " I have not spoken like the
Saviour, but only as I understood or as He permitted."
And again she says that on many occasions she did not
even hear Jesus's voice when He spoke, but that she
understood Him by His look and manner, and that she
could not find terms in which to convey what had been
manifested to her without the utterance of a word.
"Can we wonder, then," says P. Toulemont, "if appropriate expressions should sometimes have failed
her ? Is it surprising that a poor peasant girl should
not always have spoken with theological precision of
language, when reporting, after an interval of two years,
a course of instruction which fills more than a volume,
and which treats of the most delicate and difficult
questions?" The wonder is all the other way. Her
almost invariable accuracy appears to us something
miraculous.

If any one should be inclined to ask why our Lord
was not pleased to make His miracle perfect, leaving no
flaw, however slight, we may remind the inquirer that
herein lies one of the differences between private revelations and such as were intended for universal reception
and are presented to us for acceptance by the authority
of the Church. These last, which must be received and
believed by all, not only were divinely inspired, but
their writers enjoyed a special assistance of the Holy

Spirit, whereby, as the chosen instruments for transmitting God's word, they were preserved from all error. So it was, for example, with the Evangelists. Private revelations, on the other hand, have for their immediate object the spiritual profit of the individual who receives them, and it is only in a secondary sense that they are intended for others. A special assistance, such assistance as should infallibly preclude any error or mistake, was not indispensable in these cases, but rather the reverse, were it only to guard the humility of the recipients of those high favours. God, it is true, enlightens such souls supernaturally, and manifests certain truths to them, but He permits the faculties to exercise themselves concurrently upon them. It is admitted that the most real and heavenly communications do not in general exclude the play of the natural powers; and in visions, especially, the imagination may unconsciously add something of its own; for, since the imagination confessedly acts, the work must be regarded as conjointly divine and human, and it is very hard to define the limits of each element. Now the human element, it is evident, must be, like all that is human, liable to error. This, with other reasons which it is not necessary here to develop, will be sufficient to account for the contradictions to be met with in visions which different saints have had of the same mysteries; *e.g.*, of the Passion. And if saints have sometimes confounded their own thoughts with divine inspirations, we have no reason to take serious exception should there be cause to surmise that on one or two occasions this may have happened in the case of Marie Lataste.* Thus much

---

* This remark has, in fact, hardly any apparent ground for application except on one occasion. Some of her reported communications from our Lord, with directions how to apply for

has been said that we may not seem to have passed by any criticism which has been made. It all amounts to very little.

To proceed with the favourable appreciation with which her works were received in so many quarters. An eminent ecclesiastic, of the diocese of Aire, who had been directed by the bishop to examine the works before they were printed, wrote thus to the Abbé Darbins :—" I cannot tell you what I experienced on perusing, as I did two or three times, the first sheet which you sent to me. I esteem it a great favour which God has done me in placing this admirable work under my eyes. Apart from all that is supernatural in these communications of the Saviour with the humble peasant girl of Mimbaste, there is in her writings such a breath of inspiration, such peace, such a sweet simplicity and richness of unction, and they produce so deep an impression on the soul, that, in my opinion, one cannot fail to discern in them God and His Holy Spirit." As he proceeded with his reading, we find him writing again in the same strain, and with ever-increasing enthusiasm.

The following is the testimony rendered by that distinguished theologian, P. Ramière :—"A simple country-girl, who scarcely knew how to read and write, is found to have composed within a short time,* and

admission to the Sacré Cœur, had never any actual fulfilment. It was never necessary, for instance, to apply to the Archbishop of Paris on her behalf; and, moreover, certain reported expressions of our Lord seemed to fall in with the erroneous idea, which she and others at first entertained, that the classification of the Sisters was determined by the portion they brought, whereas, as we have seen, it was dependent on their education. It was just upon such an occasion as this that Marie might possibly be led into some trifling mistake, for her mind must have worked intensely on the subject of the carrying out of her vocation.

* Less than three years.

that only by devoting to the work a few hours stolen from sleep or snatched from her daily toil, what the most learned theologian, the most practised writer, would hardly have been able to accomplish in the space of many years and with great labour. It seems difficult to me not to discern herein a manifest proof of the supernatural origin of these writings, especially when it is considered that their authenticity is supported by incontestable evidence." Another theologian, after having read and carefully examined her writings, declared that they might be placed side by side with the most remarkable and useful books of piety of a like order. The Carmelite Nuns of Aire, the first Religious to whom they were communicated, were alike charmed and edified ; and their Superioress, writing on the subject to the Abbé Darbins, thus concluded :—" Oh, how admirable is God ! He has made use of this little creature, in whom He could freely act, to speak of the great truths of religion, and to confirm, as it would seem, what saints and doctors have written of them, but whose sublime thoughts might by some be attributed to their own personal spirit and genius. Here it is impossible to see anything save the Spirit of God ! "

The writings of Marie Lataste (as has been already said) were not seen by the nuns of the Sacré Cœur until after they had been published. The impression which they produced has been recorded in a number of letters from their different communities in France and other countries. They all speak the same language, and bear testimony alike to the admiration excited by them and the spiritual profit derived from their perusal. The Abbé Darbins says that he has also in his possession a considerable number of letters received from ecclesiastics in high station, as well as from others remark-

Y

able for their learning and piety, who had transmitted
to him their appreciation of these works : grand-vicars,
superiors and professors of seminaries, eminent theologians, religious experienced in the direction of souls.
Their very number hindered him from attempting to
quote them all ; besides, their judgment for the most
part closely coincided with that of P. Toulemont.
The Abbé, however, selects a few, which he generally
abridges. We must be yet more concise. A chaplain
of one of the houses of the Sacré Cœur concludes his
contribution of high praise in these terms : "If this
work was placed in the hands of a man versed in
theology, the name of its author being concealed from
him, I believe that the judgment he would pronounce
would be that the work was the fruit of consummate
science." M. Allain, a former superior in the seminary of Rennes, belonging to the Society of Priests
of the Immaculate Conception, gave it as his opinion
that Marie Lataste's book was quite unique in its
character, and totally unlike anything written in the
ordinary way ; such, at least, he declared, was his
feeling whenever he read any passage in it. The work
of this humble peasant-girl, he says, is "a compendious
treatise of religion viewed in all its leading points.
Dogma, with its most exalted mysteries, evangelical
morality, in its most important and practical applica-
tions, spirituality, with its fundamental rules, all is
treated there ; and with what vigour, what simplicity,
what serenity !" There is much more to the same
purpose which we omit.

The words of the Bishop of Aire, however, which he
subjoined to his episcopal approbation, must find a
place. Bishops, as we know, are necessarily cautious
in giving their opinion, and are never heedlessly lavish

of their encomiums. This circumstance confers all the higher value on their testimony. "Yes," he says, "God will more and more bless this book, which is dear to His Divine Son, and it will be the substantial aliment of those souls which are simple and upright in their ways." M. Houet, a canon theologian of the diocese of Rennes, sent the Abbé Darbins, at his request, his judgment in writing of the works of Marie Lataste. His approbation is strong, and his remarks on the criticised passages coincide with those of P. Toulemont. He does not think that, the sanctity of her life and the authenticity of the writings being pre-supposed—and those two points he considers to be incontestably proved—any objection grounded either on the form of these communications, strange as it may at times appear, or on their substance, can be reckoned sufficient to interfere with their claims on our belief. Inexactness of language he considers to be extremely rare, and as regarded the one or two passages which might be taken to convey something positively erroneous, it was not impossible to interpret them in conformity with the general teaching of theologians ; as was done in the case of two passages in St. Bridget's Revelations, as well as in others similarly approved. (See Benedict XIV. "On the Canonisation of Saints," book iii.) So far negatively, as regards objections. He then states some of his positive reasons for crediting Marie Lataste's revelations, and, amongst them, he specially alleges, 1. the prediction of the Definition of the Immaculate Conception and of the very form in which it was made ; 2. that of her own death, which was literally fulfilled ; 3. her superior understanding of Christian dogma in its highest expression ; 4. the sound morality and wisdom of the rules which she lays down. He quotes

M. Guitton, a Vicar-General and former professor of
theology, as thoroughly agreeing with him.　For both
of them, he says, the decisive test of the truth of her
prophecies will be the triumph of the present Pope and
the deliverance of Rome.*　The Abbé Darbins also gives
a most favourable judgment sent to him by another
Vicar-General of Rennes.　All lay much stress on the
worth of the moral as well as the dogmatic portion of
her works.　We may add that (as Marie's biographer
has observed) it is, humanly speaking, inexplicable
how a young girl, isolated from the world, should have
displayed the comprehension she does of the chief
wounds of society in our day and the remedies which
they call for, of its false maxims and the antidotes
which should be applied to counteract their fatal
venom.　Again, it would have been difficult for anyone to paint in more striking colours the deplorable
results of religious indifferentism, the ingratitude of
men abandoned to the dominion of their passions, and
the misery of families, cities, and empires which forsake
God.　Where did this child of poverty, this unin-
structed denizen of a secluded village in the most
isolated of districts, whose feet had never wandered
beyond the wild solitary pastures where she tended her
flock, or the road which led to her village church—
where did she acquire this knowledge of an outer
world which she had never seen, and of its cankering
plagues—the insatiable love of wealth and of pleasure,
the luxury entailed thereby, the ambition which infests

---

* We have already observed, with reference to her well-known
prophecy of the three years and more during which Rome would
be in the power of its enemies, that we are scarcely entitled to say
that the restoration of the Pontiff to his rights at the close of that
period is necessarily included in the terms employed, although
the conclusion was a natural one to draw.

all classses, the over-estimate and immoderate pursuit of science and art, which so often turn away hearts from the study of the only indispensable science, the one thing necessary, the knowledge of God, of His Will and His commandments, and of the means which lead to the attainment of our only true good?

Her appreciation of the grandeur and dignity of the priesthood and of the proper qualities of a director of souls is not less striking; indeed, there is not a situation in life concerning which she does not evince the most penetrating discernment, and offer rules of conduct which may be studied with great profit by all. M. Fallières, a Grand-Vicar of Amiens, whose opinion had been asked, but to quote which would be but to recapitulate in substance the judgment of others, says, " It was a few days ago that a distinguished Superioress of a community (not of the Sacré Cœur) said to me, ' I am at this present reading the works of Marie Lataste. Oh, how beautiful it is when she speaks of the priest! Assuredly, I always venerated the priest, but it appears to me as if I had now a higher esteem for him and a deeper respect.' What charms me," continues M. Fallières, " in the midst of so much profound and solid doctrine, so sublime and yet so practical, is the perfect simplicity and the deep humility of the writer. Never do you find her occupied, still less pre-occupied, with self. In obeying, she has manifested no other desire save that of fulfilling the will of God, and of rendering, so far as was in her power, honour and praise for ever to Jesus in the Most Holy Sacrament of the Altar." Then, recalling to mind how her humble and obscure life in the Landes was followed by a life still more humble and obscure in the community which she joined, and where she succeeded in hiding herself and in almost disappearing amongst her sisters, this Religious adds, that she feels a great confidence in the sanctity of those souls who make humility their chief delight. " I have an instinctive love," she says, " of those little ones of the earth to whom the Lord reveals Himself ; and I willingly listen to them when, moreover, it appears to me that their words carry with them a light which illuminates the soul and a perfume which pervades it."

A venerable Religious, P. Barelle, of the Company of Jesus, thus expressed himself concerning Marie's works :—" These volumes are full of admirable doctrine ; on every page one recognises the touch of the Word made Flesh, and the absence of the creature, who has received only in order to give. It is very desirable that this work should be circulated, and be read, if possible, by a large number of people ; for it is not written for any single class of persons, but for all generally ; such is the conviction derived from their perusal. I hope that the price may be sufficiently reduced to bring it within the reach of all ranks, so that the majority may be able to gather from this tree, which is truly a tree of life planted in the Paradise of the Heart of our Lord Jesus Christ."

The venerable Curé of Dax, Marie's director, heard with indescribable pleasure of the general admiration and appreciation of her works. He himself read them with unflagging interest, and shed many tears over the chapter which related the illness and death of this pious girl. Who can be surprised at this ? In the pastor's love for the members of his flock there is a deep tenderness which in a certain sense none can share, not even the nearest friends ; for, with the exception of the God from whom nothing is hidden, no one has so nearly approached them, or has been admitted to such intimacy; no one has been so profoundly acquainted with every fold of the hearts of those committed to his care, with their affections, their temptations, their sorrows, their trials, and, if with their sins, so also with their worth; no one has been to them the dispenser of such precious benefits: and who does not dearly love those whom he has benefited?

"Poor Marie Lataste!" he exclaims, in a letter written in 1866; "how good she was, how pious, how truly holy! How often in her presence have I had to humble myself, to blush for my cowardice, my lack of faith and of zeal for my own sanctification! I say it in all truth, her writings, her letters, her conversation, her whole conduct, in fine, have done immense good to my soul. The memory of this saintly girl will never be effaced from my mind. Every day, as I recommend myself to her prayers, I feel within me an impression which allows me to entertain no doubt but that she is specially interceding for me."

A year later, her holy director had gone to join her, as we have every reason to trust, in the abode of everlasting bliss.

We have learned, on the best authority, that, notwithstanding the prudent reserve enjoined by the Church in the case of persons on whose sanctity no authoritative judgment has as yet been passed—a reserve sure to meet with due observance among Religious—confidence in the intercessory power of the sister who gave such edification to their community thirty years ago continues unabated in the Rennes house. It will be remembered how great was the affection and reverence elicited in the hearts of the pupils towards Marie while she was yet among them; and it is, therefore, perhaps, worthy of remark that the young girls receiving their education at present in that community frequently beg her aid, and, especially when about to pass through one of their school examinations, will make a *novena*, or ask leave to burn a lamp, in her honour, to obtain a favourable issue. It is still more worthy of remark that their prayer is granted, and this even when some circumstance has rendered their success doubtful.

We are also assured that, in spite of the most diligent inquiries, the exact spot of Marie Lataste's interment has not been discovered. Our respected informant says that, unless some special miracle should hereafter point it out, no reasonable hope can now be entertained of its identification; adding these words: "Has her prayer to remain hidden after death been granted? To this question the future must reply."

# QUITTERIE LATASTE.

# QUITTERIE LATASTE.

QUITTERIE LATASTE was worthy of being the sister of Marie. Eleven years her senior, for Quitterie was born in 1811, she early manifested a serious and deeply pious disposition. At eighteen she went to try her vocation with the Sisters of St. Vincent de Paul, passed her noviciate in the mother house in the Rue de Bac at Paris, and in the year 1830 was placed at the foundling hospital, the *Enfants Trouvés*, where, as the reader will remember, we made a brief acquaintance with her. She appeared to us on that occasion chiefly in the light of a censurer, although a kind one, of what she regarded as imprudence in her sister's conduct. In this, however, she acted blamelessly, from ignorance of Marie's peculiar vocation ; for she was distinguished among her sisters in religion, not only for her solid virtues, but for her tender charity. At the close of the year 1844, only a few months after Marie had entered the Sacré Cœur, Quitterie was sent to Turin by her superiors. Here she was terribly tried, in what way we do not learn, but her devotion to the Passion sustained her ever under her cross. She was after-wards sent to Genoa to found an institution. Here, again, troubles and trials awaited her, and she was seen to practise such countless acts of deep humility that the administrators of the institution could not but be struck with her merit, and were heard one day to exclaim that they had never before met with any women of that kind. In 1859 we find her superioress of the hospital at Perugia, and the nuns of the Sacred Heart, who had a school in the place, often heard of the great esteem in which she was held, and of the power which her truly heroic virtues and her reputation of sanctity gave her over the hearts of all who came within the sphere of her influence. Even the enemies of the Church, and of all that bore the stamp of religion, felt and acknowledged this power, for many of their wounded, who had been carried to the hospital at the time of the capture of the city, could not refuse her their respect and admiration. "There is nothing remarkable about her," they said, "and yet she pleases; everything she says is appropriate and good." The usurpers of the Pontifical States were striving under one pretext or another to secularise every institution. Accordingly, the Sisters of Charity were marked out for expulsion; but, as things could not be carried with so high a hand as they are at present, an excuse had to be sought in the mismanagement of the hospital. One who could render personal testimony to the fact afterwards declared that to Quitterie Lataste, the Superioress, it was owing that the design was defeated. Every attempt was made, by the closest and most vexatious investigation, to catch the Sisters in some fault which might seem to justify their dismissal; but the Superioress, with a marvellous calmness and rare presence of mind, knew how to give such perfect satisfaction to every inquiry, down to the minutest details, that these irreligious men, agents of an impious Government, could make out no cause of complaint, and went away confounded, reluctantly confessing that this sister was "a great woman." Some of the ladies in the town, however, conceiving a mistrust of the impartiality of the daughters of St. Vincent de Paul, and fearing lest the wounded of the Piedmontese army should be treated with less attention than others, came to nurse them themselves; but they no sooner saw Quitterie at her labour of love among the sick than they were thoroughly undeceived. From that moment, the clamour which had been raised against the Sisters ceased, and it was no longer question of removing them.

Quitterie, like her saintly sister, had an ardent devotion to the Blessed Sacrament: when she was praying before the Tabernacle you might have supposed her to be a statue, so immovable was she and so incapable of distraction; on leaving the chapel the expression of her face was like that of a seraph. Moved by a pious curiosity to know what passed between God and her soul at the foot of the altar, the Religious more than once hazarded some questions on the subject. A humble and modest smile was all they could elicit, except that on one occasion she was betrayed into saying to a Sister who had been specially importuning her, " Jesus and I, we understand each other." She was peculiarly exact in all that concerned divine worship; nothing was too minute to claim her attention, and the least negligence or omission distressed her to the greatest degree. Indeed, she carried her conscientiousness on this head to a point which others whose faith was not so lively might have judged to be scrupulosity, but it was not so : her solicitude proceeded from her very present sense of Him whom we serve, and who abides on our altars. From the same sentiment of love and reverence, she personally undertook the cleaning of the chapel; and those who beheld her thus employed were reminded of the Blessed Virgin in the house of Nazareth.

Quitterie was distinguished from the first by her love of obedience, her attraction for the interior life, and her humility. This last virtue shone with peculiar lustre when she exercised the office of Superior. She availed herself of her authority only to reserve for herself whatever work involved the greatest trouble, or was from its nature the most repulsive. She was ever ready to confess herself in the wrong, to humble herself before her inferiors, and even to repair their faults. One of the officials was much struck with this trait in her character. She had been making some excuses to him in the name of one of the Sisters, and, speaking of her afterwards, and narrating the charity with which she had discharged this kind office, he said, " I always had a high esteem for the good Superioress, but now I hold her to be a saint." She would throw herself at the feet of all sorts of persons, no matter who, either to beseech those who were quarrelling to cease offending God, and to be mutually reconciled, or simply to humble herself when she was in no way to blame, as she was seen to do in the case of an infirmarian, sixty years of age, who was so touched that he in his turn fell on his knees and with tears begged her forgiveness ; or, again, to pacify a sick person who had been teased by one of the others. Regarding herself as the servant of a God who, so to say, annihilated Himself for the love of men, she thought she could never descend too low in imitation of His self-abasement. She was as desirous to hide and eclipse herself as others often are to display themselves and attract attention. To this motive must be attributed the silence she sedulously maintained concerning her sister Marie, even after her Life and Works had been published. She never either saw or alluded to them, and people used to wonder whether the two were really related to each other.

An ecclesiastic who knew Quitterie well said that he had met with very few souls raised to so high a degree of perfection; her union with her Divine Spouse, he added, was continual; and such faults· as she might commit were only those into which human infirmity will betray the holiest while still in the way of probation. When she spoke of the mysteries of the faith and of the love of God, it was with remarkable unction. During the hours allotted to recreation, she would not suffer any conversation of a trifling character, considering such purposeless talk to be unbefitting persons consecrated to God. Yet she knew how to make the time pass agreeably as well as profitably ; often availing herself of the opportunity to answer the questions of inexperienced sisters in a familiar and pleasant way, or to prepare them for the practical work of their vocation. Her fervour was contagious; it animated all to press on to the attainment of those virtues which befit daughters of St. Vincent, and the more so because her language and her sentiments never outran her practice. She was uniformly unruffled in temper, calm, silent ; never under the dominion of any mere natural movement, a defect which is sure to reveal itself in overeagerness, precipitation, or some passing shade of worry or irritation; her exterior, in short, was under as strict regulation as her interior, as of one who always remembered the presence of the Lord of all; her voice was never raised, her tone was always moderate. " Let your modesty be known to all men," said the Apostle ;* " the Lord is nigh." And as the overwhelming sense

* Phil. iv. 5.

of this awful presence restrained the tongue and kept in check every gesture of this holy woman, so she communicated like feelings to her sisters. She spoke so little and in so low a voice, that, when in her company, they almost fancied it was one of the hours of silence, when nothing is said but what is strictly necessary. This was particularly the case when she was in one of the passages, still more if in the vicinity of the chapel. But her silence was also the fruit of that recollection which her close union with God rendered habitual to her. Hence also her love of her duties, for in all things she constantly sought God; hence also, when her tongue was unloosed, it was only to speak of the love of God or of the love of that sacrifice of self which brings us nearer to Jesus. The thought of Jesus was the nourishment of her soul; she was ever feeding upon the remembrance of the mysteries of His Life and Death, and drawing thence that fervour which supported her through all her labours and troubles, and that ardent zeal for the salvation of her neighbours which expressed itself often in precious and salutary counsels. But her example was still more effective. Sister Quitterie, according to the testimony of one who had been under her charge, " spoke few words, but gave many examples of humility, of charity, and of all those virtues which distinguish the true daughters of St. Vincent."

Like her sister Marie, she was a great lover of the Divine Will; this was the source of her perfect resignation in the most trying circumstances. " Everything is a permission from on high," she would say when any trouble fell upon them; then she would hold her peace, accepting all and submitting herself to all, adoring with deep self-abasement the hidden designs of Providence. It is scarcely necessary to say that she excelled in love for the poor; for what Sister of Charity but dearly loves Christ's poor? In them Quitterie's faith beheld the Person of her dear Redeemer, and this was sufficient to draw forth all the tenderness of her heart. The poor were quite aware of being the objects of her predilection, and had a love for her in return which love only can obtain. Benefits may win gratitude, but love alone can win love. They would go and sit on the steps at the hospital door, for the pleasure of just seeing her as she came out. "When we have seen our mother we will go away," they would say; and if some one told them that they could not see her yet, they would reply, "Well, patience; we will wait till we do see her pass." No service that she could render to them, whether it were mending their rags or waiting on them in their sickbeds, but she performed it, not only willingly, but with love and respect, always seeing in them her adorable Lord. Then she would help the infirmarians to clean out their rooms, and that, too, when she was so foot-sore from fatigue that she could scarcely bear her stockings. The time she bestowed on these rough occupations was saved out of the multiplied employments which her office laid upon her. It was thus she filled up leisure moments. If, for instance, any one looked for her on Saturday afternoon, they would probably find her seeing after the coal-cellar, or setting in order the large store-rooms of the hospital. She would emerge covered with dust and cobwebs, with her face so begrimed that you would hardly have known her, and so utterly exhausted that she could scarcely stand. This rude mode of life she never gave up until illness at last compelled her to take to her bed; the remonstrances of the sisters, urging upon her the expediency of reserving her failing strength for more important

z

work, having been of no avail. Quitterie would reply that Sisters of Charity ought not to be waited on ; they were servants, and therefore such offices appertained to them of right.

She was truly, indeed, the servant of the poor, whom she regarded as her masters. She made nothing of any sacrifice or fatigue in their behalf. She also exhorted those who were under her charge to act towards them in the same spirit of faith, and insisted upon the utmost care and punctuality in the preparation of the food which was to be distributed to the sick and indigent. Even in the closing days of her life, when she was racked with most acute pains, she would recur to this subject, and inculcate the love of the poor on all who approached her, promising them that they would thus secure for themselves a holy and happy death. "No, no," she was heard to exclaim on her bed of suffering, "God will not banish me from His presence, for I have striven not to banish Him during my life, and have desired Him alone and the poor."

Her companions had also an abundant share of her overflowing charity. Besides labouring unceasingly to enlighten, advise, and instruct them by word and example in the path of virtue and in the discharge of their duties, she had also a heart of tenderness for them. Her own entire detachment from earth and from all earthly solicitudes, which were to her as so much smoke, had not caused her to lose any of her delicate sensibility for the feelings and wants of others. She would forestall their smallest needs, she nursed them affectionately when they were ill, compassionated their infirmities, and whatever additional fatigue might fall upon herself, she always managed to procure some rest for those who, without this tender vigilance on her part, would probably have sunk from over-work.

Notwithstanding all the trials which, both physically and morally, were perpetually trying her generous courage and patience, Quitterie was ingenious in seizing additional occasions for mortifying her senses. She would always reserve for her own share of labour what was most repulsive to nature. After having fatigued herself much in nursing the sick, instead of taking any rest, she would go and shut herself up in a garret to put together the dirty bandages which were lying there. The stench of this room was so intolerable, in consequence of this great accumulation of linen which had been used in dressing every manner of wound and sore, that no one could remain in it long. A girl belonging to the house, entering one day accidentally, and shocked at finding the Superioress engaged in such an occupation, offered to help her in spite of the great disgust she felt; but Quitterie would not allow her, saying that a work of that sort was not suitable for young people, while it was no inconvenience to her. A sick woman in the hospital had been given up by the doctors. She was literally one gangrene from head to feet; her bones were coming through her flesh, and the sores on this poor sufferer exhaled an odour so insupportable that the infirmarians refused to attend on her any longer. So Quitterie undertook the charge, and waited on her for above a month. The dressing her ulcers used to take a full hour each time, and, while the sick in the same ward would be calling out to beg she might be removed further off, for that the smell was unendurable, this excellent sister seemed to take a delight in her charitable work, lavishing on the poor sufferer the most delicate attentions, while endeavouring to persuade others that she was not herself incommoded in the slightest degree. If tasks of this kind had become easy to this fervent sister, it may be conceived at what price she had purchased this facility, and by what inward battles she had triumphed over the rising of nature. As she always chose for herself what was likely to prove the most repulsive to others, so it was with any exceptional fatigue. She has been seen sitting up an entire night, without varying her position, by the bedside of a sick person who required constant assistance, and this although she knew that it would be quite impossible for her to rest herself on the coming day.

But it was during the last painful illness of this faithful spouse of the Crucified Jesus that her heroic patience and love were specially manifested. For, like her sister Marie, Quitterie died a death of extreme and prolonged torture. We have already noticed her reserve in speaking of herself or in manifesting any token of her intimate state of union with her Lord. It pleased God, however, that at this time she should make this remarkable avowal to her confessor : " Our Lord has willed that during my whole life I shall represent Him in the exercise of works of charity towards my neighbour; and now, at its close, He wills that I should represent Him in my sufferings." Then, after a pause, she added, " I see Him present, my dear Jesus, waiting for me with the Cross laid on His shoulders, and inviting me to follow Him ; yes, I see Him here before my eyes." These words serve to confirm those which Marie heard in vision, when our Lord manifested to her His designs in regard to the three sisters. Quitterie had certainly never seen her sister's writings, and during the few days which they spent together at the *Enfants Trouvés*, it is more than improbable that Marie ever confided to her anything concerning her own interior life, a subject which she strictly reserved for the ear of superiors, and which she had withheld from father, mother, and the sister with whom she had lived in familiar association for so many years, and whom she called the guardian angel of her childhood.

Every effort was made by the community to preserve a life so valuable to them as that of their Superior. Change of air was adopted, and some amelioration ensued, enough to enable Quitterie to resume her work ; but the reprieve was very short, and, when all hope of restoration had vanished, she was moved from the general to the military hospital. Its inmates welcomed her as a blessing from Heaven, and the situation of the house was favourable to recovery, had such in her case been possible. But Quitterie well knew that nothing remained for her but to prepare to meet her God. The crises became more frequent, and sometimes extorted from her cries of agony ; but she generally succeeded in stifling them with her handkerchief. This state of violent pain lasted a fortnight, to the consternation of the doctors, whose every attempt to alleviate her sufferings was completely baffled. If, however, they could give no relief, they, like others, received much edification as they heard her, in the height of her paroxysms, content herself with saying these words : "Lord, since it is Thy will that I should endure these pains, increase my patience, for I fear lest I should offend Thee." And then she would affectionately press to her lips the crucifix which she constantly held in her hands, and cover it with kisses. Although these attacks left her like one almost bruised and crushed to death, they never robbed her of the sweet look with which she welcomed all who attended on her, nor hindered her from addressing expressions of gratitude and kind counsel to all. Her companions would eagerly

take their turn by her bedside to hear her last words
and treasure up in their memory her saintly example.
When, however, they wished to procure her some relief
by changing her position in her bed, she declined to
move, alleging that our Lord had no such alleviation on
the Cross, and that she wished to remain fixed like Him.
Being asked in what she was occupied, she replied, " In
awaiting the hour of my deliverance."

Quitterie was denied the blessing of the Last Sacraments, for she refused to communicate with the government chaplain, who alone had access to the military
hospital, but when her sisters were commiserating her
for this loss, and for not enjoying the assistance in her
last hours of the priest who had her confidence, she
tranquilly replied, " The Lord has so permitted it;
you will assist me, and He will Himself, I hope, assist
me." Her peace was undisturbed. Ejaculations to
God or to His holy Mother were all that ever escaped
her lips; her eyes remained habitually closed, as if she
had bidden farewell to this earth; she only opened
them from time to time to fix them on her crucifix.

Feeling her last hour approach, she asked for the
recommendation of the dying, which her companions
recited several times. She followed the prayers, uniting
her sacrifice to that of her Saviour, and, when these
words were addressed to her: "My sister, place your
trust in God," she said, " I am in His hands." Soon
after, she entered on her three hours' agony, if by that
name can be called what seemed like a peaceful slumber.
Her real agony was past, and nothing remained but to
loosen the tie which bound her soul to the body, and
allow it to mount towards heaven. "She died like
one predestined to glory," said the witnesses of this
blessed death, " after living like a saint." The priest

above alluded to, writing to the sisters who had enjoyed the happiness of being under her charge, observed, "This holy soul has finished her purgatory, I hope, and now receives in the bosom of God the reward of her love and perfect self-oblation. You are happy, my dear sisters, in having enjoyed her presence amongst you for so many years, in having witnessed her example, and heard her instructions. Rest assured that it was from the Crucifix, sole object of her love, that she drew all that she taught you. Oh! if you could but know all that she imbibed at the feet of Jesus! If for a few instants you could have penetrated into her interior, how would your esteem and veneration for her be increased yet more! In the last conversation which we had together, I recognised more fully than ever the riches of this soul, and the loving predilection with which Jesus had first chosen her for Himself and then adorned her as His spouse."

Such was Quitterie in life and death, according to the brief record which is all that we possess of her; so like to her sister Marie in many ways, although her vocation was so different. We have our Lord's own testimony that Marie's was the highest, as representing His interior life, but who can say, had we possessed as abundant means of knowing Quitterie as we do in the case of Marie, that we should not have seen that she as faithfully corresponded to the grace of God, and as perfectly, in her measure, fulfilled her vocation as did her blessed sister? Be this as it may, they were well worthy of each other, and, though separated on earth, where each followed her appointed path, we may confidently believe that they are now united eternally in glory.

## Note to Page 163.

It is interesting to compare with this statement of Marie Lataste's, respecting the mode in which she received divine communications, the description which St. Hildegarde gives of the supernatural light with which she was favoured from her infancy. It is not surprising that knowledge thus imparted should be difficult to render in words. St. Hildegarde expressly says that, when writing what had been revealed to her in this light, she uses other words than those which she had heard, adding that she does not hear these words like those which audibly proceed from the mouth of a man, but that she sees them like a flame, like a luminous cloud. in the pure ether. Anne Catherine Emmerich apparently enjoyed a similar gift. Even the instructions which she received textually during her visions were not communicated in language addressed to the ear, but were imparted "in the form of irradiations, or of floods of light emanating from the living light. Now, as in order to communicate what she had perceived in contemplation, she was obliged to translate it into ordinary language, that which she reproduced in this manner was frequently very defective. Scarcely ever could she do more than give a slight sketch ; often she would say (speaking of our Lord), 'He gave a beautiful instruction which, unfortunately, I am unable to repeat.'" *

## Note to Page 358.

It does not appear on what precise grounds Quitterie Lataste refused the ministrations of the chaplain attached to the military hospital. It may be that he had been suspended by the ecclesiastical authorities, and was sustained in his office by the usurping Government.

* "Vie de N. S. Jésus-Christ, d'après les visions d'Anne Catherine Emmerich : traduite par M. l'Abbé de Cazalès." Deuxième Édition, 1875. Tom. i. pp. 27, 28, 124, 125.

𝔅𝔞𝔩𝔩𝔞𝔫𝔱𝔶𝔫𝔢 𝔓𝔯𝔢𝔰𝔰
BALLANTYNE, HANSON AND CO.
EDINBURGH AND LONDON

# LIBRARY

OF

# RELIGIOUS BIOGRAPHY.

EDITED BY

## EDWARD HEALY THOMPSON, M.A.

---

Now ready,

VOL. VI. THE LIFE OF MARIE LATASTE, Lay Sister OF THE CONGREGATION OF THE SACRED HEART, with a brief notice of her sister Quitterie. Cloth, 5s.

---

In preparation,

THE LETTERS AND WORKS OF MARIE LATASTE, 2 vols. Translated from the French by Edward Healy Thompson.

---

Also in preparation,

THE LIFE OF HENRI-MARIE BOUDON, ARCHDEACON OF EVREUX.

---

Volumes already published.

I. THE LIFE OF ST. ALOYSIUS GONZAGA, S.J. Second Edition. 5s.

"The life before us brings out strongly a characteristic of the Saint which is, perhaps, little appreciated by many who have been attracted to him chiefly by the purity and early holiness which have made him the chosen patron of the young. This characteristic is his intense energy of will. . . . . We have seldom been more struck than, in reading this record of his life, with the omnipotence of the human will when united with the will of God."—*Dublin Review.*

"The book before us contains numberless traces of a thoughtful and tender devotion to the Saint. It shows a loving penetration into his spirit, and an appreciation of the secret motives of his action, which can only be the result of a deeply affectionate study of his life and character." —*Month.*

## II. THE LIFE OF MARIE EUSTELLE HARPAIN; OR, THE ANGEL OF THE EUCHARIST. Second Edition. 5s.

"The life of Marie Eustelle Harpain possesses a special value and interest, apart from its extraordinary natural and supernatural beauty, from the fact that to her example and to the effect of her writings is attributed, in great measure, the wonderful revival of devotion to the Blessed Sacrament in France, and consequently throughout Western Christendom."—*Dublin Review.*

"A more complete instance of that life of purity and close union with God in the world of which we have just been speaking is to be found in the history of Marie Eustelle Harpain, the sempstress of Saint-Pallais. The writer of the present volume has had the advantage of very copious materials in the French works on which his own work is founded, and Mr. Thompson has discharged his office as editor with his usual diligence and accuracy."—*Month.*

"Marie Eustelle was no ordinary person, but one of those marvellous creations of God's grace which are raised up from time to time for the encouragement and instruction of the faithful, and for His own honour and glory. Her name is now famous in the Churches; . . . and her writings have imparted light, strength, and consolation to innumerable devout souls both in the cloister and in the world."—*Tablet.*

## III. THE LIFE OF ST. STANISLAS KOSTKA, S.J. 5s.

"An admirable companion volume 'to the 'Life of St. Aloysius Gonzaga.' It is written in a very attractive style, and by the picturesqueness of its descriptions brings vividly before the reader the few but striking incidents of the Saint's life. At the same time it aims at interpreting to us what it relates, by explaining how grace and nature combined to produce, in the short space of eighteen years, such a masterpiece of sanctity."—*Dublin Review.*

"We strongly recommend this biography to our readers, earnestly hoping that the writer's object may thereby be attained in an increase of affectionate veneration for one of whom Urban VIII. exclaimed that, 'although a little youth,' he was indeed 'a great Saint.'"—*Tablet.*

"There has been no adequate biography of St. Stanislas. In rectifying this want, Mr. Thompson has earned a title to the gratitude of English-speaking Catholics. The engaging Saint of Poland will now be better known among us, and we need not fear that, better known, he will not be better loved."—*Weekly Register.*

## IV. THE LIFE OF THE BARON DE RENTY; OR, PERFECTION IN THE WORLD EXEMPLIFIED. 6s.

"An excellent book. We have no hesitation in saying that it ought to satisfy all classes of opinions. The style is throughout perfectly fresh and buoyant. We have great pleasure in recommending it to all our readers; but we recommend it more especially to two classes of persons: to those who, because the dress of sanctity has changed, think that sanctity itself has ceased to exist; and to those who ask how a city man can follow the counsel, 'Be ye perfect, as My Heavenly Father is perfect.'"—*Dublin Review.*

"A very instructively-written biography."—*Month.*

"We would recommend our readers to study this wonderful life bit by bit for themselves."—*Tablet.*

"A good book for our Catholic young men, teaching how they can sanctify the secular state."—*Catholic Opinion.*

"Edifying and instructive, a beacon and guide to those whose walks are in the ways of the world, who toil and strive to win Christian perfection. We earnestly recommend these records of the life of a great and good man."—*Ulster Examiner.*

## V. THE LIFE OF THE VENERABLE ANNA MARIA TAIGI, THE ROMAN MATRON (1769–1837). With Portrait. Third Edition. 6s.

This biography has been composed after a careful collation of previous Lives of the Servant of God with each other, and with the "Analecta Juris Pontificii," which contain large selections from the Processes. Various prophecies attributed to her and to other holy persons have been collected in an Appendix.

"Of all the deeply interesting biographies which the untiring zeal and piety of Mr. Healy Thompson has given of late years to English Catholics, none, we think, is to be compared in interest with the one before us, both from the absorbing nature of the life itself, and the spiritual lessons it conveys."—*Tablet.*

"We thank Mr. Healy Thompson for this volume. The direct purpose of his biographies is always spiritual edification. The work before us lets us into the secrets of the divine communications with a soul that, almost more perhaps than any other in the whole history of the Church of God, has been lifted up to the level of the secrets of Omnipotence."—*Dublin Review.*

"A complete biography of the Venerable Matron, in the composition of which the greatest care has been taken and the best authorities consulted. We can safely recommend the volume for the discrimination with which it has been written, and for the careful labour and completeness by which it is distinguished."—*Catholic Opinion.*

"We recommend this excellent and carefully-compiled biography to all our readers. The evident care exercised by the editor in collating the various Lives of Anna Maria gives great value to the volume, and we hope it will meet with the support it so justly merits."—*Westminster Gazette.*

## SELECT TRANSLATIONS FOR SPIRITUAL READING.

## I. THE HIDDEN LIFE OF JESUS, A LESSON AND MODEL TO CHRISTIANS. Translated from the French of Henri-Marie Boudon, Archdeacon of Evreux, by Edward Healy Thompson, M.A. Second Edition, 3s.

"This profound and valuable work has been very carefully and ably translated."—*Weekly Register.*

"The more we have of such works the better."—*Westminster Gazette.*

"A book of searching power."—*Church Review.*

"We earnestly recommend its study and practice to all readers."—*Tablet.*

"We have to thank Mr. Thompson for this translation of a valuable work which has long been popular in France."—*Dublin Review.*

"It is very satisfactory to find that books of this nature are sufficiently in demand to call for a re-issue; and the volume in question is so full of holy teaching that we rejoice at the evidence of its being a special favourite."—*Month.*

# By the same Author and Translator.

## II. DEVOTION to the NINE CHOIRS of HOLY ANGELS, and ESPECIALLY to the ANGEL GUARDIANS. 3s.

"It may be doubted whether any other devotional writer of the French Church, not marked for reverence by authority, is more highly or more justly revered than Boudon. . . . Faith assures us that we are surrounded on every side by a world of spirits, which, by the permission or by the command of God, interfere in earthly events and in human interests, and with which, therefore, we are in truth much more really concerned than with the great majority of those earthly events which we so often allow to engross all our attention and all our thoughts. We need, then, hardly say how valuable are works like this in the present day and in our own country. They show us how near the invisible and spiritual world appeared to men who believed only what we believe, but who lived in a country and an age where faith was more universal and more fresh. We do not know any English book which in any degree supplies its place, and are heartily glad to see it put within the reach of English readers."—*Dublin Review.*

"We congratulate Mr. Thompson on the way in which he has accomplished his task, and we earnestly hope that an increased devotion to the Holy Angels may be the reward of his labour of love."—*Tablet.*

"A beautiful translation."—*Month.*

"The translation is extremely well done."—*Weekly Register.*

---

## III. THE HOLY WAYS OF THE CROSS; Or, A Short Treatise on the various Trials and Afflictions, interior and exterior, to which the Spiritual Life is subject, and the means of making a good use thereof. 3s. 6d.

"If some of our statesmen out of work could spare a little time from their absorbing occupations of blowing up the embers of insurrection abroad, or of civil discord at home, for the study of this little publication, they might learn, even in their old age, some plain truths about Christianity, and avoid the sad blunders that overwhelm them whenever they attempt to deal with any question that has a supernatural bearing. . . . If this work becomes as well known as it deserves, its circulation will be very wide."—*Dublin Review.*

"Boudon is fortunate in his English translator, and we may feel sure that these little volumes will long hold their place among our spiritual classics."—*Month.*

"The author of this little treatise is well known as a master in spiritual life, whose writings have met with the strongest commendation. . . . It comes to us with the best introduction, and with no slight claims upon the attention of every one."—*Tablet.*

"An infallible guide-book, to be commended to every Christian pilgrim."—*Weekly Register.*

"A perfect gem of safe devotion, and of priceless value as a sound spiritual book."—*Universe.*

"Precisely one of the very best kind for spiritual reading."—*Catholic Times.*

"Eminently adapted for spiritual reading, and beautifully translated into terse and vigorous English."—*Catholic Opinion.*

www.ingramcontent.com/pod-product-compliance
Lightning Source LLC
Chambersburg PA
CBHW021543110726
47902CB00004B/1005